Mixed Blood
LAST WINTER IN AMERICA

Mixed Blood
LAST WINTER IN AMERICA

"There is a Reaper whose name is Death, and since no one can tell us when he will thrust in his sickle and cut us off from life, now is the time to take your picture at Whitney's Gallery in Saint Paul."

— Advertisement in the window of Elfelt's Dry Goods Store, Saint Paul, Minnesota Territory, February 1853

Polyverse Publications
Santa Barbara, CA

Polyverse Publications and the colophon are trademarks of
Polyverse Publications, LLC.

Book and cover design by Louis F. Torres
Original interior art by Tim Anderson

Library of Congress Control Number: pending
ISBN: 978-1-7378832-3-4 (paperback)
ISBN: 978-1-959111-98-6 (ebook)

Printed in the United States of America
1 2 3 4 5 6 7 8 9 10

First Edition

Contents

Author's Note

This is a work of fiction. In the winter of 1853, William Whipple Warren, a mixed-blood Ojibwe, set out from Minnesota Territory to cross the Great Lakes and overland to New York City, a manuscript in hand. How he accomplished this is unknown, but he made the journey. He returned in June and died the next day at 28 years old. His manuscript, *History of the Ojibway People*, was lost and rediscovered, published in 1885, then lost again. It has been republished many times.

This novel is based on documented history of Warren's tumultuous life and times. Some characters existed, some were invented. The author takes full responsibility for their descriptions and expressed ideas.

Note on language: In the early 19th century, the people in this story were referred to by different terms. Language has evolved, reflecting the changing perceptions, politics, and social realities concerning the origins of America's many peoples. Negro (or colored) was the widely accepted term for those who are now Black, or African American. Indigenous peoples of all origins, Native Americans and First Nations from every corner of the continent, have been broadly called Indians ever since that fateful day in 1492. Whites are still whites, regardless of their mixed origins. In this novel, the language used and attitudes thereby reflected could shock the sensibilities of some readers. Rest assured that it is the author's concern to depict the historical reality of the times through the language of that era. And even in fiction, to be true to history.

I first heard my great-uncle's story from my mother's family, his Ojibwe/American descendants from the White Earth Chippewa Reservation in Minnesota, which did not yet exist when his story took place.

William Whipple Warren's *History of the Ojibway People* and some surviving letters attest to the reality of his journey.

Le Havre, France April 29, 2022

Back cover portrait by Chicago artist Tim Anderson is a study done in 1994 from a daguerreotype, the only existing image of William W. Warren. The Preface to Warren's book published posthumously in 1885, as well as acknowledgments, are included in the appendix hereto.

Prologue: Homecoming

Minnesota Territory, May 31st, 1853

THE ONE MAN THEY HAD GIVEN UP FOR LOST at Galena would be the first to disembark at Saint Paul. He stood stiffly on the top deck, gripping the rail. It was sunup, chilly, a light mist hanging over the Mississippi River, the green of spring lushing the banks.

The landing was already madding with immigrants as the *Dr. Franklin's* whistle screamed high and loud coming in under the bluff. Five other steamboats were already docked. The pilot found a slip among the new quays, and the steamer dropped its ramp to let the impatient Germans off, then the Swedish contingent, all from the same village. Exhausted at the end of their long journey, they could not get past the cord below.

An official and two armed deputies held them at the bottom of the ramp, where they spoke to the Captain. The sickness was moving upriver. A city health ordinance held the ship in quarantine. Two more deputies stood armed on the shore. Word of the cholera deaths on board had reached the territorial capital ahead of them, even as more bodies had been put ashore and burned every night.

The sequestered passengers on deck moaned and harped; a young woman with a baby began to wail. A tall blond Swede who spoke English stepped up and demanded a doctor to examine his people.

"I am a doctor, ya lout," said the official. "You'll do as I say!"

"I do not know lout, Doctor. But our women and children need food. We have come very far. We can pay."

There was a harangue from the deck. The throng on the ramp parted. A squarely built, hatless young man was kicking his way

1

through, shouting everyone away in a language no one understood. People let him pass. He carried in his arms the man who was not lost, wrapped in a black cloak with a wide-brimmed beaver hat shading his head, visibly still alive.

He grasped his protector, struggling, and held himself high to address the Sanitation Committee. He looked young but ravaged by time. He wheezed when he spoke.

"I live here, Doctor. I am William Warren. Territorial Legislature. On my way home."

"He ain't sick, Sir." By his brogue, the protector was Irish. "Least not like these others. Just ailin' a wee bit. He knows the Gov'ner. I'm takin' 'im ta his sister's house."

"I know who he is, Paddy!" The doctor felt the sick man's nodes and checked his neck. "This man's got Indian and Yankee blood. He's not dead yet."

A man in a visor and spectacles pocketed his notebook and made his way through the crowd on the quay. "William! Thank God you made it home, lad. You look... well." There was no answer. He spoke to the examining official.

"Colonel D.A. Robertson, Doctor. The *Minnesota Democrat*. We've published this man's work."

"I wasn't born in a wigwam, Colonel. I read the papers. Now get this man to his sister's." The doctor pushed the Irishman and his charge past him.

Robertson had his buggy on the landing. They loaded Warren in.

"Billy," Warren breathed, "My case...the luggage."

The Irishman saw the first-class baggage being unloaded and went for it.

Among the stacks of lumber and barrels were huddles of blanketed Sioux. They barely looked up. The meat roasting over a barrel fire smelled like dog.

The landing was swarming with foreigners, wagons, furniture, trunks, workers, and animals. Standing still on the bluff were small gatherings of Ojibwe observing the happenings. Warren gazed up at them and nodded with something like recognition. Robertson squinted at him.

"William, it's over. The removals are stopped. Governor Ramsey's been fired. He and Watrous are under investigation. The Ojibwe can all go home."

Warren looked around and through all this, then leaned back in the buggy.

A husky foreman loading barrels onto a wagon spotted them and walked over. He looked up at Warren, who had dozed off. He introduced himself to the newspaper editor as Edward Price, his brother-in-law. His wife was Warren's sister, Charlotte. Robertson said Warren needed rest. His sister was expecting him.

"I know," said Price. "We'll go. Good God. Charlotte ain't gonna like this."

Billy came back hefting two bags and a small wooden trunk secured with a leather strap. Price loaded it all in the black two-wheeler and jumped on the back. The big horse carried them up the slope to the new neighborhoods under construction.

Billy took a flask out of Warren's coat pocket and nudged him awake. "Time for a nip o' yer tea, Captain. Ya want ta be fit to greet yer sister, now don't ye?"

He swallowed what he could and seemed better for it. He sat up. He knew it would not last long. Billy arranged his waistcoat and cravat and told him he looked like a regular gentleman.

Charlotte saw them from the window and ran out drying her hands. Warren was standing on the ground, hat in hand, propped up by Billy. His long hair, stringy and matted, and his extreme thinness made him look even taller than his six feet, albeit slightly bent. Sister and brother embraced. Charlotte leaned her head on his chest, looked up at him, and began to weep.

"I brought you some coffee from New York. In my bag." He spoke raspingly, nearly whispering. "I want to see Matilda, the children, and Julia."

"I'll send a runner," said Price. "A Chippeway. They go fast."

"And Hole-in-the-Day," Warren added. "Send for him."

3

This seemed to finish his list.

Billy picked him up and followed Charlotte to the back room, where he eased him into a bed, placed him half sitting up, and loosened his clothing like a nursemaid.

"Wouldn't he be better lying down?" Charlotte asked, still weeping.

"Can't lie him down, Missus. He'd never get up. Can't breathe."

Warren slept, propped up on pillows, under a quilt his sister had just finished for his homecoming. They let him rest.

Outside, the spring sun was peeking out to warm the Mississippi River Valley. Charlotte's sprouts were just coming up in the garden, under a flowering dogwood that had survived the construction mayhem. A mild winter it had been.

Robertson remarked that Warren's writing chest was lighter; he must have left the manuscript for publishing in New York. He would spread the news. And yet there was a pall on the small gathering before the modest white house the Prices had just built.

"Don't print anything unless he tells you to," Charlotte told him. The editor agreed. Price asked Billy what he knew how to do.

"Engine mechanic. Boiler man. But I take to any honest work."

"Can you handle a hammer and saw?"

"Aye, if that's what needs doin'."

"Then come on with me. You can board downtown. Food's passable."

"I thankee. Would ye mind me comin' tomorrow morning ta see the Captain, Mum?"

Charlotte was going to say, of course, when Price said, "He's barely half the weight he had when he left last winter. He might not even be here in the morning."

Charlotte Warren Price turned on her husband, yelped, and with both her fists struck him hard on the chest so that all could hear the thump. Then she shrank him back with her dark, shining eyes.

"I told you once," she hissed, "I'll tell you again. You don't know my brother. He'll bury us all!"

4

PART I
THE FRONTIER

Chapter 1: First Kill

Lake Superior, August 1831

AT THE END OF A LONG, windless day on the big lake, head factor Lyman Warren raised his arm to signal the pose. Four high-crested canoes with painted prows glided to a stop and held together. The air swirled. As the canoes sat, their wakes went flat and vanished on the sheen of clear blue water. Three buzzards came out from the wooded shore and circled. The metallic tang over the lake drew closer as the sky deepened. The trader's party included his French-Ojibwe wife Marie, their two young sons, a dozen voyageurs, and Ojibwe braves from the La Pointe band. They all rested their paddles and watched the changes conspire around them.

Above the western horizon where there was no land, they saw a thin strip of oxide green as sometimes seen on chunks of copper. The green ray spread wide and sharp, then gave way to a fiery sheen of red-orange where the sun had sunk below the cool blue and Venus burned through the sky.

The boy William felt his heart race. He went lightheaded as he felt himself rising above the surface, watching the green line fade away. A weightless vertigo made him grab the gunwales. Then just six years old, he thought of the lake as endless. To the west and north it was like the sky, or like the ocean he had never seen, infinite and round. He could not envision that the canoes would ever reach the edge. He could not imagine that he would ever die.

Distant gull cries made the only sound on the lake other than the whimpering of William's little brother Truman, called *Makons* or Little Bear, who lay limp in his mother's browned arms, weakened from the flux. William was all right, or so he told his father. Sits

Alone, the old Midé with five feathers and beads of glass strung into his braids, whispered a chant and held something in his fist over the boy's stomach. He blew on him through a piece of hollow moose bone, shooting his medicine into Makons to force out the illness.

Packing his pipe, Lyman Warren kept a keen eye on his point scout, Little Raven. The nearly naked youth still wore the blood from this morning's kill on his chin and down his neck. On this day he had lost his boyishness. He was fuller, sharper, his skin a darker red. He had a first-kill eagle feather in his tangled black hair. The fresh scalp on his strap drew the buzzards. His ropey torso twisted as he peered toward the shore two miles distant. They all saw it.

The slip of white smoke rose behind the tall pines and flattened out over the Porcupine Mountains. Little Raven touched his knife and grunted at the other braves. He spoke to Sits Alone who studied the smoke pattern and the northwestern horizon. The Midé did not like it for two reasons. First, it was likely not Ojibwe smoke. It could be a taunt from the Sioux party, intruders too far north in Ojibwe country. The other reason, he motioned to Warren, was that the smoke told him the sky was falling.

Daniel Dingley in the side canoe said, "Hogwash. What you reckons in them boys' heads, Lyman?"

"More scalps. Wouldn't be Chippeway smoke; they'd sign us. Midé says rain tonight."

"Rain my ass. Sky like this, water flat, we could go all night. But if them over there is Sioux, our Indians hanker for a fight. Killed one for a rat's tail this morning."

"They'd just as soon swim two miles and kill a few more. We'll wait here for the others."

Warren spent a match, lit his pipe, and the Canadian paddlers, all seasoned voyageurs, followed suit and made ready for the pose. The braves broke off pieces of dry *legalet* and chewed, glaring towards the shore.

Behind them, coming into view beyond the last point of red ferrous rock, came a fleet of several Mackinac batteaux loaded with trade goods and their human cargo. They carried a schoolteacher named Frederick Ayer, a mixed-blood interpreter Elizabeth Campbell, and the two white missionaries, the Reverend and Mrs. Sherman Hall, all rowed by Canadian Bois Brulés and Mackinac voyageurs. Lyman smoked and waited while they drew near to form a whole with the canoes.

Intentionally, their convoy was visibly white: the women all wore ample cloth dresses and shawls common to the frontier, the traders wore three-point hats except for Dingley, who wore a coonskin winter and summer and never left his buckskins, while the voyageurs and coureurs des bois favored red bandannas, Hudson Bay shirts, feathered woolen hats, sashes, and ample pantaloons. The Ojibwe scouts, young men but for the Midé, were all naked save their straps, weapons, and deerskin breechclouts. They wore blankets against the insects and chill at night. Around their necks, some wore beads or porcupine quills, small medicine bags, bone jewelry, and some were painted or tattooed. Little Raven, in Warren's party, now had the only eagle feather among the young braves. Indians outnumbered the whites by thousands in the Northwest, but there was no mistaking this as a white man's convoy.

Their route led either over open water, directly west toward the island, or for another two days along the south shore—into the mouth of the great diving fish that formed the tapered end of Lake Superior at the headwaters of the Mississippi. The Island of the Golden Breasted Woodpecker, Monigwunakauning, as named by the Ojibwe (they called themselves Anishinaabe, the People), was home to the Warrens as well. They now called it Madeline Island after the baptismal name of Equaysayway, the mother of Lyman's wife, Marie Cadotte Warren. Chief White Crane had gifted the island to his daughter when she married Michel Cadotte, Lyman's first employer in the Northwest trading business. Since Lyman Warren had married Marie, his father-in-law Cadotte had transferred a good portion of his gifted land to him and his children. Now the old fur trader was waiting for them, no doubt watching for them every day.

The faster native canoes had broken ahead, lookin for a night bivouac before reaching La Pointe. Warren, however, was not keen on stopping. Not since that morning's encounter with a party of Dakota Sioux, one of whom was unceremoniously beheaded by Little Raven. It could not be considered murder since the 1827 Treaty of Fond du Lac—an attempt by the American government, however futile, to stop the Indian warring, secure mineral rights, and extend the rule of law over Indian lands. The so-called treaty defined the territorial boundaries between the Sioux and the Ojibwe, who had for two centuries fought to drive their enemies westward out of the lakes and into the far plains beyond the Mississippi. They had just about succeeded.

Little Raven had simply killed an intruding enemy, a common practice in the Ojibwe-Sioux wars. However, Warren's young son William had witnessed this act from his cache in the bush, which was not so common, and preoccupied his father and mother. The boy hadn't eaten all day.

§

That morning, they were four hundred miles out from the Sault Sainte Marie, their last harbor of civilization, having left Mackinac over three weeks ago. On Lake Superior they had not seen another living soul save one half-starved Chippeway near the sand dunes, somehow exiled, to whom Lyman gave food, powder, and shot for his old British musket, then went on.

As they approached the green Porcupine Mountains two days beyond Keweenaw Point, the canoes and batteaux, ten in all, turned landward at a small stream the Ojibwe knew as a good hunting spot. It seemed idyllic, a shaded haven under big-leafed beeches, lindens, and white oaks. The flies and mosquitoes were not yet unbearable, and all were relieved that the weather bode well, and the destination was but two days away. They made fires and took breakfast, boiling up wild rice, flour, pemmican, and maple syrup.

Little Raven and two other braves were dispatched with bows and muskets to hunt game upstream. They took along young William Warren, as they had many times before on this trip. He took a bark *makuk* with him in case he found blueberries. The boy was an eager learner and spoke more Ojibwe than English, which made him a favorite with the young scouts. Although he was a mixed-blood with a white father, his mother's Indian blood flowed in his body. Her grandfather was Chief White Crane, and this made him like a little brother to them. They were teaching him to stalk, to be as silent as a fox.

At some distance up they sighted a lone Indian, not yet a man by any standard but Dakota Sioux by dress and markings, with a breechclout of antelope skin. He was far from his home, hunched over skinning a muskrat by the stream. The braves crouched and motioned to William to spread flat on the ground.

Not a shot was fired, not a noise was made. The boy watched Little Raven spring from the brush, jerk the Sioux's head back and cut his throat with a steel blade so sharp he nearly cut his head off, but it caught on the vertebrae. Blood from the jugular spewed straight up to maculate the attacker's neck and jaw. He trembled and exulted as he let his kill descend to the earth. The young Sioux quivered with a gurgling sound and bled out onto the stone stream bank.

William felt his pulse race as he witnessed the scout claim his scalp, cutting then ripping it off, and hold it up with a silent cry, his bloody mouth open to the sky. All the boy could hear then was birdsong and the rush of the stream through the green forest, so high and dense he could not see the sky. Suddenly there was a swarm of deer flies. Little Raven motioned for the others to come forward.

William went dry in the tongue. He held tight on the ground and for a few moments, covering his head against the flies. Then he looked up. He had seen death take old and young and heard of war from his Ojibwe elders, but had never seen a kill, much less a scalp taken. The three were squatted around the body, mumbling lowly, but he could not see what they were doing. They then propped the Sioux boy up with his severed head tilted against a tree, and made back for the canoes, tapping William to follow. Little Raven carried off his scalp, one severed ear, and as an afterthought, an arrow from the dead boy's quiver and the skinned muskrat. The mouths of all three braves were bloody but any further celebration was cut short, perhaps out of deference to the Warren boy who was both too young and too white. The other Sioux intruders were surely not far. Instead, they took William's makuk from him, dropped in a slice of something dripping red, and leapt off over brush and deadwood like young bucks.

All three scouts were about sixteen years of age and yet unseasoned as warriors. Leaping back with their blood running high they could not contain their ardor and forgot their rule of silence. They began to yip in shrill animal voices, thrashing through the brush, crying out their victory. They lost part of the muskrat and lost William, who had a hard time keeping up but shortly found his father's camp by following the braves' thrashing and whooping. The Indian paddlers and scouts were all in a state of high excitement. The white voyageurs and trappers looked on chewing their gruel, consternated at this display of wild jubilation.

Lyman Warren had called on the interpreter, Mrs. Campbell, to find out what happened, but the braves were blood-inebriated and heedless. Mrs. Hall, habitually watchful to preserve the whiteness of her skin, blanched even further when she saw the scalp and went sick in the whortlebush. Her husband, the Reverend, followed her seeking to be useful.

William ran up and told his father about the kill, and that every word was true, he had seen it: "He jumped, he cut him, cut his hair off and set him down by a tree. Then he cut his ear off. He was all cut up. Then his head fell off."

The boy was breathless and scratched from his run through the bush.

"Sits alone see it in a dream. He say more will come. Enemy Sioux."

Lyman squatted down close and put his rough palm around the back of his son's neck. His son looked like one of those little Indian boys. He should cut his hair. And the boy should speak more English.

"I'm sorry you had to see that, William. It was a Godless act. It's not our way. We're going home now. We'll build our new church,

12

and the Reverend will pray with us all. Go ready the canoes with your mother."

The braves would not be quelled. Little Raven yelped and brandished the blood-wet scalp to the general disgust of the whites while his band whooped and beat on a copper pot to laud his victory dance. Even Dingley, a frontiersman all his life, was repulsed, and voiced as much to Lyman.

"Nasty custom that scalpin'. It ain't enough just to kill 'im. Just like a savage."

"Whites started it," said Warren, watching the scalp dance. He was a reader of history and fond of putting things in perspective.

"The Dutch in New Amsterdam offered bounties for Indian heads three hundred years back. To set off the wars between the tribes. The wars spread farther west; the Indians found it easier to carry back scalps. They'd dry out and keep longer over the distance. Pretty soon they had a scalp market. Custom stuck with the Indians. They never took scalps before. They took whole heads."

"I never cared much for the Dutch," said Dingley.

"English and French did it too. Pretty soon they set to warring and offered bounties for settlers' scalps. Some of the old men say the Indians shoulda stuck to heads. More medicine in a head. Religiously speaking. A scalp's nothing but a prize." At this, Dingley walked away to the boats.

The scalp, by Ojibwe warrior tradition, would earn Little Raven his first eagle feather and made the other braves eager to strike out and get theirs. From the red smears on their faces and the sharpness of their eyes, they had all tasted the fresh kill. The tang of blood renewed their sinewy muscles and made their tempers run strong. They presented William's makuk to Sits Alone, who appeared impressed and went off a moment behind a large beech trunk. He came back satisfied, his strong old teeth stained red.

Mrs. Hall, now partially recomposed in her soiled gingham dress and high collar, picked her way around the reveling Ojibwe and approached the trader.

"Mr. Warren, do you think it possible to constrain these savages?" By the twitching of her gray pupils, the trader could foresee that the woman herself, if seized by fright, would be the most difficult to constrain. Warren lit his pipe and reflected a moment before answering. The less she knew, the better. What could he tell her?

Heedless of the Fond du Lac Treaty, the Sioux still penetrated Ojibwe territory, killing and mutilating Anishinaabe men, women, and children indifferently while roaming their old hunting and fishing grounds which they were loath to relinquish. War parties ran from the Mississippi up the Saint Croix Valley, to Folle Avoine and Lac Courtoreilles. Summer, with its clement weather propitious to overland travel, was the best time for warring and killing, but they had never come this far north. Perhaps it was just a small hunting party, lost youngsters. Earlier, before the treaty, Little Raven would have rallied the braves to track the Sioux into the mountains and massacre them all. A Sioux party had crossed into Ojibwe territory last spring and killed four of their women and their children in a sugar camp. Flat Mouth's son had been killed in a raid. The ceaseless drive for revenge still ruled the warriors' blood and it was in that measure, Lyman considered, that his wife's people could still, after more than two centuries of commerce with civilized beings and countless explanations of the ways of God, be referred to as savages.

That those same civilized whites decimated native peoples with disease and whiskey and starvation while profiting from their resources and labor was no more justifiable, he knew. But he said none of this to Mrs. Hall, an envoy from Vermont who would not abide living in a land ruled by such terror.

Checking his powder, Warren said, "Be assured of your safety, Mrs. Hall, the young men will calm down on the water. It is preferable that when abroad, we respect their protocol. I shall refer the matter to the authorities upon landing in La Pointe, where we'll all be in safe harbor. Please return to the boats."

That was when Sits Alone touched the five feathers earned in his warring days and stomped a few circles with the young warriors around the scalp. He then doused the fire and began to break camp

14

without waiting for the sign from Lyman Warren. He told Little Raven he had seen the attack in his dream some nights ago, and there were other Sioux to be reckoned with, but not here. Then he pulled a sixth eagle feather out of his bag and gave it to Little Raven, who donned it with silent dignity. They would hold the warrior's ceremony when they got back to the island. William translated this conversation for his father. The trader understood less Ojibwe than his young son, who spoke his mother's language like a native.

Warren considered what the old Midé said and the repercussions it would have once the La Pointe bands were alerted. Then he gave the order to pack up. He called Dingley over.

"We don't need the kind of trouble this is going to bring. Tell that boy if he's gonna paddle in my canoe, he's got to wash that blood off."

"He ain't going to. Not 'til he shows it off to old Buffalo."

"He can keep the scalp. That'll do. We want no warring here. So far it's contained down on the border, the Mississippi bands."

"Makes you wonder what's worse, givin' 'em a knife, or givin' 'em whiskey."

Warren did not reply. The knife was a fair deal. Warren had given it to Little Raven in Mackinac as payment for the trip. It was what they call a Bowie knife, named after a famous Indian fighter now down in Texas. Instead, he ordered the voyageurs to check their powder and keep arms ready. He was of a mind to disarm the Indians, but let it pass. At least they had not fired a shot that morning. Maybe they had time on their side.

And there would be no whiskey. He and the other traders on the island, Dingley, Oakes, and Ashmun, had told this to the American Board of Foreign Missions in Boston. They all wanted a mission, a school, and teachers for their children. As proof of their sincerity, they had made a pledge not to bring liquor onto Madeleine Island, neither for themselves nor for trading with the Indians.

Warren had decided some years ago to leave off trading and dedicate his life to religion, and was received into the church that summer at Mackinac, although his wife Marie followed her French

15

father's faith and was baptized Catholic. But he was still a trader and a fair man, working for the AFC, and he depended on the Ojibwe for his pelts.

As the canoes were made ready, William asked his father, in English: "Was that bad? Is Little Raven going to be punished?"

"It's between the Indians, William. They've been at it for hundreds of years and there's no bad or good to it. They say it's revenge. An Indian thing. I'll report it to Agent Schoolcraft but there's nothing he can do for it."

"There's no reason?"

"No, boy. It's senseless. Revenge begets revenge. No end to it and it doesn't bode well. It's not a good way to live. You'll be going back to Mackinac to school for a while, William. Until we set up the mission school at home. Truman will come later."

William liked to school there in summer. His cousins George and Edward were already there, learning at the Ferrys' school, and he did not want to fall behind. They broke camp and set off, sending one of the La Pointe braves back to alert the Ontonogan bands.

§

Sitting in their canoes at day's end, the sky deepening around the evening star, little Makons still sick, the party waited for Lyman Warren's decision while the buzzards circled above. The scalp was still fresh, and the birds had picked up the scent. Mrs. Hall, after understanding that Warren could not formally threaten or incarcerate the heathens, insisted on traveling behind in the batteaux. Her husband conceded and, somewhat queasy himself, accompanied her. Warren saw the convoy coming behind them, heavily laden with cargo and sick missionaries.

He was disconcerted by the flat line of smoke above the trees. Even after more than a decade of heeding the weather on Lake Superior, he was inclined to wager that Sits Alone was wrong. It was still uncommonly warm, no sign of weather bothered the horizon, and they were making fast headway. He was also firmly convinced that this particular voyage, one of many annual trade trips he made to Mackinac, had the blessing of the Lord. His petition had been

16

fruitful, he would have his missionaries, a church, and a school on the island. He had gone so far as to offer his home, describing it fully to John Hudson of the American Board of Commissioners for Foreign Missions:

> *I have a house 60 ft by 24 containing three large rooms & 5 bedrooms a considerable storehouse & other buildings that are at your service until you wish to build. This Island on which I am 2 miles from the main is say 50 miles in cir- cumference the half of which belongs to Mr. Cadotte & his heirs, which include mine & my brother's children. The land is productive and well-timbered and the fishing ground good just at my door. As much land as you want is likewise at your (disposal) plenty of wild hay a good range for cattle & deep bay partly between us and the main which is an excellent harbor. Wild rice also may be had not far distant. About 40 Indian families live on the Isle & a large body of them inhab- it the district which looks to this as the center of trade.*

The ambassadors of God's Word were in his boats. The new mission, and soon the new school at La Pointe, were within their reach. Warren's remit was to go forth and civilize, to make way for settlement on the frontier. For this, they had to quell the Indian wars and convert the heathens. Now there was this dead Sioux and the smoke line above the trees.

The open water route would take them about ninety miles west toward Monigwunakauning, avoiding another two days along the south shore. Madeline Island, the whites called it now. Safety was near. If the sky did not fall.

Sits Alone drew away from little Makons for a look at the water. The Midé knew the colors of the lake like those of the sky. He also knew that the young men, whose eyes narrowed like knives at the sight of the woodsmoke, would choose battle over flight. But in this circumstance, given the weight of their charge, the Midé hoped they would defer to his judgment. The old Ojibwe peered into the depths, smiled at William, and pointed down. Under the canoe passed a sturgeon the size of a man.

"Weeng," he said. "A good sign." He dipped into his pouch, spoke a few words to the sturgeon, and offered some tobacco to the waters. The four canoes, for some moments, hung like decorated white baskets between water and sky with only the buzzards circling above them.

Not one to embrace superstition, Warren put no value on the Midé's dealings with the sturgeon. A rational man weighed the chances of the sky falling on them if they continued overnight, due west, to the island. They had been lucky so far, seen only one bad storm, and taken shelter. He weighed the possible consequences of heading ashore for the night. It would inevitably entail bloodshed if the smoke came from a Dakota Sioux war party. With their firearms, they could easily overcome them, but this was no business of the whites, and he wanted no Indian wars near the lakes. He measured the risk as the batteaux drew near. The Reverend and Mrs. Hall would want to continue on. And Ayer hated the mosquitoes.

It was Warren's best season yet in the fur trade, having just delivered $35,076 in pelts to the post at Mackinac for the account of the John Jacob Astor's American Fur Company, in which he had a small share. He had spent some of his profit share to buy his trading outfit for the year and personal items, books he had ordered from the East, and religious tracts, bibles both Catholic (for his wife and her father's family) and Protestant, from which he would read to their children as they grew. Lyman was the soul of tolerance and saw no reason why the two faiths could not co-exist on the island—even if the Indians took easier to the black-robed Catholics whose conversions went quicker and whose bibles had pictures.

Warren's convoy carried this charge, consisting not only of his family, but a cargo of considerable value in goods and human lives, tools for their industry and education. There were provisions for the winter: salt pork and flour and salt and beans, and sundry trade goods—scores of beads, blankets, hats, mirrors, and kettles, traps and tobacco for the Ojibwe hunters who provided him with the tanned pelts that fueled the fur trade, the economic factor that had made a fortune for his employer. Also packed in were the tools and accouterments of white civilization including barrels of forged nails and axeheads, knives, carpentry tools, and twenty army-issued Springfield 1816 muskets, powder and shot, lead bars, cooking utensils, store-bought or manufactured clothing, a canvas-wrapped crate with writing materials and, even a greater rarity in the wilderness: a collection of books ranging in subject from the science of physics, mathematics, world geography, history and the classics, correct orthography and English grammar. Warren's frontier library, growing every year, was his most precious concern; it was the future generation's sole access to knowledge about science, the outside world, and the human accomplishments that defined it.

When the batteaux caught up Warren conferred with John Corbin, head voyageur, there on the water, and took stock. Four of the whites and mixed-bloods—including the two women—were sick and exhausted. Ayer was wan, suffering from bug bites, and lay prostrate in one boat. The Reverend prayed constantly. The Ojibwe scouts seemed to grow stronger and quicker and were like the voyageurs: they needed but little sleep or food to continue. Mrs. Hall was eager to continue. For her part, she had her fill of the savages. They passed around some hard bread, pemmican, and berries.

He looked to John Corbin and the voyageurs, who assured him that they were all *"toujours frais"* and ready to go the night.

Lyman looked back at Marie cradling her sick four-year-old in her arms. She had lost none of her authority as the granddaughter of Chief White Crane by marrying a Berkshire Yankee. He let his decision be known through his wife, his foremost emissary to the Anishinaabe. They were heading back to Monigwunakauning under the cover of night.

Marie Warren spoke, delivering a low, even tirade in her language directed at Little Raven and the other braves. Lyman did not understand all her words, but he caught her meaning. His wife finished by pointing at the western horizon and uttering one word, *"Marche."*

Little Raven brooded a moment, touching his Bowie knife. He then cried out, stood, grabbed his bow and quiver, flew out of the canoe, and dove toward shore. Three other braves followed him. They churned through the water in the direction of the rising smoke. Marie shouted, but Sits Alone only frowned as they grew smaller.

Dingley said, "They don't stand a chance without firearms."

"They can get help from the Ontonagon bands," Lyman said. "If they're smart." Then to Corbin: "We're four paddlers less and we might never see them again. Balance it out, John. We need three more in the canoes."

The buzzards left them, disinterested now that the scalp had vanished, and flew for shore. The Ojibwe, seldom loquacious, went mute. The voyageurs renewed their steady pace without the usual accompaniment of song. On this calm summer night with the lake as smooth as sky, Warren estimated they could reach La Pointe before dawn.

Night began to fall, a chill set in, the robe of stars rose, arched and fell into the dark water at every horizon. Just before moonrise, when no line of land was visible in any direction, the northern lights flashed above them for better than an hour. Sits Alone told William they were the souls of the dead dancing in the land where souls survived forever.

Marie wrapped Makons in two blankets and fed him boiled rice water. She had already lost her firstborn. She held tight to her crucifix, humming to her younger son.

William thought about never seeing Little Raven again, wondering if he was dead. He resumed his questioning of Sits Alone in the stern. Curious of all details of his mother's tribe's rites and habits, the boy wanted to know about the Midé's five eagle feathers.

"Five kills, Nosins. Long ago." *Nosins* meant grandson. All the elders called him that.

"But a Midé is not a warrior," said the boy. "A Midé knows medicine."

"And he knows secrets. He knows the hearts of warriors."

"Little Raven says all men want to be warriors."

"All young men, Nosins. Old men, no longer."

"What do old men want to be?"

Sits Alone was amused by the boy's assertive curiosity. He had a mind like a snare and never forgot what walked into it.

"To be young men again. Now sleep. *Weeng* is nearby. You will scare him away."

William listened to the water rushing against the birch bark hull. Soon the sky and lake were so dark and fused together that the boy could not tell whether the stars were above or below him. He dozed, awoke, and dozed again to the steady rhythm of the paddles in the night.

A half-moon rose about midnight. His father called a pose, while voyageurs and Indians lit their pipes in the luminescent band of moonlight gleaming up from the lake. Sits Alone spoke to the moon and offered tobacco to her reflection, then to the lake and sky.

They ate what they had, drank, and secured the lashings on the cargo. Then they struck out again due west. The late hour and total absence of land gave free rein to the voyageurs, who reckoned by the heavens around them. They took up their low singing in the starry night. This and the night chill rising from the water lulled the white passengers to sleep, lying in oilskin mats and blankets on the bottoms of the batteaux and large canoes. Marie alone stayed awake chanting comfort to her son and fingering her rosary beads.

In the deep night, a colder wind rippled the surface. The northern sky suddenly flashed white under electric clouds obscuring the stars. Seven seconds later thunder rolled across the water. Lyman Warren cursed. No land in sight, and the storm would soon be on them.

I was once standing near the entrance of an Ojibwe Me-da-we-gaun, more commonly known as the "Great Medicine Lodge", while the inmates were busy in the performance of the varied ceremonies of this, their chief medical and religious rite... The language and phrases used were so obscure to a common listener that it would be impossible to give a literal translation of the whole speech. The following

21

passage, however, forcibly struck my attention: "While our forefathers were living on the great salt water toward the rising sun, the great Megis (sea-shell) showed itself above the surface of the great water, and the rays of the sun were reflected from its glossy back. It gave life and warmth to the An-ish-in-aub-ag (red race). All at once it sank into the deep, and our ancestors were not blessed with its light.

-History of the Ojibwe People,
William Whipple Warren,
ca. 1852

Chapter 2: Peacemaking

Moningwunakauning / Madeline Island, Lake Superior

HE RAN DOWNHILL FROM HIS FATHER'S house on the slope to where the canoes lay overturned on the beach, hulls facing skyward, and plunged his bare feet into the chilly lake water. It felt like running on air, then the water cooled his feet. He had thorns, bruises, and cuts in his feet from running through the woods and along the shore where the shells and stones and shards of timber never fazed him.

He would soon wear cobbled shoes like his father, but on the island, he only wore his mother's moccasins. He had never worn shoes and there were none on the island to fit him. They would come later, from his grandfather's bench in New York State, far to the east near the great salt water. His white forefathers had landed there from Europe. His mother's people, the Anishinaabe, had also lived there before they followed the great Megis shell to this island. Once William saw that great white shell hovering above his island home but did not tell anyone, especially not his Ojibwe grandfathers, for fear he would have to follow it.

The boy stood with his bare feet in the water and gazed south and east over the blue face of Gitchi-Gumee. In two small canoes, four Ojibwe were setting their skein. The beaches were cluttered with drying nets and many canoes, more than any he had ever seen on the island. They had come for the payment, like every year, and to parlay. There were hundreds, big canoes, with many men. They had heard of the Sioux scalp taken on the shore by Little Raven.

The call of a crane echoed across the water. It was the only sound in the world, a trilling sound that made him shiver. He could not see the crane, but he heard it. From far away. The Indians stood their canoes, unmoving in the silence that followed. They listened for the crane.

He heard his mother call his name: "Weel-Yom!"

He did not want to go back to the cabin. Not yet. William went to find where he had traced his three initials, just as his father showed him: WWW. In the wet sand with a driftwood stick. This signature gave him a sense of being there, of leaving his mark on his home.

Now behind the rise above La Pointe, downwind from the Indian village, came the sound of drums, the chanting of the men and high ululation of the women.

Looking up the knoll, he saw three Ojibwe boys striking at a dead pine with tomahawks and clubs, marking the war post. His father disapproved of this war game which boiled down to whacking standing logs meant to be the enemy, whooping and boasting.

The bare-skinned boys saw William and came down to the sand. They stood looking at his mark. The two bigger boys were from the island, sometimes his partners in games. The boy he had never seen before was younger and had a serious mien with charcoaled bars under his eyes and a small, well-carved tomahawk in his fist. He wore a breechclout and a deer hide strip around his long hair and seemed older than his size. He pointed to the sand and asked William what the letters meant. They all spoke in Ojibwemowin, his first tongue, the mother tongue.

"It's my name: William Whipple Warren."

"You draw the treetops but not the trees," said Laughs-at-the-Fish, the bigger boy.

"It's my sign. My name. And my father's name, Warren."

"What does Warren mean in the tongue of the whites?"

"It is where the rabbit lives."

"So. You are Little Rabbit Warren?"

They all found this hilarious. Even William laughed.

The younger boy took up a stick and connected William's three W's together so they looked like a zig-zag design. Then he drew a vertical trait down from under each peak. He motioned to William to come around and look from his side. The letters now looked like six pine trees all in a row. The boy pointed to a stand of identical pines that topped the rise where the drums sounded from. William nodded and asked him his name.

The boy looked up and pointed to a small clearing in the moving clouds, a patch of blue sky. Then he drew a head with an eye, a small circle above it, and a curved line connecting the eye to the circle. *"Bagone-giizig"*.

William took this to mean that the boy could see through the heavens, that he was somehow connected to the sky. He would think that for the rest of his life.

"Bagone-giizig," said William. "Hole-in-the-Day." The boy smiled proudly, nodding his head once to affirm his declaration.

"No", said Laughs-at-the-Fish. "That is his father's name. His father calls him Gwii-wisens."

"Your name is Gwii-wisens? *Boy*?" William tried not to sound mocking.

The younger one said nothing but glared at his taller companion.

"My name is Warren, not Six Pine Trees." He laughed, and this drew another laugh from them all. "Where is your father, Gwii-wisens?"

The younger one whose name meant Boy looked at him squarely and said, "I also go by my father's name. He is a chief. Where is your father? Where is Warren?"

"He is at our home, in the white man's village."

"My father is with the People." He pointed over the rise. A gust of wind carried again the sound of the drums to their ears.

§

Toward mid-afternoon, Lyman Warren was in the storehouse, deep in his ledgers checking the inventory loss after the big storm, when he heard the drums pounding. The chanting too reached his ears, high and wild. The war chant. He lit his pipe and considered the reasons why. They'd had their payment, and their feast. Dingley came in stomping his muddy boots and cradling one of the new Springfield rifles.

"There's a mess o' Indians over there, some up from Sandy Lake, some from Flat Mouth's band. Little Raven made it back from the Porkies on foot with his Sioux scalp, Lord knows how. That scalp's got them riled up, Lyman."

"Pillager Chippewa. Who's with the Sandy Lakers?"

"That smart ass chief Hole-in-the-Day. Schoolcraft calls him Hole-in-the-Sky. Used to call him Young Buck and now he ain't so young. The one that got shot by the Sioux by Fort Snelling. The Colonel gave him four Sioux outside the fort, and he shot 'em dead on the run. Indian justice, they say."

"The Sioux killed his daughter in that ambush. Revenge is Indian justice, Daniel. You know how it works. So did Colonel Snelling."

"Flat Mouth, he's here with about thirty braves. Sioux killed his son last year and he ain't got his yet. They know you come back with these new rifles. Appears Schoolcraft tried to talk 'em out of the warpath. But now that Little Raven's got 'em hot again. They goin' out, for sure."

"What's Buffalo say?"

"He don't like it. A peaceable man, our old Beauf. But he ain't got no hand on them young bucks. They's your family, Lyman. And that Sioux scalp was took on your watch."

"I'll go speak to them."

"We oughta send Andy Jackson over with some of them soldiers from Fort Gaines. He gonna use that Removal Act to boot 'em all out, send 'em all over the Mississippi. Sioux and Chippewa alike. Just like he did with them Choctaw down south. They wanna kill each other off, let 'em do it out in the desert."

"This is their home, Daniel. By rights, and inheritance."

"Not if Andy Jackson got anything to say about it. An Indian don't know what it is to own land, and that Removal Act makes it illegal. They'll skedaddle if they know what's good for 'em. You just wait."

It was unproductive. Lyman knew from experience not to argue principles with Daniel Dingley. Or with any other trader in the territory except his old father-in-law Michel Cadotte, who had seen governments come and go in this land ever since the Revolution. In the end it was always a matter of force. The victors consistently claim ownership of the land the Indians have lived on since the time of creation. Then they kill them or push them out. When they kicked the Brits out of the Great Lakes in 1812, America claimed a country so big they didn't even know what they had. But the Indians knew. He closed his ledger.

"We don't want to upset these new white folks, especially the women. Keep it quiet. We'll pay a friendly visit to Great Buffalo. Leave the rifles here."

Outside, the drums beat louder as a gust of lake wind bent the pines and scattered the silver clouds.

§

They walked into the Ojibwe village. A great many fires were burning and much dancing and drumming came from the quarter surrounding a long bark-covered lodge recently erected. Women were preparing foods for a feast. Lyman saw several dogs being skinned and dressed for roasting, a ritual feasting for neighboring bands. Even more were gathered than at payment time. Some of the younger men had painted their faces and bodies. Two of them in full feathered regalia, red and white, were dancing to the war drums and high-pitched singing, brandishing their war clubs and hatchets, spinning and soaring like weightless birds. Their eyes and muscles emanated high excitement. The chief of the La Pointe band, Gichibishiki, was not at his wigwam. His wives told them that Great Buffalo was at the big lodge with his guests.

On their way, Lyman and Dingley came on a group of boys taking turns at striking a standing post. William was running in place, awaiting his turn, holding a small tomahawk in his fist. Lyman Warren peered directly at his son. The boy's jaw dropped as he let the hatchet fall to his side.

"Father," William said in English. "These are my friends."

27

Just then the smaller one called Boy stepped up and snatched the tomahawk from William. He looked at Lyman with a level gaze. "Warren. This is my weapon. I made it with my father." The boy ran at the post and struck it hard. He was surprisingly fast. The other boys followed, yelling their wild cries.

"William, you come with me," said Lyman. "We're going to see Great Buffalo. You will tell him what you saw by the creek. Put your shirt on."

They left the dog feast preparations and crossed the village of wigwams to the long mat-covered lodge under guard in a clearing.

Lyman was recognized and announced. The sentry pulled back the flap and allowed him to enter the lodge with Dingley and William. The smoke was dense. A flute, rattles, and a drum beat a steady rhythm while a shaman, a Midewewin, leapt and chanted around the low fire.

William had never seen so many pelts, feathers, beads, bone necklaces, and dried flesh adorning a man before—he looked like an animal drug up from the swamps. The shaman rattled and rang as he swung back and forth invoking the Great Spirit, now lamenting, now incensed. Warren kept his son close until he saw that he was not afraid, but transfixed. The boy stood still, looking all around him. No women. The tang of sweat, dog meat, cedar bark, and the scent of wild men hung in the lodge. The scalp dance was over, they were preparing for war.

Smoke drifted out the top hole where clouds were passing but the air inside was thick and rank. The lodge itself was high and dark and hung with robes and skins, carved and colored masks, blankets, and mats painted with figures and symbols. He saw stiffened hide shields, quivers, clubs, lances with feathers and scalps hanging down, and an assortment of drums and weapons never displayed in an ordinary wigwam. William had never been to a war council.

Great Buffalo, his broad face impassable, was the only chief unpainted. He sat under his headdress with the horns spreading wide above his temples, facing the entrance with several neighboring chiefs to his left and right. One was Strong Ground, then Flat Mouth, and Hole-in-the-Day, painted to the ears with a red circle around the black-smudged bullet hole in his chest. He held a long, unlit pipe tomahawk in his arms and gazed directly at Lyman Warren.

Buffalo invited the two white men and the métis grandson to sit on the mats. "Warren. You are my friend and cousin. You are welcome in my lodge."

Lyman sat with his son beside him. Dingley remained standing, wary and tensed. The flap opened and William watched as his new friend, Boy, entered the lodge, tomahawk still in hand, and stood by his own father, Hole-in-the-Day, at the place of the chiefs. Boy's father appeared to approve, and no objections were voiced. Now both boys were beside their fathers.

The younger warriors numbered about twenty. Little Raven was painted and ready, as were the other braves who had accompanied Warren on the trip to Mackinac—those who had seen the killing of the Sioux youth whose scalp now adorned a pole hanging from above. They were not yet passing the pipe, but a large, red-painted post was erected near the fire, where daylight filtered down on the shoulders of the braves as they boasted of their deeds and victories and hacked at the post with such force that it was splitting into shreds.

A young Pillager ended his turn declaring his allegiance to Flat Mouth and his readiness to die on the warpath. Little Raven then cried out, rushed at the post, and hacked off a shard with his tomahawk. He launched into a long tirade that Lyman Warren understood by his gestures as the account of his first kill, goaded on by his fellow warriors. He then presented Flat Mouth with the Sioux arrow he had taken, a sign of his allegiance and a tribute to the chief's lost relatives, urging him to raise the war party and leave in the morning. Flat Mouth accepted the arrow. Little Raven pointed to Warren and Dingley with a disdainful grunt.

Lyman turned to his son. "What is he saying, William?"

"That you would not let them fight. You let the other Sioux escape."

Warren addressed the chiefs one at a time by their names. He looked down at William, then stated, "I ask my son to speak my words in your language, that we all may understand." William stood up.

"You have all expressed your dissatisfaction with war. Flat Mouth, you refused to fight for the British. You say that the Anishinaabe do not ask the whites to fight their wars, so you will not fight theirs. Your words are wise. We all wish for peace with the Sioux. When you raise your arm to strike the Sioux, they will strike the Anishinaabe. In this manner, you kill your own people."

William said this in Ojibwemowin, standing next to his father.

Flat Mouth stood. He and his bands lived closer to the Sioux boundary line. His losses were legion, and his reputation as a war chief carried far. He had been in 25 battles and never suffered a wound. He looked at Warren as he spoke, pausing so William could tell his words to his father. The straight line of his lips moved but little, yet his voice was grave and powerful.

"I am irretrievably involved in war with the Sioux. I believe it has been intended by the creator that we should be at war with this people. I went to Detroit to talk to Schoolcraft about ending the wars. I came home to find my son was killed. We are not satisfied. We have signed the treaty and sought help from the long knives but have not been answered. The Great Father has not helped us. When the enemy killed my son, I vowed never to lay down the war club. I have sought death in battle, but have not met it."

When the chief sat, a great cry went up in the lodge. But Warren persisted.

"The wisdom of Flat Mouth, who works for peace and has never been wounded, is known and respected. Wiser yet is Great Buffalo, who has never taken a scalp and advises his young men to follow the path to peace, for the good of all the People.

"Strong Ground, Hole-in-the-Day, brothers in war and in peace, you have both told the Dakota chiefs that you wish to sit at the same fire with them and smoke the pipe you gave them. Yet still you seek them out and kill them. Where is the wisdom in this? Today you gather for war, again to avenge your losses, which I grieve along with our Great Father. But war only brings more war, more suffering for your people who already number few. They are hungry. Now is the time to harvest the wild rice. You will have no help from the Great Father in war, only in peace. Great Buffalo, advise your people."

Buffalo answered that he could advise his young men, but could not hold them back from the warpath. Little Raven could not be bridled for his actions.

"War is folly," he said. "But my brothers act in self-defense against the Sioux. On this island, we are isolated from such warfare. The elder Sioux chiefs probably do not sanction the crossing of the lines, but they cannot restrain their young men. I am old now; I do not mingle in interior battles. I have no say in what happens outside my village. The traders know me, I do not look into their houses, nor their canoes. Our children are poor. We cannot survive now without the traders. The white Father has many children, yet his breasts drop. Give us a little milk, that we may wet our lips."

Lyman understood that the chief meant whiskey. "I have no firewater, Great Buffalo. There will be none on this island. I bring useful things, to live, to work, for peace."

Strong Ground answered, "Warren, you are a trusted trader. We have given you our pelts. You and your children were given Ojibwe lands by the treaty. Now we come for payment for our furs. You have new guns from Mackinac. We need guns to hunt."

"You will have your guns to hunt. In the season. Not to kill your enemy."

Chief Hole-in-the-Day then stood. His voice was poised despite his full warrior regalia. He carried two knives, his war club, a full quiver, and a flintlock pistol in his belt.

"Trader, the People do not make war against the Great Father. The Ojibwe is the friend of the white man. We trade with the long knife. The Americans have by treaty set the boundaries of our land, and we agreed peacefully. Now we are attacked by the dogs who kill our women and children in our own land. We defend our own land."

Hole-in-the-Day signaled at William to translate his words for the white traders, which he did faithfully.

"The Sioux walked here before the Ojibwe," said Dingley. "Why not share it? What gives you the right to that land anyway?"

William hesitated before translating this, but the chief wanted to hear it. William went ahead. Hole-in-the-Day's brow lowered, he stood straighter and began to approach. He was not a tall man, but his very presence and stature made him seem like a giant.

"By the same right, trader, that your Great Father claimed this country from the British King—by conquest. We drove the Sioux from this country by force of arms and have since occupied it. They cannot, and dare not, try to dispossess us of our habitations! You will give us our rifles. We paid good furs for them."

Lyman understood what the chief wanted by his two-armed gesture; fists held forward then jerking back.

"You will have no rifles before I finish my count," he said.

Hole-in-the-Day then darkened with rage, flailing his pipe-tomahawk as he spoke, his temper spreading fast to the warriors in the lodge.

"Peace or war is not for a trader to decide! You walk now on Ojibwe land, where our fathers have walked before us long before you came. You pretend to dictate to me the law of the traders? Give us our guns!"

The entire company raised a cry, raising arms and rattles. Dingley shifted on his legs, but Warren stood fast.

The masked Midé tossed a powder on the fire that flashed light on the warriors' faces.

At that moment, young Boy darted forward past his father, loosed a wild cry, and swung his tomahawk at Warren's left leg. Lyman grabbed the wound and saw that the boy had drawn a little blood. A hush overtook the lodge. Little Raven smiled broadly. Hole-in-the-Day looked surprised, but not displeased.

"Gwii-wisens!" He motioned for his son to come to his side.

William instinctively leapt after Boy to retaliate in defense of his father, but Lyman caught his shirt and pulled him back. He knelt before him, looked into his face, and whispered: "It's all right, son. It's nothing. Be still. We want no trouble."

Hole-in-the-Day told Boy to sit, then faced Warren. There spread through the lodge a low laughter of satisfaction. The show of boyish impulsiveness had broken the tension.

"I have raised my son to be fearless," said Hole-in-the-Day. "He has yet to learn wisdom, as all boys do. The wise warrior is calm until the kill."

This last line seemed to be addressed to the entire company. There was a murmur of comprehension, or of impatience—Lyman could not read it.

"No harm was done," he said. "Children are blameless."

William translated this, but then glowered at Gwii-wisens. He then spoke a phrase of his own, in the language of the People.

"Gwii-wisens is his name. He acts like a boy. He does not act like a father." This drew a mean twitch from the Indian boy, but his father held him.

Warren gripped his son's shoulder and looked at Dingley, signaling a move. When he spoke, it was to Great Buffalo, still sitting impassively.

"We thank you for your welcome into your lodge. All bands will be paid in goods and coin in three days, when the count is finished. Flat Mouth, Strong Ground, Hole-in-the-Day, we lament your losses. We hope there will be no more losses, no more war with the Sioux."

He turned, his arm around William's shoulder, and Dingley followed. They left the lodge, where the ceremonial ranting and song recommenced as before. It lasted late into the night. The wind passed and a yellow moon rose.

§

That summer the Ojibwes' payment for their pelts was meager, as some of the trade goods were lost in the storm and the AFC would hear nothing about replacing them. Lyman made up for it as he could out of his own stocks, counting on being reimbursed from the Company, or later in another treaty agreement. It was a necessary practice to keep his Indians, as he thought of them, from starving. Over the years it would prove to be the gesture that kept a prosperous man poor.

By the time the payment was ready, the war parties were formed and some of the canoes had already left. The women left to gather wild rice. Flat Mouth and the other two war chiefs left with separate parties in three different directions. Little Raven led one party back to the site in the Porcupines where he had taken the scalp. The Sioux had fled. Lyman had softened and given one new Springfield rifle to each chief—perhaps uselessly, he realized as he told the subagent—in an effort to keep the peace. Nights on the island again turned silent.

"Will they make war?" William asked his father one night before sleeping.

"They probably will, son. That's what they know. But I had to try."

He sought sleep with the memory of the drumming in his ears, hoping the war would not come to his island home. He wondered if he would have to fight Gwii-wisens. If he had to, he would rather fight with him, not against him.

Chapter 3: White Pine Treaty

Fort Snelling, Northwest Territories, 1837

THE GOVERNMENT WANTED TIMBER and a land cession in the vast pineries south of Lake Superior. The country was inhabited by the Chippewa River and Saint Croix Ojibwe bands on both sides of the Mississippi—10 or 12 million acres, half of Wisconsin Territory. A council was called at Fort Snelling in July to make a new treaty with the Ojibwe.

It was old news to Lyman Warren, who saw it coming. The fur trade finished, the American Fur Company switched to fish packing on Madeline Island. Lyman planned on buying into a sawmill right in the heart of timber country. If they wanted to buy timber, that meant they'd want the land. The Ojibwe would be hard put to sell their homeland but without the fur trade, they'd starve. Maybe they could sell just the pine trees, as they had sold the minerals. To survive.

Treaty Commissioner Henry Dodge, Governor of Wisconsin Territory and ex-officio Superintendent of Indian Affairs, wanted the marks of all the principal chiefs on the treaty. Lyman was told to travel down with Great Buffalo, picking up the Mille Lacs and interior bands along the way since it was their lands the government wanted. The Company had interests to defend, trade debts owed to them by the Indians, and money was to be negotiated. They wanted Lyman at the council, along with other partners. He knew the Indians, and most of the chiefs.

He would take along his son William, 11 years old now, just before he left for the East with his grandfather Warren for proper schooling. The boy spoke their language perfectly, and needed to see more of the world. They'd march inland, portage on the streams until they hit the Saint Croix, paddle down to the Mississippi then upstream to Fort Snelling, a stone stronghold on the high bluffs dominating the river.

Great Buffalo told him that the mixed-bloods also had to be involved and warranted payment: they were the children of the Ojibwe and needed protection. This struck a resonant chord in Lyman's mind. His entire family were of mixed-blood, but his previous chance to secure treaty rights for them had been blocked by Congress. Lyman owned that the Indians would have to change their ways, just like he would.

The La Pointe Ojibwe delegation was put together, and in early July they set off together with Great Buffalo, Tug-waug-aun-e to represent the Crane Clan, and a handful of braves to paddle and hunt. Lyman and young William took the same canoe as sub-agent Bushnell, a man he only mildly appreciated, so green as to be completely in the dark about what the Anishinaabe needed or wanted to live. He couldn't figure why or how Bushnell got the appointment—probably through connections. John Jacob Astor, now America's first millionaire after his ventures in fur and far east trade, had sold the AFC to Ramsay Crooks. Together they had so many irons in the fire that even Lyman, a small stockholder in the Company, had no idea.

As they entered the interior country, the brush was thick. They stopped to hunt, and the portages were long and slow. At several points they waited, sending runners to summon the surrounding bands. The water was low until they reached the Saint Croix River, which finally opened up and the canoes could drift downstream unhindered. The big white pines thickened and towered above them and the dark green canopy grew dense. More canoes joined them from the bands along the river, some from the Chippewa Valley where a few sawmills, Lyman had heard, were already under construction.

Washaskkokone, chief of the Mille Lacs bands, joined them with more braves. Lyman liked his Ojibwe name and could not bring himself to call him Muskrat's Liver. He and Great Buffalo would smoke and talk quietly around their fire at night. Young William often sat with them and listened below the towering trees whose tops could still be seen, black and alive against the starry blue night. The wind was calm and the bugs were thick; they all slept close to the smoke and covered up. The only sounds were the crackling fires and the river, an occasional owl's hoot, and the big trees breathing a song that was more soothing than silence.

After the portages, paddling downstream with the high forest enclosing both sides of the river, they encountered more floating brush, then timber. They began to hit log jams in the narrower bends that they had to portage. Carrying their canoes over the fallen logs, they witnessed some of the big trees felled on the banks of the Saint Croix, leaving ragged stumps with centuries behind them.

Washaskkokone frowned and emitted a rare comment: "They do to the river what the beaver does to the stream. They will turn it into a bog and drown the rice."

Further on they met a small logging party—ropey, ragged men who appeared to live on sweat and whiskey. They were dragging brush to the fire by the bank. It was not legal to cut trees on Indian land but the cutters, French speakers from Canada, had no idea where they were. They were told it was all right. In the spring when the water rose, they would float the logs down to the Mississippi and the Indians would be paid. Buffalo said the trees would grow back, but the land would last forever, and the People would not sell it. Washaskkokone said nothing.

They stopped at a stream the loggers had dammed up to float felled logs, making another bog. The Indians opened a breach to drain it. Lyman Warren turned a blind eye, knowing they were punishing the trespassers for taking their trees without permission.

At a sharp bend still well above the falls, the canoes which now numbered thirty were stopped at a log jam. The loggers, who spoke French and Swedish, had felled a white pine maybe 200 feet long over the water, then floated more logs down to crash into it. The Indians looked at the fallen trunk, bigger around than they were tall, with curiosity, sadness, and shock. Great Buffalo turned and stood by himself looking at the river. Warren reckoned he was getting old, sentimental. Some Indians wept that way, though he couldn't figure weeping over a tree.

The obvious choice was to portage around the jam, but first, the loggers wanted help clearing it, as they had only one ox left. The other broke a leg and they had to kill and eat it. They were smoking the rest over a brush fire. The Indians were not enthusiastic about helping the trespassers, but their subagent Bushnell talked them into it. It was important to get to the council and the river be cleared, if only for the return. The loggers offered smoked ox and whiskey to pay the Indians. The jam was undone after two days. The ensuing night was boisterous, but Warren's rationing avoided useless drownings or bloodshed.

Out of curiosity, Lyman counted the rings on the fallen giant and showed Great Buffalo how big it was when his ancestor landed at Plymouth Rock, by the great salt water. It was a young tree then, about one hand in diameter, over two hundred years ago. The chief answered that his people came from the salt water, down the great river to the lakes, to live on Monigwunakauning, before the tree was born. Their fathers hunted these lands and warred against their enemies to protect them, watching the trees grow bigger.

William translated this for his father, who nodded. "Now the white father needs the trees to build his house," he said.

Great Buffalo seemed puzzled. "This is the home of the badger, the bear, the wolf, the moose, the whitetail deer, the birds you see flying above you. The forest is not mine to sell."

That evening all were encamped under pines so high and dense you could not see the stars through the canopy. Lyman walked over to Great Buffalo's fire and shared a pipe with him. His words carried great import for all the bands. Tug-waug-aun-e joined them and partook of the pipe. It was an informal council, like the many they had on the island, many a night. As he grew older, William often interpreted, as he did this night. He had a natural talent for it, his young voice flowed like water.

"Gichibizhiki," said Warren. "You know me. You know I am your friend. The island is home to both of us. We need to live. How will we live, you and me, without the furs? The beaver is almost gone. The mink, the badger. How will we buy our blankets, our fishhooks, if there is no trade?"

"The People and the traders are now like the roots and the earth. We live together. We hunt for the traders; we buy what we need from the traders."

"The Great Father in Washington will pay you money for the trees. And tools. And teach your children. You will farm your land, grow your food."

"I do not like to farm. The rice is there to harvest, the fish, the game to hunt. The Great Spirit has given this all to us to live."

"There is no longer game enough for trade. The whites in Europe no longer want the beaver. My children too must live. The mixed-bloods must be paid."

Tug-waug-aun-e said, "Your children are our children. You send my nephews, Nosins and Makons to learn the white man's ways, to read and write the word. This is good. They will teach their children. It is the way. All our children will learn the word."

"And the People must pay their debts to the traders."

"To you, Warren. You give us clothes, traps, knives, food when we are starving. You are like a father to the Anishinaabe, as you are to your children. Others are not so good." Buffalo nodded in assent.

Lyman nodded to the chief. He rose to leave.

"Your people must sell the trees, Gichibizhiki. For a good price."

In the morning he went with William to find Great Buffalo with Washaskkokone and a few braves standing on the riverbank at first light, still wrapped in their blankets, gazing across the water at a four-legged beast as big as a moose that stood its ground and watched them back. Its hide was a shaggy red and ravaged by vermin, its head long and drawn, white and snoutless, with two great blank holes for eyes. The short blunt antlers were white as bone. The boy froze and held fast to his father. Lyman turned to get his rifle, but Buffalo stopped him.

"No use, Warren," he said. "Windigo cannot be killed." The beast vanished in the brush.

They loaded the canoes and headed further south, leaving the pine forests. Bushnell hurried them on, the month was nearly over and the council had probably begun already.

Before nightfall they reached the Mississippi River and turned from the surrounding prairie lands into the island-strewn waters that they now had to paddle upstream. Hardwoods and dun-colored limestone cliffs rose high above, turning salmon-colored in the dusk. At one point they saw a settler's cabin and a small herd of cows, and a good number of caves in the bluffs. Here Buffalo said they would stop, as he would not go into Sioux country in the night, and he wanted to arrive at the council in full daylight. Lyman agreed. They selected an island, lit their fires, and posted sentinels. The river flowed by, flat, wide, and heavy.

§

The thirty Ojibwe canoes approached the fort from the south, past many small islands where the Dakota Sioux stood densely along the shores by their summer lodges and tipis, glaring at them. The Ojibwe glared back silently. They were in enemy territory, but within the jurisdiction of the US military. The Ojibwe came at the request of the Great Father for the purpose of making a treaty, to secure their lives and the lives of their children. It was not a place or time for war. Fort Snelling rose above the bluff, a diamond-shaped citadel the same dun color as the fluted limestone cliffs but more obstinate, an impenetrable fortress, a wall of stone flatness built not of any reverence for the surrounding beauty, but to express its will and might.

They arrived at the foot of a long cleared slope where they were greeted by an excited gathering of Ojibwe women and youngsters. They had sent a runner ahead and were expected at the council that very afternoon. The white father was impatient and wanted to proceed without them, urging all the chiefs present to sign the treaty, but Flat Mouth, head of the Leech Lake Pillagers, spoke for the civil chiefs and was holding fast to established protocol. Not one Ojibwe would touch the quill without the presence and agreement of the people who lived in the country the whites wanted to buy, as it would be improper and unfair interference. Chief Hole-in-the-Day, on the other hand, was urging them all to sign at the price Dodge and Taliaferro were offering, although there was still no talk of price—it was just called "fair".

On the plain outside the fort was a village of bark-covered lodges, where Ojibwe bands from hundreds of miles around now formed, for the duration of the talks, the largest community in the surrounding area. The canoes just arrived brought the number of Ojibwe encamped on the plain to 1,200. Farther back, spread out over their own allotted territory, were about 700 Sioux who had come, they said, to listen. Warren found William Aitken there, a Scotsman and fellow fur trader, along with the missionaries Brunson and Boutwell. The women fed them all a beef stew made with government cattle while Aitken filled him in.

A disconcerting bit of news was that Colonel Davenport's soldiers had been called away to Florida territory to fight the Seminoles, an emergency measure. The entire US Army consisted of 5,000 men and most of them were down in Florida. A Captain Scott was in charge of the 19-man skeleton regiment left to defend the fort, but Dodge had all the Indians, Sioux and Ojibwe, on best behavior promises.

Also in and around the fort were about 20 black-skinned people, men and women, who seemed to be doing all the domestic chores for the whites. William asked his father what tribe they were from.

"No tribe, son. Slaves."

"Reverend Ferry said there were no slaves in the Territories. They're free here."

"That's right, free according to the 1820 Missouri Compromise. Two Negro women who lived here won their freedom in the courts last year, but that was exceptional. Generally, Army officers are allowed to own them, I suppose because they move around. The Sioux agent Taliaferro owns many. He rents them to the officers."

"How can he own them here? Why are they slaves?"

"I hear they get paid wages here. But they're property, son. They were bought in states down south where it's legal. Most states down south have more black people than whites."

"Like here, where the Indians outnumber the whites?"

"That's a fact, William. But this is their country. Indians are free. The Negroes down south are slaves, like these here. But I suspect the officers treat them well."

"Better than they treat the Indians?"

Warren looked up at the walls of the fort with the armed soldiers stationed above, where the American flag waved in the wind. His son asked questions he could not explain to himself. "They're all treated badly," he said. "When you go to New York state with your grandfather next month, you'll see Negro freedmen. Slavery is abolished there." He went no further with it.

Captain Scott was no negotiator, Aitken told him, but a military man. Taliaferro the Sioux agent was there, trying to wheedle his way into Ojibwe territory. He seemed to side with Chief Hole-in-the-Sky, a Chippewa he spoiled with praise and favors and who was set on taking center stage. The Chief had his young son with him, by his side all during the council. Lyman remembered Boy, the young one with the serious look, from the tomahawk incident in La Pointe. William remembered him even better.

The real one-man show was the Commissioner, Wisconsin Governor Henry Dodge, who'd arrived on a steamboat with his bespectacled secretary, a skinny man who never stopped scribbling, and a well-dressed younger man named George Fowles. Tall and fit, a former dragoon captain, Dodge was a Blackhawk War veteran respected by the northern tribes who hated the Sacs and Foxes. He dictated terms rather than negotiating them, but was amenable to appeasing the traders by allowing them payment for the Ojibwe's' debts out of the treaty money. Taliaferro, watching out for his own Sioux, despised the traders and the American Fur Company. Allegiances, said Aitken, were unclear. Apparently, the Company used its influence to have Dodge named Commissioner, pretty confident he could get what he wanted from the Indians. Sibley was across the river in Mendota with a few more Company men, waiting to go up and stake more timber claims on the Chippewa River. Warren asked Aitken how the talks were shaping up.

"Dodge wants to go fast, but you know them Indians. All ceremony and speeches. It's important to them, poor devils, and they don't want to go away empty handed. There's some confusion about what the hell the Indians are selling. They think it's the trees, but Dodge wants the land. They think they're making a savvy trade deal. Listening to him, he's buying half the territory. Far as I can tell, them dolts they got to interpret—one's a tongue-tied Irishman not even I can understand—don't know they ass from a hole in the ground. Pardon me French."

Lyman kept his voice low and looked around. Hundreds of Ojibwe women were tending to food and the encampment, a good many children and dogs ran around just like in their villages. It was the biggest gathering of Ojibwe bands he had ever seen. The men had returned to council after the mid-day meal. All were up under the leaf bower the soldiers had built for the formal outdoor council, where women were unwelcome. They had been discussing, smoking, stalling, giving speeches for almost a week. Lyman weighed possible consequences of a refusal to sell. It would be good for no one, but the Ojibwe would suffer most. That was probably not the government's uppermost concern.

"If he wants their land," he said to Bushnell, "they'll have to remove. Van Buren is a Jackson man on removal. That's why the army's down there in Florida. If they refuse, we'll have another Trail of Tears here. Where will that lead?"

"Ain't no talk of removal," Aitken tried to reassure him. "Dodge, he's a crafty one. Wants to treat them all as what he calls one nation. We know that's hogwash. The Chippeway ain't no nation, ain't no one man can rule them. Flat Mouth told them as much. Not even a chief can decide alone, they ain't got the authority. That's their way. That Hole-in-the-Sky though, he says it's all his. That man wants to be big chief, Lyman. He's gonna be trouble, mark me words."

Chief Hole-in-the-Day, as Warren called him, was wary of traders, having known good and bad in the Sandy Lake and Fond du Lac area and now in his southern domains near Crow Wing, where whiskey abounded. The chief of the Sandy Lakers in the prime of his life was unimposing, of average height, admirably constructed but plainly dressed, unlike most Ojibwe chiefs who prized medals, highly colored beaded leathers and jewelry, and elaborate head-dresses, especially when in council. Hole-in-the-Day wore a blanket mantel that he spread like wings in his most eloquent moments, a breechclout and leggings, and a fitting but plain head crown of splayed eagle feathers, one for each kill. His war prowess and oratory powers were by now legendary, and he had a keen sense of politics as the whites saw it. He maintained that he spoke for all the People and they would do as he told them.

The Mille Lacs and Leech Lake bands present at the council did not agree wholeheartedly with Hole-in-the-Day, but recognized that he had a way with the whites. He had been known to take a paddle to drunken Ojibwes, even as he maintained cordial and sometimes privileged relationships with the whites and obtained admirable concessions, notably from Sioux agent Taliaferro.

§

The Ojibwe delegation marched up the hill to the fort at a brisk pace in the early afternoon, over a hundred from the interior bands with their banners and flags afloat in the wind, preceded by their chiefs but in some disorder, creating a commotion among the many hundred already gathered before the bower and table set on a platform in the shadow of Fort Snelling. Commissioner Dodge stood on the platform in plain view, as tall as his commanding rank afforded him. Lawrence Taliaferro stood as well, with the advisor Fowles, as did Captain Scott and his flanking soldiers, holding up the American Flag. There was a slight updraft where eagles rose. Artists had described that vast country around as paradise. The sun beat warm and the air smelled of summer hardwoods, prairie grasses, and the river. Benches were set out, but most of the Ojibwe sat on the soil or stood proud, some blanketed, many painted, with feathered spears planted as firmly as the flag. The solemnity of the occasion was marked by elaborate speeches and dress on both sides of the table.

Lyman Warren shook hands with the officials and told them his credentials as trader and American Fur Company stockholder. Sioux agent Taliaferro was cool, asking for subagent Bushnell and remarking that they had held up the business of the Commission by arriving late.

"Why did he come here with a trader?"

"Bushnell is on his way up the hill," said Warren. "He asked me to come. The subagent is new and is not familiar with the Indians he was assigned to govern."

Taliaferro grunted. "I remind you that traders are not part of the appointed Commission and have no voice in treaty dealings. You may observe, Mr. Warren, but that is all. Please take your place."

Lyman sat close to the front. It was to be an afternoon of talking and listening. Opposite his bench, among the Mississippi chiefs, stood Hole-in-the-Day and his son, Boy. The youth, as silent as his father, held no tomahawk this time but had a beaded knife sheath on his strap.

After formal greetings and smoking of the long pipe, the interior chiefs told the Commissioner who they were, who their ancestors were, and how they lived on their lands. One by one, the chiefs spoke through the afternoon, the interpreters took their turns.

Great Buffalo said that they had been given very little notice that the Great Father wanted the land, and they had to confer among themselves before anything was signed. Washaskkokone made it clear that his Mille Lacs band occupied the land:

"We are talking about the land you have come for. I have tread all over it with my war club in my hand. My ancestors and those of Bagone-giizig are the chiefs and protectors of that country and drove the bad Indians away from it."

They expressed the wish that the Great Father would treat them, his children, kindly. They were poor and depended on the traders to live in the winters when game was scarce, and their own children were sick or hungry.

Behind the platform, Dodge showed them a map of their land and the great stretch he wanted to buy. He stated over and over that their Great Father wanted the pine timber, and in any case the land was of no value to them for game or cultivating any crops. "Your Great Father wishes to purchase the pine timber for his white children. He will give you a fair price for it."

Buffalo then said, "Lyman Warren has been kind to us and given my people money, food, and clothing. We want him to be paid $20,000."

Taliaferro, incensed, drew his pistol and pointed it directly at Lyman Warren. Chief Hole-in-the-Day bounded up and yelled, *"Shoot him, Father!"*

Warren stood and faced him. Aitken and two other traders readied their guns, the soldiers aimed, and the whites stared each other down for a few moments not knowing whom to shoot. The Ojibwe maintained an admirable calm. The advisor George Fowles spoke to Dodge, who put his hand on the agent's arm and leaned over to whisper in his ear, obviously urging better judgment. Taliaferro kept his uncocked pistol aimed at Warren while he spoke to the entire gathering.

"Very well, Sir," he intoned. "I only hold for the first act of hostility, then I sell my life, if need be, after the fall of the dastard who has attempted to intimidate this Commission." He laid his pistol on the table. Lyman sat, reassured that the Sioux agent was all huff and bluff.

Commissioner Dodge pushed matters forward. He called the council to task, urging them to accept his offer of "a fair price" for the land. He stated that by morning he expected them to act as one people and to select no more than two chiefs to speak on behalf of all. He concluded by reminding the Ojibwe to remember their mixed-blood relatives and to render justice to their traders when they decided how much and in what manner they wanted to be paid for the land cession. This was all translated and written down by Secretary Van Antwerp. It caused a murmur as close to discontent as Ojibwe etiquette would allow. Hole-in-the-Day and his band abruptly left the council and Dodge formally adjourned the proceedings.

Talks were deadlocked for a day. Lyman went down to check the canoes and pondered what ties could bind a Sioux agent to an Ojibwe chief. It dawned on him that Taliaferro could be cajoling Hole-in-the-Day with favors, flattering him in order to use him in the negotiations. The Sioux were his charge, so getting a fair share for them was his main concern. Which is why he sought to eliminate the traders' debts, especially those affiliated with his nemesis, the AFC. Taliaferro was outranked by Dodge, who seemed willing to appease both the Ojibwe and the traders to get the signatures, but the odds seemed against Lyman's obtaining anything for his family, the mixed-bloods, or the AFC.

He and Aitken took the chance on a parlay with the chiefs. They did not bother to notify sub agent Bushnell. Nor any government official.

He sought out Buffalo, then Flat Mouth, and went to find Hole-in-the-Day and his brother Strong Ground. There in the camp, which was more like a wigwam village, they walked through the cooking fires, families, dogs, and games to find the quarters of the Mississippi bands. Buffalo, a moderate man, would hopefully do

most of the talking to the younger chiefs. Wanting no misunder-
standing, Lyman took William with him, as well as an interpreter, a
black slave named Jim. The Reverend Brunson had just bought Jim
from Laurence Taliaferro for $1,200. He spoke Dakota Sioux and a
smattering of Ojibwe, Brunson's main justification for purchasing a
slave in a free Territory—to explain the expense to his Board. Once
purchased, Jim was freed by the Reverend who gave him a letter to
that effect, but he stayed to interpret when needed. He and young
William got along fine, speaking English and Ojibwe.

Hole-in-the-Day, sitting bare-torso in the shade, was adamant
but even-tempered. The only paint he wore was around the blackened scar in his breast from the Sioux bullet hole he took ten years
before at this same fort. Around it were circles of red, yellow, and
purple, a reminder that he could not be killed. His only other accouterments were his chief's medals, a necklace of his enemies' dried
ears, and two brass bands around his biceps. The taciturn Strong
Ground, despite his lesser influence, wore his elaborate beaded
chief's garb every day of the council.

The talk was informal, sitting on blankets in the open. Lyman
cautioned them all against selling for too little. Annuities made a
livelihood they must count on for years, if not forever. And there
would be goods and services, farms and schools, tools and tobacco offered. They must hold out for more money. Their debts to the
traders, accumulated over years, must be paid. Those were likely
included in the terms the Father would offer, but it would be better
if they stated them first, at a good price.

Flat Mouth made the laconic comment that this was beyond his
comprehension, that the traders owed the Ojibwe as much as they
owed the traders. Their hunters were killed by the Sioux while trapping for the whites. The food the traders ate, and the wood they
burned, all came from Ojibwe land. "And they talk to us about paying their debts?"

Hole-in-the-Day mistrusted traders, he said and maintained they
should receive nothing. But he wanted satisfaction for their debts,

payment for his people ,and peace with the whites. If debts must be paid, they must be paid now, and on the Indians' terms.

Buffalo reminded him that most traders were of mixed-blood, and their children were the People's children. The tribe must provide for their own.

Hole-in-the-Day said nothing.

Lyman then told him he admired his son, Boy, and how close he held him. "A father must guide his children," he said. "It is for them that we preserve what we have." Lyman gestured toward Boy. Jim interpreted into some kind of Indian gibberish and repeated Lyman's gesture, stretching out his hand. William politely, briefly, again translated his father's words.

"One day, Boy will inherit the role of chief," Lyman said. "He will lead the People. Teach him well." That, Lyman knew to say in Ojibwemowin. It was understood.

The lad named Boy looked on with his stern face and listened. He crossed his arms in imitation of his father's posture, furtively glancing at William. Hole-in-the-Day sat implacable. Warren and Aitken got up and bid the chiefs good day. William walked by his father's side.

"You ain't tellin' him nothin' he don't know," Aitken said, "But he likes to hear it. They're leery of the traders, Lyman. But they need us as much as we need them. It's good business."

That day the bands did not go to the council but remained in the encampment talking and smoking until after twilight, roasting government beef. There was a great deal of low drumming, chanting, and speech making late into the night. This created an air of expectation, an electricity as felt before a thunderstorm, yet the nights were calm. The entire tribe felt on the verge of a moment of great importance. It was customary that treaty talks should take much time; the chiefs did not like to be hurried. Unlike many recent Indian gatherings for trade payments or annuities distribution, the Fort Snelling council was marked by a great sobriety.

An old whiskey seller named Parrant nearly broke this spell when he rolled in with a wagonload of casks, but was instantly seized by soldiers. Taliaferro had banned him from the Fort Snelling reserve and called him Old Pig's Eye for his half-blindness. He wanted to leave a cask with the soldiers on credit, but Captain Scott sent him back to his cave on the river.

The treaty Commission, the military surgeon Doctor Emerson, officers and their wives dined often at Taliaferro's agency quarters, a large fenced-in house outside the fort with many Negroes bustling about, setting a handsome table on pressed linen with Mrs. Taliaferro's gilded black and white china. They had no need of Parrant since Henry Sibley, the young and ambitious AFC trader, provided delicacies and drink from his post in Mendota, across the river. The port wine was poured by Doctor Emerson's Negro servant, a slave named Etheldredge Scott, whom the doctor called Dred.

Lyman, as he expected, was never invited to the doings at the Taliaferro's'. In the evenings he walked past the festively lit house with his pipe, taking in the vast waving plateau behind the bluffs of the Mississippi, where the Ojibwe encamped, and further on the Sioux tipis. From the ridge he saw the wooded islands below at the confluence of the Saint Peter's, where the fires of the Sioux burned brightly. This was good country, but he missed the lake.

To the west, the sky here was purple. It was the beginning of the great plains, the home of the buffalo, the Mandans, and surely in the fullness of time, the Sioux. They had become excellent horsemen, he noted, now that the Ojibwe had driven them from the forest into the plains. Most Ojibwe wouldn't know what to do with a horse. The government had once shipped forty saddles to the La Pointe Agency as part of annuity payments, oblivious to the fact that the Ojibwe had no use for them. They lay in store molding for a couple years before they were shipped back to Washington.

One morning William came to the breakfast fire leaning on an improvised crutch and favoring his left foot. He had snagged it in the woods while running with his friend Boy. Chasing a moose, he told his father, who told him it was a fool thing to do.

"For once we have a real doctor. He'll see if it's broken, fix you up." Lyman brought him inside the fort to see the military surgeon in the stone-built officer's quarters. The busy Doctor Emerson obliged, pronounced it sprained, and Lyman left to prepare for the council.

The doctor told William that if he was going east to school, he'd better cut his hair, or they'd take him for an Indian. And wear shoes. Then he had the boy's ankle bound up by his servant Dred Scott, in their stone quarters in back of his own apartments. Harriet Scott prepared a bowl of poultice and a better crutch that Dred adjusted to his height. William was impressed by their dress, their skills, and by their melodious humming as they worked. He finally asked the man.

"You always dressed up like that? You live here?"

"We both work for Dr. Emerson. Major Taliaferro used to own Harriet here, but sold her to Dr. Emerson when he married us last spring. Right here in the fort. Now we both owned by the Doctor. He let us live here with this fireplace for Harriet to cook on."

"They good to all the black people like you here?"

"Most of 'em eat and sleep down by the stables but it ain't so bad. Most of the time."

"This Territory don't have slavery," William said. "They got abolitionists here."

"Well, we come from Missouri, a slave state. Maybe someday we go back there, with the Doctor. We go where the master go, but we just fine right here. We savin' for a family." He smiled at his wife, who looked younger than her new husband and very happy.

"Two Negro women just get freed because they live here. You know them?"

"Them two ain't here no more. The good Lord blessed them with freedom, I reckon. Maybe someday the Lord bless Harriet and me."

"Not if you don't ask. You go to court, my father says. Because you're both free here."

"Until the master say we free, the Lord don't say it neither. Now you all fixed up, young man. You use this, and you step light." Etheldredge Scott stood and handed him the crutch. The smiling Mrs. Scott gave him a wrapped piece of gingerbread she had just made for the Doctor, telling him it would make him feel better.

"Thank you, Sir. And thank you, Ma'am. I hope someday you get free too."

William hobbled his way back to the encampment, where he told his father and Aitken that he'd been well cared for by the Scotts' two slaves. The kindest people he'd met at the fort.

§

The council resumed the next morning with the pipe offered to the four cardinal points and passed around in silence at a solemn cadence. Maghegabo of Leech Lake came forth painted in red and yellow and black, crowned with a spray of eagle feathers and with several silver medals placed on his chest by the different chiefs. Before the Governor's table he planted his war flag and made it clear that his words were important and those of the chiefs. He pointed to the map alongside Dodge, telling him they had smoked and shook hands four times already, and now on the fifth day, they had come to give him an answer.

"I come to tell you that I speak for the different bands of my nation, and they agree to sell you the land you want. The being that created us made us naked, but created you and your people with knowledge and power to get a living. Not so with us. We had to cover ourselves with moss and rotten wood, and you must be merciful to us."

Dodge's reply was unequivocal: their Great Father had sent him to treat them as his children, to pay them the value of their land, not to deceive them in anything he might say or do: "I tell you this now, that you may not hereafter say I deceived you. Your Great Father, the President of the United States, will be just toward you."

Maghegabo then laid an oak leaf on the table, saying that they wanted to keep this different kind of tree. It was clear to the secretary Van Antwerp, who noted this down, that despite the nonsense translated by the incompetent Irishman, he meant the hardwoods, not the pines. They wanted to hold on to the tree that gave them life, the streams, and lakes where they fish, the maple that gave them sugar. Moreover, they wanted to hunt game and gather wild rice on the land for as long as it lasted. The Ojibwe would sell the pine trees, but they wanted to stay and live on the land, their source of life. They proposed payment over sixty years, then their children would renegotiate in their time.

Dodge told them that the Great Father would probably not want the land for his white children for many years, probably not in their lifetime. But he never purchased land from the tribes for a designated time, only in perpetuity.

Flat Mouth stood and reiterated that it was hard to sell the land, but the trees would grow back. "There is some game on the lands yet, and we wish to remain on them, to get a living. Sometimes we scrape the trees and eat the bark. The Great Spirit above made the earth and makes it produce, which enables us to live. Without it, we could not live. We hunt and make sugar and dig roots on the land. We fish and harvest rice and drink from the waters."

This was noted, Dodge reassured them. When asked how much he offered for the lands, he was true to form as a negotiator and offered no figure and no payment terms. He told them to consult with their agents, Bushnell and Vineyard, to know how much their lands were worth. And to reserve part of the payment for the mixed-bloods, as a gesture of "benevolence", as well as payment to the traders.

The negotiations went on for another day, the bands again gathered in the village and talked late into the night. The next day, Dodge offered some of the payment in goods. Maghegabo said they would gladly take the money offered and the goods, not one or the other. They would sell the pines, but held out for more money and longer payments, the right to hunt and fish and gather wild rice, and to stay on their lands. Dodge consistently countered that they would not have to move, probably, for a long time. And they could hunt and fish freely on the land, which they would occupy *"during the pleasure of the President."*

He finally offered $800,000 including $100,000 for the mixed-bloods, and an additional $70,000 for the traders, specifying $25,000 for Lyman Warren and $28,000 to William Aitken, in payment of "certain claims against the Indians." The terms of the treaty were broken down as twenty annual payments to the Chippewa, partly in money, partly in goods, blacksmiths jobs and supplies, provisions, and $500 in tobacco.

Hole-in-the-Day came forth and made a final speech to dispel their hesitations, saying that he would sign or die, the dramatic import of which carried the consensus. The chiefs and representatives voiced their agreement. The treaty ceremony would take place the next day.

Lyman Warren felt some satisfaction where himself and Aitken were concerned. The business end held up; Dodge saw to that. But he did some figuring and estimated that once divvied up, each Ojibwe would get enough for a couple blankets, leggings, salt pork, and flour, maybe a pot to cook it in every year for twenty years. They could have done better.

The day after they agreed to the terms, only twenty chiefs came to council. They smoked the pipe, as customary, and the Commission waited to see if they would sign. A half-hour passed. Two fully painted warriors came up from the bark-lodge encampment bearing the Ojibwe war flag alongside the American flag. Behind them was a parade of drums, dancers, and several hundred warriors in full regalia, waving spears and tomahawks in such a manner as to cause Captain Scott to close the gates and put his nineteen soldiers on full alert.

Maghegabo stepped up to the bower and shook Dodge's hand, telling him they agreed to the terms and would sign. While Secretary Van Antwerp busied himself writing out the terms, including the names of forty chiefs, the Commission, the witnesses, and five Company men, the great dancing festival went on all day in the sun and then in the shade of the fort.

At the signing the next day some chiefs were visibly reluctant, but Hole-in-the-Day with his customary flourish stepped up and signed first. Some of the chiefs would not touch the quill if it were in the hand of the Secretary. It had to be set on the table. They were superstitious and "queasy" about the written word, Warren told Bushnell. It was sacred to them and had close to magical powers. That night 1,300 Ojibwe feasted on 10 cattle slaughtered by the slaves at the garrison. Dodge wanted them to leave Fort Snelling with full bellies.

§

The Treaty of Saint Peters, however inadequate and disputed, was signed on July 29, 1837. Penned by Van Antwerp, it totaled three pages. How the annuities were to be distributed among the bands, Dodge declared, was a matter of tribal judgment and not for him to decide. This was another matter that would cause years of ill will among the bands. La Pointe was the designated venue for annuities payments in the fall—the best hunting and rice harvesting season. Some of the Mississippi bands had hundreds of miles to march. Many figured it was not worth it and did not bother to come.

The Ojibwe were granted the usufruct, as it was termed, to continue to hunt, fish, and gather wild rice in abundance on the ceded lands, for a given time that was nonetheless unspecified. Governor Dodge conducted the treaty officially with the "Chippewa Nation of Indians", an entity unknown to any Indian at the time, thus eschewing any notion of conflicting desiderata among the many bands and imposing for future negotiations a term that would allow the United States to deal with any smaller bands on a piecemeal basis.

Secretary Van Antwerp took abundant notes, sometimes interpreting himself what was translated by four interpreters, noting on one page of his treaty journal that Maghegabo's speech was rendered literally in English as "nonsense" and that the interpreters were "unfit to act in that capacity." As the Ojibwe could not read what they signed, they had to trust what they heard on the lips of the whites who entertained them.

Lyman reported later to Schoolcraft that Taliaferro used Hole-in-the-Day's influence to get them to sign their lands away for a pittance. The Ojibwe had no idea what thousands of dollars were, nor how annuities were to be divided among them, nor who owned what land, nor what was bought, nor what was actually sold. They were told of mineral rights and timber that the whites wanted, not the land. They called it the White Pine Treaty. Perhaps the Indians thought they were leasing pine trees, as Flat Mouth understood, to be cut on the stump. But not the land. And they must keep the resources they lived on, the game, the fish, the rice, the roots, the bark of the trees, in perpetuity.

Dodge had listened carefully and spoken carefully, dictating the terms. The word removal did not appear on the treaty, nor did he utter it. He conceded, in Article 5 of the treaty, that the Ojibwe should be guaranteed *"the privilege of hunting, fishing, and gathering wild rice upon the lands and the rivers, and lakes included in the territory ceded...during the pleasure of the President of the United States."*

When at the end of the day the chiefs and band representatives finally touched the quill, unwilling to break the consensus, Dodge issued a promise and a warning. He was apologetic about not having brought them flags and medals, but would do so at the first treaty payment next year. The warning concerned the Dakota Sioux camped around Fort Snelling: they were to refrain from attacking them, for any blow would be felt by himself and their Great Father.

The 1837 Treaty of Saint Peter's struck the first wedges among the Ojibwe bands by treating them as one political entity. Dodge obtained what the government wanted—to clear the way for removal by ending a way of life.

Henry Sibley and his associates left immediately after the signatures and laid more timber claims on the Saint Croix and Chippewa River valleys. Lyman Warren, with his share in a lumber mill there, counted on timber from the whites and the Indians, who also needed the money. Those bands not mentioned in the treaty would also have timber to sell. They had to sell whatever they had; such was the march of civilization. At least they could live.

Chief Hole-in-the-Day, still feeling the wound in his spine from the Sioux bullet ten years earlier in the attack that killed his daughter, left Fort Snelling peacefully and with vows to kill no more Sioux. Instead, he would lead his people to civilization.

Chapter 4: At Oneida

Southwest view of Oneida Institute, Whitestown.

Oneida Institute, located near the Mohawk River in upper New York State, was an abolitionist college run by the Reverend Beriah Green and supported by the Presbyterian Church and fervent American abolitionists from 1832 to 1843. The most radical school in the country educated students of all races and was known as a hotbed of the growing anti-slavery movement. Oneida county served as a pass-through for the Underground Railroad.

1839, Oneida Institute, New York State

THE RUNAWAY WAS BARELY OLDER than William, but younger than Kunkapot. He was a big, strong boy that Reverend Green had brought to their room because when they came—and they would come—they would first search in the black boys' dormitories. The runaway was safer with them. They hid him under the bed.

"I can't keep him anymore at my house, boys. So this one's up to you. They won't suspect Indians. Do your duty to God."

The runaway was dressed in an old black suit a couple sizes too small and had a bowler hat but no shoes. His feet were hard as wood and scarred and scratched.

"Slaves sometimes don't have shoes," said Green. "You boys find him a pair. His name is Elijah. A fine name. Elijah brought down fire in the Hebrew Bible."

Under the bed, his feet looked large. William kept watch while Kunkapot went off to look for shoes. The black students would find a pair. They could find anything.

"Where you come from?"

"Georgia."

"They chasing you?"

"I expect. Where's Canada?"

"Just across the lake. Reverend Green got a boat for you."

"They got people there? People like you?"

"People like me, Indian, and people like you, but free. They got whites there too, but not bad. They'll find you work, teach you to read."

"I can read some. I can write my name." He would not come out from under the bed.

There were footsteps on the wooden stairs and in the hall, boys coming in from classes. William tried to work on a map he was drawing, but he could smell the fear coming from Elijah and could not concentrate. Maybe it was his own fear.

He opened the window that gave onto the green before the Oneida Institute. A black transom was coming up the road. It was the sheriff, who had come here many times, and a man with him under a wide-brimmed hat. William slid some satchels under the bed and pulled the blanket down to cover them. That better do, he thought.

"Anybody come in here, you don't move. No noise. Stick your feet in."

Kunkapot came running in with shoes and gave them to Elijah under the bed.

"Keep them for later," said Kunkapot. "Don't move around. We put a kitchen knife in there. Real sharp."

"I thankee."

Green came back at suppertime. It turned out that Elijah couldn't wear the shoes they found him. He was better off without, but the stockings fit.

"You'll have to walk through the night," said Green. "The slave-catcher will be back tomorrow with a warrant. Black people are not enslaved here and do not go barefoot in New York nor in Canada. You have to wear shoes." Then the Reverend took off his own shoes and handed them to him. "Put these on. I have others."

"I can't do that, Sir. It ain't right."

Beriah Green looked at him steadily. "The Lord sets it right."

Elijah said nothing but did not touch the shoes. William kneeled down and whispered to him under the bed.

"You better take them. He won't leave you alone if you don't."

The Reverend Green, a slight but straight man, stood staring at Elijah.

Elijah's long hand slowly reached out and took the Reverend's shoes.

"I thankee, Sir."

"You thank the Lord." He turned and walked out of the room barefoot.

§

Night came on dark, still and owly. Green sent William, who was part white, and Kunkapot, who could fight, to take Elijah to the next link, a wagon on the way to Oneida Lake. There would be a man in a wagon to take him to Lake Ontario, where there would be a boat for him. Kunkapot, who knew the country well because it was once his people's country, took the knife.

They headed northwest through the woods and along the river, skirting any farms or cabins over a trail nobody but Kunkapot knew was a trail. The idea was to meet nobody until they found the wagon. The man in the wagon had been paid and Green assured them that he was an abolitionist.

They had to cross a pond where there was a cabin on the shore with a lamp lit inside. The night was chilly, so the cabin had a fire burning. Kunkapot said they'd have to swim to the far side. The moon was rising. They could see the dark line of trees. The wagon road was just past that, but they had to avoid the cabin.

"I can't swim," said Elijah. "Never nobody showed me how."

"I see a canoe," William said. "You wait here, I'll get it."

"They catch us, they'll turn us in," said Kunkapot.

"They won't catch us." William took off his clothes and waded in. The two older boys watched him swim very silently to the canoe and push it back.

"We can't make noise," said Kunkapot. "They'll hear the paddles."

"I'll push you. My people taught me."

William pushed them across the pond with a strong leg stroke. They beached the canoe and William dried off and dressed himself in his dry clothes.

"Thankee, Elijah whispered. "I ain't seen that, ever. Who your people?"

"Ojibwe," he said. We live on the lakes. We have to swim."

"I expect. I ain't never lived but on a plantation. But I can run."

"That's what we do now," said Kunkapot. "Where's your shoes?"

"Back there. I didn't want 'em to get wet."

They all ran Indian style, keeping low and fleet through the brush. When they reached the road, the wagon was not there. They waited. Finally, they saw a flatbed arrive. The man in the seat was white, and there was a woman in the back who looked white, maybe mixed. The woman looked at the three of them and spoke to Kunkapot in a language he seemed to understand. Kunkapot nodded.

"Get under that blanket, boy," the man told Elijah. "You others, you can find your way back, I reckon. But not before you put that canoe back where you found it."

The woman gave them all a piece of cornbread before he snapped his whip at the horse. The woman in the back sat still as standing water. The wagon creaked ahead. Elijah waved goodbye from under the blanket. William asked Kunkapot what the woman said.

"She said we should know better. She spoke Iroquois."

§

Some weeks later the Reverend came into their room and stood by the windowsill, where the light was getting weak. "You stole a canoe. That was imprudent."

Kunkapot said nothing but William stood up from his chair.

"We put it back, Sir. Elijah couldn't swim. We just borrowed it."

"Elijah might never swim now. He never made it to Canada. He'll be back in Georgia. If he's alive." Green gave them the stern look that they had come to know. "We lost that one, boys. It's not your fault. But you two boys are Indian, you should know better. You can't trust anyone out there."

"You told us the man was an abolitionist."

"He was not the man we paid, nor was the woman in the cabin."

"We're sorry, Sir," said William after a moment. "Sorry for Elijah."

Green walked out. He was wearing the same shoes he had given to the runaway, which had never been wet, thanks to Elijah.

Chapter 5: Moose

*View of La Pointe, Madeline Island ca. 1843, attributed
to a young Native American artist*

IN THE WINTER OF 1846-47, La Pointe sub agent James P. Hays
took a party out to survey the Indian country west of the Mississippi
and north of Crow Wing on the orders of Henry Dodge, Governor of
Wisconsin Territory and Superintendent of Indian affairs. The government was interested in more land, for the natural resources, and
for the masses of settlers arriving. Hays's mission was to meet the
chiefs, feel out the Ojibwe bands concerned, and know how much
land was out there, and how much could be bought.

It was a severe winter with the ice setting in early which made for good sledding. They struck out after Christmas with horse trains and dog sleds, supplies, trinkets, buffalo hides, flour, sugar, coffee, salt pork, and two caskets of Hays's whiskey against the freeze. Veteran AFC traders still controlled La Pointe trading and knew that whiskey brought in more Indians at payment time and made them spend their money.

The party consisted of Bois Brulé voyageurs, two Ojibwe scouts, and Hays's official agency interpreter, William Warren, a young half-breed of 21 who spoke the language like a native. Warren was educated like a white man and had interpreted for several treaty negotiations since he had come back from the east. He knew the chiefs well and word had it that the Ojibwe trusted him as one of theirs. It was not known if the whites could trust anyone with Indian blood, but he was a useful go-between. As a mixed-blood Ojibwe, he was in fact one of theirs. When he said goodbye to his wife and children in La Pointe, he began the chain of events that would change his young life definitively.

They moved west and south into Minnesota Territory, bivouacked under blizzards, taking shelter among the traders and the Ojibwe at their wintering camps and moving on river ice and unpacked snow. They ate their stores of salt pork and flour and hard bread and hunted when they could. Sometimes Hays traded for frozen meat and fish from the Indians. When the snow got deep they had to snowshoe. They could feel the cold freeze in their lungs but kept moving. The interpreter spent a good deal of time in the lodges talking to the chiefs—too much, Hays thought. Warren said he was asking them for their stories and their history, how they got there. The old men told many different versions of the same story, sometimes hodgepodge, and he kept a notebook. Hays told him he was working for him, not the Indians.

The men warmed up and fed the horses below Crow Wing where Warren's father-in-law William Aitken kept a trading post at the mouth of Swan River, close to the Sioux line—a country Hole-in-the-Day the Elder liked to think of as his. The chief was there with his son Gwii-wisens, a friend of Warren's since boyhood. They had seen more of each other since Warren came back from the east. They found many things to talk about. Warren still called him Boy by habit, although it did not quite seem to fit now.

They all ate hot stew, then Hays was having whiskey at the bar. Hole-in-the-Day liked it too, but they drank apart. Warren and Gwii-wisens, as his father still called him, were playing cards, low stakes. He asked Warren if the government intended to purchase his father's land.

"I don't think so. Dodge is looking to the north. If the bands agree to sell."

"The Anishinaabe do not always think as one. Starlings think as one, they all turn and fly as one. It is not so with the bands. They must council first."

"They must decide together, Gwii-wisens. Those who disagree will be left behind."

"They will not be left behind. They need to be convinced. You vote for your president. The majority vote wins, then he decides for all. In our custom, all must agree as one."

"What if they don't think as one?"

"They must all be convinced by one man, one chief. Like the president. A Great Father treats his children fairly. Does he not?"

"Some do. If he doesn't, we choose another president. Democratically."

"My father says the president treats the Indians like starlings because he wants our nesting tree. The bands will never agree, there are too many. They need one chief. The chief must decide. The chief must convince them. They must change. Or the soldiers will come."

"Your deal, Gwii-wisens." Warren won a little money that night, and Boy left the table to help his father to their wagon. Outside the hotel, they had a vociferous altercation and Chief Hole-in-the-Day the Elder wound up covered under bear coats in the barn.

"The Chief's a sore loser," said Aitken. "Not the first time."

In the morning the survey party pushed on. They slept wet some nights and dried their boots by the fire as Warren interpreted for the chiefs and headmen. He wrote down the different versions of the same story and other stories while sub agent Hays took his survey figures.

The sub agent determined that the unceded Ojibwe lands east of the Mississippi amounted to 10 million acres, the lands west about 12 million. Purchasing the land would not be difficult, he would report to Dodge upon his return to the island, but the terms of the pending treaty must include immediate removal. He thought at the time that it was no use purchasing the land south of the Crow Wing River, as that would leave not enough land for the Chippewa. It could be bought, but if so, it would also necessitate immediate removal.

It seemed that staying on their lands at the pleasure of the president had come to an end, even for those Ojibwe who had not signed a land cession treaty. This gave Warren cause to reflect on the comparative merits of civilization and the consequences of removal for the Ojibwe. They would be heartbroken, and it would change their way of life. They may not survive it. This was not his job, so he kept his ruminations to himself.

§

They were camped on a snowy clearing between the lower Saint Croix and Chippewa Rivers when Warren saw a moose standing at the tree line staring at them. Many Hands, the scout, said not to move, the moose would come closer. The men were hungry, so Warren's head told him to go ahead. He checked his powder, mounted a horse, and took off after it. The moose thought it was odd how the horse moving toward him had grown a man with one long arm.

Don't come this way, little brother, the moose told him.

We are hungry, said the horse-man. Have you anything to eat?

The moose turned into the pine trees and loped away. The snow was wet and heavy. Warren pursued at a gallop and cocked his rifle on the run. The horse did not stop when a pack of snow fell from a bough, blinding the rider. He raised his arm to his face, still galloping and hoping not to lose the moose but the forest was blurred and white. Riding blinded, he took a blow in mid-torso and spun backwards over the horse's rump. The rifle discharged in the air, and he lay stunned under the big drooping branch that felled him. He could not breathe. He rolled over and spat blood to clear his lungs. The horse went back to the tree line, riderless, and stood there. The moose stopped on a rise and looked back at him and said, *you were foolish, little brother. Now your children will go hungry.*

A voyageur named Petit Pierre went out in the dogsled to get him. Warren was barely conscious, lying under the pine branch spitting blood on the snow. Hays checked him military style, determined there were no broken bones, and fed him hot coffee spiked with whiskey for the shock. He admitted after a cup that it helped a little, but he still spit up blood and rasped with embarrassing difficulty. Hays stood over him, his breath steaming.

"He's no good to me now," he declared. There was a gash below his sternum that they cleaned with boiled snow and whiskey before they bound him up. Hays sent Petit Pierre up the frozen Chippewa River with Warren on a dog sled. The driver did his best not to jostle him. Warren remained prostrate under a pile of furs for the five days it took them to reach La Pointe.

Doctor Norwood diagnosed that he had a couple broken ribs, but rest alone would heal that. The blood he coughed up was internal, from the stomach region, and it would do him good to lose it. That would heal by itself with a diet of wild rice and meat broth. For the pain he gave him a tincture of laudanum and said not to overdo it. It worked better than whiskey, for which William had a profound distaste, as did his father. It would be the perdition of the Indians and for that it disgusted him. Norwood said to mix the laudanum with tea— sassafras or peppermint.

"You're lucky that branch wasn't a little higher, young man. You might have wound up like the headless horseman in your book there."

It was too painful to laugh, but it drew a smile. He had told that story in Buffalo's lodge one night, likening the horseman to their *Windigo*, evil as the child-eaters that still lurked in the swamps of the island. He had lit the candle in the gruesome pumpkin he had carved out for the occasion, like the horseman's head, and tossed it into the fire.

"As you tell it," said Buffalo, "the children will remember it forever."

"It is written down," said Warren, "like in the Bible." He showed them the book by Washington Irving, with the engravings. "This is why I remember it," he told them.

The next morning, he wrote down what his great-uncle Tug had told once him about the Windigo. It began like that. Now he wrote down, on whatever paper he could find, all the stories the old ones would tell him.

§

Hays returned and by mid-February 1847 made his report to Superintendent Dodge with his observations on the desired Indian lands, their features, the contemplated cessions, and removal. Warren was unable to work, bedridden for two months and dependent on Matilda and her sisters, who shared their Indian Service cabin with them and their two small children. This did nothing to assuage his dour mood at his forced idleness.

He began to gather his notes on the Ojibwe stories and histories the elders had told him over the past few years. They were rough, written on bits of anything, even wrapping paper from the stores. The women too had stories, but he was closer to the old men. The stories, they said, were true. It was, he knew, oral history, with its vagaries and pitfalls. Every old warrior had his own heroic tales, and tales of suffering, and there were tribal secrets they were not telling him. He could try to put the histories in a semblance of order, and double-check some facts with the chiefs, to determine how they counted time. When the old men died the histories would disappear, or they would change again and again, depending on who was telling it. Sometimes the different versions muddled everything and became a pack of nonsense that resembled more the present than the past.

When spring came around he was able to move again and went to visit Chief Great Buffalo and the elders he had listened to. He held a public council then in his own home and told them that he intended to write their histories down so that, as Buffalo said, "they could last forever." At the time he had no idea of a book, but it would be good to write them down on paper.

Tug-waug-aune was gone now, but before he died he had shown his nephew Warren the copper plate with the eight markings that marked the generations passed since the first Anishinaabe, following the Megis shell from the shores of the big salt water, came to Mo-nigwunakauning. After the third mark on the copper, there was the figure of a man in a hat, the first white man they had ever seen. Most likely they were trappers, and explorers, from about when Jacques Cartier came into the Saint Lawrence, before the first Jesuits. It was a gesture of great trust on the part of his great-uncle. No white, to his knowledge, had ever seen it. The Ojibwe marked a generation on the death of their elders, most of whom lived long lives before the epidemics came. William did some figuring and estimated a genera-tion at about forty years for the Anishinaabe. When Tug-waug-aune died, a ninth mark was added to the copper plate. This gave Warren a theoretical starting point for their history on the island, the begin-ning of a timeline to order their recollections.

As his strength returned and he became inured to the pain, he began to visit the chiefs more often. Their trust now being with him, he marveled as they recounted traditions and histories never before revealed to white men. He took copious notes, writing hurriedly, endeavoring to put them into some form of readable pages at home, where now Matilda, nursing their baby daughter, and William's two young sisters Julia and Sophia doted on him. They made him poultices and bark teas, administered wintergreen rubs, and fed him stews and soups to cure the insistent cough. At times he thought the bleeding was finished, then he would have another coughing fit that opened the internal wound. Norwood and another visiting doctor gave him elixirs and asked him about his digestion. They gave him paregoric. He must have caught a bad cold when out in the wilder-ness with Hays last winter, which prolonged the healing process. The more clement spring weather eased the affliction somewhat.

§

His father Lyman was heard saying that misfortune arrives in the midst of happiness, of which there is not much to be said, and it comes when least expected. There was nothing to mar the contentment of the young couple whose infant children were healthy, whose cedar bark roof was intact, and whose livelihood was ensured by Warren's job as an interpreter for the U.S. government. As there was not much official interpreting to do, he rarely saw his superior that spring. Matilda's sisters and his own came regularly to help with the never-ending chores made more imperative with their growing family. Warren often visited the Ojibwe lodges.

On a mild day in June, Henry Blatchford ran up to him as he returned home from the Ojibwe village. "You get home quick," he panted. "Hays has gone crazy."

They both hurried down to the small agency house on the row before the lake where they heard the women's cries. As he burst in Hays was tottering, pursuing Matilda's sister around the table while his wife cowered half exposed by the fireplace with the girlchild Anna crying at her breast. Matilda's blouse was torn open.

"He hurt my baby, William! Get him out!" A cousin of his named Michel Dufault stood by her with an iron poker in his hand. Warren grabbed Hays. The older man was bloodshot red, drooling, and reeked of whiskey. Hays tried to swing at him but missed and fell.

"Mr. Hays, Sir! Get a hold of yourself! Leave my house immediately!"

"He tried to choke me!" Cried Matilda, "He smothered the baby!"

"You're an insult to your station, Hays. Get out!"

"Goddamn you, Warren. You think I want that half-breed squaw o' yours? With a pussy stinks o' bear fat? She'd take it kneelin', I'll wager." Hays stood up and spat.

"Get out! You're drunk and insane!" He pushed Hays towards the door, but he grabbed the younger girl again and tore her dress. Warren and Henry wrenched him outside and into the sandy lane.

The few onlookers, Indians and voyageurs, held their distance. Hays suddenly stood and faced him.

"I'm your superior, Warren. You'll regret this." Hays turned and staggered back to the Agency with the few Indians and whites watching him go.

"He made to hit her, William. Then he fell on her," said Michel. "You got here just in time." Matilda and her younger sisters were shaken, but all right. The baby calmed down.

Warren did not. He went to the agency office and vented his anger at Hays, calling him a drunkard and degenerate in front of both Indians and whites and forbidding him from entering his home again. That evening a messenger delivered a scribbled letter from Hays. Warren was dismissed from his post as interpreter for insubordination.

He immediately wrote to Superintendent Dodge, including sworn affidavits from Michel and Henry as witnesses to the debacle. He accused Hays: *"For most shamefully abusing my family and strangers under my roof, I have talked to him in a manner which he calls disrespectful and for which he had suspended my from by duties and wages as U.S. interpreter and otherwise endeavored to hurt me."* Henry Blatchford, the interpreter for the Protestant mission, wrote before a Justice of the Peace that Hays had *"most shamefully and grossly abused not only the interpreter's wife but also her sisters."* Michel added that Warren had been hurt on the winter mission and was mostly confined to home, but had always performed his duties faithfully and well.

There was nothing further said. Warren sent the letter to Dodge, then mulled it over. His father became ill, lost his belongings and papers on the way to Detroit for medical help, then returned to La Pointe to be taken in by his Cadotte in-laws and began a slow descent. Young Warren was jobless now, his father destitute, insane from his depression, and his sisters confided to the care of himself and others.

A La Pointe trader one day told him he had no more credit with him if he couldn't pay. That was Hays's afoot, he was certain. He went to talk to Sherman Hall, who advised him to compromise, but his complaint was already lodged and on its way to Washington. It was not the only complaint involving the sub agent's recurrent intoxication. He swallowed his pride, went to see Hays and apologized, telling him he had always treated him and his family kindly, they should let the incident pass.

But it did not pass. Despite Dodge's support, Warren was not rehired. The AFC traders in La Pointe gave Hays their full approval and he remained sub agent for several months after that. Warren's future as a government interpreter came to an abrupt close. They packed up the household in a wagon and left for Matilda's father's trading post on the Mississippi while he contemplated how to support his family. As a half-breed, his white education seemed all he had to sell.

One morning he found himself in a swampy stand near the Saint Croix river at very first light, still wrapped in his blanket, gazing through the shady woods at a four-legged animal he first thought was a moose. But he had seen it before, when he was a boy. The shaggy red beast stood its ground and gazed back at him, immobile. Its hide was pocked by vermin, its head was drawn and snoutless with two great holes for eyes and short blunt antlers as white as bone. Warren did not have his gun with him.

"Do not come this way, Windigo, " he said. "There is nothing for you here."

The beast turned into the brush. Warren returned to the wagon.

Chapter 6: Gosiwin

Gull Lake, Minnesota Territory, June 1850

TWO WHITE MEN APPROACHED HIS FARMHOUSE on horseback. They both wore dark hats and mutton chops. Warren, hoeing his garden, was clean-shaven which revealed his high Indian cheekbones and gave him a youthful look not widely cultivated by white men in the Territories. The taller man rode straight with a brown arrogance in his dress and chin. The other hunched down and peered forward from beneath his wide hat brim, sucking on a pipe. When he saw who it was, he went inside for his coat and hat and came forward to his gate where they dismounted. One of Warren's black oxen lumbered behind them, paused, turned his head, and stared at their backs.

"Governor Ramsey, it's an honor, sir." All shook hands.

"Likewise, Mr. Warren. A fine few acres here. I hope these Indians are learning something. I've read your articles on these damnable Dakota-Chippeway wars. This is Major John Watrous, retired, the new sub agent at La Pointe. I trust you've received my proposal?"

"I was just preparing to answer. The mail is better, but still slow."

"And what, sir, were you prepared to say? You will agree, I trust. You are by all accounts the most qualified and best situated to assist me as an interpreter in this task. You know these Indians. As a sort of tribesman."

"Yes. Family connections. I interpreted for the Treaty of Fond du Lac in 1847. And I was in La Pointe for the negotiations of 1842. I interpreted thereafter for the Department under sub agent Brunson. On Stuart's recommendation."

"Is that so? You must have been but a boy."

"Young. The chiefs have always treated me as a grandson."

"Well then. Will you help us find a suitable area for these Indians? It will surely pay better than government farming. I can arrange for your leave with the Indian Department."

"I am pleased to do what I can to help. For the Ojibwe people and all concerned."

"Excellent. You shall report to Mr. Watrous here. We shall have to look at all fitting locations. Mr. Watrous has already made arrangements to establish a temporary agency at Sandy Lake. It may present some advantages. I have been contemplating Leech Lake, but we lack a treaty there. I hear you are on good terms with Flat Mouth."

"The greater part of the four thousand to be removed are Wisconsin bands, Governor, half the existing tribe in the country according to the last census, which I helped to compile. They do not want to remove. The Leech Lake bands are Pillagers, they were not included in the 1847 Treaty and cannot support thousands more on their grounds. The only satisfactory way to satisfy all the bands, and provide for them all, would be to establish a new treaty, a fair one, prior to the removal. With perpetual annuities."

Watrous removed his pipe and spat. "New treaty? Whatever for, man? This removal is ordered by presidential decree. That's the law."

The ox moved on.

§

Appointed Territorial Governor by President Zachary Taylor, for whom he had campaigned vigorously in Pennsylvania, Alexander Ramsey arrived from the east in May of 1849—just days after Minnesota became a territory. Ramsey's reward post included his remit as Superintendent of Indian Affairs for the territory. He was to prepare for statehood, opening the way for settlers, investors, and the unprecedented tide of European immigrants to enjoy the fruits of their predestined paradise and the benefits of United States citizenship. This entailed setting up lawmaking institutions, ending the incessant Sioux and Ojibwe wars, purchasing land from the Indians, and removing them. A plan was afoot to pay the Dakota Sioux to move to reservations west of the Mississippi, but this left mainly the Ojibwe. Part of their lands would be used to move in Winnebago bands from Wisconsin, setting up a buffer between the warring peoples. According to the 1849 census, there were 8,000 Ojibwe living on their ancestral lands, far outnumbering the whites, half of whom were to be removed. How to deal with their removal was largely up to Ramsey; Congress would deal with the money.

William Warren and his young family were looking smart despite the chest wound that had not healed since his fall from a horse in the woods. He clerked for Henry Rice's trading concern and held a position as a government farmer for the Ojibwe near Crow Wing. Besides his interpreting, he had 43 acres improved, livestock, his Indian corn, and their comfortable cabin. He saw the old men often and persevered in writing down their stories. Warren and his wife Matilda took in boarders, mostly Rice's men, and served a good table. He wrote to his cousin George that he missed his relatives and didn't like the country as much as the Chippeway River country or La Pointe. He did not want to believe that he had the consumption, but he thought he was hard on to it. In one letter his mood could go from dark to bright and back again.

The Indian Department had launched an extensive inquiry into the Indian tribes of the United States. Ojibwe agent and scholar Henry R. Schoolcraft devised 350 questions and sent them to Henry Rice, who entrusted it to Warren, judging him the most qualified to answer as he had been collecting their histories and traditions for the past six years. The elders were reluctant to tell them to whites, but Warren had blood ties to the principal chiefs. He held a council at his home in La Pointe, where Great Buffalo told him that he had become one of them, and reached the age of thinking and discretion and could see far around him. The chief trusted William Warren to hear their words and write them down as he now knew to do, like the whites, to pass on to future generations and to last forever, long after the elders were gone.

Having lost the chance to become interpreter for the new subagency in La Pointe, still in control of the American Fur Company traders, Warren set to work. Disregarding his fragile health, he questioned all the Ojibwe elders he could meet, from below and above the Mississippi River to La Pointe. After a year he gave his copy to Rice to send to the Indian Department.

In September of 1849, he came across the first part of his *"Answers to the Inquiries"* in the *Minnesota Pioneer.* It was a shock, however pleasant, to see his name and words in print—Rice had sent it in to the Saint Paul newspaper of his own initiative. This raised his spirits and his energy. Here was a way he might make some money, with his knowledge and with his pen. He wrote to Schoolcraft to offer any information he could, as he was deeply interested in the Ojibwe and closely connected through his family, describing himself as a quarter breed having been born and brought up among them at La Pointe.

§

With the pressing matters of State, Ramsey needed someone the Indians trusted. Warren fit the bill, which was evident from his insistence on a new treaty and fair treatment of all the bands—and from his knowledge of their traditions and habits of which Ramsey himself knew nothing. Although there was no specific agenda, removal had been the order of the day since February 1850.

"They'll have to be convinced to go," Warren said to his cousin George on a rare visit. "Maybe Hole-in-the Day can do it. I told Ramsey that the Wisconsin bands would resist moving north and east of the river. They see it as barren, unhealthy land."

"It can't sustain thousands more," said George. "But the number of soldiers in the territory is increasing. After Fort Snelling and Fort Gaines, they're building Fort Ripley. It might be unavoidable, William. We don't want another Trail of Tears. Removal could be their only hope for survival."

"At least they'd be out of the reach of the whiskey traders. That's the most important, George. What makes those traders rich will kill the Indians. And it could end the wars with the Sioux. Nothing else will."

The removal plan began to circulate among the agents of the Indian service, and eventually to the Indians themselves, who were puzzled because no mention of this had been made in the treaties of 1842 and 1847. The chiefs understood that they were selling minerals and timber to the whites, but their lands were always theirs and they could stay and live as always for as long as it was the pleasure of the president. Their Great Father would not need the lands now. Most likely, said Commissioner Stuart at La Pointe in 1842, they may not have to remove in their lifetimes. Stuart had pushed them to sign quickly, in three days. Many were reluctant to sign and called it the bad treaty. They received $25,000 over 20 years, four cents per acre. Some, like Warren and Rice, began to suspect what was coming.

§

In summer, 1847 Henry Mower Rice, then a well-connected independent trader, was called to assist the treaty commissioner, General Verplank in negotiations. He was on his way to La Pointe when he met William Warren and his family on the way to his wife's father's post at Swan River. Warren introduced himself as a government interpreter who had just suffered the injustice of being dismissed by sub agent Hays from his position. Rice had heard of William Warren already by his reputation among the Chippewa. He asked him to turn around and go back with him to La Pointe, which he did. Rice determined that they needed the services of this young man of irreproachable character for the treaty negotiations in Fond du Lac, as he was the only correct interpreter in the Chippewa Nation.

Both Rice and Warren would be remunerated. Rice arranged for provisions while Verplank and Warren left for Fond du Lac, where the commissioner hoped to deal with as many Chippewa bands as possible, far from the La Pointe traders and their whiskey.

Hole-in-the-Day the Younger, groomed all his life by his father to inherit his role as chief, was among the first to arrive at the Fond du Lac trading post where a leafy bower was set up outside the log-built stockade. He and Warren had a short conversation, mainly about their recently deceased fathers, before the council began.

"I am glad to see you here," the young chief told him. "You will speak well for the people. Rightly."

"I've lost my post in La Pointe, Gwii-wisens. And my home. After the council, I go to my wife's father's house. I have no way to make my living. Maybe I can become a farmer."

"Call me Bagone-giizig. Hole-in-the-Day. It is my name now, since my father died."

"So be it."

"You have a home among my people. Your mother's people, *Ni-sah-yan*. Remember that." He had called Warren *Ni-sah-yan* since they were boys. It meant older brother. They had grown closer since Warren's return from his eastern schooling.

"I never forget, Bagone-giizig."

Several hundred Ojibwe had arrived for the council. All the elder chiefs were there, but Hole-in-the-Day the Younger declared that he would be first to speak. He and Rice had already reached an agreement when his father was still alive, and here it would become official.

The next morning, after the pipe was raised to the four directions and smoked by Commissioner Verplank, Henry Rice, the dignitaries, and the principal chiefs, speeches were delivered and all were formally introduced. Hole-in-the-Day then rose. His face still bore his black mourning paint, but he was dressed not as a warrior. He wore a white man's frock coat with a clean white shirt and a woven scarlet sash, his furred and feathered turban advertising his war kills, and elaborately beaded high-top moccasins. He used his green blanket like a Roman toga, lifting one arm to the sky for emphasis, his pipe-tomahawk cradled in the other. As he spoke calmly and measuredly, he trained his sharp eye on the entire council, the commission, the chiefs and headmen, while Warren interpreted alongside Peter Marksman. Warren wrote it all down:

"Our Great Father instructed you to come here for the purpose of asking us to sell a large piece of land, lying on and west of the Mississippi River. To accomplish this you have called together all the chiefs and headmen of the nation, who to the number of many hundreds are within the hearing of my voice; that was useless, for they do not own the land; it belongs to me.

My father, by his bravery, took it from the Sioux. He died a few months ago, and what belonged to him became mine. He, by his courage and perseverance, became head of all the Chippewas, and when he died I took his place, and I am consequently chief over all the nation. To this position I am doubly entitled, for I am as brave as my father was, and through my mother I am by descent the legal heir to the position.

Now, if I say sell, our Great Father will obtain the land; if I say no, you will tell him you cannot have it. The Indians assembled here have nothing to say; they can but do my bidding."

His discourse flowed like gospel. The elder chiefs present, some of whom criticized even his father's audacity, were bluffed by Hole-in-the-Day the Younger's bravado. He was obviously the man to reckon with. The new chief's speech carried the day among the Mississippi bands, and they agreed to sell the land but at the initial price of $80,000. The Lake Superior bands should receive nothing, Hole-in-the-Day maintained, as it was not their land. Verplank negotiated $17,000 for those bands, the rest to be paid to those who inhabited the ceded land, beginning with one identical cash payment to both groups. That balance would be paid to the Mississippi bands alone in annuities and goods, along with farming and blacksmithing services, including schools.

For the lands northeast of the Mississippi, the Indians living there set a price of one million dollars, intentionally too high. Verplank did not get everything he wanted. He would have to deal with the Leech Lake Pillagers later.

Hole-in-the-Day insisted that his bands' annuities payments be moved from La Pointe to a new agency in Crow Wing to avoid traveling 600 miles and spending it all at once during the hunting and harvesting season. Verplank included this in Article 5. By virtue of Article 4, the 1847 treaty was the first to allow mixed-bloods to participate in annuities, if they lived with the Indians. No allowance was made for traders' debts, which rankled the La Pointe triumvirate.

The Lake Superior Ojibwe felt cheated by the treaty. They received too little, and no annuities, no goods, no services. The Mississippi bands got at least the price they first dealt for with Rice. A rift was thus cleft among them. Despite this, Hole-in-the-Day persuaded them to touch the quill and like his father, made some enemies and some friends but impressed every man there. It was concluded in three days, too fast for Great Buffalo. Around the walls of the Fond du Lac post the Indians huddled in their bands and kept to themselves. The Lake Superior head men walked bent and brooding under the low cloud cover.

The incensed AFC traders voiced their complaint to the Commissioner. If the payments were transferred south, they would lose their business in La Pointe. The Indians' annuities were their main source of revenue, as there were still too few whites in the territory to make a profitable enterprise. Verplank had been previously informed of the ways of the La Pointe traders and the influence of the AFC. He did not flinch.

The August weather was cold, blustery, and wet. Warren's chest wound began to smart. Every chief made a speech before touching the quill. Late in the day, Verplank called the last council adjourned and told the remaining chiefs to get dinner, then go to the farmer's house to sign. It would be open all night. William Warren, whom they knew well, would be there to witness and mark their signatures.

He stayed late into the night. Hole-in-the-Day and Nodding of the Snake River band were the last to sign the next morning. Hole-in-the-Day wanted his signature on a separate piece of paper to distinguish him from the other chiefs. He saw that William too had signed as a mixed-blood and first chief, along with Corbin, Roy, and Marksman.

"But you live like the whites, Ni-sah-yan."

"The blood of the Ojibwe runs in all my family. I have lived like a white, but among the Ojibwe, since I was born. You know me well. So it is for my children and my wife. You told me yourself that you wanted to teach your people the ways of the whites. Soon you will live in a house, learn to farm and harvest like the whites. By the terms of this treaty."

"This is inevitable," the chief said. "We both know it. My father knew it. Or we could fight it and die. When I think of our children dead it makes me weep as I wept for my father."

"Buffalo says he wants to share the payments with the mixed-bloods, as family."

"I will share with no traders. They share nothing with us. They put us in their debt."

"Many traders are mixed-bloods. My father was white, yet he shared all his life with his Ojibwe family. Where are we to draw a line when lines are always crossed?"

The young chief said nothing to this, as crossing lines was a delicate matter now.

"Did I not make the Great Father's words clear yesterday?" Warren insisted. "Did the People not understand?"

"I understood. The Anishinaabeg will never again be all in agreement. Some will never understand the words the whites use in treaties. We depend on your words. You spoke well, Ni-sah-yan. Even the trader Beaulieu says you spoke Verplank's words correctly."

"And are you satisfied?"

"The Mississippi bands are satisfied."

"Then let us again part as friends," said Warren. He extended his hand and Hole-in-the-Day shook it. The chief even smiled at the friend he considered more white than Indian.

§

Congress struck Article 5 from the treaty before it was ratified the following spring. AFC traders had lobbied successfully in Washington, wanting to keep the Indians' payments close to their posts. Payments would still take place at La Pointe. The chief rode to Warren's farm for help in writing a letter of objection. With a copy of the 1847 Treaty in hand, Hole-in-the-Day questioned him about another word, what it meant and how it was pronounced.

"Removal, " said Warren. "Stuart wrote that into the Treaty of 1842—"

"The bad treaty. Stuart said that it was not necessary for all to sign, the majority rules. For the Anishinaabeg, everyone must sign. That treaty was a sham."

"Removal means *gosiwin,* in Baraga's dictionary," Warren said.

"That is inaccurate. The People understand *gosiwin* as moving from lake to lake, from summer to winter encampments, as they do every year with the change of seasons. The Ojibwe have no notion of selling or abandoning our homelands, because there is no word for it. And what does this mean, *"during the pleasure of the president?* "

"That you can live there as you want, until it is needed by the President.

"Verplank said for as long as we live. They want to deal with us as a nation, yet they treat us like children. I cannot allow them to treat me like a child, William. Why make a treaty with us if our Great Father can alter it without our consent? Why make children of us?"

Hole-in-the-Day's trust in the spoken word was greater than what was written. He could not understand how they could alter the treaty without asking them. He then began to see that the whites could say one thing and write another, with no bearing on their sense of honor.

"If that is true, our Great Father can take our lands without asking us, or without price."

"Perhaps it is not his intention," Warren answered, not without regret. "But yes, he can."

"No. First, he must keep his word. If not, those Indians will not move. We must go see the President, to hear him speak these words. You will come with us. He must hear his children."

Warren wrote to the Governor requesting funds to send a commission to Washington, but Ramsey had other preoccupations. White settlers arriving in droves were terrified by the violence of the Indian wars. In isolated raids, Sioux warriors attacked and took the lives of Ojibwe women and children, and the Ojibwe retaliated. They never bothered the whites. The wars were ancestral; attempts at brokering peace between the tribes had no effect on the centuries-old cycle of revenge. The Indian Affairs bureau in Washington thought that distance between them would be the only remedy. The tribes must be removed and contained so settlers could move into the lands free of Indian violence. The main obstacle was purchasing Indian domains.

In October 1849, seven months after Minnesota became a Territory, the first Territorial Legislature drafted a resolution to revoke the Ojibwe's rights to hunt, gather and fish on the ceded lands, contravening the rights guaranteed in Article 5 of the Treaty of 1837, and to remove them from the lands ceded thereby, and by the treaty of 1842, "to ensure the tranquility and security of the white settlements in an extensive and valuable district of this Territory."

§

In Spring, 1850 President Zachary Taylor cooperated with his governor's strategy by signing an executive order in February of 1850, referred to as the Removal Order. Ojibwe living on valuable lands destined for settlement were to be removed to their unceded lands near the northern headwaters of the Mississippi, in the Territory of Minnesota. Most of the Ojibwe concerned were Wisconsin bands but the traders wished to keep them, and their annuities, close to the Mississippi. Agents were fired and replaced. The Ojibwe were informed that future payments would take place at Sandy Lake. If they did not come, they would not be paid.

Warren by now felt bold enough to advise Ramsey in a letter about the Dakota-Chippewa wars, recommending that he summon the chiefs, headmen, and young men to a peace council with the Sioux at Fort Snelling, in an attempt to deflect a June meeting of the bands to march against the Sioux villages. He wrote that Hole-in-the-Day had secretly formed a war party a week ago and headed to Saint Peters. Warren rode after him, as he had done before, to dissuade him, but they traveled in the night and he could not catch them. He closed with: *"It will be a difficult task to pacify the Chippeways, as they are very much exasperated."*

Warren managed to secure a modicum of trust with the governor, who called the council for June 9, 1850, and asked Warren to interpret. Hole-in-the-Day was again chief spokesman.

About ninety Ojibwe were present. According to a Saint Paul newspaper, the eleven Ojibwe chiefs Warren introduced at Fort Snelling looked like the finest body of men ever assembled, models of grace and perfection for an artist. A day later, 300 Sioux rode whooping and yelling across the plain in a spectacle that both thrilled and frightened the St. Paul women present, most notables' wives, who preferred the classic elegance of Hole-in-the-Day. The tribes faced off under the boughs set up outside the fort where the chiefs shook hands ceremoniously but suspiciously. Feathered spears were held high, soldiers surrounded the gathering, and the American flag wafted at the council table. The Indians sat. Both sides presented a list of injuries going back for decades, demanding reparations for the most recent killings which numbered in the dozens.

The governor opened by saying it was time to bury the hatchet forever, the whites had their fill of their warfare. When Bad Hail of the Sioux declared they would not condone the presence of women at the council, Hole-in-the-Day requested that they remain, to cheer on the Ojibwe. This show of gallantry won him the favor of the Saint Paul women and made him a darling of the press.

The imperative of peace was clear: if this treaty was broken, the offending side would surrender the guilty chiefs to the soldiers. Ramsey repeated that the 1843 peace treaty held firm, and they would have to remove when ordered. Terms of reparation were discussed. The Ojibwe claimed $29,000 for the lives the Sioux had taken, the Sioux refused to pay a cent. Warren tried to interpret Ramsey's words with the firmness intended, but the chiefs appeared not to take the governor's words seriously. Edward O'Neil wrote that Warren rolled off the euphonious sentences in the Chippewa tongue with utmost fluency. Ramsey promised an answer in three months. They all left the council on tenuous but civil terms.

On the steamer hired to take the Ojibwe back upriver, Hole-in-the-Day drew Warren aside to thank him for his advice and interpreting, adding that he had told his people not to drink the water or touch anything on board. He described the boat as a filthy shit hole, it was no surprise that the whites brought disease everywhere they went.

The Ojibwe were granted reparation, since their losses were greater, and the Sioux were the first to attack after the Treaty of 1843. Total damages of $5,000 was deemed fair after the council. They eventually received $1,500 as Ramsey thought that the symbolic value of reparation was more significant than the sum. In August, the Sioux raided a hunting party near Otter Tail Lake and killed four children while the women gathered roots.

John Watrous, the official removal agent, sent messages to the Wisconsin Ojibwe that if they wanted their annuities, they would all have to come with their families to Sandy Lake in the fall. He told them if they wanted to be paid, they had to come. His messages contained no mention of the word, *gosiwin*.

Chapter 7: Making History

GOVERNOR RAMSEY'S QUANDARY AS TO how to implement the presidential removal order was compounded after the 4th of July celebrations in 1850, when President Zachary Taylor died abruptly after eating cherries and milk in Washington. The entire removal matter was to be handled by Orlando Brown, Commissioner of Indian Affairs, who turned it over to Ramsey. The duration of the pleasure of the president had manifestly ended. Ramsey conferred with John Watrous, official agent for the removal, who wanted to proceed unhindered. Payments at La Pointe were to be moved to the upper Mississippi, where the Wisconsin and Lake Superior bands were to remove. Those who did not participate would forfeit their rights to treaty annuities. The government would pay expenses and provide subsistence during the time of removal. At the time, Ramsey had agreed that Hole-in-the-Day had considerable influence among his tribe.

Copies of Warren's request for a delegation of Ojibwe chiefs to hear the president's words from himself went on to Washington, where they wound up in the hands of Henry Sibley, there lobbying for removal as a Minnesota delegate. Sibley, with his rich historical connections to the American Fur Company, told Ramsey and the new Indian Commissioner Luke Lea that Warren was untrustworthy and disloyal, "a blatherskite with just enough education to make him mischievously disposed...no confidence can be placed in his statements."

That same summer, Warren was asked to represent Benton county on the upcoming second territorial legislature. His reputation was growing as one of the more educated and well-spoken men in his district, and after all his white father was of Mayflower ancestry. Already a popular figure in Saint Paul through his historical articles published in the *Minnesota Democrat* and the Ojibwe stories told in his melodious voice, he became known as an articulate intermediary between the Ojibwe and white civilizations. He was elected in September.

His brother Truman and cousin George hurried to Gull Lake to congratulate him. They contrived to gather their sisters to come as well and managed, with Matilda's help, to keep it a surprise. Truman shot a deer, the pumpkins were ripe, it felt almost like a holiday in the crowded cabin.

Late in the evening while the women cleaned everything up and Julia read to the children in the sleeping loft, the three Warren men had a chance to sit and talk. George and Truman had a hot toddy in hand and cigars, blowing the smoke into the open hearth. William refrained from smoking, feeling his lungs, but conceded to a cup of spirits—more symbolically than willingly. After all, this was family. An unspoken undercurrent ran through their hesitant conversation. Finally, George pierced the boil and brought up what they were all thinking.

"This removal business is nasty," he said. "They'll push them over the river, one way or another."

"They'll push them all the way out west, by God, by the time this country gets settled," Truman added.

"They cannot," said William, "Not the Chippeway. They won't move onto the plains; it would kill them."

"That might be the point," said Truman.

"You're quite the cynic tonight, little brother."

"You know Ramsey, William. What do you think? The government will just give up and let them live in peace?"

"No, surely not. But they'll have to negotiate as one large tribe, not just isolated bands. Force in numbers."

"That's what Hole-in-the-Day is trying to do. As the sole chief of the Anishinaabe."

"I doubt he'll be able to. He's got political savvy, maybe more than his father, but he's made some enemies in the tribe. Still, they must join together, present a united front, to resist any further machinations."

George tried to change the mood. "The good news is now you're an elected representative in the Legislature. The first man of Ojibwe blood to be elected to office, do you realize? You've got Benton county and you can defend the Anishinaabe in the Legislature!"

"The Anishinaabe didn't elect me, George. They can't vote! Over half the people in this territory are mixed-blood now. And a mixed-blood, for the whites, is still Indian."

"You'll be at the heart of things in Saint Paul, next to Ramsey. Be proud. This is an important moment in history! You can defend our own Indians better than you can help the Negroes and Abolition, like during your school days, back in Oneida. Where's your fighting spirit?"

"What I did then may have been useless. That runaway Elijah may have never made it to Canada, we don't know. He was just one, but I regret we lost him. And the Blacks are still slaves. Some whites would kill the Indians just as quick as they'd kill a black slave."

"They can't, they're on their own lands, said George. "They're free!"

"Free to starve," William grumbled. "They take their lands by treachery and deceit couched in bad treaties. Then they kill them slowly, by starvation, poverty, and whiskey."

"Who's the cynic now? But you're right." Truman drank from his toddy.

"The Indians will resist. I'll defend the Ojibwe until I die, I swear. That's why I can't die too soon. Just pray that I resist too." He scowled and turned away.

There was a silence. He had said it aloud, but it was no time to speak of that. Briskly he stood up, suddenly animated, and launched into his tirade with the toddy cup in his hand.

"I'll be in the political soup, George. This is only the second territorial legislature, with twelve Democrats and maybe six Whigs, but the Governor is Whig-backed so that could change. Ramsey has already tested my loyalty, I'll warrant he'll do it again, and you cannot remain in government without loyalty. Even with Taylor gone, Washington under Fillmore is still removal bound. Now with the treaties, the steamboats are running faster, the settlers are arriving, the capital is wide open for the taking. Last census count in the Territory is nearly five thousand, mostly new settlers, but a swarm of speculators, lawyers and businessmen. Over a thousand now in Saint Paul. You've got land speculation and the trade war, all counting on the Indians' annuities and timber money. There are more taverns than churches in the capital, and no schools to speak of. Yet. The rules have to be redressed here, that's the business of legislation. We can't have mayhem. The big division is Sibley and the AFC against Rice and the other traders. Rice and Sibley fell out last year, now they're in a battle of influence. Sibley was elected Delegate to Washington, but only barely. Who controls the Indian lands and where they pay out their annuities is mainly a question of who controls the money flow. There's enough money for all, except the Indians. We have to get them a better deal. Good lands, lifetime annuities. And we have to get them away from these...grafters. It'll kill them."

William coughed, spat into the fire, raised his cup and drained the toddy.

"By God, you've got me drinking liquor. Another drunken Indian."

"Hog swill! You sound ready to go, Brother!" Truman laughed. "Listen, buck up. Your articles in the papers have got you a name in the territory now. Those Indian histories… now you can do more than write history, you can *make* history!"

"You're a household word there," said George. "People trust you. At least the Indians do. Better brush up on your parliamentary procedure. When do you leave for Saint Paul?"

"The session opens January first. Rice is behind me. I can live at his American House, big and comfortable, for a song, with Matilda's help there. You bring the girls down later, Truman—we can all live there during the session. About three months. Meanwhile, you'll watch the farm here, won't you?"

"Count on me. Until something better comes up. Matilda's father says he's got something for me down near Crow Wing—they call it Aitken's Ferry now. He's doing a booming business at that hotel, even trading. You've resigned your position here as a farmer?"

"Effective end of March 1851. I have my government pay, the Legislature, and a bit of back pay from interpreting coming up if my claims come through. Maybe I can make a little more money writing. I'll do my best, but I can't manage farming anymore. Getting too weak."

"Blather. You look fine to me. Here, have another shot of this, that'll fix you up."

Matilda walked over and blithely filled his cup with hot tea. Warren smiled up at her, considering himself saved by his wife once again. Truman for once felt awkward with a full raised cup and looked over to their cousin for support.

"Eh, George? Don't he look like a fine future congressman, ready to tackle the world?"

"Hell yes, he does. A Warren never gives up. You just keep on. Do your best!"

William touched his cup to those of his brother and cousin. It was good to hear their voices in his house. And it did the children good to speak English with their family. After all, the future was theirs, and they must be prepared.

He glanced at Matilda standing at the basin, a thick braid of black hair falling down the middle of her back, held behind her neck with a finely beaded medallion. To celebrate, she wore her long-fringed doeskin robe tonight with the flowered breastplate and her best beaded sash.

The patience it took to fashion those marvels, Warren thought. There was nothing to match the beauty of her elaborate dress, except the woman herself. It was near midnight, and her hair was still shiny. He had a fleeting thought that he rarely allowed himself: who would take care of her, and the children, when he was gone?

George saw him admiring his wife and declared that he was a lucky man, he'd found himself a jewel of a woman. Not only did Matilda have the prettiest eyebrows in all the Northwest, but she also did the work of three women.

Julia heard this as she brought over the bedrolls. "And she's half Ojibwe," she quipped. "That means she does the work of ten men."

Matilda looked back at them under the lamplight and gave William a wry smile. She seldom spoke English, but she understood everything they said.

§

Despite his disagreement with removal, Warren was convinced it was inevitable and, as the agent Livermore had intimated, futile to resist. He was now inextricably involved. Not only did Ramsey count on his advice, but so did the Chippeway River bands who wanted him to accompany and speak for them at the payment that fall at Sandy Lake. He could not refuse.

It was still unclear whether it was a payment or a removal, especially in the mind of Alexander Ramsey who could not get a decisive answer from Washington despite his frequent letters. Brown answered only that appropriations would be made late in the season, so it would be best to time the removal to accompany the payments.

"If they are removed early in the season," Brown wrote, "many will no doubt be inclined to wander back to their old haunts..." Ramsey contemplated the timing, but no funds were forthcoming.

The bands would receive subsistence but would not be paid unless they took their families, prepared to remain there permanently. Indian Appropriations were the last item on the list in Washington. More urgently, a divisive debate was ongoing in Congress concerning whether slavery would be extended to the territories and new states. Then there was the matter of communications between the territory and the capital, and the transport of funds. The removal order remained in force. In August, after the death of President Taylor, the new Commissioner of Indian Affairs Luke Lea authorized $1,500 out of the Chippewas' Sioux reparations fund for subsistence during the payment, ignoring Ramsey's pledge that the government would sustain them. Funds for payment itself had not yet been appropriated.

John Watrous went ahead and told the Lake Superior bands to come on October 25th.

"They'll never go if they're afraid of starving," William told Matilda, trying to assist her in the ripe cornfield. "They have to gather the rice, to hunt, to prepare. Watrous is determined. He's told Ramsey it's all ready, the supplies are headed for Sandy Lake, and he's leaving for Saint Louis to fetch the money for the payment. Meanwhile, Ramsey has no confirmation from the Indian Department. No one knows if it will be now or later, in the spring."

"The People will have to go," Matilda said, "and so will you." She'd harvested a bushel of corn while he stood contemplating his third ear. "They'll force them to remove. They'll bring the soldiers. Someone must convince them. You said yourself that you wanted to get the Saint Croix bands away from the whiskey. Did you not tell that to Ramsey?"

"I did. The lumbermen are as bad as the traders, they'll kill them all with their alcohol. That doesn't mean I can convince them to move. Maybe they should just go for their annuities and see if they like it, then come back. If they do not want to remove there, they will not have to. There are other choices. But they know they can't all live at Sandy Lake. Not enough rice, no game. They won't like it. Still, you're right, Matilda. They have to go. For the payment."

Warren asked Ramsey for expenses for the trip and set out by canoe to assist the Chippeway River bands. Passing through Saint Paul, he found there were no expenses to be had; he had not been hired by the government, it was his own decision to assist the Ojibwe. They would have to sustain themselves until they got there.

Chapter 8: Sandy Lake

Fall, 1850

WARREN HIRED MEN AND CANOES with his own money in Saint Paul and started his journey up the Chippewa River in early October to collect the bands willing to go. The fall weather was still mild. He arrived at the house of his aunt Charlotte and her husband James Ermatinger at Chippewa Falls, near his father's old farm. His sister Julia was now living with them. "Little Money", her Ojibwe name as a girl, had grown into a fine and able young woman of eighteen. Refined and sharpened by her eastern schooling, she venerated her brother, often helping him and his family during his bouts of illness in La Pointe. She was still not married, but Warren was sure this would come soon—when she found a worthy man in these territories where most were Army soldiers. She still had the roundish face of her childhood framed by her dark hair and high-button dresses. Her eyes were soft and caring but revealed a character as obstinate as his own. Charlotte suggested that it would be a good idea for her to go along and help her brother. Julia perked up. She had been thinking about it, but dared not mention it herself.

"I can help, William, you'll see I can. Please let me come."

"It's no trip for a girl, Julia. We'll have to march and carry the canoes, the portages are long, winter is coming on. Look at the leaves already. Red and yellow but almost gone."

"Mother's made me be strong. And Aunt Charlotte. I'm stronger than you now!"

"Don't be silly."

"At Sandy Lake I'll see Matilda and the children again—you said you'd send for them."

"That's the plan. But it's long way yet. Maybe 300 miles all told."

"It's not far from your house at Gull Lake. We can go there afterwards."

"Julia..."

But she won out. She always did. She packed up her things and a beaded pouch of herbal teas and medicines for her brother, who might need them in the days to come. Warren was secretly relieved that she would be coming along, as he knew his sister to be constant if he needed her. He sent word to the bands. Julia's own account of the journey still survives:

> *There was a great many Chippewa at that time at Chippewa River. He had to send for all of them, and council with them for a few days, and when ready to start, issue out pork, flour, and tobacco to take with them on their journey. My brother was in very poor health. He was taken ill in Saint Paul after leaving his home, but he was feeling better. My aunt tried to persuade him not to start until he felt stronger. She said she would feel better if you would take your sister with you. She can take care of you if you get sick on the way...*
>
> *We were soon ready to start. My brother had bought a canoe and hired two stout men to paddle, and pack it through the woods. Two Indians to pack our tent, bedding, and food. We journeyed up the Chippewa River to Lake Cotra old French trading post with several mixed-blood families dwelling there. The Lac du Flambeau Band of Chippewas were all waiting for my brother. We were there one day. Pork, flour, and tobacco had been brought in canoes from the falls, to be issued to the Indians that were going. The next day we started on our journey through the woods. The Indians packing their canoes, they all had packs of some kind on their*

backs. We had to walk nearly all day. We came to a lake and camped for the night. Our tent was put up, with branches of spruce and cedar spread on the ground inside, which made it quite comfortable. In front of the tent, a small fire, where I cooked our evening meal. The Indians built several large campfires and fixed places to hang their kettles over the fire to cook their evening meal, which was large kettles of wild rice and water thickened with flour and seasoned with pork. It was always their evening meal, as it took a short time to cook. On each side of the fire, they stuck small poles to hang long rush mats for a covering where they slept. A number of them were hunting through the woods as we traveled along. They killed all kinds of game, such as deer, geese, ducks, and other animals. Some of them would cook by the fire all night, both game they had killed during the day, and legalet, bread made with salt, water, and flour, kneaded quite hard in round flat loaves fastened on a stick and placed before the fire. They did this when camping for the next day's lunch... When starting in the morning at noon we would rest for a short time and eat a cold lunch, when we walked all day we traveled only a few miles. We traveled along occasionally crossing lakes and rivers. After a few days reached Saint Croix River after journeying through the wild country and dense forests of the then Wisconsin Territory. We were there for two or three days, waiting for the St. Croix and Pokegama Chippewas to come. We then started for Lake Superior. After a few days we reached Iron River, which empties into Lake Superior. The river was dangerous with canoes. There was many small rapids and rocks. Some of the Indians had traveled it so often, they knew exactly where to go. When we came to a bad place, one canoe would go ahead, and the rest follow, we arrived safely at the lake. We camped on a sand point opposite where the city of Duluth now is, with seven hundred Wisconsin Chippewas. My brother was taken ill with hemorrhage from the lungs that night. His friends the old chiefs were much worried about him. They did what they could. They were all very kind, they thought so much of him. My brother was quite ill. After keeping quiet and resting for four days he felt able to travel. The Indians had a good rest, with their nets caught all the fish they could eat, such as trout, whitefish, and game they killed. We were ready to start our journey up St. Louis River to Fon du Lac. As the Indians were getting into their canoes, my brother told them to wait. He wanted to say a few words. Pointing towards where the city of Duluth now is, he said: over there will be a great city. The lake near it will be full of all kinds of vessels. Pointing to where Superior is, will be another city, but not so great as the city over here. I will not live to see those cities. Some of you young men will live to see them. I want you to remember what I am now telling you. Some of the old chiefs who were standing near him, shook their heads as if they though he was losing his mind. It was hard for me to believe my brother's words, that a city would be built on such a desolate rough spot where the city of Duluth now is. We started for Fon du Lac which was a small village and trading post. We stopped there one day, then went from there to Sandy Lake. On our way we had to cross a three day portage. We traveled very slowly on my brother's account. It took us nearly five days to cross the portage, when we at last reached Sandy Lake. After having a pleasant weather all the time for three weeks my journey with the Chippewa Indians ended. I have often thought during the years that have passed away of that hard journey, and wondered how I ever went through it. I remember of being very tired when we camped at night, after walking nearly all day, but never once regretted coming with my sick brother, the trip was much harder for him. We had to go across the lake to the agency. All the Mississippi Bands of Chippewas and Leach Lake Indians with their families were all there, waiting for their payment. When we came in sight of the agency there was great excitement amongst them. A

great many jumped into their canoes, came to meet us. There
were a great many Chippewas at the time. I don't remember
the exact number.

"My Journey with the Chippewa Indians",
Manuscript dated 1921,
Julia A. Spears & Family Papers

More than 3,000 Ojibwe had gathered at Sandy Lake awaiting their annuities. The great enthusiasm of seeing Warren's 700 arrive was also the promise of more food, they hoped, but the little rations left from the trip lasted only one day. Game was scarce in this country. Watrous was not there and there was something wrong with the supplies he'd provided. The flour had gone rotten and the pork was spoiled. People fell sick eating it. It was too late to find any rice now, the marshes were frozen and snow covered the ground. Waiting for their payment and more supplies, the Ojibwe walked slowly between the fires, shuffling in the snow and keeping their blankets close, stirring the rations silently. There was nothing to do, no meat to smoke, no furs to scrape, only an occasional fish in the lake— not enough to feed the thousands waiting. The smoking wigwams looked like dark beasts hunched against the snow, overshadowed by the boney gray fingers of the leafless trees above them. The only birds left were the cawing black crows. The sky was an impenetrable steel gray infused with smoke from the fires.

Warren found his family living in a tent near the agent's house, along with his sister Sophia. Sickness, dysentery, and soon measles ran rampant among the Anishinaabe. Winter had set in, most of the rations had been consumed, the bands were surviving on a pound of half-rotten flour and a half pound of pork apiece. A dog ate the pork and died in the snow.

Hole-in-the-Day arrived late October, dressed in his otter headwear with eagle feathers straight up, a clean frock coat and blanket, with an added accoutrement: he was riding a shod bay horse with a military saddle. His entry was in stark contrast to the decimation around him. Bodies were being burned or buried. Measles was running wild. The cries of the children and mourners were heard day and night. The chief mutely stared at his people's desolation, the cold, the starving, the children and old people dying, four, five, even six every day. Even the whites present, Oakes and Hall, stayed in their tents. He went to the agency house and saw Warren by his tent there, with his family. Mrs. Watrous had taken his younger ones into the house to warm up. His mixed-blood brother, Ni-sah-yan, was looking peaked, in stark contrast to the vitality coursing in the young chief's blood, which Warren could see was running high.

"Where is the agent?" He demanded of Warren. "Where are the supplies? These Indians need food. Good food." He threw a ration of rotten flour into the fire, where it smoldered. "A pound every three days. This is not fit for your pigs to eat. Where is Watrous?"

"We do not know. On the way from Saint Louis. With the payment."

"What can they buy with their money, more rotten food? These people have been here too long. They must go back."

"They can't go back, Gwii-wisens, they have no rations, and the rivers are frozen."

"My name is Bagone-giizig. Why did you bring them here? To have them starve? I should have kept those two oxen. I would slaughter them here myself."

That night there were two head of cattle stolen from a nearby prairie where the white settlers let them roam free. They fed the Ojibwe for two days while Hole-in-the-Day went down to Saint Paul to demand provisions from Ramsey, who seemed unconcerned and left the matter in the hands of his agents. Apparently, John Watrous had encountered delays in Saint Louis, where the annuities did not arrive, then there were further delays returning. They had already spent the $1,500 from the Sioux reparation settlement on more spoiled rations. Ramsey did nothing but wait.

The agent finally arrived in Saint Paul and for a few days exchanged letters with the governor, who said there were rumors about starvation at Sandy Lake. The newspapers were given to be dramatic about it, but he feared the consequences. Agent Watrous went on to Crow Wing, ordered more supplies, then set out in a canoe for Sandy Lake. He did not go far before he had to leave the canoe and continue on foot; the freeze was on.

Watrous walked through the wigwam village at Sandy Lake on November 24th and saw the decimation, the rows of frozen bodies awaiting burial. Fires were burning low. There was a small gathering of whites and mixed-bloods at the agency building. Warren's family was huddled on the floor of the agent's house where a hot stove warmed the rooms. Warren had been out talking to the chiefs. He came in relieved to see Watrous, but the agent was preoccupied with recording figures in a ledger.

Watrous gave instructions to the traders Oakes and Borup to distribute food, flour, and pork from the stores.

"We got 3 or 4,000 Indians out there. We can't feed 'em all," was Oakes' assessment.

"Not so many now," said Warren. "They're dying by the dozens."

"They came with nothing. We gave 'em what there was. Turned out not much good."

"More supplies will be coming by wagon," said Watrous. "Give them what we have, and keep track. They'll pay out of the annuities. Give them blankets."

"Did you bring the payment?" Warren asked him."

"The money never came to Saint Louis. They'll get it later. Feed them. Start with the Pillagers, then the Lake Superior bands, and Saint Croix. Write it in the ledger, Warren. Dr. Borup and Mr. Oakes will charge it against the money when it comes. Those who stay will be paid. Those who leave will be struck from the roster. When they remove here in the spring, they will be paid here. If they bring their families."

"Many did bring their families. The children and the feeble will die first. Do we sacrifice them?"

Watrous kept his eyes on his ledger. "Sickness. Looks to be about 70 bodies piled up. They never do eat right in the winter."

Warren, feeling sick himself, and beginning to fear for his own family, took them home to Gull Wing. Sophia, down with the measles, had to stay with the agent's wife, as did Julia. All of his family survived, but Warren himself had to return to Sandy Lake for the distribution of goods in payment. The traders Borup, Oakes, and Nettleton sold the bands supplies at inflated prices, but the annuities were gone. More Ojibwe had died in the meantime.

Why were they not paid? Why were they not fed, as agreed? They had come peacefully, on the strength of the Great Father's promises. Now they were trapped in this desolate place, they told Warren, and even further into debt to the traders. They could not believe the Great Father would treat his children this badly. Neither could Warren believe that a government agent would willingly imperil the lives or poison whole bands of Indians. He was their chosen speaker, their close advisor, but he was powerless to save them. His efforts had been useless.

The bands resolved to go home despite the winter, abandoning their canoes. John Watrous called a final council and told them they would have to remove next year, and Sandy Lake was now their agency. The Chippewa River chief, Big Wolf, answered for them all:

"We are all of one mind. We will not remove. We cannot leave our part of the country, where we have always lived, where our forefathers lived and died. We do not like Sandy Lake, nor this part of the country. We will never come to Sandy Lake for our annuities."

They slowly began their march through the snow, Indians faltering, some dropping, as they headed northeast to the big lake or south the Saint Croix River. Those heading for the interior had the longest trek.

Watrous made his report saying at least 150 had died and the rest would have a hard time making it home. He was not far from right, but had no way to count. Chief Buffalo said 170 were left dead at Sandy Lake. 230 more had perished on the way home. The removal, despite the efforts of John Watrous to keep them there permanently, had failed. No one remained at Sandy Lake but a few stragglers and the bodies, piled up and frozen in the winter silence, disappearing under the snow. Four hundred dead, no violence, not a shot was fired.

The Sandy Lake disaster reached the newspapers in Saint Paul as *"devastating reports from the upper country"*, raising a great tide of sympathy for the Indians and strong tempers among the editors and debaters. The *Minnesota Pioneer* blamed the starvation on delayed payment and the *"shameful negligence of the government."* In mid-December, the *Minnesota Chronicle and Register* published a letter with the headline *"Dreadful Sufferings of the Indians"* decrying the deaths, *"most of them half-dead for want of food—not less than 85 dead at Sandy Lake—and since the payment some five or six die every night."* It further claimed that the Indians were left without their agent in the winter: *"destitute of clothing, provisions, guns, ammunition—they were helpless. All this suffering and distress has been occasioned by the inefficiency of the present administration"*.

This induced Ramsey to express his doubts about such rumors, and to investigate personally. He went upriver and met Borup and Oakes who told him it was disease that killed the Indians, and this provided some relief for the governor. He then met Watrous and other semi-officials who had been at the payment and they all blamed it on disease, not starvation.

They resolved to put the incident behind them. In official reports and to the newspapers, neither man mentioned the original plan of delaying the payment to keep the Indians at Sandy Lake. The official version stated that an outbreak of disease had coincided with administrative delays, and the Indians lost some of their number despite Watrous' increased expenditure on rations to remedy the situation. The fall payment had been affected, but removal had not yet begun. Ramsey was now preparing for the second session of the Territorial Legislature, and Watrous requested 60 days' leave.

The party went back downriver to Saint Paul in time to celebrate Christmas at the Ramsey's' temporary residence, where his wife did her best, there on the desolate frontier, to set a silvered table in grand Philadelphia style. John Watrous presented the governor with a pair of long fur-lined gloves and a fancy cigar box as his gifts of the season.

Flat Mouth, before leaving Sandy Lake, had spoken to all present and wanted his words sent to Ramsey. It was a detailed account of the ordeal even before it was over, closing with an accusation that the governor could hardly misinterpret.

"...Tell him I blame him for the children we have lost, for the sickness we have suffered, and for the hunger we have endured. The fault rests on his shoulders...The Governor promised to feed us while here. He has not done it. We have been stealing all we have eaten from our fellow Chippewas: of this we have been accused and made a laughingstock thereby. I have always been friendly to the whites. I see nothing behind me to cause regret. I have always said what I thought and kept nothing back: it is for this reason I am not ashamed. I speak to our Great Father at a distance: the words that you now hear will be carried to him. When I saw him, he spoke to us about farms and other matters of interest to us. I believed his words would be verified in this respect, but instead of this, they have been falsified. And I blame him for this. My friend, it makes our hearts sore to look at the losses we have sustained while at Sandy Lake. You call us your children, but I do not think we are your children. If we were we should be white. You are not our Father and I think you call us your children only in mockery. The earth is our Father, and I will never call you so. The reason we call the earth our Father is that it resembles us in color; and we call the sky our Grandfather. We did not sell the ground to our Great Father. We gave it to him in order that he might follow our example and be liberal to us."

Chief Flat Mouth at Sandy Lake,
December 3, 1850
Ramsey Papers

Chapter 9: Cigar Store Indian

Saint Paul, January 1851

ARRIVING IN SAINT PAUL TO take his seat in the second legislative session, Warren saw that the territorial government had made advances in style. For the occasion, he purchased a new frock coat, a warm and elegant black cloak, and a wide-brimmed beaver hat. Matilda sewed him two cravats. In this attire, he arrived at the American House, one of the very first brick buildings erected by Henry Rice, now finally finished and appointed with pine furniture throughout, cotton mattresses and glass lamps, a fine big Franklin stove in the lobby, and smaller ones in the rooms. Three stories high, spacious and comfortable, two rooms were at the disposal of the Warren family for a modest rate, and Matilda could defray some expenses by helping in the kitchen. It also served as the new seat of the second Territorial Legislature. The legislators commenced with procedural questions, appointing officers, reviewing the election process, and erecting regulatory obstacles to keep rival factions from moving the capital from Saint Paul.

There was also a matter of selecting a printer. James Goodhue, editor of the *Minnesota Pioneer*, was in line for the contract. Another newspaper, the *Minnesota Democrat* (the very title establishing its political loyalties) had been founded by DA. Robertson, who was also a candidate for the contract. Robertson, a forthcoming man, was enthusiastic about Warren's Ojibwe writings and encouraged him to publish more, even in book form.

"Well, I've pretty well completed a more accomplished version of some histories."

"Then I'll publish them, in serial form and for payment, in my paper."

"The stories are not yet in order, but I'll surely consider your offer."

James Goodhue, however, was the first publisher of William's *Inquiries* two years earlier in the *Pioneer*. He was also the official Democratic candidate for the printing contract, and already had a good brace of supporters amid the legislators. He sent Warren a personal note proposing to house him and his family in the capital for half what he was paying Rice. Such offers, he was told, were common in the legislature; private contractors needed House approval. He was hesitant to tell Goodhue that he was considering a deal with Robertson to publish in a rival paper. When they met to discuss the housing offer, Goodhue was more explicit.

"Of course, I should like your vote on the printing contract, tit for tat as it were."

"Well, Sir. I think that you should have part of it. I cannot pledge it, though. That would not be appropriate in my present office." He felt it coming; he was already in the thick of it.

"I'd like that note back from you in that case, Warren."

Here, he did not hesitate. "I can't do that. But don't worry, I won't hold you to it."

"Unfortunate, Warren. Here I thought you were a man to know who your friends are."

He wanted no such notes with his name on it floating about the capital. And he made it no secret that he was supportive of D.A. Robertson as printer. He had made his first blunder and secured an enemy in the press—probably inevitable. And he knew Goodhue would not hold back his venomous pen.

During the week of the first session, Hole-in-the-Day announced to the legislature and to the *Pioneer* his intention to address the Saint Paul community in the First Presbyterian Church the next evening, on Friday, January 8th. Citizens of the capital had already been kept abreast of the Sandy Lake disaster by the newspapers. The debate over the blame was still fresh in their minds. Ramsey, when informed of the "rumors", doubted greatly that they were true and still held that newspapers always tend to exaggerate. He went upriver intending to investigate and met Watrous and some traders who had been there. They all declared it was disease, not starvation, that caused the unfortunate deaths, and resolved to put the matter behind them. The party then returned to the capital relieved, with the peaceful holidays in mind. Watrous was invited to the Ramsey's home for the festivities, where he presented the Governor with a pair of gloves and a carved cigar box for Christmas, and requested a two-month leave.

§

The Chief drew a crowd at the new church, freshly built, painted white inside and out, admirable for its simplicity, and still smelling of fresh pinewood. Most of the legislators attended, as well as the prominent citizens of Saint Paul and traders from the territory. The notable exception was Alexander Ramsey, busy elsewhere, but his brother attended.

All the town citizens had heard of the young chief's exploits and diplomatic savvy during the recent treaty negotiations at Fort Snelling. Also known as an immortal warrior since his daring raid on the Sioux at the gates of the city, Hole-in-the-Day had gained even further notoriety by striding through town just days after he was reported killed by a Sioux bullet, wearing a bright scarlet sash around his neck and a new black holster for his Colt .45. The *Pioneer* had gone so far as to publish an engraved likeness of the chief dressed like a white man with no headdress. It hardly did him justice, many concurred as he took the podium with William Warren at his side to interpret. As the audience quieted down Warren leaned over for a word with him.

"Gwii-wiseṅs—"

"Bagone-giizig," he replied. "Bagone-giizig is my name."

"Yes. Of course. Pause sometimes so I can say your words."

"You know already what I mean to say. You know I am here to speak for the Anishinaabe. But I will pause."

The chief's customary otter skin turban sported a full spray of standing eagle feathers, his blanket was crimson over his long frock coat, and his shirt under the beads, bear claws, and medals that adorned his chest, was pink calico.

"Cleanest Indian I ever saw," said a man in the audience.

His wife added, smiling, "There is certainly something almost majestic about him."

The wood stove and the crowd heated the room sufficiently for him to leave his blanket aside and speak to the public in the white man's clothing, except the two large silver medals inherited from his father, his ear jewelry, and beaded leggings. He left his pipe-tomahawk on a bench. But there was no mistaking, by his features and direct eyes on his audience, that he was a regal presence and though still a young man, versed in the art of public speaking.

"Bagone-giizig is my name, as was my father's name," he began as Warren interpreted. "You know my father was a fair man, a good man, and a friend to the whites. So it is with me. I speak in the name of all Chippewa people, as I am their sole chief."

He then told them what was on his mind: the suffering of the Chippewas, the deaths and disaster at Sandy Lake. His speech was lengthy and eloquent with reason and tragedy, giving pauses for Warren to translate as he spoke.

"The more treaties we make, the more miserable we become," he said. His examples were many, but mainly now was the recent blundering treatment of his people at Sandy Lake, where for months in the prime hunting and gathering season they were forced to live in squalor and fed spoiled rations, musty pork head, rotten beef, and a portion of bad flour per day that would not fill his two hands. This, while waiting for their paltry annuities, which never came.

"These provisions made them sick, and a great number died. I was among the last to arrive, and four, five, six died every day." He echoed the words of Flat Mouth and wondered why the Great Father did not send someone "who will be a father to his red children and report to him their wrongs and sufferings."

Then, with the same reasoned and measured voice, he said: "If the present state of affairs continues, the existing friendship between us will, I fear, turn to hatred." He paused. Warren paused for a moment, searching for a better word than hatred, but then went ahead. He would be faithful to his friend's thoughts.

When Warren spoke the chief's phrase in English, an offended rumor went up in the crowd. Especially among the most prominent men, gathered in the legislators' corner. William and Hole-in-the-Day glanced at each other. The distress in the room was palpable.

The chief then explained that it was the suffering that he feared might break the peace between them. Was the Great Father aware of these things?

"They are driven to extremities," he intoned. Death is on every side, and in the minds of our young men…They are like some poor animal, driven into a hole and condemned to die. To them, one death is as good as another."

The chief asked how the Great Father expected his children to survive after such treatment. He could not understand how he could allow it. Hole-in-the-Day thanked the congregation, draped his blanket over his shoulder, and left the church through the center aisle. After the silence, there was still murmuring in some corners. The speech was effective, but had caused some disgruntlement. Warren thought he knew why, and took the stand.

"Ladies and Gentlemen," he began. "By the young chief's talk, you will probably be disposed to lay the whole of the blame of the sufferings he has narrated, on the officers of the Territory, who are placed in charge of the Chippewas, by the General Government. It is true that the tribe has suffered severely, they have lost many lives and bad provisions have been dealt out to them. Many of them are under the impression that our Government wishes to poison them off, to hurry their removal from Wisconsin. (He paused, but got no reaction). Things could not have happened more detrimental to the carrying out of the policy of our Government towards this tribe. The fault of this, mainly lies with Congress, at Washington, for making their Indian appropriations late in the fall. The Chippewas were summoned at their usual time, at Sandy Lake, and were unavoidably kept from the payment of their goods for a long time. The measles and dysentery, assisted by the cold, for want of their goods, and also through bad provisions, cut many of them off. Their agent had been summoned to Saint Louis, to procure their money annuity. He was gone nearly two months, and returned without the money. It was not his fault. The bad provisions were taken to Sandy Lake, and dealt out to the Indians, while he was absent. On his return, it was too late to remedy the evil, but he immediately procured for them good provisions.

"Being aware of these facts, I have thought proper to make this explanation; it is a duty I owe to the officers, on whom some people are disposed to lay the whole blame of the sufferings of the Chippewas."

The response came readily after Warren's intervention: Henry Rice, Borup, and Justus Ramsey, the governor's brother, quickly formed a committee to collect contributions for Hole-in-the-Day's band, and money was raised. Warren looked around the room, saw Henry Sibley, a tall man of unparalleled influence and ambition, talking to Charles Oakes and his wife, and felt that he had calmed some tempers. Blame, he knew, must be defused in this situation. Allegiances must be clear. To his surprise, Sibley called him over.

"You did well, Mr. Warren, to defend the Governor's actions, and those of Mr. Watrous. I'm sure Governor Ramsey will be pleased with your clarifications. They did what they could to help those poor Indians, as did yourself. We all want the best for them, now don't we?"

"It's reassuring to see the generosity of our citizens," Warren replied. "Even though the chief did say he was speaking for all the Chippeways, not just his band."

"I suspect these contributions will benefit the Crow Wing traders more than anyone," said Sibley, who had no operations there. "That's where the chief will purchase his supplies. Morrison over there will surely profit. A shame we couldn't have spread it around further."

It struck Warren that profit hunger brought out the worst in the traders. He held no sympathy for Sibley, heir to the AFC interests, but he was the Washington man and a Ramsey ally. He held his rancor in check, but could not help a more down-to-earth aside.

"The worst off are the Wisconsin bands. They marched home in the snow empty-handed. Except for their dead."

"Horrid," Mrs. Oakes interjected. "One wonders how they survive the winters up there. Mr. Warren, I must tell you how much I've enjoyed reading your accounts of the Indian stories in our newspapers. It's just like being there. I do hope to see more."

"I expect you will, Mrs. Oakes, time allowing."

"And tell us, why are these Indians called the Ojibwe?"

"They call themselves Anishinaabe. Simply put, it means the People. The original People, the spontaneous People, some have ventured."

"But what about Ojibwe? Or Chippeway, as the papers say?"

"*O-tchip-we*, with the accent," he gently corrected. The lady and the entourage listened with smiling interest. "Chippeway is a variant. There are two theories, Madam. One is that it refers to their moccasins, the particular style of sewing the seams, as if puckered up. Always made by skilled women."

"Charming," said Mrs. Oakes.

"The second and more likely meaning, etymologically speaking, is literally 'to roast until puckered up'. It refers to their custom of roasting their enemies."

"Oh. Well..." Mrs. Oakes asked if any refreshments were being served.

Diplomatically, despite such candor, the evening ended well, on a note of cordial approvals. Warren had tried to shift that blame away from Watrous and Ramsey, as Sibley remarked, thus saving the necks of the authorities in charge. He also considered that he had softened the impression left by Hole-in-the-Day's warnings. The good citizens of Saint Paul would not dig into their pockets for an Indian they considered an enemy.

The next evening, Hole-in-the-Day visited the Governor at his house with the trader Morrison in his company. It was a small gathering, at Ramsey's invitation. They were met by a black woman servant in her apron and bonnet who was quickly dispatched to the kitchen by Mrs. Anna Ramsey. The hostess was delighted to meet the chief and offered punch to her guests.

Warren was already at the Ramsey house, called upon to assume his usual function as interpreter, although he felt a certain awkwardness this time. He was, after all, an elected official, a territorial representative, as well as in the employ of the Indian Department. Ramsey was, effectively, his immediate superior. And Hole-in-the-Day, a full-blooded Anishinaabe chief, was his close friend. They had not spoken since the previous evening at the Church. He had rarely felt so compressed between two men of different bloods. He could not have expressed it clearly, even to his cousin George, but he felt that evening in Saint Paul that his allegiance was being exacted by both sides.

Ramsey himself shook the chief's hand, then drew him aside. He addressed Hole-in-the-Day directly, directing Warren to translate, which he did, looking straight ahead at the papered wall, hardly even seeing the framed landscape of the Mississippi bluffs.

"See here, Sir. I was told by my brother about your speech last night. It is astonishing and ill-advised for such a famous chief to speak out critically against myself and the government in a town meeting. This business about delivering the annuities this fall. It could not be helped, as Mr. Warren said, due to delays in Washington. Your people were given supplies, as promised. The disease was tragic. The annuities will be paid as soon as possible. But the government and its officers cannot tolerate such criticism at a public meeting. It serves nobody's purpose. Please consider that before any future actions."

Hole-in-the-Day stood silent at this, glancing at Warren who saw a dark cloud passing over his eyes. He offered the Governor his most dignified smile, reminding him he was his friend, as he was the friend of all whites. He said no more, and bowed slightly to shake

Mrs. Ramsey's gentle hand as he left the Governor's house. He did not shake the hand of his friend William Warren, nor did he bid him goodbye.

Walking back to the American House in the cold January night, a light snowfall blowing up, Warren passed a storefront—a newly opened tobacconist—where two men were setting up a stiff, blank-faced effigy of a standing Indian in a feathered headdress, painted garishly, offering wooden cigars to potential customers. A small group of white citizens were admiring it and congratulating the cigar store owner on an advertisement so fitting to the city. Warren slowed as he walked past, lowering his hat brim to the flurry, burying his face in his muffler.

"He's like that little darkie holding the lamp at the Sibley's residence in Mendota," said one lady. "But this one is our very own Indian. And very hospitable!"

"Old Injun Joe we'll call him. Might be here longer than those other Indians. A historical reminder, in some ways." They all laughed.

Warren heard, and continued past them, cloaked and silent.

"Oh," said the woman brightly. "Isn't that the young man with the Chippewa stories in the newspaper? I recognize that dashing cloak of his!"

"Why I believe it is, the Chippeway in the legislature. Mr. Warren! Oh, Mr. Warren!"

He kept walking, head down. Something about the wooden Indian revulsed him. He wanted at that moment to be just as invisible as any good servant. Now a man of the government, he had to play the servant's role. But he did not have it in him to turn around.

§

One week later he sat reading in their comfortably heated rooms in the American House when he stood and snapped his copy of that day's *Pioneer* in his hand. He paced furiously.

"Matilda, listen to this. I can hardly believe it. Bagone-giizig has published a letter."

"Mr. Editor—The day after my speech in the Presbyterian Church, I was informed that Mr. Warren, the interpreter, said that in justice to the Chippewa agent and the government officers, that it was not the provisions that were the cause of sickness and death of the Indians. Had I understood Mr. Warren at the time, I certainly would have proved to the meeting, his double way of acting, which I will now state to let the public know, that I did not come to this place to impose upon them a falsehood, as Mr. Warren says or insinuates..."

The letter then accused Warren of not telling the whole truth about the agent's actions in order to keep his place as an Indian farmer. Thus he had kept quiet about the spoiled rations that killed the Indians at Sandy Lake, which the agent made them sign for. If he had spoken up, then lost his place because of the agent,

"... he would have explained the truth in favor of the Indians, who have given him bread ever since he has been born. To those very Indians he owes his livelihood, but no, he is one of those men who can be bought at any time for a small sum of money...I also say that the agent refused to have the bills and invoices compared with the goods and provisions brought to us. The Chippewas were compelled to sign papers because of hunger and want... All the Whites know me, and knew my father to be friendly with them. I wish them to know that I am still one of their friends, and hope that Warren's words will have no weight with them..."

"That cannot be him," said Matilda, "Not Bagone-giizig. It's a trick, William. There are things in that letter that would not come to an Indian's mind. Those are not his words."

"Who would do this? Who would make him sign it? He didn't even know what he was signing. We've known each other so long…"
He collapsed in his chair, incredulous.

"They're in league against you, afraid of your influence in the Legislature. The traders. They're using him, William, because they can't use you."

The personal nature of the attack laid him up for a full day, then another, coughing blood as he ruminated. It hurt his attendance record at the legislature which further made him wary of Goodhue, who had already used his vitriolic pen to lambast two office-holders for absenteeism, Col. Mitchell and Judge Cooper. In plain print, he called the judge a sot, a brute, an ass, and a profligate vagabond. What would he reserve for William Warren, an opportunistic half-breed?

Matilda was right, those were not the words of his friend. He recognized the AFC at work here, endeavoring to oust Watrous and put in one of theirs as removal agent. The Chief was being manipulated to openly accuse Warren and Watrous. Someone else wrote the letter, not Hole-in-the-Day. Oakes? Sibley? Someone with AFC trader connections at the church.

Warren wrote this and more in his response two weeks later, filling a full page in the *Democrat* and accusing *"certain designing individuals"* of using Hole-in-the-Day as a tool to further their own interests. These were in fact the same contractors that sold spoiled pemmican to the Ojibwe at Sandy Lake for 17 cents a pound, aggravating the rampant disease and deaths while they were awaiting their payments that never arrived.

> *"It is these same contractors, or those connected with them, that have persecuted me for the past several years because I would not be their tool and slave.... These men have advised Hole-in-the-Day to the measures he has pursued, and have made him sign papers among which the letter above referred to is one. They are, and always have been since they came into the country, the worst enemies the Chippewa have ever been cursed with. In treaties and other matters of vital importance, sacrificing the best future and interest of the tribe, for their own."*

If his response could not win back his friend, it would certainly earn him more enemies.

Now that he had defended both Watrous and Ramsey, he could not back down and had no inclination to. The rub was, removal was still on Ramsey's agenda. The only way to fight that now would be by the proper channels. He would help the chiefs take it to Washington and see the president, who would certainly listen to their reasons. There was nothing in the 1837 or 1842 treaties stipulating forced removal. It was up to the president to tell them. The Great Father was the only one whose spoken words they would believe.

Chapter 10: Second Chance

Saint Paul, 1851

"YOUR HEART IS WITH THE OJIBWE, WILLIAM. But your head is with the whites." His wife's words stung, but rang true.

Warren's response to Hole-in-the Day's letter was that the accusations, all false, proved nothing; he had done his duty to the government and the Indians, but only too well. It went unanswered. Obeying the dictates of both sides of his mixed-blood was more difficult than he had foreseen. He felt that he had to remain in his position in order to do something for the plight of the Ojibwe, if anything at all could be done. The legislature, now a hotbed of political intrigue and rivalries, could be his only way. He was known as a man of duty. But duty to whom?

He wrote to his cousin George from Saint Paul again during the winter session, sending him a package of local papers and telling him that he and his family were comfortable and all enjoying pretty good health.

> *Hole-in-the-Day was down here to raise a contribution. He represented himself as the head chief of the nation. For Mr. Aitkens' sake I interpreted for him to a crowded church. He was so excited that he could not talk reason and I had to smooth down his talk. After his speech, I made a few remarks... I spoke in the name of the Wisconsin and Lake Superior Chippeways over whom Hole-in-the-Day could claim no chieftainship, and a contribution or help given to him would not help these bands who were the greatest sufferers. I made other remarks which Mrs. Oakes told to Hole-in-the-*

Day and wrote a letter which he signed abusing me, and had it published in the papers. Of course, people knowing where it comes from, it does me more good than hurt, and the contribution for Hole-in-the-Day has been stopped. Gov Ramsey thanked me for the course I had taken and refuses any longer to recognize Hole-in-the-Day as chief.

He went on to explain how he told Ramsey the Chippeways would not remove unless they saw the president. Ramsey, still with removal in mind, asked the Department for $25,000 more to finance the removal and for soldiers to help him. Warren had asked for a delegation of twelve to go to Washington in the spring, himself and George included, paid for by the government if not by the Indians' coming annuities.

...They have got to remove—and our only course is to get it done as well as we can and in a manner which will conduce best for to the interests of the Indians as well as our own. If you have any advice to give me on this subject do so.

The Gov has informed me that he will supply us for the removal. And I told him that I would not move a hand to say a word in the removal unless it was to be done in the right way, and unless my opinion was listened to and carried out.

...Come here as soon as possible without fail. You will not be sorry for it. Mr. Rice is anxious to see you. He is going in heavy at Red River this spring and says you are just the person he wants to take charge of his business there...

Don't forget to bring Nancy with you. Don't let want of funds deter you. I have some and will divide it with you. I board at a private house & have two fine rooms. Will be able to accommodate you.

Love to all,
Your Aff Cousin,
Wm. W. Warren

This plan was launched. The next day he was descending from the American House into the freezing mud streets of Saint Paul after the Legislature had finished business. He passed a small crowd just in time to observe an altercation, a fairly common occurrence in the capital, but this one involving some well-known figures. He wrote further to George:

Yesterday I witnessed a very bloody fight as our House adjourned for the afternoon—between the Editor of the Pioneer, Mr. Goodhue, and a brother of Judge Cooper's. Judge Cooper is gone away this winter, and Goodhue, who is an unprincipled scoundrel, wrote and published an article in his paper defaming him bitterly. He also attacked Col Mitchell and E. Rice and inserted an article in his paper signed by Hole-in-the-Day against me because I would not vote for him as public printer. Yesterday young Cooper met Goodhue near the steps of our House. He asked him if he had written that article*. Goodhue immediately pulled out a pistol and pointing it at Cooper told him it was none of his business. C. pulled out a long revolver, at which moment persons stepped between and requested them to deliver weapons. Cooper gave up his revolver and Goodhue fired his pistol immediately at him but missing him he dropped it. Young Cooper ran at him and hit him with his fist. Goodhue turned and ran, in doing so he pulled out another pistol and turned on Cooper who was following him up. As G. was about to fire Cooper hit him in the stomach with a stone. G. ran at C. pistol cocked again and when about to fire he slipped and fell. As he was rising Cooper ran at him, but someone caught him by the arm and Goodhue shot him in the side, not three steps off. Cooper held his hand to his side and said he was shot. At the same time he pulled out a small dagger and running at Goodhue he stabbed him three times in the guts and back. Had he not been held he would have dispatched him on*

116

the spot. I witnessed the whole performance. Both are badly wounded. Goodhue will probably kick the bucket, for young Cooper I hope he killed him. He is a brave man. The excitement in town against Goodhue has been great, and had he not been hurt, his printing office would probably have been mobbed. ...

...Be of good cheer and don't allow anything to trouble your mind. Particularly take good care of yourself. Since the death of our brother Edward, you owe it to your friends to guard well your life. My words are few but you comprehend my meaning fully.

Yr Aff Brother,
Wm W Warren

Correspondence was often held up for months in the winter, and he got no answer. As often in his letters to George, he was writing what he felt most deeply about himself. He was, he feared, growing weak. Losing his cousin Edward to a freak hunting accident still upset him. His ruptured friendship with Hole-in-the-Day affected him dearly, Matilda could tell. This was no time for weakness.

He wrote his lengthy report on the 1850 removal to Ramsey, as well as his views on any future removal and his request for a delegation to Washington, assuring him:

"...it is better for the Chippeways to remove, always provided, they are moved to a country adapted to their wants and habits, and with sufficient means for a livelihood thereon. A country in which they could live under the humane guardianship of our General Government, and which be guaranteed them forever. Which last is, in my opinion, the first and necessary step towards their eventual civilization."

This was, Warren knew, also the goal of Hole-in-the-Day. It was inevitable for survival.

He assured the Governor that he would always be ready to help the officers of the government, in respect of the Indians, in performing the instructions of their Great Father. Ramsey dispatched the report to Commissioner Lea with the highest recommendations, stating that Warren's suggestions were entitled to respectful consideration. Washington, in winter, was more than one month away.

The governor was also busy preparing the forthcoming treaty to be made with the Sioux, which would secure a great portion of their lands west of the Mississippi and give Saint Paul the western riverbank. It would also provide the Dakota Sioux with much-needed cash, which would flow into the streets of the city as gold through a California river. Ramsey was the architect of this coming monumental deal.

The House took care of its business, and Warren actively participated, all the while working diligently on his writings, by which he hoped to make the Ojibwe people better known to the white population. In February, he reached an agreement with D.A. Robertson and saw this notice of introduction in the *Minnesota Democrat:*

The History of the Chippewas

The Hon. W.W. Warren, of the Minnesota Legislature, has commenced in our paper, a History of the Chippewa Indians. His narratives are intensely interesting. Mr. Warren is descended from the mingled blood of the Chippewa and adventurous white trader. His maternal great grandfather was one of the first white traders in the Chippewa nation.

Mr. Warren, now twenty-six years of age, has spent his life among the Chippewas, and is better qualified than any other man in the United States, to write their history. His communications will be a rich repast for our readers, and cannot fail to attract the attention of the literary world.

Thus began the series of articles, appearing on the first page of the *Democrat* in the first week of February 1851, advertised as written expressly for that newspaper, entitled *"A BRIEF HISTORY OF THE OJIBWES IN MINNESOTA AS OBTAINED FROM THEIR OLD MEN."* His published histories did more than anything to solidify Warren's popularity in Saint Paul; people would stop him to converse on the street, wanting to hear more, and men of importance had to recognize him as an eloquent, knowledgeable writer. Somebody had to defend the poor Ojibwe, and William Warren it would be. Some went so far as to say that it was a shame about his Indian blood—he was a good man, and should be white.

Alliances in Saint Paul were becoming clearer. A new newspaper, the *Minnesotian*, appeared as the recognized Whig Party instrument. Goodhue's *Pioneer*, following the bloody gunfight, was absorbed in February along with the *Chronicle and Register*, by Robertson's *Democrat,* proudly presenting Warren's articles in its first weekly issues. The *Minnesotian* supported the Ramsey and Sibley faction (and John Watrous, appointed removal agent, also a known Whig), while D.A. Robertson used his *Minnesota Democrat* to further the cause of more liberal legislation in favor of the Indians, the independent traders, and the settlers.

All Saint Paul merchants, tradesmen, and investors brightened with the coming Traverse des Sioux Treaty, Ramsey's current brainchild, which would accompany the wave of settlers expected with the hundreds of steamboats landing at the capital in the coming summer. The population of the town and the territory was on the verge of explosion. Cash was needed as well as land, and the Dakota Sioux's removal meant both, immediately. The Ojibwe removal would play out later; for the moment, it seemed altogether secondary on the agenda.

John Watrous returned from his holiday downriver and immediately called on Ramsey to organize another removal plan. The door was answered by Mrs. Ramsey.

"Why Hello, John. So good to see you back in our city."

"Just stopping by for a meeting with the Governor," he replied. "We have business that can't wait much longer, I'm afraid. No rest for the wicked, they say."

"Well, not all of us are that wicked," she laughed. "You know Mr. Warren here. He's been publishing the most interesting articles on the Chippeways, and I'm lucky to have his company this morning. In fact, a few of the chiefs were just here to see Alex."

"How are you, Mr. Warren? You have business with the Governor?"

"He asked me to interpret for the Chippeway here to talk of a trip to Washington."

"Hmm. I see. We'll have to plan our schedule. Still on good terms with these people?"

"Yes, Sir. More so since…since I now sit on the legislature. They feel safer with someone to represent their interests."

"Good. I'm certain you could be of great service. We need someone they trust."

The subject of removal was studiously avoided outside Ramsey's chambers. The governor gave Watrous general instructions, wrote to request more funds for provisions and left the details to the sub agent. Watrous thought it more judicious, this time, to wait until after the sugar making was completed in the spring. But he would instruct them not to plant, but rather to prepare to remove. The governor appeared to give little weight to Hole-in-the-Day's impertinence or the Indians' invectives against his inaction on the first attempt, and proceeded as if it had never happened. The real removal would begin right after the Treaty with the Sioux, the governor's foremost preoccupation at this time.

Watrous set out to mount his communications and select his agents and conductors. Both he and Ramsey knew that certain factions would try to sway the Wisconsin and Lake Superior Ojibwe and advise them against removal, mostly AFC traders. Warren appeared to support removal, if only to get them away from traders and their liquor. Watrous was determined to complete his assigned mission as dictated by Thomas Ewing, the Whig Secretary of the Interior in Washington. Watrous must induce them to remove, and to make them stay. The way to do this was through promised money and goods.

Toward the last of the second session, legislators voted on Ramsey's proposal to consolidate representation of Benton and Cass counties, which were melded into one district, thereby reducing the number of representatives. Seven members tried to block the measure by abstaining from the quorum, but the vote was taken anyway and passed 10-0 on March 29th. Those seven members, including William Warren from Benton county, accordingly resigned from the House at the end of the second session. In essence, his office no longer existed, and he was again unemployed.

The Warrens returned to Gull Lake, where they remained for another quarter while he concentrated on regaining his health and seeking a way to make a living. He wrote reclaiming back payment for services performed during his position with the Indian Department, compiling the Inquiries, interpreting, and counseling the Ojibwe. Fletcher and Rice wrote in support of him. The long wait for administrative response commenced, but Ramsey too agreed to procure him a further $250, so he was encouraged. The money would come from Saint Louis.

In the summer they moved to a house in the woods at Two Rivers, near the fork of the Mississippi and the Platte, not far from where Matilda's father lived and ran his trading hotel at Aitken's Ferry. They all found it lovely. What he had now, in lieu of his health and a job in the capital, were his histories, his knowledge of the Ojibwe, the acquaintances who supported his efforts, and his growing family. He gathered his writings, as more than one of his supporters encouraged him to publish them in a book. But how was he to earn his living in the meantime?

In June, shifting manuscript pages around on his bed, he opened a letter Matilda handed him from John Watrous. It began with "Friend Warren," and offered him the position of conductor for the removal of the interior bands. This time he would be paid by the government: three dollars a day plus expenses. His wife busied herself inside the cabin, awaiting his reaction.

"Matilda, they're announcing another removal attempt to Sandy Lake. Of course, they won't go there, but this may be a chance for all of us, and a perfect way to get all the bands to La Pointe, to form a united front, and negotiate with the government. They will have to remove, but to the right place, at the right time, with good living conditions and support they could count on from the government. I'm going to accept."

"The People trust you, William. You know that. But do you trust the whites?"

"I'll have to. Ramsey has heard me. He knows where I stand. He's Watrous' boss."

To cement his will, he received a letter from George at the same time, telling him he too was recruited as conductor, along with Alex Corbin, to help him. He wrote back, excited again, explaining his new appointment and at his stated terms:

He has taken me up on all but the pay, but he promises to make up all right...He also sends a draft to pay part of my expenses. Notwithstanding all this, I was somewhat dubious about taking the appointment, as I felt quite independent, having regained my health, a beautiful place, and good crops to attend to and feed my children, a claim of $300.00 just allowed me by Govt to clothe me and buy stock, and having just completed an arrangement to take a stock of goods to payment, all this induced me to send the removal to the old Harry, but your letter from La Pointe which I received the same day with Watrous' had changed my mind And I have concluded to throw myself into the Breach... I believe we both fully understand the arrangement and will act accordingly. My main objective is a complete and full organization of the tribe—and Half Breeds if possible after this year. "United action" must be our motto.

Warren wrote this while was already on his way to the Chippewa River after securing supply vouchers from Ramsey. He would go up to the Ermatingers' place, take stock, and collect the bands there, then make their way up to join George and the Lake Superior bands. "*Above all*," he told George, "*arrange it so that not one Indian shall leave La Pointe till I get there* and let waiting for us be their excuse... I hope to see you in a few days I will wait, and then we will understand one another perfectly. I write this from Charlotte's house. She and Julia live in town, in good health. I left my family all well and perfectly happy and comfortable."

Thus began, with great expectations, William Warren's second mission to assist in the removal of the Ojibwe, which in his mind was his attempt to consolidate them all together as one nation. His great regret was that he would have to do it without the help of Hole-in-the-Day who was, he knew, of the same mind. But his friend, as he still thought of him, also wanted to be the big chief of all the bands at the same time. William told him this was not the way of the Anishinaabe, it was the way of the white man. Hole-in-the-Day had looked at him with a nod and smirked. "Then it serves my purpose."

In any event, this was not to come about. Hole-in-the-Day's bands were not summoned to Fond du Lac, nor to Sandy Lake. Watrous would go to Crow Wing to pay them. He was too wary to let the young chief get near enough to make more trouble among the Indians who were slated to remove. Warren suspected that agent Watrous was also wary of his own influence on the Ojibwe. The agent had waited until late in the day before contacting him, but in the end, Warren concluded, Watrous finally realized that the Chippewa River Indians would not move without his help. Warren knew his Indians well, they knew him and trusted him. Still mourning for their dead and fearing the same consequences as the first removal attempt, they still had to go for their payment, but they did not trust Watrous. After all the suffering and manipulation they had undergone, all the broken treaty promises, Warren thought it doubtful that they would trust any white man.

Chapter 11: What They Could Not Know

WE ARE NOW COMPELLED, in the name of historical accuracy, to cite documented evidence in order to apprise the reader of facts and actions of which our protagonists could not know in 1851, but which were later discovered by historians who delved deeply into the Ojibwe removal attempts of 1850 and 1851.

Blame for the deaths and suffering needs assignment, if only to determine the motivations, methods, and accountability of those responsible.

The roles of Governor Alexander Ramsey, Removal Agent John Watrous, Conductors William and George Warren, a handful of implicated traders, and the United States government have been disputed and interpreted at length and can only be seen in perspective by using the same method as William Warren when he determined which versions of the Ojibwe elders' stories were closest to the truth: by comparison.

This was done exhaustively by several seasoned scholars and compiled by James M. McClurken in <u>Fish in the Lakes, Wild Rice, and Game in Abundance, Testimony on Behalf of Mille Lacs Ojibwe Hunting and Fishing Rights,</u> (Michigan State University Press, 2000). This multi-disciplined research constitutes the principal argumentation examined by Supreme Court Justice Sandra Day O'Connor, who ruled against the State of Minnesota in the 1999 landmark decision stating that the Chippewa shall retain their rights to hunt and fish and gather on ceded lands, as granted by the 1837 Treaty of Saint Peters (*aka* the White Pine Treaty). Most of the information offered below is intricately detailed and fully documented, principally here by Bruce M. White, in that excellent study.

The Sandy Lake Tragedy, as it is often referred to, has not received the attention of the Cherokee Trail of Tears, where administrative and military cruelty was put to use to expel and kill thousands of Native Americans. Nor is it as well-known as Wounded Knee, a gratuitous massacre that became immediately emblematic of indigenous peoples' systematic elimination, a sort of final solution envisioned in high places. We could liken it more to the blatant violation of the rights of First Nations in the 21st century, namely the usurpation of Lakota Sioux lands endangering the entire Nation's water sources at Standing Rock in North Dakota.

This is because at Sandy Lake, the actions of very few men affected the fates of many, without physical force, without a shot being fired, quietly, almost invisibly.

It has been observed from their actions and declarations that the Ojibwe bands were consistently friendly towards the whites, peaceful, that they complied with the wishes of the Great Father, and conducted their affairs based on the trust they had for their interlocutors. They listened, weighed their words, negotiated for their survival, and touched the quill with the same respect and sanctity as when swearing to a sacred oath.

The Ojibwe always had implicit faith in the word of the Great Father, the President of the United States. A treaty is a matter of honor. They learned, over time, that they could not rely on that word when it flowed from the mouths of elected or appointed officials. They learned to do as the whites: to write it down, and keep it, in order to prove it when necessary.

§

Some facts from documented history:

The strategy behind the first attempt in 1850 was expressed in a letter written from Governor Alexander Ramsey to the new Commissioner of the Indian Department, Luke Lea, dated July 16, 1850:

> *"I am assured by a gentleman of intelligence that to secure the cheerful movement of the Chippewa into the Mississippi county, it will be necessary to convene them on the way,*

say at Fond du Lac, and there hold them with a talk. To this it is my purpose to invite them at once, so soon as I receive directions from your Department to proceed with the removal. From that point we will convey them to Sandy Lake, and there, time the payment in such a way as to interpose obstacles to a return to the county they left."

Ramsey to Lea, National Archives Microfilms,
hereafter NAM;
Bruce M. White in McClurken, P. 187

This strategy of entrapment failed, at the cost in Ojibwe lives that we have seen, arousing suspicions of duplicity, deception, and fraud among the perpetrators. Chief Flat Mouth and Chief Hole-in-the-Day could not have been clearer on who was at fault. William Warren, advisor to the Chippewa River bands for the payment, just elected to the 1851 territorial legislature but not yet in office, was at the time prone to believe it was due to inefficiency and unfortunate circumstantial delays on the part of the Washington administration. Chief Hole-in-the-Day, disappointed in his life-long friend, openly accused him of playing along to protect his job.

When the same strategy was deployed again in 1851, Warren was hired by Removal Agent John Watrous to assist in the removal, but this time was suspected of counteractions. As he expressed in his communications with his cousin, William Warren was determined to gather the bands together in a "united front" to counter any manipulations and secure their demands. Ramsey was preoccupied with the Traverse des Sioux treaty at the time, and gave Watrous discretionary power to handle the Ojibwe removal. The removal attempt again failed and removal was suspended, but Watrous persevered.

John Watrous, after the removal attempts ceased, was the subject of multiple charges of deception and fraud brought principally by the L'Anse bands of Ojibwe, the La Pointe bands, Leonard Wheeler, and William Warren, openly in the Saint Paul press and officially to the Indian Department. An investigation was opened in Washington. Ramsey gave his support to the agent, who had longstanding ties to the Whig political machine in the capital (appointed under deceased President Zachary Taylor). When Franklin Pierce was elected President in 1853 and appointed Willis Gorman as Governor of Minnesota Territory, Watrous tried to be recognized as a lifetime Democrat and gathered support to that effect.

John Watrous was deposed as an Ojibwe sub agent in 1853.

§

Ramsey himself underwent investigation for fraud and usurpation of funds in the Treaty of Traverse des Sioux, but was exonerated by the Senate after paying, irregularly as maintained and proven by the investigating committee, $210,000 to traders, including $60,00 to Henry Sibley of the American Fur Company. The alarming discrepancy between the condemning evidence against Ramsey and his subsequent exoneration went unexplained, but this was and still is a recurring outcome in Senate hearings. Two years later Ramsey returned to become Mayor of Saint Paul, where he made a fortune in real estate. He was later elected State Governor.

Ramsey wrote in his diary on May 7th, 1852 during the Watrous investigation: "Maj. John Watrous—*loaned me one thousand dollars without interest*" (Ramsey Diaries, vol. 23—original emphasis). No further mention of the loan was found, nor mention of its nature or purpose. Later that month Ramsey sent the findings of his cursory investigation into Watrous' behavior in the removals, and his answers to William Warren's charges, to Commissioner Lea in Washington. It was accompanied by (a) favorable cover letter and arrived in Washington with John Watrous. (see Bruce M. White in McClurken, P. 243).

§

Prior to the 1851 removal, Watrous wrote to Warren by runner while he was in Chippewa River country, waiting for supplies:

La Pointe
Aug 9th, 1851

Friend Warren,

    I am now very anxiously waiting the arrival of yourself and the Indians that are embraced in your division to come out to this place.

    Mr. C. H. Beaulieu has arrived from the Lake Du Flambeau with nearly all that quarter and by an express sent on in advance I am informed that P. H. Beaulieu and Edward Conner will be here with Cob-wa-wis and they say the entire Wisconsin band, there had some 32 of the Pillican Lake band come out and some now are in Conner's Party.

    I want you should be here without fail in 10 days from this as I cannot remain longer, I shall leave at the expiration of this time for Crow Wing to make the payment to the St. Croix Bands who have all removed as I learn from letters just received from the St. Croix. I want your assistance very much in making the Crow Wing payment and immediately after the completion of this, (which will not take over two days) shall proceed to Sandy Lake to make the payment to the Mississippi and Lake Bands.

    The goods are all at Sandy Lake and I shall make the entire payment without delay, and as much dispatch as can be made; it will be quite lots enough for the poor Indians. Perish is the bearer of this and he can tell you all my plans better than I can write them. Give My respects to your cousin George and believe me Your friend J. S. Watrous.

    P. S. Inform the Indians that if they are not here by the time they will be struck from the roll. I am daily expecting a company of Infantry to be stationed at this place.

JSW
(Warren family papers 1756-1907,
Wisconsin Historical Society)

The identity of the runner "Perish" is not known. Warren waited for supplies for his Chippewa River division to depart for La Pointe, where George Warren was waiting for him, with several hundred Ojibwe, to form a block. As supplies did not arrive, Warren waited for the Chippewa River bands to hunt and gather wild rice so they could feed themselves en route.

Reporting to Ramsey on September 25, 1851, Watrous wrote that he would make the 1850 and 1851 payments to the Mississippi and Lake Superior bands in two or three times, at Sandy Lake and later at Fond du Lac.

He declared that it was his: *"intention to delay (unless otherwise instructed) the money payment of the present year to the Chippewas of Lake Superior, until after navigation closes, which is done to throw every obstacle in the way of their returning to their old homes."*

In the same letter, wanting further support from Ramsey, he spoke of his wariness of Henry Rice and problems with William Warren: *"He was doing me so much injury by writing letters into the Indian country and sending the Indians in different directions with tobacco to stop them from removing that I was forced to give him a place in the removal hoping thereby to silence him in a measure or at least that he would be so situated that he could be held accountable for his course."* (Watrous to Ramsey; see Bruce M. White in McClurken, P. 215)

Reverend William Boutwell, assisting John Watrous in La Pointe, reported to Ramsey on September 18, 1851 describing the council held to persuade the Ojibwe to go to Fond du Lac. Watrous had already left. At the end of his letter he writes: *"I would only add, on the 3rd of Sept. a telegraphic dispatch came to hand viz. 'Suspend active operations in the removal until further orders.' The purport of the order remains a secret & as the Inds. are ready to go I shall start them."* (White in McClurken, P. 209)

The ignored telegram, forwarded to Watrous by runner to Sandy Lake, was sent by Commissioner Luke Lea of the Indian Department in Washington. The exact wording recorded in the letterbook, dated August 25th, 1851, reads *"Suspend action with reference to the removal of the Lake Superior Chippewas for further orders."*

Watrous signed the voucher to pay the runner, Yellow Beaver, at Fond du Lac on October 9th: $16.00, at $1.00 per day, express to Sandy Lake. Normally this would include his return to La Pointe. Active removal continued. It is not known when he actually received the telegram; Watrous told no Ojibwe nor even his superiors about it. On September 20th, he stated in his report that there was little left to do, the removal effort was an accomplished fact. (White in McClurken, p. 210)

Watrous continued his efforts for the next three months until he was able to state to Ramsey on December 15th, using the same terms as Boutwell in his September letter, that all *"active operations"* had ceased. (White in McClurken, P. 218)

During the entire aftermath and investigation of the removals, John Watrous never mentioned receiving the telegram ordering suspension, nor did Ramsey. Both men got on with it and reported that the removal was successful. Both subsequently had to reduce their stated estimates of the number removed, several times.

Missionary Leonard Wheeler, in his report to Selah Treat of the ABCFM in Boston, qualified the removal as a failure, stating that the Bad River bands would not remove, and only 200 Indians at most had removed in 1851.

The only other telegram involved in the removal effort was sent earlier that summer by Watrous himself requesting military assistance (which never came, and never found a response from his superiors). The telegram was mentioned by Reverend Sherman Hall in a December letter to Selah Treat, and in Washington by an official in the Indian Department, where no trace was ever found.

§

In his report to Ramsey on December 24, 1851, Watrous was unclear as to how many removal resisters were paid. He states that *"reliable information has been recd. that a portion of the Indians yet remaining on the ceded lands will remove of their own accord in the coming spring, and their portion of the money & goods has been retained."*

There remained, according to his accounts, $8,040 in annuities money at the agency. At $5.00 per person, this would mean that 1,608 were not paid. Hardly a successful removal, as reported by Watrous. (Watrous to Ramsey; White in McClurken, P. 262).

The goods Watrous set aside for the La Pointe bands were kept at the agency in Crow Wing, which burned down in January, as recounted by Benjamin Armstrong of La Pointe in his reminiscences, *Early Life.*

> *Some time in the latter part of the month we were surprised to learn that the new agency had burned down, and, as the word came to us, "had taken the goods and money into the ashes". The agent immediately started down the river, and we saw no more of him for some time. Crowds of Indians and a few white men soon gathered around the burnt remains of the agency and waited until it should cool down, when a search was made in the ashes for melted coin that must be there if the story was true that goods and money had gone down together. They scraped and scratched in vain. All that was ever found in that ruin in the shape of metal was two fifty cent silver pieces."*

> *(see White in McClurken, P. 264).*

According to Watrous in his report, the annuities money was not lost, but he lost $750 of his own money. However, he wrote, the *"annuity goods intended for the Lake Superior Ojibwes who removed in the spring were destroyed...: The late unfortunate fire will of course prevent me from fulfilling my promise as far as the goods go. They are all in a very distressed condition, have received nothing for a year and I feel anxious that the first who comes should not be disappointed."* He included a list of supplies to replace the goods, requesting Ramsey to purchase them in Saint Paul from trader Charles Borup. (John Watrous to Ramsey, January 28, 1853; White in McClurken, P.262).

Several fires occurred at the agency, Watrous being the subject of many accusations of fraud and misconduct. Later, William Johnston wrote to Commissioner Manypenny seeking a job as agent on October 20, 1855. At the time he complained of the claims of the traders on the Mississippi—Borup, Oakes, Beaulieu, Nettleton et al. He commented on the relationship between Watrous and Borup:

The agent for the Indians in those years, made money. He deposited $20,000 with Borup & Oakes, Bankers. When the agent went for it the Bankers refused to refund or pay, as they believed the money was taken from the Indians. The agent cannot & is afraid to take legal measures as the matter might be exposed. Therefore now both parties keep the matter hushed. The burning of the agency at Crow Wing was done intentionally to bring an imaginary loss on the U.S. and upon the Indians. My information came from the Chiefs and white people of known veracity.

(NAM, Correspondence, Office of Indian Affairs; White in McClurken, P. 264.)

An annuities payment took place in January 1852 at Fond du Lac, as Watrous was finally instructed by Ramsey. The government blacksmith there at the time was William E. Van Tassell, who was in the payroom. Also, there was Vincent Roy, a trader. In an 1855 investigation, Roy said two traders were given privileged positions at the payment, George Nettleton and Clement Beaulieu. The two men *"got most of the money. One stood at one door and one at the other of the payroom and no Indian was allowed to go out until he had paid most of his money to one of them. The chiefs and the head men were bribed to consent to it."*

Van Tassel helped count the money. The Fond du Lac Ojibwe were paid $10 each, the La Pointe and Wisconsin band members were given $8.00 each the next day:

"I saw one woman paid $80 as the share of herself & her children. It was paid to her in gold. She put it in her blanket. Beaulieu took it away from her. Gave her some silver in change. Don't know how much. It was not much. She held it in her hand. The same woman came to me the next day to borrow 50 cts. and said they took it all. She was a widow woman with a large family of children. I knew her well. Sometimes the Indians would try to go out the same door they came in and the Agent Watrous would not permit them. The woman I spoke of was a very poor woman and the traders were not in the habit of crediting her."

(Claim 63, special file, NAM;
White in McClurken, P.234-235)

However, the above words, facts and actions can be seen only in hindsight, from the perspective of informed history. We shall now return to what happened to those who could not see them coming, on their way to Fond du Lac and Sandy Lake for the second removal attempt in the fall of 1851.

Chapter 12: Change of Heart

La Pointe, Monigwunakauning, Fall of 1851

WARREN'S FLEET OF TWENTY CANOES with nearly one hundred of the Chippewa River people arrived at La Pointe in good weather. It was early October—much later than he had hoped. George Warren was still waiting for him with 500 Lake Superior Ojibwe, but the expected numbers were not there and the agent was gone.

"Where's Watrous? Why are all the bands not here? Where is Buffalo?"

"They've taken off to Fond du Lac. Maybe 150 of them, with Watrous. These here are supposed to follow, with you. Why the delay?"

"I didn't have enough supplies for all these Indians, I had to find them tobacco and food, they had to hunt and dry the meat. Ramsey was too busy with the Sioux treaty. Then we had to wait for the wild rice harvest, and many did not want to go. I couldn't convince them all."

"Not surprising. When some of their chiefs came ahead in June, they found no provisions here, nothing for them. Watrous wasn't here then either. They got disgusted and turned around. They'd rather starve at home. They don't trust him, William. This is the second time. We hear the L'Anse and Ontonagon bands got a letter from the president telling them they don't have to remove. Must have been that petition from the whites, the mining people. Looks like we're not going to get that united front, cousin. They're all dispersed."

"Why Fond du Lac? What happened to Sandy Lake?"

"Watrous held a long council here, it lasted days. Buffalo refused to go, they all refused, then they put some conditions to him. They want $200,000 to remove, and they'll go no farther than Fond du Lac. They want twine, nets, hooks, and food all year round. They want to go see the president in Washington. When Watrous finally agreed to all that—I'm not sure about the first pledge—they up and left like a cloud of birds. I got some to stay and wait for you and your bands. Sandy Lake, I don't know what's become of that. He did agree to pay them everything they were owed at Fond du Lac. But I know, as you know, that the goods and money are at Sandy Lake or Crow Wing. Sounds fishy."

"We'll have to go," Warren said." Most of the Chippewa River bands are behind me. I'll go on ahead, see what I can do, and we'll meet at Fond du Lac. You bring my stragglers too."

On the way to Fond du Lac, Warren met many Ojibwe coming back to La Pointe, convinced that the agent was not going to pay them as he promised. He arrived to find the same wariness among those still waiting for payment. They had to purchase food from the traders on site, Nettleton, Oakes, Beaulieu, Lynde, and others, at high prices. Watrous paid some of the bands their 1850 annuities, but if they wanted their goods they had to go to Sandy Lake, and then return to Fond du Lac, where he would pay them for this year. Later, and only if they'd brought their families. He'd tried to trap them again, Buffalo said. He again broke his word.

At Fond du Lac, Warren found Watrous writing a letter. He quickly covered it with a list of names. Indian names, and figures.

"What is happening here, Mr. Watrous? Why have you not paid these Indians?"

"Where have you been, Warren? The payment will be made when all the Indians, including yours, are present. As instructed. Where are your bands?"

"They were delayed. Many fell sick, we had no supplies. They're on their way, about a week behind me, but from La Pointe, where you summoned them in the first place."

"Then you go back and get them. Hurry them up if they want to be paid. I'm leaving for the agency at Sandy Lake now, to pay the Mississippi bands. Those Lake Superior bands who are willing to come there can do so, and will be paid there. If not, they must wait here for my return. And there will be no goods distributed here, the provisions are at Sandy Lake."

"My division will get here in time. No need for my returning."

"That was an order, Mr. Warren, from your supervising Agent. I've hired you as conductor. I expect you to do your duty to your government as ordered."

Warren held his tongue with great difficulty. Instead, he returned to his campsite and began a coughing fit. The days were still warm, the white birch leaves turning gold, the maples blood red, the wind was dry, but the nights were chilly. Time was closing in. He went to talk to Buffalo. They had built small lodges of reed mats, insufficient for the coming winter. The campfires were cooking pork and flour stews, bought from the traders on credit while they awaited their payment. At Fond du Lac, they could at least share the rice and the fish.

Watrous had not paid them, nor had he paid Warren in full. He was loath to abandon the Anishinaabe at this point. Maybe they would remove to Fond du Lac. It was better than Sandy Lake, more like home to some. But the traders were there with their whiskey, waiting to scoop up their dimes. The elder chiefs, for the most part, did not want their people to stay where the whiskey was—they knew the dangers, as did Warren.

"We will not go to Sandy Lake, Nosins. We will never go back there," Buffalo told him.

"But you can stay here. For the winter. Your families are here. You will be safe. You will have food." He knew this was a weak suggestion, especially to Great Buffalo. The island, Monigwunakau-ning, was his home, his peoples' home, and any trust in the agent to provide for them was broken. Warren felt torn once again between allegiance to the Anishinaabe and his fear of their inevitable fate under the thumb of white men.

"The traders are here," Buffalo said. "As soon as my people touch the money, they will sell them fire water, and the money will be gone before we return home. You know this, and your father knew it. The agent has lied to us. I will tell the others not to come. There is nothing for them here. We must go see the Great Father, tell him how we have been treated. He will tell us, as he told the L'Anse bands, that we do not have to remove. You, Nosins, will go with us."

"We shall go, Buffalo. But first I must complete my mission here. I must go back to La Pointe and bring the Chippewa River bands to the payment. I must go now, before it's too late."

"Then we go with you, Nosins. But we will not come back." Buffalo rose.

He went reluctantly back on the trail to La Pointe to gather his charge, the Chippewa River bands, and hurry them on. Old Buffalo and many of his La Pointe Ojibwe left with him, but with the intention of going to their homes. George's bands from La Pointe also turned back when they heard from Buffalo what to expect in Fond du Lac. Warren tried to persuade them to come to the payment, as they had come this far. Many defected despite his efforts. In all, 1,000 or more went back to La Pointe or never came. He and George finally found themselves at Fond du Lac with a few hundred scattered Ojibwe, weary and resigned to wait.

"Our whole plan is falling apart, William. The agent is splitting the bands up."

"They've got rations here, they're safe."

"They're paying the traders, Nettleton and Beaulieu, for the rations. Watrous pays them. Out of their coming annuities, not out of the removal fund. He's putting them in debt again. How much can they expect? What are they waiting for?"

"Twine, kettles, hooks, blankets. Pork and flour, hoping it's good."

"And the money?"

"They are owed some unpaid annuities from last year, plus this year."

"How much is that? Per person?"

"Maybe four dollars apiece, after paying the traders."

"Four dollars? They should have stayed home and fished."

"I don't know who's been lying here, or why. I am of two minds, George. I do not know whether to stay or go. I don't know what to tell the Ojibwe."

"The Indians are telling the truth, William. They have no reason to lie."

But Warren persisted. He led what was left of his own bands as far as Sandy Lake, where they expected their cash payments. Watrous dismissed him on October 28th, the very day he arrived with his bands. His services were no longer needed.

"I will stay through the payment!" Warren insisted.

"You have no right, as a half-breed, to any payment here. Get out of my sight. I should have never let you into my sight."

As for the Ojibwe, they were again deceived. Watrous gave them only flour, salt pork, sugar, and tea. The agent stalled by going back and forth, to the Crow Wing agency, to Sandy Lake, back to Fond du Lac, never in one place for very long.

Warren trod back to La Pointe, where he crumbled onto a mat of furs. "Watrous somehow slips through your fingers," he said to George. "They'll be trapped again, but in Fond du Lac with their families, until it's too late. I can hardly believe this..."

"John Watrous," George told him. "Has no intention of paying any Indians who did not remove permanently. Open your eyes, William. We've been duped again. He's used us."

The bands dispersed, his own division heading back down the Chippewa River before the freeze. The removal was over. There never were the 3,000 Indians counted by Watrous at Fond du Lac, nor at Sandy Lake. In his annual report he wrote that the removal was mostly successful. 2,000 had removed permanently. He later changed the figure to 1,000, and the rest would come permanently in the spring. By the traders' estimate, about 150, mostly Lake Superior Chippewas, stayed on the upper Mississippi that winter, then returned in the spring to their homes. Watrous changed his report several times, but it was not until December that he reported to

Ramsey that removal was accomplished, and all active operations had ceased.

§

George did what he could to quell his cousin's remorse. Warren marched despondently back to the Chippewa River country with his bands, to help them formulate their grievances. He did not stay long. He wanted to get back home to Two Rivers before the river froze.

Paddling upriver on the slow-moving Mississippi, where on the banks the leaf-stripped ash trees rose gray and black against the metallic sky like desiccated fingers, he tried not to look at them. He thought he might go as far as Crow Wing to see Hole-in-the-Day. But no, he wanted to see nobody. He wanted his wife, his children, his fire, his bed. He was no longer divided, but enraged at his own misjudgment. The rage kept burning. The Anishinaabe fingers reaching to the sky seemed to claw at his already bleeding heart. He coughed, spat phlegm into the freezing waters, and paddled homeward.

Warren gave up on more than just the agent and removal; he gave up on the good faith that he had brought to the government's removal efforts. How deeply Ramsey himself was involved; he did not know. He had been a pawn; the trust the Indians had in him had been used. How could he be so damnably naive? He knew now that Watrous was behind the suffering caused last year as well. The delays were intentional, as was the agent's refusal to pay. It was all manipulation, his promises, his absences, his lies, and deception, to entrap them. It was criminal.

The La Pointe bands formulated their complaints, echoing those of the L'Anse bands against Watrous who had broken his promises, and specifying that they wanted their future payments in La Pointe. They wanted a delegation, chosen by them, to go to Washington. The letter took up Buffalo's earlier words:

"Especially, we would like to have our friend and half-breed child Mr. William W. Warren, go. In his truth and friendship, we have confidence. He is well acquainted with our affairs and has ever advised us to listen to the words of our Great Father."

Twenty-nine chiefs signed the letter to Ramsey. It was witnessed by missionaries Wheeler and Hall, along with Henry Blatchford, interpreter, and the mission teacher.

§

In Saint Paul, the *Minnesota Democrat* reported on 19 November, after the news reached Ramsey, that the second removal attempt had again failed. The Whig *Minnesotian* promptly reported that the blame was attributable to certain traders and to one of Watrous' assistants (a relative of the Indians), who advised the tribes (most likely for pay) not to remove.

It was near the end of the month when Warren reached the capital to visit the governor, laying down his complaints against Watrous. He wrote an article published in the *Democrat* that completely demolished the reports of the removal in the *Minnesotian*.

This launched one of the most lengthy and voluminous newspaper battles recorded in Minnesota Territory. Warren was compared by the Whig instrument, the *Minnesotian,* to Judas Iscariot and Benedict Arnold, calling him *"a man possessed by all the duplicity of the Indian race (which is, perhaps, inherent) rendered active and acute in practice by a partial education, and association with the worst class of a frontier white population."*

Warren worked furiously, submitting payment details, figures, muster rolls, affidavits, and letters of support along with a full account of his movements with his division in the removal, up to Sandy Lake. D.A. Robertson stood by him, publishing faithfully every letter and defense against the attacks that drained his already weakened resistance. He was especially disappointed when he realized that his family's old friend, Reverend William Boutwell, responded with a letter in the *Minnesotian* defending Watrous and blaming the absence of payment on Warren, directly due to his negligence in arriving late, stating *"he is known to be a man devoid either of truth or moral honesty."*

He flooded the pages of the *Democrat* in response, venting his anger by providing a full account of the removal actions in meticulous detail. The *Minnesotian* refuted with more assaults on his character, saying it was all lies. It seemed there was no shelter from the barbs of Watrous, who had Ramsey's open support, and the Whig newspaper. He could only conclude that Boutwell was also being used. A respected man of the cloth, a white man.

After Christmas, Ramsey told Watrous to pay the La Pointe bands without any strings attached. Watrous was reluctant, asking if he should also pay the half breeds, as it would form a precedent and they did not intend to remove. Ramsey said to pay them. The bands finally were paid what they were promised for 1850 and 1851 in late January 1852, with which they paid off the debts they had incurred for supplies, stopped by the traders at the payhouse doors.

§

The winter wore on. Elections for the third Territorial Legislature, held in October, turned out dubious. Both newspapers gave the early victory to William Warren in Benton County, 92-49. When the official returns came in, he lost the smaller districts to James Beatty by a narrow margin. Warren recovered sufficiently to engage an attorney to contest the result in January. The appointed committee investigated and found in his favor; Beatty was improperly elected by non-resident voters in Cass County. The next day, the House discredited the report and refused to hear Warren's lawyer. Had the illegal votes been discounted, he would have won. He had exhausted all legal recourse, and himself. It was no use seeking justice.

Still anxious about supporting his family, he tried to secure back pay for his removal duties by writing to Governor Ramsey. Watrous owed him more out-of-pocket expenses and per diem pay as removal conductor. He again filled pages of foolscap with details and sums. He was paid in 1852, but only after tedious efforts to induce Ramsey to act.

He launched a formal complaint against John Watrous through the Indian Department, securing support from his supporters, compiling evidence. Watrous secured favorable letters. There were attacks on the agent from Boutwell and Captain Todd now, also accusing him of dishonesty and deceit. Watrous defended himself in

141

letters to Ramsey, who forwarded them to Washington, stating that the agent deserved commendation rather than censure.

William Warren was *persona non grata* in the circles of political power. The machine had beaten him down until he saw the futility of fighting. Perhaps it was the wrong battle.

He wearily retreated, withdrawing to his house in Two Rivers to regain his health, and put his notes in order. Matilda, always surprised by his ability to recover from his bouts of illness and depression, cared for him and supported his plan. He set his mind to it. The History…he must finish his History of the Ojibway people. In a book. There was much work to be done.

§

Continuing to clerk for Henry Rice, he and Matilda took in boarders for meals at their house in Two Rivers. The children were growing, a joy. Julia was married and living nearby at Swan River. Charlotte's husband built a house in Saint Paul and worked as a carpenter, while Mary still boarded with the Wheelers in Bad River. George and Truman found situations and grew close enough to advise the Ojibwe around them.

A trip to Washington with an Ojibwe delegation was still being discussed, but he no longer spoke of it to Matilda and did not pursue it. He seemed to lose interest, considering that the task was insurmountable. He sought medical help and advice, but could not afford to go south for the winter. Hole-in-the-Day sent some of his band down to cut wood for them. The gesture appeared to patch things up between them, but the Chief never stayed long. Writing, or as he told his children when asked what he was doing, "scratching paper with the quill", was now his sole endeavor. He was the only Warren without a job, and too weak to work as a farmer.

He heard of the arrival of William Wood that winter, a young lawyer from the East and newcomer to the territory, living in Sauk Rapids with his wife Julia. Warren had seen a poem she'd had published in the *Democrat* in December. As he slowly withdrew from the newspaper turmoil and attacks around him, he began to lean more towards literary matters. Impressed by her poem, *"My Home in the West"*, he paid them a visit. Julia Wood later wrote:

> *One January Night our silence was invaded by a knock on the door. As this had been preceded by no sound of steps, we were somewhat startled. Our visitor proved to be Mr. William W. Warren, a young man of note in this upper country, of whom we had heard often. I recall the favorable impression he made as he entered, his tall figure was enveloped in a graceful cloak; he doffed his hat, and made salutations with the polished ease of one accustomed to the usages of polite society. Naturally we gave a cordial welcome to one who deserved deference from newcomers, on account of his father who had been a man of influence, and on account of his own worth, intelligence, and truly manly dignity of character and manner.*
>
> *Almost the first words he addressed to my husband were these: You will pardon this intrusion, but on reading your wife's poem on Minnesota in this week's Pioneer I resolved to make your and her acquaintance, for I was prouder of Minnesota since a stranger can so clothe it in beauty and poetry.*

It was the first of many evenings spent with the Woods. Later, at the end of that winter, William Wood paid him a visit in Two Rivers. The naked branches were greening. He found William talking while writing on a low cedarwood box, sitting outside with the old Pillager chief, Flat Mouth, camped there for several days to visit the man he called his grandson.

In June he wrote George one of his loquacious letters:

> *You have doubtless by this time received my long letter in answer to yours of March. Yesterday I received another from you and make haste to answer, hoping you will follow suit and write oftener, a letter from you is worth $5.00 any time.*

Mr. Watrous was at Washington on 6th June by a letter I saw from him. He was to remain until the 10th inst trying to have the removal continued...The fraud has been found out and is the present scandal about the country. It will effect Watrous and may even remove him, it is a clue to the whole plan of his villainy in partnership with the Company.

I got a letter from Truman in Fond du Lac, he got through safe. Old Beauf with others having V. Roy for Intrp have gone on to Washington. All nonsense. They can effect nothing going off like fools with poor interpreters and representing only the Lapointe band.

Patrick Conner has been poisoned by an Indian, his brother Joe shot the Indian dead soon after....

I am gaining strength bodily every day, and also in influence with the Indians.

Take care of your Indians keep them under your thumb. I will attend to the Minnesota Chippeways. Truman may help us at Lake Superior and we will all by this combination hold the great balance of power, and within a year or two reap a rich harvest....

My crop looks fine, and everything now seems to smile on me. I will write you again soon more at full and open to you a <u>dream</u> of mine...

Capt Todd is now a bitter enemy of the Co and Watrous. He has found them out. Hole in the Day also, he has cringed around me till I consented to make another trial of him.

Old Flatmouth came and camped at my house ten days last winter. The old man is right. When these poor devils flock around a poor man like me from whom they can expect nothing by counsel, it means something. They often give me presents of mokoks of sugar and canoes, in fact they begin to know that <u>I am their friend</u>, without interest. If your Indians can only feel towards us like these here do, I will consider that my trip last summer has not been thrown away.

I will expect a letter from you in a few days, on account of the proposed delegation. We now have regular mails and stages and letters come quick.

Your Cousin
Wm W Warren

He was nominated for the legislature again in the fall. He won the informal ballot but backed away, saying he felt too sick to go to the meeting. He lost to George Egbert and considered it good riddance.

There was no money for the half breeds that year. He went to the Crow Wing payment in the fall, for a pittance. He set aside the little money he could, when he could, while Matilda ran the kitchen to feed the mid-day boarders. Sometimes he felt well enough to hunt. His sister Julia was a frequent visitor to Two Rivers, lending an able hand to Matilda or tutoring the young children. She had the soul of a teacher, Warren told her, not a nurse. But still she doted on him, more than Matilda did. Her brother was constantly writing, either by the window or by candle even into the night, surrounded by his notes and papers, letters, boxes of quills, and bottles of ink, propped up on pillows in his bed under a buffalo robe. He was unstoppable now. Writing the Ojibwe history became his sole obsession, the only way left to him to save at least their memory from disappearing. Even in winter, he ran the postal services ragged.

Flat Mouth, on his visits to see Warren in Two Rivers that year, said he had come to tell him more stories. He had come to trust him, as did Great Buffalo when he began to write his stories down in La Pointe some years ago. Warren had recorded Buffalo's words at the time.

"My Grandson," said the old man "You have now become as one of us, you have now arrived at the age of thinking and discretion, and you can see far around you. You are able to watch and guard over the interests of your poor ig-

*norant relatives. We have found in you a guide in our blind-
ness, and a support to our weak and tottering footsteps.*

*Since the whites have come and resided among us our
young men have become unsteady and foolish. They are
fast forgetting the usages and customs of their fathers and
when the Old men of the tribe who are fast falling into their
graves, shall have all disappeared, the traditions and customs of their fathers shall be buried with them...*

*"My Grandson," continued the old chief, "you had often
asked me what I knew of former times but I did not open my
heart to you for you was then a child. You are now a man and
you know how to write like the whites you understand what
we tell you. Your ears are open to our words and we will tell
you what we know of our former times. You shall write it on
paper that our words may last forever."*

Warren then wrote:

*The old man thus expressed his willingness to give me
the information I desired. He talked on telling a long story
materially different from any he had before told me. The ice
of their reserve being thus broken I succeeded thereafter in
procuring from them the traditions pertaining to their past
history.*

Flat Mouth told him that winter yet more histories, stories that
he had never told him before. He was getting old, nobody listened
anymore. The chief watched as Warren's quill flew across the sheets
of paper as he spoke, then as he stacked them in his cedarwood
writing chest.

"Your mind is strong," he said. "It has been trained by the whites.
You will write our words, Nosins, in the language of the whites.
Make them travel far."

"That is my wish, Grandfather. I hope my heart is strong enough
to carry them far."

Flat Mouth raised his wizened fist to his forehead, then to his
chest, and leaned forward to touch Warren's hand.

"To do this," he said, "your mind must be one with your heart."

For the rest of the year, Warren remained silent about the removals, remained at his home and did nothing but write. His bed, the big table, even the basswood floor became white with sheets of foolscap that floated and piled up like the great light snows that fell around him.

PART II
MISI-ZIIBI

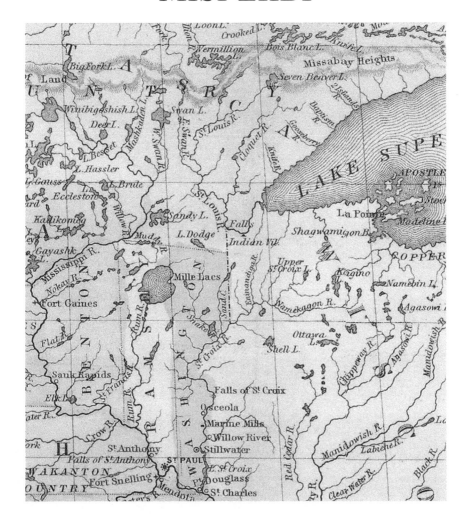

— *By sleigh along Mississippi River Road south from Two Rivers to Saint Paul; north by stagecoach on the Saint Croix Valley road to Bad River; then by canoe to La Pointe (Madeline Island, Lake Superior)*

Chapter 13: False Thaw

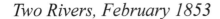

Two Rivers, February 1853

AT THE FIRST SIGN OF AN IMPROBABLE THAW in deep winter, William Whipple Warren rose from what otherwise would be his deathbed to follow a water droplet descending an icicle through the wavered glass of his cabin window. Outside, the morning air shone bluegill gray as shafts of sunlight struck the ice-braced branches with white fire. He gazed at the brilliant world in the droplet moving slowly, then faster, toward the snowy ground below. The power in a man, Sits Alone had told him, sleeps until he rises.

He pressed his last notes into his case and told his wife and children by the fire that he would leave the next morning. First to Saint Paul, then north to Bad River to see his sister Mary. There he would find a boat, cross the Great Lakes to the East, then travel overland by railroad to New York City, by the big salt water.

Silence.

His wife Matilda looked at him disbelieving and said, "You planned this."

"The big salt water," he said again. "Maybe two thousand miles, all told."

"How long?" Said Cordelia. Her child's eyes were clear green.

It is possible, he explained. Doctor Rae made 500 miles from Pembina to Saint Paul in five days by dogsled last winter, and three men just made it on snowshoes. Old Chief Hole-in-the-Day once ran 35 miles down the Mississippi, killed three Sioux, then ran back north to his home, all in one day.

"I, your father, can easily cover two thousand miles to New York by steamboat and then by train. They make sixteen miles in one hour. They travel all night. I'll have a warm bed all the way and be home for planting in the spring."

His two young children looked up at him, then at the brooding fire. The baby slept. Matilda went to stir a kettle where his blood-stained handkerchiefs were soaking in ash.

She spoke into the kettle, in a low voice, in English. "How will we eat?"

"Alfred will trap. The People will help." He knew this was not her real fear.

"You could wait until spring."

"I'll be back by spring."

Here she frowned and jutted her chin at him. An Indian gesture of disdain.

"You can lie to your children," she said. "But not to me."

He walked again to the window. The icicle cracked and stuck upright in the snowbank. Uncommon acts, the Midé told him, unlock the path to the soul. Yet the chill he felt from his wife caused his soul to shiver.

The icicle stood planted. It would not topple. He took this as no sign, but considered bluntly that he had no business being dead at twenty-seven.

He would be running for his life. No choice. He was too weak to work. He had tried to get his back pay from the Indian Department, it was all too slow. He was a writer now; his Ojibwe histories had appeared in the press and been praised. The only way to stay alive, to keep his word, and to feed his family was to take his manuscript to a publisher. And see a doctor who knew what he was talking about.

Just beyond the shroud of leafless winter trees, the Mississippi River was frozen but breaking up under a foot of snow. Patches of ground were visible in the clearing around the cabin, but Rice's man told him that the River Road was passable for a dogsled or sleigh and the mails were running. A letter from the Wheelers in Bad River, where his sister Mary was boarding, said the shore ice was so thin this winter that the Indians would not cross it to La Pointe. Steamers were running to the Sault with ore from the copper mines, the rush was on. Mary was looking smart and learning fast, but she missed her family and would be happy to see him on his way to the East. If that was his decision.

He could reach Saint Paul in two days, see Governor Ramsey who still owed him money, and maybe borrow some more. He had backers. In a week or so, with luck, the St. Croix stage line would be open, running north on the timber roads. He could board a steamer to the Sault, make a fast boat down to Detroit, then across Erie to Buffalo and on to New York, a city he had never seen except in a dream.

William Warren assembled his tools—ink, quills, blotter, and wax—in the flat case that fit into his writing chest with his graphite pencils and manuscript. The trip would afford him the time to write an introduction to the book he now called *History of the Ojibways*.

Of paper he had plenty, one of the benefits of clerking for Henry Rice's trading concern. He was indebted to his employer on more than one account as the encroaching consumption sapped his strength. Rice had also advanced him sums against promised copies of his future work. Such debts would be settled when his book was published. He would not disappoint.

As a gesture of husband-like conciliation and to make himself useful, Warren stoked the fire. Matilda knew his decision was final and did not look up from the venison stew she was stirring beside the fireplace. She was not one to waste words. Instead, she called to Cordelia to stop her doodling and set the table for the mid-day meal. Alfred was coming back early from the mission school and there were things to wash if their father was leaving in the morning.

His wife of ten years tossed her thick braid back from the fire. She was a handsome woman he still liked to think of as his bride, the daughter of the river, with more of her Ojibwe mother's looks—soft eyes like willow leaves—than those of her Scot father. She spoke with their children in Ojibwemowin, the language of her mother and grandmother before her, as it was with Warren's own mother.

His childhood, he could say, was one of an Ojibwe boy, although he'd lived in a cabin, not a wigwam. His mother's tongue was his first language, then French. The old Ojibwe said he mastered their language better than they did. He would speak for the Ojibwe. This he would tell the publishers. He had the voice of the Crane, his mother's clan.

His English came later, by dint of reading and study. Especially his schooling in the East, which he owed to his father and his grandparents, American and Yankee to the core. Now they were gone, and he had his sisters to look after, to educate. That is the way it would be, or should be, with his own children. Education, to prepare for the white world inevitably coming. Learn the language and the ways of the whites, his father had said, or your mother's people will perish. The whites will swallow them as they come. You make sure that does not happen.

Matilda, who learned English at the mission school, obstinately held to her mother tongue. It was sometimes a bone of contention between them.

"When I'm gone," he said, "You will speak to them in English? So they don't forget?"

He realized the slip instantly, but too late. Matilda wiped her hands on her apron and turned away.

"I speak to them in the language of the Anishinaabe. So they don't forget." Here she turned and commanded." You come home. You speak to them in English."

When he tried to take her hand she held out a sprig of wintergreen. "Chew this," she said. "Don't swallow. Too much can kill you."

His breath carried the smell of the blood in his lungs. He chewed the pungent green leaf that mixed with the smell of woodsmoke and sweet stew.

"I'll be seeing the best specialist in New York. You'll see."

Matilda, like all women on the frontier, had to endure her man's absences and tolerate his cursed optimism. He watched her silhouette by the window, another child already beginning to swell her

154

belly, becoming against the stark winter trees outside. Her will was adamantine, but so was his. He would prove her wrong. He would come back singing.

Cordelia, the one red-haired child with a visible trace of her grandfather's blood—her brothers were as dusky and black-haired as their parents—jumped off the bench and showed him the slate she was practicing on.

She had traced her initials in big block letters. This earned the girl a kiss on her brow from her father.

"Write it every day. And by spring you will write your full name."

"I'd rather write your initials." She spoke correct English. At least he had taught her that.

And she did so, in straight lines on her slate: WWW, with all the letters attached. Then she turned the slate upside down to turn it into the zigzag design painted on birch bark canoes.

"Like you wrote in the sand, on the island," she said. "Then the boys turned them into pine trees." It was an old story, a good story he liked to tell his children.

Cordelia added the trunks of the trees and then the ground beneath them, as he had shown them. He kissed her again and she jumped down to show her mother, who wondered if it was true or if he'd just invented it. He knew so many stories.

"And who drew the trees, Cordelia?"

"It was Boy," she said. "*Gwii-wisens*. He calls you *Ni-sah-yan*, his brother."

"Older brother. A term of affection."

Matilda clanged the lid on the stew pot. "He is not your brother. He insulted your father and he maligned you in public. He is not family."

"That's over, Matilda. He was being used."

"He is a bear, not welcome."

"A bear?"

"Big head, big mouth."

Warren turned away to hide a smile. That was accurate.

"But now," said Cordelia, ingenuous," we call him *Bagone-giizig*. He became the second Chief Hole-in-the-Day. He took his father's name. Like you. Like me."

He heard the door open. Matilda was in her furs, snowshoes in hand. "I'm going to get Julia," she said. "Stir the meat." Out she went.

She was going for reinforcements. His wife and his sister Julia were thick as thieves. She would want to nursemaid him. Or worse, convince him to stay. Self-justification had never been one of his strong points. Only cousin George knew the real reasons. He remembered what he told him four years ago, from Crow Wing. His situation was no better now. Maybe worse.

Crow Wing, 1 March 1849

Dear George,

I must own that I have been rather negligent in my correspondence with you this winter. I have not had any good news to relate is one reason I have not written before. My health has been poor all winter and of late I have been confined to the house. I don't want to believe that I have the consumption, but I think I am hard on to it, and have no doubt that my days are numbered. Through my ill health last fall I was not able to do as well as I expected at the payment. The Indians paid me about $400.00. The traders with the exception of Aitken's paid me none as they did not get paid to the full amt of their claims. So far as living is concerned I have got along quite well this winter. It cost me something to commence House Keeping and provisions have been dear, but I have lived well this winter and within means.

My wife and children and the girls' have enjoyed good health, but have been lonesome this winter. I have heard from Truman two or three times, he got some trouble with the Nettleton about a debt and has given his watch as security for $80.00, which sum I have concluded to send him by first chance. To tell the truth, I don't like this country as well as

I do Chippeway and La Pointe. The Indians are better, and probably the reason is that my health is so bad and no relative nearby. I am satisfied that were my health good I could make money, but under present state of health it is a charity of Mr. Rice to keep me in his employ...

Yr Aff. Cousin,
W W Warren

With the gentle hypocrisy required for the exercise of self-persuasion, Warren justified his dead-of-winter departure as a necessity for survival, despite his own painful reproaches for leaving his family to fend for themselves: if he did not leave now, he might never leave. The consequences of that failure would bring upon them a peril so dire—his own ruin, his family fatherless and penniless—that he himself, even dead, could never bear the shame. He would rather be shot like a quail on the wing than potted like a rooster too useless to fly. That was one reason.

To temper his regret, he told himself that his wife and children were safe and comfortable in their cedar-barked house at Two Rivers, near the Mississippi and the Platte. They had fifty dollars in the larder, her family was near, the People were near, and the Anishinaabe always took care of their own. He made a packing list and stirred the stew, ruminating on his course of action which could prove fatal but must produce tangible results.

Pain bloomed in his chest. He dropped the wooden spoon, sat, and listened to the baby's cooing. He must not cough. The pain was old. It would come and pass again. To calm himself he assessed his blessings, few but good.

The fire in the riverstone hearth provided ample heat for the 30-foot cabin and the children's sleeping loft. He and George had worked hard rebuilding the house two summers ago and the basswood floor was just beginning to shine. The hot-burning hardwood, the berry- tanged meat and the long table they shared with occasional boarders would be his sustaining memories during this trip into the mutating world of the East that intimidated and fascinated him. His wife and children would plant judiciously, as he had shown them, in spring. The season would bring much work. He would miss the rise of the maple sap, the sugar-making, and their fourth child would be well along the way. He could not be gone long.

The wracking cough came and went with regularity. Alfred and Cordelia now carried the wood, water, tended the fire and the baby while Matilda did the heavy chores. They were used to this, since Warren spent most days and nights sitting up in bed writing by candlelight with his notes surrounding him, pages laid in a basket on the floor, a legacy from his mother's hands.

Bending with difficulty under the bed frame, he slid out the small wooden chest that served as a writing desk and began to pack in the manuscript he would show to publishers. His *History* was yet incomplete, hurriedly written and in need of correction, but true and valid. Time was short and he often worked to exhaustion. By mid-month all the preparatory business in the capital would be done. He would head north over the timber roads to Lake Superior and sail from La Pointe on Madeline Island.

Hope at this juncture was William Warren's lifeblood. Having avowed only to George that his bleeding fits would not stop until they took him to Kingdom Come, a sometimes forced affability was his chief defense against despair. One night, he knew, he would never see daylight again. But it was not death itself, it was the waiting as time ran out. His greatest fear was not seeing his work to the finish. He was through with waiting. He had done the work. Now to see it to print. That was another reason.

He scraped candle wax from his wooden writing chest, which would become his traveling trunk. He would also take his carpet bag for fresh clothing and sundries. Nothing too heavy—Except his thoughts—and even those he would train himself to leave behind.

If sleep was merciful, he would awake refreshed and sufficiently sanguine to convince all persons—primarily himself—that he was gaining in strength every day. His manuscript, together with his ambitious plans for future works, would convince publishers of his legitimacy as a scholar and marketable author. All he needed was a first book to propel him forward, fresh wind in his sails. As there was no adequate press in Saint Paul, nor yet in Chicago, his friends and encouragers had written letters to publishers and men of influence in New York, now less than a month away. Those letters awaited him in the capital. Everything was ready. This redoubled his resolve.

He stacked his five hundred manuscript pages in two sections containing thirty-five chapters, wrapped them in canvas and bound them with deer hide strips softened by the wives and daughters of Flat Mouth, who presented them to him with a Pillager blessing, a canoe, and a pack of smoked whitefish for his family. Flat Mouth had camped for several weeks at Two Rivers to tell him more of the history. He had seen his library and listened to Alfred read from the Declaration of Independence while Warren translated. The old chief held the conviction that the Ojibwe history, as he told it and Warren wrote it down, held power. The words would last forever, even if the People disappeared beneath the massive oncoming of the whites.

Now he tucked those words into his writing trunk, a traveling escritoire made with cedar planks from his father's mill, although Lyman Warren did not live to see it. The hinged top was made to slide off and form a table over his lap while he sat up in bed. Alfred had lined the inside with oiled sailcloth while Matilda made a buffalo-hide strap. The pearwood medallion with his initials, W.W.W. had come unstuck last year when Alfred spilled boiling water on it. Now the rounded inlay, missing an edge, resembled a waning moon.

You live with your scars. Hole-in-the-Day the Elder painted circles around his bullet wounds to enhance their magic. So it was with his writing trunk, with its ink stains, candle burns, and gouges. He used it on the trail, winter and summer, and when well enough to sit by the window. Or outside under the oak, writing down Flat Mouth's stories of the People's migrations, sufferings, wars and conquests, the clans and the spirits, tales of Manabosho, and the coming of the whites that over the centuries had changed their lives irreparably. His escritoire had borne the scratching of his quills as he wrote those stories down and would now bear them to press. He closed it, latched it, fastened the strap, and stared at it. His future.

This one could not be lost, like the trunk he lost in the lake squall on his first trip east with his grandfather. Several years later his own father lost his trunk with all his prized belongings and business papers. That loss sank the final nail. Already driven insane by ruin, his wife gone to illness, Lyman died six months later.

Warren tested the weight of the packed trunk. He resolved that en route, he would go stand at his father and mother's graves in La Pointe and tell them that he was on his way to publish his *History*. As he'd promised. For the Ojibwe—his mother's people. For his family. For his own damned good. That was the third reason.

But he knew that none of those reasons would provide any solace to Matilda, nor to his sisters, nor to anyone but himself. He would keep his mouth shut.

§

At noon by his watch, Matilda had not returned. He peered out the window, his breath fogging the pane. The low winter sunlight now shone full on the wet limbs of the maples, ash, elm and linden surrounding the clearing. It was one of those years when everything would happen early.

Up the slope rode a man on slow horseback, bending under the branches, his curved war club shielding the spray of eagle feathers crowning his turban. An Ojibwe on horseback was a rarity, but so was this rider. Warren considered his options on this, his last day at home, expecting Matilda back any minute. It would do no good to spoil his farewells. He donned his boots and pulled the bolt on the cabin door.

"Set another place, Cordelia. *Gwii-wisens* has come to visit."

To the Legislature and citizens of Saint Paul Presbyterian Church, Quoted from the Minnesota Democrat, January 1851

"My Friends, we believe that our Great Father wishes to treat us kindly, and that he does not know the wrongs that we endure...

My heart aches when I think of my people. They come to me for food, in a starving condition; they go to the door of my friend, who is standing by me (Mr. Warren,) but we are poor. We cannot feed so many mouths, and we are obliged to send them away empty-handed. It pains my heart to remain in my own country, to witness the sufferings of my people...

The time has come when something must be done to ameliorate our conditions, by our white friends, and to prevent our being pushed to extremes.

I consider it a duty I owe to myself, and to you, to inform you, that the hearts of my people are bad and aching. They are starving!

Many of them come to me and propose to fight the whites. It is getting to be difficult to keep my young men within bounds. I am afraid they will soon commit some foolish act which will forever break our friendship.

They are driven to extremities—Death is on every side, and in the minds of our young men, one death is as good as another. They wish to throw themselves away. They are like some poor animal driven into a hole, and condemned to die. To them one death is as good as another..."

Hole-in-the-Day the Younger (his X mark)

Chapter 14: The Bones and The Blood

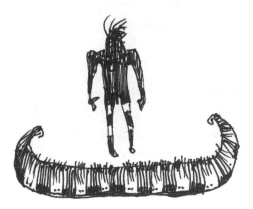

A WAFT OF HUMUS ROSE up as he stepped through the thinning snow. Above the shifting mist, the barely visible sky was a deep blue that dulled to gray as the mist thickened. Droplets hit the softening crust, the rich soil. The forest floor released an odor of beneficent decay.

Topping a knoll stood a clutch of peeling elms, their trunks and skinny branches reaching for the sky. All winter those trees had haunted him. They brought back a sharp image—of the People trapped that winter at Sandy Lake, the sickness upon them. He saw emaciated hands rising from the forest floor, their boney fingers raised in supplication.

Warren smarted. That was the Ojibwe in him. The Indian mind saw the world in images, not in words. His white blood told him to right himself; a tree was a tree. Yet the Ojibwe in him would not let go. The naked branches were his ancestors' hands.

Hole-in-the-Day the Elder, now buried on a bluff above the Mississippi, once said why the Anishinaabe held so hard to their land: *The bones and the blood of our ancestors are now sprinkled in this soil...*

Behind the horse and rider, a dense fog was moving up from the river. Soon they would be swallowed up. The horse heaved steam as the rider approached, stopped, and stepped sidewise some ten feet from where Warren stood before his woodpile. A ceremonious distance. The roan bore the brand of the US Cavalry, no doubt from Fort Ripley. Hole-in-the-Day the Younger held his mount, raised a hand, and said "Ho, Ni-sah-yan."

His long braids were shiny black, hooped and tied at the back of his neck. He wore a green blanket over a broadcloth coat of better quality than Warren's, a pink shirt bedecked with copper chains, bear claws, and two silver chief's medals inherited from his father. His face was unpainted, his dress and person impeccably clean. The curved pipe that doubled as a war club was cradled in his arm. With his strong jaw, high cheekbones, and keen, mocking eyes, the self-declared sole Chief of the Ojibwe Nation dressed to enliven his image as the Brummel of the forest. Let no man or woman deny the elegance of his person.

Here he was, calling him Ni-sah-yan again.

The fog was nearly upon them, diffusing the blue light and shrouding the trees surrounding the clearing. Warren's oldest, Alfred, had come home—his three children watched from the window, the baby in Cordelia's arms.

Warren stepped up and extended his right hand. Hole-in-the-Day leaned closer in his effortless, benevolent way and grasped it in the manner of the whites. A concession to Warren's upbringing. He gestured upriver.

"I come from my father's grave," said the Chief. "He sends you greetings."

Both men had lost their fathers in 1847. The mourning had deepened their bond. The sons swore to die fighting on their feet if for no better reason than to honor their fathers.

That was before Sandy Lake, before the failed removal attempts, the hundreds of deaths, the winter of deceit. Hole-in-the-Day had blamed the white government in his inflammatory speech at the Church in Saint Paul. Warren, interpreting, tried to calm the white audience, but only piqued the Chief's ire. Conspiring traders used Hole-in-the-Day to sign a bogus letter in the Whig paper accusing Warren of pandering to the whites to save his government job. Enraged that his friend could be fooled by the traders, he filled pages denouncing their lies in the *Democrat*. This drew more fire from the Whigs, blaming him for the failure of the Ojibwe removals—Warren was a half-breed with just enough education to stir up trouble. Too much Indian to be trusted.

Then Hole-in-the Day called him out for being too white. They did not speak for over a year. Warren lost his strength, his seat as Legislator, his old friend, and his will to fight. He finally backed away from it all and left politics to the scavengers. He had writing to do.

Old Flat Mouth, since he came to Two Rivers, had spoken with the younger chief. Whatever was said, the chill had dissipated. Warren wrote to George that the Ojibwe still trusted him, and even Hole-in-the-Day had cringed around him until he consented to make another trial of him. Now the Chief was before him at his home with his war club held like a scepter and an easy smile creasing his cheek.

Warren began in English.

"They said you were killed by the Sioux and thrown into the river near Fort Ripley. Then you were seen walking through Saint Paul with a bullet hole in your neck."

"Perhaps," he nodded. Both rumors and truth were valuable tools.

The men were young—Warren just two years older—but their copper faces held the ruggedness of their lives in the wooded Northwest. There were no blood ties between them, yet each man's left eyelid was heavier than the right and sloped off toward the cheekbone. The right eye in both shone immediately and directly, while the narrower left eye seemed to scrutinize the distance, prompting observers to inquire if they were not brothers. Both possessed the gift of eloquence and mellifluous voices that captivated listeners whether Indian or white, male or female, for them or against.

Since his father's death, when Hole-in-the-Day the Younger had assumed his father's name and unilaterally declared his leadership of all the Ojibwe to facilitate negotiations, the native bands had raised vociferous objections that would last his entire life. Warren himself considered it absurd—the Anishinaabe had never had one chief, but many. At the time of this declaration he told his friend that his aim was overly ambitious.

"You, Ni-sah-yan, live like the whites and sit on their councils."

"No more."

"But you once did. For what? To be outcast, like an Indian? And you accuse me of ambition?"

"You are as ambitious as your father. Maybe more."

"I have but one ambition. Like my father, I am a leader. A leader is loyal to one master. His people. Ambitious whites serve any master. They lie to the Indian with every breath they take, even when written in their treaties. They have no honor in war or in peace."

In addition to the nature of the Chief's intelligence—shrewd and intuitive as opposed to the bookishness of his mixed-blood friend—there was one prominent trait that set him apart from William Warren: his latent violence. A visible reminder was the deep-cleft scar on his chin, just under the left corner of his full mouth, where he had taken a blow from a Sioux tomahawk that he had neglected to remove from his enemy's hand before he took his scalp, forcing him to kill the brave with the scalp only partly severed before he could loose his cry of revenge. This mishap never sat right with the Chief. The scar had never healed cleanly and reddened when his passions rose. Today the scar was calm. Although he spoke passable English, he remained mounted and addressed Warren in Ojibwemowin, as the old friend he had been since they were boys.

"Ni-sah-yan, I come to recount to you a dream I had. No animal came to me in this dream. This is what I saw: You and I walked together, heading east to the place where the sun rises on the shore of the great salt water. In this dream, the Megis shell was once again shining, but above that eastern horizon, as if the world had turned itself around. There I stopped, but you went on. This I dreamed just two nights ago. Now I ask you, Ni-sah-yan. Would you be so foolish as to go to where the world is turned around? Is it true there are men in New York who sit on their heads with their asses to the sky?"

Warren reflected, the wet snow soaking his boots.

"You are both right and wrong. The world is turned around. I am going east. But for the Anishinaabe, the Megis shines forever in the west. There is no turning back. And that dream is a bald-faced lie. But it is true that some men speak with their asses and shit with their mouths."

The young chief laughed and took from behind his blanket a woven bag that looked to contain about ten pounds of wild rice.

"Flat Mouth tells me you will go now to the East, with your written words that are the words of our grandfathers. Will you see the President?"

"No. I will not go to Washington unless we go together. I am going to New York. To see the book publishers. But first I go to Saint Paul. Governor Ramsey owes me money."

"You expect him to pay you? The man who let the People die in the cold like dogs at Sandy Lake, sick on spoiled rations, rather than pay us our treaty money?"

"That was Watrous' doing. And the Fur Company traders. They want all Indians to remove to where they can take your treaty annuities."

"Ramsey supports Watrous. He refuses to allow us to see the President. Ramsey does not care if the Anishinaabe live or die."

"He is weak. But he has supported me before. And he owes me money."

"He is a politician, not a leader. He supports those he needs." Hole-in-the-Day straightened on his horse and his face turned stony. "Or those he fears."

"He's not smart enough to fear you. He knows nothing about your ways."

"Then we must educate him."

"I see another eagle feather on your head. Soon you will have as many scalps as your father. The feathers will flow down your back.

You were just a child when you struck my father in the leg with your tomahawk, while he spoke of peace with the chiefs."

"He insulted my father, who taught me to act first, speak later."

"I wanted to thrash you for it, but my father stopped me. He taught me to think twice before I act. You will make yourself more enemies than your father had."

"My father had more enemies than friends, yet none could ever harm him."

"Except the one that killed him." Warren immediately regretted his words. That the elder Hole-in-the-Day had fallen drunk from a wagon to be crushed under the wheels was not something he needed to recall. Still, he was convinced that the traders' whiskey would be the ruination of the Indians. Either that, or war with the whites.

Hole-in-the-Day the Younger stood his horse and let silence fill the shifting fog before he spoke again. Then he talked to the fog.

"Flat Mouth was a great warrior, like my father. He told me: When you are a child, you know the true path. Then, to survive, you learn to fight. When you are very old, you understand again, and no longer wish to fight. You and I, Ni-sah-yan, we are still in the fight."

His horse shuddered, shifted, then settled again with his legs planted on the earth. "You cannot educate with the gun and the knife, Gwii-wisens. It is not by waging war that you win peace. But you are right, you must resist. To protect the People. You must obtain the best treaty you can, the best terms, the best lands, to last forever. To outlast the white politicians."

"You of all people know that my father was a man of peace. The Sioux would not let us live in peace. The Ojibwe want to lay down their arms. This is my ambition, as it was my father's. They must take up the plow and hoe, to live like the whites. We both know this. The Great Father must know this and help his children. Politicians must be educated. Even your President."

"I trust you can do that. It might take some time. I'd like to help you...," Warren stifled a cough and spat a little blood on the snow. The horse whinnied and looked toward the river.

Matilda walked into the clearing, snowshoes in hand, her head covered in furs. She walked past the two men without greeting and turned at the door to announce that Warren's sister Julia would come later to say goodbye. She looked at the chief, blinked, and went into her cabin.

"Forgive her rudeness," said Warren. "I'm leaving her alone."

"Rudeness is woman's privilege. But hear me. She will not be alone, Ni-sah-yan, nor will your children. The People are here."

Warren looked down, trying to control his labored breathing.

"You will help me when you return," said the Chief. "We will go to Washington together in the fall and explain our plans to the president. You are the educator. Maybe the President can learn." He held out the *mashkimod* of wild rice. The finely woven reed was beaded, finished with red-dyed horsehair tassels.

"Take this. You once kept me from starving. I can do the same for your family."

"You were fasting for the wrong reason. You never shamed your father."

"You said I was worth more alive than as another dead Indian. The same is true for you, Ni-sah-yan. Come back to your family."

Warren stepped forward to accept the rice. He knew how precious it was to the People in winter, but he could not refuse his friend's gesture.

As he put one hand on the horse's flank, a coughing fit buckled his knees. He grabbed the Chief's legging and held on. Matilda, watching from the window, tightened her arms around her baby and whispered to the children to stay put. Warren did not fall. Hole-in-the-Day held his horse steady.

When the fit passed the two men looked at each other, ignoring the spray of red on the snow. The chief handed down the bag, revealing the butt of the Colt .45 revolver in his sash. This was a recent accoutrement, uncommon in Minnesota Territory except for Army officers. No further word was said until Warren extended the proper invitation.

"Will you not come inside and sit at my table?" He looked around and saw Matilda's firm disapproval through the window. She quickly turned away with the children.

"Not today. Be with your family. We'll come in the spring, when you return, to till and plant your earth in the manner of the white farmers. You will show me how this is done. I will show the People. Godspeed. Is that not what you say?"

"Godspeed, Gwii-wisens." He liked to call him by his boyhood name, despite Hole-in-the-Day's objections.

They clasped hands. Hole-in-the-Day the Younger turned his horse and left, following his own tracks, vanishing into the thick fog faster than when he came.

Warren returned to his table and found that the place for the chief was still set. He put the mashkimod of wild rice beside the vacant plate and they sat down, the baby Tyler still in his mother's arms, Matilda harboring a satisfied smile as she let her eyes go soft. She suckled the baby as he rested on the swell where their next child lay growing.

Untypically, Warren said a brief grace. His thanks were addressed more to their friends, to the Ojibwe people, than to any god beyond this world.

Chapter 15: The Ploy

THE EVE OF HIS DEPARTURE was blunted by the women's subdued preparations and Warren's own brooding. Matilda was still distant, and Julia had come by with a few things for his trip and to stay the night. To keep his mind off matters, he retired to bed and wrote some lines of a preface, over and over. An herbal mixture Julia had brought settled his nervous lungs, and she said it would help him sleep. He was restless, but dozed off.

After his sister went up to the loft with the children, he awoke. Matilda came under the blankets in her nightshirt with her hair down. They lay there, he half sitting, she on her back, resting softly while the fire burned low. He snuffed his candle.

In the dark, she turned and held his arm. Lightly, then tighter. Her breath was sweet.

She shifted under the heavy buffalo robe and slid her naked thigh over his. He started. "We should be careful," he said. "Don't you think?"

"This is careful." Her hand moved down and held him there. "The last time, I could not finish right."

"You finished. You finish everything you do."

"I may start to cough. Wake the children and Julia."

"No matter." She was convincing. He grew quickly in her hands. It always surprised him. Even exhausted and bloody in the lungs, he had wanted Matilda since the first time he saw her naked in the river and it had never stopped.

"You won't leave me a dry old woman, will you?"

"You are everything but dry, my dear."

"Then come and see."

And he did, in the dark, with his hand in the lustrous fur below the swell of her belly, her strong thighs tight and quivering, then opening. They had found ways, since his infirmity, to satisfy each other's urges, to feed the bond of their skins, and mend their hearts with their bodies. They did this silently, with bated breath in the blackness where the fire lit only the moving hump of the buffalo robe on their marriage bed.

Afterward, Matilda rose while he calmed his breathing. She washed, revived the fire, and brought the trade pan and a wet warm cloth. She washed him thoroughly as he lay there accepting her administrations. Her hand lingered lightly over the bird-shaped scar on his chest. His injury sustained in the forest was still tender after six years.

"You do that nicely."

"Who will do this for you when you are... away?"

"There will be no one. You know that. Unless it be the doctor."

"Then come back. You have a wife and a family here. I can do what the doctor does."

"You can do what the doctor cannot."

"Then come back," she concluded.

She built the fire to last the night, stacking logs in the shape of a wagon wheel. They both slept then, as the fire ebbed into glowing coals.

He was relieved, spent at last of his angst at leaving, but awoke somewhat restless as he suspected more nursemaid meddling. He was groggy while Alfred rekindled the fire.

Dawn came late. The thaw had not lasted. The low gray sky bore down on the dark treetops, it was well below freezing. He rose and tended to his work papers to leave with Henry Rice along the way. His carpet bag was already tightly packed by the women. Matilda made sure everything was clean and he had plenty of handkerchiefs and linen.

Before breakfast he took another fifty dollars in coin from his pouch, without telling Matilda, and put it in the larder jar. One hundred for his family. One-quarter of his yearly earnings would have to keep them until spring. He was leaving with barely fifty dollars himself. But he had prospects, where his family did not. Julia made griddle cakes and fried rabbit which he doused with their own maple syrup.

§

The previous night, Julia, now married and living nearby with her husband, had come in after dark with her nursing bag. She was all abustle, considering it her remit to care for her brother on his official voyages, brandishing a satchel for just that purpose with poultices, camphor, healing herbs, tea and maple syrup and a vial of something bitter from the doctor. This trip was not official but the sendoff entailed more preparation than any mission of state.

Three winters prior when his sister was eighteen, she had trudged over two hundred miles with her brother by foot and canoe to accompany seven hundred Wisconsin Ojibwe to Lake Superior and west to Sandy Lake—the first of two filed removal attempts. The chiefs asked Warren to come along to speak for them. Sick as he was, he could not refuse, and the winter trek had just about killed him, but he survived where many of "his" Indians perished. Julia attributed this not to a miracle but to her meticulous care of her brother.

After supper when the women were packing, Julia told Matilda in a hushed voice that with her permission, she was ready to go with him all the way to New York.

"You need his permission, not mine," she answered. "You know you'll never get it." He will leave us all behind. All for his book."

"No, Matilda. It's for you, for the children. You must understand him. He's trapped."

Matilda frowned but said no more. She glanced over at him, propped up in bed in his writing posture, by all visible signs asleep. Julia opened her nursing satchel.

"He won't take care of himself, he's too weak. We have to make sure he takes this."

She poured a dark liquid from the vial into a small flask of maple syrup, then two teaspoons of that elixir into the pint flask of herbal tea prepared for his morning departure. "It's from Doctor Borup. For the pain, and a cough suppressant. Sweeten the tea with this mixture, and he'll rest. There's some rum in it but he'll never know. I don't want him to refuse it, you know how he is about alcohol. Two teaspoons of syrup to a pint flask of tea, no more, no less." Then she packed all the makings of the brew—herbs, teaspoon, the spiked maple elixir, into a cloth bag with a waxed note of instructions for sister Charlotte in Saint Paul, who would then pass it on to Mary at Bad River, his next stop. Matilda felt quite satisfied by the secrecy of the plot. She put in a second, smaller flask of tea aside to use as a chest warmer, for his coat pocket. Together, the women would get him in comfort at least as far as Lake Superior and off to the Sault. After that it was up to Providence.

§

An hour after first light Rice's driver, a gray-haired Ojibwe in thick leathers, hooded and cloaked in a bear skin, drove the mail sleigh into the clearing. He had made good time from Aitkin's Ferry, just upriver where Matilda's father held a hotel and trading post, and the team looked still fresh. Warren knew the route: one hundred miles by the river road. On good packed snow they would make Sturgis' place by nightfall with a change of horses at Rice's post, then the long haul to Robert's Ferry, and finally Saint Paul on the third night. The mail sleigh was open and light, built for speed as were the horses. Halting before the cabin, the team of twin blacks steamed and stamped as the runners of the sleigh cracked the snow crust.

The children loaded his chest and bag in the sleigh while the women bundled him in double breeches, boots and leggings, his ample black cloak, a muffler, and his flat-crowned legislator's hat firmly on his head. He tolerated the care but could not help quipping that he wore more than he carried. The sleigh provided buffalo hides to protect passengers against the elements, but the driver, a Pillager named Three Hands, preferred his bearskin against the dry cold.

As Warren crunched through the snow, Julia brought out her handkerchief on the verge of tears. Matilda intentionally paid more heed to directing Alfred and Cordelia, eschewing any emotional display. He saw that she was consternated because, despite her loving

173

administrations, she had lost the battle of wills that marked their marriage—he was having his way and traveling in midwinter. Julia made one last attempt to climb aboard, pretexting her desire to see her sister Charlotte. He vetoed it immediately.

"You must stop this damnable fuss! You women fret too much. You have things to do for your own families. You are a married woman, Julia, stay by your husband. I want to proceed by myself. I'll write from New York. Children, come give your father a kiss goodbye." They did so. It seemed almost familiar, just another departure.

"River Woman, come..." He touched her belly and whispered something in Matilda's ear that made her smile, or at least pretend to. Then to them all: "Expect me in the spring."

"You will publish your book. I know this," she said. "You come home to us." He could see the look in her willow eyes that asked an unanswerable question.

She slipped the smaller flask of herbal tea under his coat, close to his chest, and instructed him to drink some while it was still hot. Charlotte would make him some more with the package in his bag. He repeated his promise to write, the principal display of attachment between the spouses and the only instance of cracking voices. He turned and boarded.

The sleigh jumped off at a guttural yell from Three Hands and headed down to the River Road with disconcerting speed. With just enough packed snow to carry the runners high, the vessel was faster and smoother than any wheeled vehicle. Warren looked back once to wave, and saw them all together before the log house. He touched the warm flask next to his chest.

It entered his mind thus: the freezing fog, his family huddled before the cabin, the white ground, the darker naked elm branches reaching for the implacable sky.

Chapter 16: A Crane In Winter

HE TURNED TO LOOK AHEAD, strangely exhilarated to be propelled with such urgency through the frozen wash of winter, speeding south along the River Road to the capital. He had succeeded in setting off alone, as was fitting to his mood and mission. He took a long draught of the warm tea. It was very good with the maple syrup from his own trees. He covered up and dozed off almost immediately.

Further on, Three Hands picked up two ragged, hunched-over Ojibwe Warren did not know, but who knew him and asked him for money to pay the driver. He gave them a dollar. As it happened, they got off at a trading post and saloon a few miles downriver, Three Hands drove away and charged them nothing. Warren wondered how long the coin would last before it was entirely spent on whiskey, the two Indians out in the snow again.

The sleigh continued on, now on the riverbank road, now losing sight of the widening Upper Mississippi, lined on both banks by the lace-thin upright branches that had pursued him since the day before—his ancestors' bones rising from the soil coveted by the whites.

The only other sign of movement that morning was a lone dog-sled heading north on the white expanse of the frozen river, one fur-clad man driving behind. No doubt it would stop at the tavern upstream where the two nameless Ojibwe were now drinking the rotgut reserved for Indians. He remembered then his tea, which he found well sweetened with maybe a bit too much sassafras. Matilda favored sassafras. And forest peppermint. He savored the warmth that spread quickly.

Then, as the low clouds deepened, his thoughts turned dour. He had to advance into and against adversity. Again, no choice. His education and principles, his pigheadedness, and Yankee blood rebelled against falling victim to the same fate as his father, or that of his mother's people. All his life he had fought injustice. His father had given in to the Company and lost everything. Lyman Warren had left him only what he owned himself when he struck out for the Territories as a young man: his learning, language, determination, and good sense. And maybe his hard luck. But William Warren, over the years of enduring his own changing fortunes and hardening to the ways of men, had come to think that luck had nothing to do with it. It was merit, earned by perseverance, that would triumph in the end. You get what you deserve, so make sure you deserve it.

His younger brother Truman said that was all hog swill—it wasn't a matter of merit. You just had to keep on.

Warren slept again in a fog.

§

There was a change of horses at Rice's post where the sleigh took on a sack of mail. William left a bundle of accounting papers for Henry Rice, who was in Washington at the time, and found a letter addressed to him from his employer. In it was a draught for fifty dollars on a Saint Paul bank. The letter itself was terse but warm: "A small advance for published copies. Godspeed, good luck, and come back."

He was in business again.

As they made headway, the dark mood left him. By late morning they were well past Olmstead's trading post and William had dozed off after eating some legalet—pleased to be cracking hard-baked trail bread again—and finishing his tea. He found the brisk pace to his liking and not at all laborious for his ailment. Indeed, he felt as close to comfortable as he could get beneath the buffalo robe, lying half prone in this fast-gliding box, protected from the wind. He felt no urge to cough. This augured well for his voyage.

He had been up and down this road several times in the past two years, since his term as Territorial Legislator, traveling with his family. The bleak and somewhat monotonous winter landscape beyond the riverbanks, fringed here and there with gray hardwoods, was not new to him. Today, the naked trees could talk. He could feel their stifled voices.

He moved constantly, it seemed, on foot, by canoe, horseback, stagecoach, buggy, and sledge, first for his interpreting duties even before he married, then as a government agent, farmer, and adviser for the Ojibwe. He would never stop, Truman told him one afternoon as he took his adze from his hands. They had been shucking bark for floor joists when Warren suffered a coughing fit.

No, he'd said, spitting blood. By God, he would not stop. Not until he joined his father, his mother, and cousin Edward, rest his soul, and that was a choice he could not afford. Nor could God choose it until his children's future was assured.

Edward had died the year before, shot in the chest falling on his own rifle in the bush. Warren's parents already gone, his family was being further diminished. Death struck relentlessly, in waves. The freakishness of Edward's accident had severely shaken his already tenuous faith in a benevolent God. He had wept for months, in private, but he spoke such thoughts to no one. Instead, he kept moving.

§

Three Hands stopped to water and rest the horses after they forded a small stream and the ice broke, forcing his passenger to wade through to lighten the load. The driver seemed less than sure-footed for some reason, so Warren thought it best to grab the harness and lead them up the bank, surprising himself with his sudden strength and prowess. He stood to catch his breath, and realized he was breathing easy. The cold air seemed to revive his lungs and warm him inside. He had not felt like this in some time. He felt clear, if a bit lightheaded.

At that moment he heard a crane call—high and shrill, only once. He searched the sky above the branches but could not find it. Why a crane this far north in winter? Without a mate. Did he really hear it? Was it his grandfather, Chief White Crane? Or was it the trees talking?

The sudden rush fled and left his body slumped, his vision skewed. He looked down at the varicolored river stones where his boots were tenuously set and felt that the ground was closer, unstable. He steadied himself and got a hold. The vertigo quelled, and the stones assumed their assigned distance. He was all right.

When the driver took the reins back Warren got a good look and saw he was not only old but passably drunk and smelled of rum. There on the bank, he offered to share his meal of dried venison and rice gruel, which the man downed with great gusto before climbing aboard. He asked him why they called him Three Hands and the old Indian told him with a toothless grin, "Two for horses, one for firewater!" He took a swig from his bottle and slapped the team into a trot.

Nearly every Indian he knew was half starving in the wintertime, but few complained if alcohol was at hand. Along the river it was everywhere, in every trader's pack, at every rest stop, in every village and logging camp. There was nothing to it but to hope the horses knew the way.

The old Pillager managed to sit up in his sleigh until they reached Sturgis' farm at day's end, when he fell flat in the stable. His bottle was empty, a good sign for the rest of the trip. Warren covered him up with the bearskin, was fed a stew by Mrs. Sturgis, and given a pallet in the back room, where he drank more of his tea warmed on the stove. Three Hands, passed out drunk, was at least sheltered for the night.

Had he been traveling with his family, he reflected, even on the way to lucrative business or legislation, he would have given only fifty cents to the two Ojibwe. That way they wouldn't have had enough to get drunk and freeze in the snow. He should have known better. What was it about traveling alone that made one looser with one's money? He would have to be vigilant and strict with himself. No more of those high-stakes card games for William Warren. Not until he sold his book.

He dozed off on a pallet by the stove, fully clothed, visiting a vivid dream of strolling between cliffs of bound books in an enormous room where it snowed paper flakes.

§

Fort Gaines, Minnesota Territory, 31st March 1850

Dear George,

Since I wrote you last I have been out to Long Prairie and saw Hon. David Olmstead, who has confidentially informed me of the intended Chippeway Removal. There is no doubt at all but the whole annuity will this year be paid on the Mississippi. Gov. Ramsey has the whole matter in charge, and is coming up to locate the agency &c. about 1st May.

An appropriation has been made for the removal and subsistence. Olmstead recommends to the Gov. to pay 10 or 15 dollars a head and have the Indians removed by contract. What think you, can't we get a number to come this summer to their payment and if they did not like the country return in the fall. Hurra for a spec! Keep this in mind and act accordingly until you hear from me again.

The country is not fit for our Indians to live on, and I apprehend difficulty unless a first-rate Treaty is made with them, a perpetual annuity &c. The Govt will not do this unless they are forced to it by resistance &c on the part of the Indians. Rest assured that I am not sleeping but at work to carry the measure through. In case of a Treaty, I intend that the Half Breeds sell the right to soil and annuity which the Fond du Lac Treaty has given us, for a large sum, say $200,000 or more. Think on this and mention it to Corbin and Gauthier &c.

Your Aff. Cousin,
Wm W Warren

He slept through, for once. There was activity in the farmhouse, a quick gruel for breakfast and he warmed more tea. In the dark morning Three Hands was already aboard with a fresh team hitched. They were off at first light.

He had dreamed, he thought, of his father's library on Madeline Island. Maybe a hundred and fifty books, described by the missionaries and explorers of the day as the largest they had encountered in the wilderness. He had kept many, so had his sisters and Aunt Charlotte, as a hallmark of the day when La Pointe was a learning center where scholars and missionaries would flock to write and teach the growing generations of the nation, be they Ojibwe, white or mixed-bloods like himself. That library left its mark on him even as a small child when he spoke only Ojibwemowin and French.

He saw his father bending over a candle at night, showing his children how the print formed sounds, recounting knowledge and stories as he read to them in the purposeful cadence of the written word. At the age of six, when his schooling began in earnest, first in Mackinac then at the Mission school on the island, he was already eager to read them all. Soon he would have another book to add to that library—his own *History*. The knowledge of the elders, the chiefs, Flat Mouth, his own mother and grandmother, and the stories they told him throughout his life. Those stories were now bound for New York. And there were yet more to write.

There were two changes of horses that day as the weather held fast. The driver seemed to last well too, on legalet, jerky, and coffee. Warren's tea was only as warm as his own body could keep it, the flask close to his chest. It kept him dozing as well, for which he was thankful. The night spent at Robert's Ferry was warmer. Warren ate well at the post tavern, where Three Hands found whiskey as long as he had the coin to pay for it, but that only lasted a few glasses before the tavern keeper corked the bottle and told him to sleep in the stable. The old man came over to Warren and asked for money.

"Tomorrow," he told him.

"You paid those other Indians, for nothing."

"You have a job to finish. Take me to Saint Paul, with the mails."

180

"Hungry," said the Pillager. "Your breasts are full. Give me some of your milk."

"Keeper," said Warren, "Give the driver some stew. I'll pay. No whiskey."

He bade him sit down at his table, but Three Hands ate at the bar and left for the stable. Warren expected he could keep him sober until they arrived, but no longer. He couldn't save them all. He couldn't even save one, despite his years of trying.

Dawn came quickly and there were more mail stops on the last leg to the capital. The air was warming, the snow wetter, the pace slower.

As the sleigh passed near Saint Anthony just above Saint Paul, where floes of ice were breaking up under the falls, the road turned muddy and his driver stopped the sleigh when he met a stagecoach. Three Hands, who had found a bottle at a stop along the way, somehow managed to transfer his luggage before crawling back into the sleigh and passing out under the buffalo hides. Rice had paid the man ahead of time, he knew, but Warren could not help leaving him a few coins for his trouble even though he knew where it would go.

He boarded a new Yellow Line coach which would take him into the capital for only 25 cents. Two years ago the Red Line charged 75 cents, but competition had sparked a trade war and forced prices down.

When he first went into Saint Paul years ago it was no more than a cabin settlement called Pig's Eye, next to a large Sioux village, with more tents than cabins in any season. Then came the steamboats, the first settlers, followed by merchants, lawyers, and speculators, the land rush, the Territorial formation, and talk of the land the Sioux would sell to the government. What choice had they, now that they were a beaten tribe and settlers were flooding in? Thanks to Governor Alexander Ramsey. They had no choice but to take the government's money.

The Traverse des Sioux Treaty secured the vast Lakota hunting lands covering the Territories of southern Minnesota, South Dakota, and Iowa. They were now for sale to settlers at $1.25 an acre. The

Sioux were paid 3 cents an acre, over a million and a half dollars, all of which would funnel into the hands of traders as they, the first people to live there, were pushed west into the plains. The reservation lands were poor for hunting. The government promised them more reservations, more annuities. But the Sioux were now rich, drinking themselves into a stupor in the capital, in the trading posts, the taverns, buying up parlor chairs, ornamental fans, and trinkets they would never need. Soon, he feared, this would be the fate of the Anishinaabe.

That fear was no good. It would paralyze him unless he shook it. Warren had spent the last two years writing down their history in order to counter it. Or was it to bury the sense of doom he felt for the Ojibwe People under the oncoming domination of the whites? He never spoke of it. After his short rise to politics, after Saint Paul, the Legislature, the insidious deceit and creeping deaths at Sandy Lake, he withdrew from all that. He had learned the inevitable: the People could never trust the whites. They must outsmart them. He had tried, and failed.

Going into Saint Paul, high above the river, the light was fading. Warren could just make out the steeple of the white Episcopal Church above spreading rooftops on the bluff. Hammering, sawing, clinking, men's shouts and horse whinnies came from the city under construction. The stagecoach jostled and slid in the mud below the deepening red of the winter sky. Workmen were lighting their lamps. A few clutches of Indians, probably Dakota Sioux, loitered in the shadows along the riverbanks, huddled around small trash fires among the woodpiles stacked for steamers at the landing.

Others were huddled on the high bluff, blanketed, bent, looking down at their brethren on the riverbank. Those Indians stood like statues, immobile, watching the frenetic bustling and hefting and hammering of the white builders transforming their world, now the white world, the world of their ancestors that once was their home. They hovered above the specters of their own past, watching their ghosts disappear.

My Friend,

When I saw the Governor last spring in our own country, I listened attentively to all he said and believed he would make his word true. He saw our nakedness and wretchedness and promised he would help us. But now I am called upon to mediate. We have been called here, and made to suffer by sickness, by death, by hunger and cold. I lay it all to him. I charge it all to our Great Father the Governor.

My friend, it makes our hearts sore to look at the losses we have sustained while at Sandy Lake. You call us your children, but I do not think we are your children. If we were we should be white. You are not our Father and I think you call us your children only in mockery. The earth is our Father and I will never call you so. The reason we call the earth our Father is because it resembles us in color, and we call the sky our Grandfather. We did not sell the ground to our Great Father. We gave it to him in order that he might follow our example and be liberal to us.

Flat Mouth,
Chief of the Pillager Ojibwe Sandy Lake,
December 1850

Chapter 17: Saint Paul

THE STAGECOACH KEENED AND RATTLED through the slush and detritus of Saint Paul at dusk. To Warren it looked like a shipwreck after a three-day storm—boards awry, tents soaked and drooping, bare roof joists hammered up awaiting cover. A few lanterns lit the ruts freezing over in the falling darkness, then streets began to appear. Small shop windows glowed along Third Street. As the air thickened, the structures of a town took shape—gaping windows, stacks of board lumber, scattered timbers, an occasional lone facade, then the finished frames. Pulled stumps lay with their roots up, slowly burning. Wagons were left horseless in the streets. Here and there a dog scavenged.

He saw a saloon, lamp lit and smoky. A clutch of blanketed Indians stood outside by the horses. A banjo and piano tinkled through the window. One staggered down the steps, lost his feathered hat and fell face down in the mud. His tribesmen gathered him up and tossed him in a wagon, covered him with his wet blanket and went back into the saloon. They were Sioux. One picked up the hat. At least they still took care of their own.

The coach passed another tavern. A big-hat man backed out and fired two shots from a pistol through the doorway, then disappeared up a muddy alley. Nobody pursued, but someone closed the door. The coach rolled on.

THE TAVERNS THRIVED ON THE sudden fortune of the Sioux, the money from Ramsey's negotiated treaty for their lands west of the river. To Warren it was obvious who got the better deal. The terms delivered Saint Paul and 21 million surrounding acres into the hands of settlers and businessmen. The payments to the Sioux provided every merchant there with an immediate source of free-flowing revenue that the now homeless Indians spent primarily on liquor. Then on anything striking their fancy, from hats to guns to pots and mirrors, beads and fishhooks, calico, fur-lined boots, and boudoir furniture they sat on around a rubbish fire. White men's things. The traders received $400,000 directly—a good share to Henry Sibley, it was said—in payment for the Sioux's debts. There was an investigation opened, he had found out, on Ramsey's handling of the money.

As for the Sioux, they still had trouble with the notion of "owning" land. How could any man buy or sell the earth? The land was given to the people and the animals by the Great Spirit, to use, to live on.

Money itself had no value for the Indians. The impoverished Sioux were suddenly the *nouveaux riches* with one idea in mind—spend it. Perhaps better, just get rid of it. It was dirty money, not an honorable trade, as they had no choice. It was either that treaty or war with the U.S. government, certain death and extermination. The only things they could purchase came from traders, including whiskey, so the annuities flew back into white hands. Cash was flowing, and Saint Paul had grown from an outpost to a bonanza overnight.

It would be a city, he thought, though nothing like those he had seen in the east. The new capital was being set up on the ground like a pole lodge. He had not been here in over a year, and already he did not recognize it. Tomorrow he would see the changes. He coughed and spat up out the door of the coach, not bothering to inspect the color of his spittle.

§

The driver delivered Warren and his baggage to the small house finished just in time for the first born of Charlotte and her husband Edward Price. Charlotte had been forewarned by Julia of his weakened state. The short walk up to the steps was yet another tax on his resistance but he disguised it well. His sister was overjoyed to see him again in his city garb. She looked well, a bit thinner perhaps, but happy. As she embraced him, he stifled a cough and winced. The stage driver noticed his condition, and lugged his writing chest and bag inside her door.

"You got river rocks in there?"

"A few centuries of history," he said, "Heavy, though. Thanks."

Warren paid the driver and eased into a chair by the kitchen table. The stage ride had jostled his lungs, so he asked Charlotte to warm a cup of this excellent tea Julia and Matilda had prepared for him. It did him good. She fed him hot chicken soup and bakery bread and listened to his praise of the white clapboard house she and her husband had built and outfitted in so short a time. Charlotte herself had whitewashed the plaster walls while her baby slept.

"The whole town sprang up in a season," she said. "And to think now they're calling it the capital. Makes your head spin."

"You should be proud," said Warren, raising an eyebrow. "You're now in the vanguard of white settlement, the model of modern citizenry."

Charlotte could not tell if he was being sincere or ironic. No one could blame him. She was well aware, from the newspapers, of his being ousted from the Legislature, and of his enemies in the capital. Governor Ramsey was the kingpin, but pretended to remain above it. Charlotte did not pursue the issue. He was defeated, but politics were behind him.

His sister cleared the table while he picked out a few packages from his satchel. "These are for you, Charlotte, from Julia and Matilda. As for me, I bring you only the extra burden of myself for a few days. Nobody else in the city will have me. Who wants a used-up pauper at their table?"

She gave him a puzzled look. He must be out of sorts. William Warren was known in the city as an effervescent and optimistic young man, proud of his Mayflower and Ojibwe ancestry, his education at the progressive Oneida Institute in the east. He was a natural and astute public speaker who regaled one and all with his stories of trapper history and Indian lore, a promising figure in the life of the capital, a defender of the Ojibwe. Then the politicians took his seat in the Legislature and defamed him in public. He left it all behind, to finish his book.

Or to brood, thought Charlotte. But he did finish his book. It had cost him his health over the last year. Maybe the greatest cost was yet to come.

He shied away from his sister's eyes. This show of self-pity would not do. It must be the fatigue, the dull pain. He must get a grip. He rummaged through his bag.

There was a pound or two of the rice given to the Warrens by Hole-in-the-Day, some maple sugar from their trees, and the wrapped package from Julia with her note inside. Charlotte brought it to the fireplace lamp to read when her husband Edward came in, rambling on about the building, the security it promised and the schools still lacking in Saint Paul.

"A town with six churches and twice as many saloons can't see a way to vote a bill for a new schoolhouse? At least the new courthouse will stand, and the Legislature's in planning, but the jail's all pegs and pasteboard. It could be kicked in by a sickly mule. With all these murders and thievery going on, we need a brick and bar construction, and quick, with a big wing for the politicians!"

Warren, who appreciated Price's progressive notions, found more maple syrup and the smaller flask of tea he had forgotten to drink, which brought Charlotte back to the table.

"Here, I'll warm that up for you." She did, and set a bowlful before him. "With syrup from your own trees, dear Brother. Concocted by Julia and Matilda for yourself, Sir. Plants from the lakes. Drink up. Edward and I will have coffee."

"Does me good, I'll warrant," he said. "Slept like a rotten log on my way down. I think the driver did too, drunk as he was." By the time he finished his bowl, his mood was better, and he was soon nodding off.

After she put Warren to bed with a hot camphor poultice in the back room, Edward Price took her aside and whispered that he had never seen him looking worse, she should be prepared.

"You don't know my brother!" She darted. "He's indestructible."

187

It appeared she was right. The next morning Warren slept long and woke feeling and looking haler. Great plans always had a beneficial effect on his health. He breakfasted copiously on pan bread, eggs, and steaming cupfuls of Charlotte's coffee. Mr. Price was gainfully employed in the carpentry trade, she explained, and since she was schooling their child herself, they allowed themselves a few luxuries. Warren detected the shadow of embarrassment in her downward glance—they had both been raised in their father's Presbyterian ethic of frugality and their mother's Indian way of sharing whatever they had with those in need. Luxuries were unknown on the frontier in their childhood. Perhaps, once in a while, there would be calico or a forged steel shovel from Mackinac. And their father's precious books. But never coffee. Warren held out his cup for yet another dollop.

"You deserve every drop of it," he said. "And by God so do I."

Warren reminded her that he had come to collect money for his voyage and had some convincing to do. He washed and groomed himself meticulously, borrowed some of Edward's toilet water (a wedding gift from Charlotte), donned his fresh shirt and went to call on Governor and Mrs. Alexander Ramsey. Before he left, Charlotte slipped the flask of warm tea in his coat pocket.

"For the warmth," she said. "Does you good."

§

Picking his way through the mud and building debris, he passed the new Ramsey Court House. It stood alone on a treeless lot, a tall boxlike structure with a cupola and Doric columns in the Greek revival style so typical of the East, in great contrast to the little board-built jailhouse which for the time being was the only other edifice—save the gallows—representing the territorial concept of civil justice. Had there not been so much jetsam and hazel brush clogging the streets he would have sworn he was walking through a city as promising as Buffalo, which was also on his route to New York.

Apparently the east had changed in the past ten years, and he was anxious to see it again. He was barely sixteen when he left the Oneida Institute after four glorious seasons of higher learning and wild oats. The only period of his life he had spent outside the Northwest frontier, and indeed it had turned his head around. The architecture, the conversation, the ideas, even the females were different. Eastern girls smelled of perfumed powders and starch, as if they had always just stepped fresh out of a spring-flowered family parlor. Here in Saint Paul the morning air smelled of mud, sawdust, hogs, the river, pitch, tar and woodsmoke.

The Governor's temporary residence was a whiteboard cottage hardly bigger than the Price's but somehow sturdier with a front garden space, a wooden porch three steps up from the ground, and plenty of glassed windows for light. At his knock, Mrs. Anna Ramsey, well- groomed and no older than he, opened the door with an air of pleasant surprise.

"Ah, such a pleasure to see you again, Mr. Warren. That melodious voice of yours has been sadly missing in our capital of late. What brings you back to us today?"

"Truth be told, Madame, I am only here in transit to the East where I have urgent business to attend concerning the publishing of my manuscript. The Governor is expecting my visit. It is indeed a pleasure to see you again in such fine health, and in your own lovely abode."

She smiled and bade him enter. A waft of warm air flowed out the front door as she took his arm to show him in. Her shoulders were straight, her dark hair drawn back over a blue-gray crinoline dress that she wore with the grace learned in finishing schools. He noticed a few strands waving loosely behind her ear on one side. No doubt an oversight. He wondered why he should notice this— perhaps because the rest of her was so prim. And she had that faint floral scent about her.

As she took his cloak and hat and sat him down in the cozy parlor, Warren was again pleasantly fascinated by the proximity of a gentlewoman who savored her own cultivated charm. She also wore with a certain pride her liberal arts education, a rarity among women on the frontier (she was from Pennsylvania), and had once privately expressed her admiration for Warren's eloquent defense, in his characteristic sing-song voice, of the poor wretched Indians thrust so suddenly and unjustly under her husband's charge. This confidence was spoken in hushed and hurried tones to Warren alone, one sunny afternoon a couple of summers ago, before the office of the Minnesota Democrat, where she had seen his early articles on the history of the Chippewas.

He recalled the scene vividly. Under her horsewoman's hat and parasol, she had spoken with firm conviction:

"You are very right to defend the poor natives, Mr. Warren, but this does not mean that I condone the position of your editor with respect to the Governor's official duties. My husband did what he could to support the Indians during the removals, and was profoundly affected by their tragedy. The *Democrat* has taken a political position against his party. That is quite another matter." She adjusted her parasol, ill at ease before the little newspaper office, and bade Warren to accompany her a few steps down the dusty street.

"Still, you must persevere in defending the Chippeway and your own reputation. My husband has his orders as the appointed Governor of Minnesota Territory and he is bound to do his best with limited means. At least the Dakotas have listened to reason."

"They're selling their lands," Warren interjected. "They will disappear. Is this the reason of the government?" He was careful not to overstep his bounds.

"They have been paid and will be paid more. If they don't spend it all on folly, they will go west to the lands reserved for them, and learn to farm as a civilized people. The Governor has every intention of being just as equitable with the Chippeway, but he is not the only force at work in the removal efforts. *Au fond*," she told him, lowering her voice again in strict confidence, "My husband, like myself, has profound regrets about the unfortunate fate of these Indians. But who can impede the march of History?" Warren had found himself frowning and nodding at once. He had no answer.

She knew her station. That was the extent of her foray into politics, an arena which was best left to the whiskered gentlemen in the legislature and the newspapers. Still and all, she gave him a look before taking leave, a bit contrite, as if imploring him to understand.

Warren was pleased but puzzled. Mrs. Ramsey, who had obviously pondered the morality of the "Indian problem" more than most men in the Territory, was telling him he was right to disagree with Ramsey but wrong to disobey him. A wife's position. Dutiful.

In fact, there was nothing to disobey. During the first attempt in 1850, he was not in Ramsey's employ—the chiefs asked him to go with them as an advisor. He had asked Ramsey for funds but never got any, and spent his own on supplies to Sandy Lake. The spoiled rations once arrived were delivered by the traders. The 400 deaths that winter Ramsey described as "unfortunate", but Warren now understood and placed the blame on Watrous and was almost certain, like the chiefs, that the governor shared that blame.

Again, in the fall of 1851, Ramsey did nothing to stop the next attempt to remove the Lake Superior and Wisconsin bands—despite the fact that the deceased President Taylor's removal order had been suspended even as it was being executed for the second time. Warren was a paid agent then, contracted by Watrous, but unaware that the order had been suspended. Suspecting foul play, he turned back with his bands, avoiding another disaster. By far most of the bands had still not removed. And Warren still had the trust of the Ojibwe. They would have to remove, he knew, but far from the liquor traders, and under the right terms. Or so he hoped. More than a year had passed. He bowed out of the tumult after exhausting his energies writing letters to the *Democrat*. Governor Ramsey finally sided with Watrous, his archenemy. The machine was too powerful. Finishing his *History* was more useful than engaging in politics, where honesty and equity were not required these days. He was untouchable, not in the government's employ, but he wanted what money was due to him for his services. That, of course, was no business of Mrs. Ramsey—he would take it up with the Governor.

On that uncommonly mild February morning as she welcomed Warren with small talk, avoiding any reference to their previous conversation, Mrs. Ramsey was looking radiant and treated him with the warmth and deference reserved for guests in her house, those of her privileged class.

"I'm afraid Mr. Ramsey is *très occupé* with his secretary this morning, Mr. Warren, but I shall tell him of your arrival and I'm sure he'll grant you a few minutes." She very much enjoyed using these French phrases with him, but Warren knew she did not speak it fluently. It was their secret. It put a veneer on their conversation and gave him the impression, when he was with Anna Ramsey, that they were both figures posing for a painting, in a sudden burst of sunlight coming in through the window to raise the moment.

It was fixed this way: she in her prim dress and piled-up hair, her chin up framing her smile, he in his black legislator's suit, collar tied high, set against the vase of dried purple flowers on the doily, the fire in the wood stove, the glass pitcher of water and decanter on the dark lowboy, the paintings from (he believed) France on the blue-papered walls—it was all arranged to flatter the composition of their exchange and to remain stark in his mind. He needed to say something appropriate and memorable.

"I shan't need more time, I assure you, Madame, as I am on my way to New York. The Governor has drafted a letter on my behalf which I'll need when speaking with the publishers."

Why did he say "shan't"?

"Yes, of course. For your book. The *History* you spoke of. I should like to reserve a copy immediately. Several, in fact."

"Well, first we'll have to see it in print. But according to those who've read parts of it in newspaper form, it stands an excellent chance—"

"Of course it does." She smiled as if to persuade him of this gentle truth. "And it shall be. I believe that writing history, Mr. Warren, is your true vocation. I'll just tell Mr. Ramsey you've arrived."

She rose and disappeared into the back room where Ramsey had his office. Warren was confirmed in his impression that she spoke fast and assuredly because her answer was ready before the question was posed. This somehow left him speechless. Was he more at ease talking to men? Or was he just a fool for a woman's charm?

Now that she was gone, he took another look at the room as the sun disappeared behind the low cloud cover, and the window darkened. The small parlor was overheated by the enameled wood stove and stiffly formal despite the signs of hasty building that all the houses in Saint Paul displayed—loose joinery, the pine doors still seeping sap, cracks in the plaster. Yet it had the touch of a Yankee woman in printed wallpaper, the lace curtains, embroidered cushions, and the elaborate green settee on which he sat. It took him back to his Grandmother Sweet's meticulous house rules in Clarkson, New York, where a visitor must see nothing out of place. Although it was modest for a governor's lodging while awaiting the two-story frame house on the bluff, Mrs. Ramsey had imbued their temporary residence with the air of efficiency and opulence that must necessarily accompany the administration of political power.

There were also personal touches, most surprisingly the framed daguerreotype portraits of the two small children the Ramseys had lost to pneumonia two years ago. Mrs. Ramsey, devastated, had blamed this on the severe winters in the Northwest Territories, but Warren was given to believe that lack of modern medical care was the cause. His uncle Truman had died of the same affliction years ago on the boat to Detroit, while seeking last-resort medical attention that was unheard of anywhere in the wilderness. The Midé remedies may work for his mother's people, but the Warrens were of educated Yankee fabric and put their stock in science. Warren still wore the Megis shell that Sits Alone had shot into him once to cure him of the flux, but this was more through loyalty than conviction. If he stood any chance of overcoming his own lung condition and continuing his literary career, it was with Dr. Trall in New York City.

This thought made him feel constricted and he longed for a glass of water. He would not want a coughing fit when talking with Ramsey. There was a glass pitcher and service on the lowboy. He walked over. In the framed mirror behind it he caught a glimpse of himself in full legislator's suit with a starched shirt and a soft silk tie at the neck. He was not used to seeing his own image, as there was no mirror in his house, and Matilda used her small glass mainly to amuse Cordelia.

He stood straighter. Strong-jawed, mellow-eyed, somewhat drawn but still young, and dignified. Perhaps he should get an image done by that new daguerreotype shop in town, for posterity. Even Hole-in-the-Day had done it, in full regalia. Warren the writer. The historian as a young man. Just as he stood and reached for the pitcher of water, Mrs. Ramsey floated back into the room with a courteous smile.

"Oh, how rude of me. Do excuse me Mr. Warren and let me pour you a glass." He thanked her and sipped, looking at first straight into her level brown eyes, then into his glass. Her eyes belied something stern and forthright about her. A woman with a purpose.

"I'm afraid Mr. Ramsey has been too busy with territorial affairs and must ask you to come back tomorrow for the letter. Would the morning suit you?"

"*Bien sûr, Madame. A votre convenance.*"

This drew another smile from his hostess. "I have the intention of visiting Mr. Le Duc at his bookstore this afternoon. You've been to see him no doubt?"

"Indeed, and I must see him again."

"Perhaps I should accompany you," she said in a lower tone, handing him his hat and cloak. Warren stood stymied for a moment, then followed her lead as she headed for the front door. When clearly out of earshot, she spoke rapidly, sometimes glancing toward the hall.

"I believe you would agree that we are in dire need of a cultural and historical institution here in the capital, Mr. Warren. It goes hand in hand with educational institutions, of which there are none as yet, but of course they are in the planning. I should like to confer with you and Mr. Le Duc about the matter. And with other persons whose political affiliations center more around intellectual and... humanitarian concerns. Like yourself. I understand you studied under the Reverend Beriah Green at the Oneida Institute?"

194

"I had that opportunity, yes. In my formative years, before the Institute's financial difficulties. Unfortunately, the Reverend Green fell out of favor with the New York Abolitionists. You are familiar with the Institute, Madame?"

"I was raised Quaker by my Abolitionist family, Sir. My father, a congressional Representative, knew Reverend Green and his unmitigated stand on immediate emancipation of the Negro slaves and educating black people. You must have been schoolmates with some."

"Many, in the preparatory section. Along with some Indians, and some of mixed origins like myself. We numbered about twenty at Oneida. There was no distinction as to race, and we all labored alike, red and black and white. It was an experiment to found a new working society, Madame, an America where all are men are treated as equals and educated as such."

"Yes. And women?"

"The first young black woman was enrolled in the last year of the Institute. But there were others. We harbored some in our lodgings as they made their way to freedom."

"Ah. To Canada, I presume."

"The Institute served as a safe house for escaped slaves. Yes, some were helped in their flight to Ontario. The black slaves found a champion in Reverend Green. And there were others like him in the Burned-over region of New York State. Unfortunately, not enough. But even fewer champions defend the red man."

"And so you took up Green's fight. Commendable, Sir. But it sounds as if you spent more of your youth defending the Negro's cause than the Indian's."

"For me it is the same cause, Madame, for human equality and justice for all races. And the Ojibway are my family, I shall defend them to the end of my days. They are furthermore being unjustly used and decimated by those in power, as we saw at Sandy Lake. The history of this country, even this Territory, is being built on the bones of the enslaved and the dispossessed."

She bristled. "What are you implying, Mr. Warren? That it was my husband's fault?"

He had gone too far, feeling fired up by remembering his time at Oneida and the runaway black boy he had hidden in the dormitory. Those too were dangerous times. He backtracked.

"No Madame. As I stated, that was due to the slowness in Washington. I'm sure your husband had another goal in mind," he lied. "My concern is that the Ojibway retain their right to live as they choose on their land, and to be paid a fair price for its use. I defend them as I can. And I write to preserve their history before they disappear."

"My husband attends to his duties of state. It is our duty to the Lord, Mr. Warren, to defend those left behind."

"Red men will not be slaves, so they are caused to suffer and die out. Here in the Territory, slavery is prohibited under the Northwest Ordinance and the Missouri Compromise. Yet there are black slaves still. I have seen them. All this as part of Manifest Destiny? Ordained by God?"

"Those Negroes working for Army officers who owned them previously are treated more than fairly. They can even work for their own account."

"Like Dred Scott and his family at Fort Snelling? My father and I met him and his wife there in 1837. Even then he was enslaved in a free territory. Property of an Army surgeon. Now he is suing for his freedom in Missouri."

"The courts shall decide. Nevertheless, outside the fort the Negroes are free in this territory, and my sentiments still lie with the Abolitionists who defend them. As yours lie with the Chippeway people. Our causes are united, Mr. Warren. They both reflect the teachings of your Reverend Green."

"He has his convictions, and I daresay his humanism."

"Then I've nothing to add to yours, good Sir. I'm sure you are well acquainted with the responsibilities we face in such matters as race. These are my concerns as we construct the Society I have in mind. Colonel Robertson, despite his own convictions, is unable to contribute given the position of his newspaper with regard to my husband's actions in conducting the Government's removal efforts.

We shall need people inclined to temperance and progressiveness, like yourself, and those connected with civil government on amicable terms. I have spoken to Mr. Ramsey about it, and we could possibly secure funding. Perhaps you would give this some thought, Mr. Warren?"

Warren, sufficiently puzzled to remain speechless once again, heard the voice of the Governor himself down the hall, barking a list of orders to his secretary. Mrs. Ramsey suddenly opened the door, took his arm, and led him outside.

"Shall we meet at Mr. Le Duc's shop about five?"

"Five," he said. "*Mais oui, Madame. Avec plaisir.*"

"*Excellent*! And we'd best keep it confidential for now. Have a very good day, Mr. Warren."

She offered her hand. Resisting a foolish temptation to raise it to his lips, he took it in his own and shook it gently. He felt a surge of something—perhaps a covert complicity despite their differences—as he was overcome by the soft and foreign texture of her palm. They bade goodbye and Warren left the steps, mulling over her words. People like himself? Confidential?

When he reached the mud street, he realized he had forgotten his next destination.

Chapter 18: Windfall

CORNER OF THIRD AND ROBERT STREETS IN 1851.

Corner of Third and Robert Streets, IN 1851.

Saint Paul, Minnesota Territory, ca. 1851-52

WILLIAM WARREN CONSIDERED HIS MARRIAGE a good one. Then again, he had never had the occasion to reconsider. On this morning, slowly progressing through the edification of Saint Paul, he felt a pang in his chest and paused for a draught of his tea and weighed the worth of the life still left in him, on which he was now gambling to take him to New York City. To new health, successful authorship, something to leave his children, for his mother's people, hopefully something to help the Ojibwe to live forever. In his sudden lightheadedness, he assessed such a life as one of struggle, fortitude, and dedication but ultimately ineffectual when placed opposite the wispy strands of auburn hair floating on Mrs. Ramsey's neck.

Her name, he knew, was Anna. A name he favored, in fact the name he first chose for his own daughter before bowing to family pressures. He walked to the river, the swelling in his chest seeming to epitomize the constriction of his life as it closed in on him. He found a secluded spot behind a lumber stack and took another draught of tea, sat on a crate, and watched the sleeping ice floes drift downstream on the Mississippi. They too would soon disappear.

He had spent the past ten years, since he came back to La Pointe at age sixteen and set to work as an interpreter, living at an industrious pace and taking care of others. First his mother, his mother's people, and then his father and younger sisters. His filial love underpinned his determination to do Lyman proud even as the old trader lay in his grave.

He owed Lyman his progressive values and education, and had moreover spent his father's borrowed money the minute he had a small sum in pocket, on a youthful spree the last year he was boarding out in Clarkson. The Oneida Institute was facing hard times, enrollment had slacked off and the Warren boys received 170 dollars from Lyman to ensure their studies and board. Young William's first experience with financial freedom had an inflammatory influence that lasted as long as it took to spend the money. He went back to Lake Superior after the money ran out, infuriating his father, saying only that he was giving up his studies to come home and work. The loquacious and now educated young man, fluent in Ojibwe and close to the chiefs, impressed a treaty commissioner who hired him as interpreter on the strength of hearsay. This put an end to his short-lived youth.

It was also the end of the fur trade, and the end of what seemed to him to be a simpler life on Madeline Island. His mother Marie took sick, devastated by the death of her last infant child, and died soon after. This rude stroke further undermined his father, already ruined by Ramsey Crooks' American Fur Company and struggling to maintain a living with a sawmill in Chippewa Falls. Lyman plunged even deeper into depression, sold all his holdings, and abandoned all recourse against Crooks, along with any hope of securing land for his children from their 1837 Treaty rights. When he lost his personal papers in the steamer trunk, his father gave up, fell sick, and died in a few months leaving his shattered life behind him. He no longer even knew or cared what happened to his library.

William Warren, now with the charge of his younger sisters, was a working man when he was still young. He made a good impression on everyone he met and was happy to marry Matilda Aitken, fairly well the most attractive prospect on the island, when he was eighteen and she twenty. He did what was expected of him, much like his father but better than most because he had a way of winning people over through his sociability, his natural generosity and youthful effervescence. His steadfast loyalty to the Ojibwe people was an admirable quality to good Christian society that would later make him many enemies.

Matilda, with more Ojibwe blood than himself, was a fine wife who admired her husband and his convictions. What she lacked in education she made up in good sense and industry. He had needed her in the most dire way to counter the loss of his parents and the old way of life on the island, and Matilda had a gift for intuiting his every need and desire. Their ebullient marriage seemed to solidify the new future that Warren had to make for himself.

And yet, he ruminated as the river flowed by, it was somewhat ironic that the wife of a public figure, and the author he had become, did not speak fluent English. Matilda had never gone beyond basic English and would not accept his tutoring her as he did his children. She was a frontier woman, both soft and hard and silent, an exemplary mother but without the background, enthusiasm, or intellectual capabilities of a woman like Mrs. Ramsey, who had recognized immediately his vocation as a writer. It was the first time a woman had told him that. It certainly bolstered one's sense of self-worth. In fact, it flattered him more than he would stoop to admit. (He would have to tell George. Or maybe not...). He found himself looking forward to their appointment at Le Duc's bookstore that afternoon. The bookseller most certainly had contacts in New York, and he was given to believe that so did Anna Ramsey--after all, she was from the east, and an ally. She was also a white Abolitionist who knew he embraced the radical views of Beriah Green. Now she knew that Warren had helped runaway blacks escape to Canada, to freedom, back in New York State. Here she was proposing that meet at the bookstore, and that they keep it confidential. Was she sincere? Or did it have to remain confidential because Warren was part Indian, and in opposition to her husband's purpose?

Then, with no warning, from deep beneath the waters of the river, or somewhere deep in his own soul, came the question: What kind of man leaves his family in winter when he is on the brink of death?

He abruptly attributed these unpalatable thoughts to fatigue and got back on track.

Another swallow of tea and he stood up. He must see about more funding.

He stopped by the office of the *Minnesota Pioneer* where D. A. Robertson was typesetting obituaries for the next day's edition. Smells of ink and oil wafted up from the mechanical press. He looked at it and imagined his own words being set in the rows. Robertson had already typeset many of his articles. The editor had upheld and published his defense against his detractors during the removal debates and the unsavory aftermath when the Whigs resorted to calumny. Warren revered the newspaperman as a sort of personal oracle. Now his book was ready for the printer, but books were of another realm, out of Robertson's capacity. Mass printings required industrial presses now, and capital, not to speak of promotion. Robertson handed him his ink-stained canvas sleeve to shake and looked at him gravely, bespectacled from under a dark green visor.

"By God, William, this trip is insane. Wait for the spring. You'll kill yourself, man. You could send a copy. We could surely find someone..."

"There's no time for a copy, nor to send it. By the time I get an answer, it could be too late. We both know that." He paused, attempting to laugh. "I'm going to do this myself, Colonel. If only to show you that for once, I'm not heeding your advice."

He went through his justifications. Publishing the book was Robertson's idea in the first place, and he was bound to see it through. He would be home by the spring, the clement weather was a sign, steamer travel was comfortable, the new railroad through New York State ran at top speed; there was no time to waste. With a little more money he could book a cabin. He let this last phrase linger, examining the screw mechanics of the manual press. Robertson wiped his hands and went to a drawer.

"I have here my letter of recommendation and copies of your first articles that you must show the gentlemen on this list. I'll write to Judge Daly. He knows several influential men in the publishing field. Will you be going through Chicago?"

"I see no point. No possibilities there. New York is the publishing center and I can get to Buffalo faster by the lake route."

"If Lake Superior is open to navigation."

"It is. I have news from Wheeler up in Bad River, and I must see my sister Mary there."

"Then take this and use it wisely. I wouldn't want to be remembered for laying down cash money on your demise." He slipped a gold coin into the younger man's waistcoat pocket. "Many thanks. You'll be repaid, Sir, many times over. My oath."

"That's all the thanks I'll need, William. Come back to us."

Robertson, who as his first publisher considered Warren his protégé, was still dubious about the northern route but well aware that Warren was not easily dissuaded.

They shared his editor's lunch of reheated bean stew and Warren returned to his sister's house to rest and freshen up a bit before his next meeting. He would not sleep during the day but the slowdown, propped up on pillows to ease his breathing, did right by him. He restored himself with some of his tea before he borrowed some more of Edward Price's cologne.

At five, dusk falling, he was at the small white corner shop recently opened by Le Duc & Rohrer, displaying "BOOK STORE" above the single window. Being the smallest of the structures in the area, tacked onto the back of an inauspicious one-story house, not unlike his sister's, it seemed dwarfed by the barn-like buildings going up beside it. In the window he noticed five copies of *Uncle Tom's Cabin*, a recent Anti-Slavery novel become a sensational best-seller. It was a small corner of paradise for the burgeoning writer, with its lined bookshelves, however scant and mostly stocked with classics, best-selling authors and topical essays, recent fiction, or imitations thereof, plus an orderly array of pens, quills, and stacks of boxed stationery. This impression was mightily reinforced when he entered and saw Mrs. Ramsey, demure in her afternoon dress and hat, standing straight beside the fading daylight before the window, perusing a magazine entitled *Putnam's Monthly*. He bade her "*Bonjour!*"

"Ah. Mr. Warren, *bonjour*. I was just thinking that this periodical might be of interest to you. The publisher, Mr. Putnam, has a thriving concern in New York. Indeed, perhaps you've read *The Wide, Wide World*? Elizabeth Wetherell? It appears that the book has universal appeal and has been translated into several languages. The author's real name is Susan Warner, and she has fairly well made Mr. Putnam a rich man."

"Good for her. And for him. I haven't read the book you speak of. What is her subject?"

"The trials and tribulations of a young woman left to her own devices in Europe. A moving account of adversity and acquiring the strength to face it, through her faith in God. But I believe there is another underlying theme, the plight of women in a man's society." She looked at him with that fixed, level gaze again. "Having to fight for recognition every step of the way. Not unlike your Indians."

"Yes. But the Red Man has lost his homeland and nearly his entire existence, whereas women are gaining ground. And rightly so, when we witness such books as Mrs. Stowe's here, another eloquent defense of freedom for the Negro race. Yet in this modern world, no statesman defends the Indian's cause."

"Aside from Cooper, Hawthorne, not to speak of Rousseau..."

"The noble savage? I'm afraid the romantic argument has not been effective. Literature rarely affects government policy. My purpose is not so ambitious. I have simply transcribed the history of a disappearing people, as they tell it. Their struggle to survive will continue. I hope to further our knowledge of Ojibwe history and thus contribute to their just recognition."

"You are too modest, Mr. Warren. Your cause is deeply felt, and I know what you have done and said to defend it." She drew closer to him and lowered her voice. "This is why I intend to help you."

His dark eyebrows rose at this. How on earth could a woman—the Governor's wife at that—help him? William Le Duc entered from the back room with a kerosene lamp that he set on the table beside them. The glow lit them generously. Mrs. Ramsey shifted her position so that her back was turned to the window, where the fading winter light enhanced her posture.

"Ah, two privileged customers. I'm not interrupting?"Mrs. Ramsey deftly turned her face to him. She had a fine chin line and Warren saw that she was slightly rouged, and used kohl. Not unattractive.

"Of course not, Mr. Le Duc. In fact, we were just talking about sponsorship for Mr. Warren's New York venture. I believe his Chippeway history will be a grand success and as you know, I should like our future Cultural Society to participate and eventually share in the profits. The Le Duc Book Store should most certainly be first on the list of sponsors, don't you think?"

Warren was dumbstruck by the woman's pluck for the second time that day. He would not have had the gall to ask Le Duc outright.

"The Society? An excellent initiative. I take it you've discussed our idea for a Cultural Society with the Governor, Mrs. Ramsey?"

"I think it should have more substance before soliciting government support. Mr. Rice has agreed to sponsorship, *n'est-ce pas,* Mr. Warren?"

"Er, yes, Mr. Rice has generously contributed an advance toward publishing the book, in addition to his letter of recommendation."

"And he is wholeheartedly supportive of the Society. He has agreed to help me draft the by-laws."

"Excellent. So, William, you aim to knock George Copway out of the running?"

"To be honest, I haven't read the Reverend. I'm told he's quite the poet. And he has written something on the Ojibway as well."

"A man of Christian values, yes. He also sells quite well." Le Duc picked a volume out of his stacks. "As a contribution to your voyage, I'm more than happy to give you our last copy of his book on the Ojibway Nation. You should always measure the competition." He extended the book with both hands and a slight bow. "I have no doubt yours will surpass it."

"Thank you, Sir. I'll read it before I arrive, I assure you. I think my *History* is of a different nature. A transcription of oral history. Told, as you know, by the elders themselves. I thought it best to go to the source."

"A fresh approach, I'd say. And a damned good read, Warren, if anything at all like what I read in the *Democrat*. I'm sure they'll find it interesting in New York."

"To be sure," Mrs. Ramsey interrupted, "but first we shall have to speed you there and with adequate funding. What say you to a one-hundred-dollar investment, Mr. Le Duc? Against future sales? If Mr. Warren is agreed."

Warren opened his mouth but found his tongue mute.

"A bit out of range for a mere bookseller," Le Duc defended.

"But surely not for a lawyer and investor," she cajoled.

Le Duc smiled somewhat blandly and looked at Warren under half-closed eyelids. His dealings in land speculation were no secret in St. Paul, which boasted over a dozen lawyers. Women were normally ignorant of such business, or so it was thought.

"Indeed. Advancement of cultural literacy warrants such initiatives." He drew from his pocket an envelope and an oversized business card, wrote on the back, and handed it to him.

"And Mrs. Ramsey is entirely right about investing. Contact either one of these two gentlemen in New York. They are very keen on investing in any... holdings in the new territory. Call on my behalf, Mr. Wickes and Mr. Lyons. I daresay, Mrs. Ramsey, that the Governor himself may be interested in contacting them. Professional investors can greatly benefit our growing city. And I've prepared this draft for you, fifty dollars, as a partial advance against my firm order for one hundred copies of your future book. As a contribution from the future Society."

Looking at Mrs. Ramsey, he handed him the envelope. Mrs. Ramsey suddenly beamed, clapped, and executed a slight bow, then lifted herself on her tiptoes in an almost girlish attitude that embarrassed Warren even more than Le Duc's gesture. Spontaneity being contagious, he took a step toward her and seized her hand but again withheld a primary urge to kiss it.

Warren did not dare look in the envelope. He slipped it with the card between the pages of the gifted book and shook Le Duc's hand vigorously. He thanked the man over and again and bade him good evening after Mrs. Ramsey purchased a copy of the monthly she had in her hand. Gracious to the end of the interview, she promised to talk to her husband about investors but reminded Le Duc that the Cultural Society was still to be kept secret. Until established, she wished to keep it beyond the scope of territorial government. It would then be a pleasant surprise for the Governor to see such an institution already founded, and investing in the future of the city. Le Duc wished Warren the traditional "Godspeed" and showed them out the door of the overly cozy shop.

They found themselves outside under the dark canopy of evening already gathering, a lamp lit here and there as if to celebrate their new and awkward complicity. They walked, seeking hard ground in the mud, Warren slightly dizzy but feeling exceptionally elated. Saint Paul was more than ever alive, with shouts coming from carpenters still knocking on the roof frames, horses steaming, pulling overloaded carts through slushy ruts in the street. Warren lowered the brim of his hat, and Mrs. Ramsey fumbled with her parasol before she realized that in the gathering dark, there was no need or pretense to justify her opening it. They began to walk slowly, once composed, up the street towards the town center. Without boardwalks, he reflected, Mrs. Ramsey's dress would be rimmed in mud before he got her home. She was still beaming with satisfaction. But propriety was her watchword.

"Excellent then. I shall continue on alone, Mr. Warren, thank you. Sponsorship is underway. With Mr. Le Duc's contribution, you have the full support of the Society. I'm so pleased to have been of help to you. Shall I expect you tomorrow morning? The Governor will have your letter about ten. Have a very good evening, Mr. Warren."

He bade goodbye and realized he had no words to thank her. He tried to flag down a carriage for her on an impulse of gallantry, but she would have none of it. She had another call to make before returning home. When she extended her hand and leveled her eyes once more at his, he thought he detected a change, a gleam, a softening in her gaze. That was how he would describe it to himself later that night. The *au revoir* took less than five seconds and she was off, holding her hooped skirts above the mud. He watched her vanish around the next corner.

Warren felt a sudden drop in the air pressure. The night went drab, the street seemed to close in on him, the air was dampening, growing colder. His boots were heavier with the weight of the sodden earth into which he sank, sucking mud and air as he pulled them out. The whole mess would soon be frozen over during the long February night. He felt Le Duc's envelope in his pocket. He would wait until he got to Charlotte's house to open it. Fifty dollars would likely cover his expenses to New York. He already had Rice's funding; his employer and benefactor had secured contributions from other influential friends. George had sent some money too. Now if only the government would pay him his due, he could say that indeed things were working out. He understood that Anna Ramsey had discussed this contribution beforehand with Le Duc. She was on his side. But he could not fathom why she should be.

He passed the lamplit window of Elfelt's Dry Goods store with the panel advertising Joel E. Whitney's photography studio upstairs, specializing in portraits and landscapes. The notice boasted that many reproductions could be made from one image under the new Daguerreotype process invented by a Frenchman. The equipment was imported from Paris, and a special opening price was proposed for studio portraits. Warren was given to think, like Anna Ramsey, that any invention from Paris was surely a harbinger of genius, and this tempted him. What decided him, however, was a phrase set in bold print at the bottom, obviously clipped from a newspaper:

"There is a Reaper whose name is Death, and since no one can tell us when he will thrust in his sickle and cut us off from life, now is the time to get your Picture taken at Whitney's Gallery in Saint Paul."

He stepped in, inquired, and was ushered upstairs where there was still just enough day filtering through the large skylight, with help from the phosphorus bar, to take his immortal image. The photographer, a Mr. Pepper, arranged Warren's straight hair, recently trimmed by Matilda, baring his high receding hairline on only one side, and fluffed up the bow of his tie. During the pose, a great fatigue overtook him, half closing his eyelids and tilting his head to the left. The phosphorous flashed and made his heart jump. Pepper took, in his words, "only one shot." It was sufficient. He could stop back in the morning for his Picture.

He judged that it would be imprudent to mention Mrs. Ramsey's intervention to anyone, not even his sister Charlotte that evening. But the cogs in his head were turning and despite his fatigue, sleep did not come easily. Her husband had heard that wagonloads of timber were due to arrive soon from the Saint Croix Valley. The building push was on. Business ventures, faulty planning, betrayed partnerships, and foolhardy gambles were reaching a fever pitch already in mid-February. Money was changing hands up in the copper veins along the lake. Ships would be bolting to the Sault, then on to Detroit and Buffalo. Coaches would be running north on the new military road as soon as tomorrow. He could possibly make Bad River in two or three days. He only had to clear this business with Ramsey in the morning. The prospect of imagining Anna Ramsey opening the door and smiling upon him brought a modicum of peace in the last hours of the night when he began hearing horses and men moving in the streets, and he slept.

In his dream he was driving a sleigh along the melting Mississippi, reins in hand, the big horse's back gleaming before him. Beside the track stood Anna Ramsey in her hat and flared cloak, still as a statue. He passed her wondering if he should stop, but he did not. He rarely dreamed of things that could have been.

§

The next morning after a stop to get his Picture, which shocked him, he arrived promptly at ten. It was not the governor's wife but his secretary, a balding man with the look of a mortuary assistant, who saw Warren in. The parlor did not have the same floral scent, nor did the secretary, who told him Mrs. Ramsey was called out on an errand, but the Governor was expecting him. He swallowed his disappointment and took on his Dignified Statesman posture as he was shown into the office. Ramsey, a tall man with long mutton chops, appeared distracted. He extended his right hand while with his left, he handed him an envelope.

"Your recommendation, Warren, as requested. You may find it rather short and to the point, but that's best in any circumstances. You may show it to whom you please, I'm glad to be able to help."

"Most grateful, Sir. Mr. Rice told you about my publishing efforts? I expect to leave for New York tomorrow, taking the lake route by way of the Sault."

"Excellent. Henry told me about your book. It pleases me to think that I had an early contributive role in its genesis—that it all started with that historical article I asked you to write some years ago. A grand idea to leave now. No time to waste, I have reports that navigation has begun early, just as with everything else in the territory this year. Busy times, Warren, busy indeed..."

"It's why I would like to leave with maximum funding, Sir. Perhaps an effort on your part, say ten dollars, towards liquidating the government's payment for my services, pending a final statement?"

He was owed more than that, he knew. The figure of ten dollars seemed ridiculous, and hovered for a moment between the two men. He had actually intended it to be somewhat insulting to Ramsey. How could he refuse such a pittance?

"Services? I was under the impression that Watrous paid you in full."

"I remitted a statement of dates and expenses for escorting the Ojibwe over a year ago. Some monies are still due."

"I've forwarded that to the Indian Department."

"And concerning my article for your 1850 Report? The twenty-dollar remittance of last year constitutes full payment?"

"Of course. And I acknowledged your authorship in the report. My apologies for the delays. Budgeted monies are always checked in Washington. As for your escorting the Ojibwe, you know as well as I that despite all our efforts and expense, they refused to remove." Ramsey moved behind his desk and, still standing, motioned for Warren to sit before him. Which he did not do.

Instead, he insisted: "They will refuse so long as the annuities are not made perpetual."

"The annuities will be fixed by treaty. As with all Indians."

"The treaties limit their annuities to 10 or 20 years. The Canadians agree to annuities for perpetuity. This seems to me only fair in view of the richness of the ceded lands and the deplorable conditions our Indians live in at present, purely the result of the Removal Act."

"What's the point, Warren? It is our duty to provide for the future of the nation, and avoid legal imbroglios that could compromise that future in any way." Ramsey sat and began rummaging through a drawer, visibly impatient. "In ten or twenty years this wild territory will have become part of a great nation, and there won't be a hundred Indians left to claim any annuities. They will be sufficiently indemnified until that time."

"Is that an official position, Sir? Or a personal conviction?"

"What are you insinuating? I'll have you remember that your Indians, as you call them, have been guests in my house and eaten at my table! None of us can fight against the tide of progress, Warren. None of us."

This last platitude, become a credo for Whig political circles, served as a cap and bolster against any argument. Its true purpose was to end a conversation, which Ramsey reiterated by closing the drawer and crossing around to Warren, who was still standing and unmoving. He put a five-dollar piece in his left hand.

"A personal contribution." Ramsey displayed his Benevolent Father smile, took Warren's elbow, and walked him toward the door. "You of all people know the futility of impeding progress, Warren, which is why you were hired to help with the removal. A pity that some refused. Things will evolve, I assure you, and your Indians will evolve with them. Gently." He opened the door and called for his secretary. "Have a good trip, stay well, and good luck with the book."

He found himself in short order outside on the Governor's stoop with the coin still in his left palm and the impression of having begged for a handout.

He turned into the street and made for the river, where he was hopeful that in the hullabaloo of the workers, wandering Indians and roustabouts, he would most likely not cross paths with Mrs. Ramsey, to whose conversation he would be at a loss to reply.

Wide wooden steps took him down to the shores of the lower landing where makeshift boardwalks were set on timbers to span the mud flats, softer than the higher ground where the main streets of the capital were being traced day by day. One side-wheeler, the Governor Ramsey, lay hemmed in by ice at the quay, waiting impatiently for navigation to open. Then all hell would break loose from here down to Saint Louis. The town would be flooded by yet more immigrants.

Kegs of powder, nails, whiskey, flour, salt pork, and hardware goods were piled up beside stacks of firewood and lumber, bundles of furs and salt fish. Wagons and carts rumbled among them behind straining horses, oxen, and bearded men. Armed guards strolled, rifles across their chests. A few canoes slipped slowly among the ice flows.

Speculators now bought up the town lands quicker than they were laid out, giving the alleys along the bluff a crookedness that made city planning more dependent on ownership deals than on civil engineering. Ramsey himself had made a considerable sum already on land he bought and then quickly resold to settlers and businessmen.

Warren walked down toward a small cluster of blanketed Sioux, drunk before noon, huddled around a fire. They were passing a bottle, crouching over something close to the fire. One was skinning a dog.

He wondered where they might have found the dog, usually saved for feasting. They no longer hunted. There was no end to the abjection. He felt again the looming fate of his mother's people. The doom. Yet some Ojibwe chiefs would never cease to fight the treaty cessions.

He had hoped to ease the pain of their removal. He worked to unite them in one nation, to negotiate with the government from a stronger position. Now that was Hole-in-the-Day's fight, not his. Warren knew that no tribe could resist the whites and their will to possess. A tragic pride, obstinacy, and love of their homeland made the Anishinaabe as ready for a death march as for battle. Sooner starve or freeze than give in. Yet they never abandoned hope that the Great Father would be merciful towards his children. They were mistaken. The Great Father was indifferent. Sandy Lake was the morbid proof. He walked back up the slope.

He cashed the drafts at the bank, knowing they may not be honored outside the Territory. Stopping by the big livery at Fourth and Roberts, he found that stage fares were much lower than the previous year. A half-breed Winnebago driving a Red Concord told him in French that he would take him through Stillwater and up the Saint Croix as far as Taylor Falls, maybe farther depending on the road. He had passengers bound for the pineries. The stage left at dawn.

Leaving the livery, bound again for Third Street, he came face to face with Anna Ramsey. She was coming his way with an Indian boy, a Sioux, following twenty paces behind her carrying packages. The boy stopped when she stopped and so did Warren. He took off his hat and bowed, but thought it better not to shake her hand in public. Mrs. Ramsey gave the boy a coin and gestured to him to bring the packages to her house. Then she turned to Warren.

"I'm so pleased to have found you here, Mr. Warren. I suspected you might be dealing with your transportation. Forgive my absence this morning, it couldn't be helped. I've come to deliver this." She drew very close to him as if to shake his hand, but instead thrust a small leather pouch into his waistcoat pocket which, judging by weight and ring, contained gold coin. Then she stood back.

"To further the official contribution of the Cultural Society. I was able to arrange things." She drew back, smiling demurely, with purpose and a certain satisfaction.

"I'm afraid I cannot accept, Madame. You have done so much..."

"Certain parties would be very disappointed were you not to accept, sir. We hope to be investing in the publication of your *History*. The Minnesota Historical Society will also be called upon for sponsorship. I assure you I am not acting alone. Were you able to find a coach?" She turned and walked briskly toward Third Street. He could do nothing but follow.

"Yes. Tomorrow at dawn. *Ecoutez Madame, votre générosité me comble!*" He found he had to strain to keep up with her short steps. She stopped and offered her hand.

"*C'est tout naturel.* But I'm afraid we'll have to part ways here, Mr. Warren. You understand that for confidentiality's sake..."

"Of course. *Au revoir*, then, Madame, *et merci infiniment*. You shall certainly have news from me while in New York. With your permission."

"I'd hate to lose your correspondence among official territorial business, Mr. Warren. There's so much, you know, at the home office. I'll have news from Mr. Le Duc." She shook his hand, wished him bon voyage, and was gone again.

He stood stock still. A four-horse rig sped past him, the driver whipping furiously, ignoring his presence, spraying mud on his cloak. Warren had heard nothing. Indeed, he felt somewhat invisible the moment Anna Ramsey left his field of vision. Their encounter there on the street had not lasted two minutes.

§

That night at Charlotte's house, packed up, poulticed, and with a fresh cup of his hot tea next to his bed, he took stock, and counted his money. The purse she had given him held fifty dollars in coin, no note. A secret. He had in all just over two hundred in coin, plus the cashed drafts. It would get him to New York and support him, maybe even pay for medical treatments. He could already see himself back in Saint Paul in the summer, placing his bound *History* on the shelves at Le Duc's bookstore, and into the soft hands of Anna Ramsey. Then there would be the book sales. His fortunes had reversed in Saint Paul.

The success of his mission kept him awake when he sorely needed the sleep. He concentrated on the silence and darkness. In the room adjacent, he heard the voices of Charlotte and Edward Price talking in low tones. He was saying that her brother's mind was unsteady, he wasn't thinking, that it was madness in his state to attempt such a trip in winter. All that for a book about Indians? Couldn't it wait a couple months?

Charlotte's harsh whisper came through the door to cauterize his will: "He can't do otherwise. He'll publish it."

After a moment, he heard Price's resigned voice: "If he gets there."

After three hours of half-sleep, he woke in the dark, lit a candle and wrote:

> *Dear George,*
> *Much regret at not having time to visit you in Chippewa Falls before I leave, but as we discussed I must see Mary and settle with the Wheelers. Heading up on Ste Croix stage this morn, hope weather holds for a few days. Crossing Superior and down the Lakes. You recall the route from our old school days. Then the train. I should be in New York in a pair of weeks. Charlotte, her new baby and husband Price in fine fiddle, my business here successful and I don't mind telling you I feel flush for a change, which dispels my late trepidations about expenses. I should come back with pockets*

full, health restored, book under way and perhaps see you in Saint Paul at that time. Matilda and children all safe and in good health as am I. New herbal remedy doing wonders. I'll write from the City. If you feel churchlike on Sunday put in a good word for...

Yr aff. cousin,
William W Warren

Chapter 19: Overland

DAWN WAS SHARP AND FOGGY. Men started the work fires with piles of frozen branches stacked in the streets. The stage was rigged with four large horses still under their blankets, restless as Edward Price heaved Warren's chest and bag onto the roof and the driver roped everything down under canvas. The horses, the livery, the greased leather, the freezing air, all smelled of travel. Warren settled onto the blanketed seat in his cloak and muffler.

The three other men in the stage, all German, were headed for the lumber camps, or maybe the mines. Price had heard that up in the mining country there were as many as four or five new steamers operating between Superior and the Sault, hauling copper and iron eastward. After logging took hold in the Saint Croix valley, here was another new boom along the south shore—copper fever. They pulled a four-ton piece of pure copper ore out of a mountain near Ontonogan. Indian country, strewn with Ojibwe lodges and trappers' cabins, was the next El Dorado. Investors were staking claims and founding townships on the shores of the big lake. These young Germans would be extracting the minerals, cutting the logs, and building the new cities. Tomorrow was near, there was money to be made.

The driver yelled the departure. Price shook his hand through the coach door, wished him a safe trip, and walked off with his hammer in his belt. The coach bolted forward.

Halfway to Stillwater, the Germans were dozing, and Warren watched through a crack as the weak sun tried to break through. The gray light enveloped all but the black limbs reaching for the sky. The ancestors. A forest of ghosts. How many more would die before the whites took it all?

The jostling coach stirred the congestion in his lungs. Why these dark ruminations? He was starting his voyage sufficiently funded, had posted the letter to his cousin, and was on his way to see Mary. He had every reason to cheer up. Stifling an urge to cough, he spat blood into his handkerchief. He drank half of one flask of the warm spicy tea Charlotte had prepared with Julia's instructions. He nodded off. His mind paced wearily back and forth on a distant bridge between memory and dream.

He awoke in a thicker fog and realized the coach was stopped; the door open. Ahead, the driver and the German passengers were chopping upended roots out of the road. He could be of no help so stayed put and drank some more tea, and had a biscuit. At least the jostling had stopped. His lungs were calm. He entered into his half-dream, which brought him sometimes to pleasant memories and places, and other times, to places he never wanted to be again.

He remembered especially the six oxen he had as a farmer at Gull Lake, and his horse, his milk cow, and forty-three cleared acres, earning good money from the Indian Service and from Henry Rice. The chest ailment was at bay, and he and his family were doing well. His writing had begun to pay, from the government's Indian Inquiries and his published articles in the *Minnesota Pioneer.* Ramsey himself asked him to write part of his report that summer, based on his knowledge of the Ojibwe. This largely made up for his weakened physical state. He could have continued on and lived a healthier life, sheltered, paid, and making faster headway on his book—although at the time it was not yet a book.

Instead, he made the ill-fated choice to help his Wisconsin Ojibwe friends when they asked him to accompany them on the trip to Sandy Lake. The bands along the Saint Croix were in utter despair, falling quickly into alcohol from the white traders and lumberjacks. The old ways were doomed. He thought he could persuade his friends of the necessity to get away from the scourge. To save themselves from the whites.

He wrote to Ramsey then to explain his reasons for going, and asked for government provisions to feed the hundreds of Indians for the journey. Whatever made him think it would work? Maybe being elected to the Territorial Legislature that summer went to his head. When everything seemed to be falling into place—a new life as a legislator, scholar, and historian. A published writer, a man of influence, and a respected defender of the Ojibwe. He was comfortable, living at Rice's American House in Saint Paul with his family, debating the finer points of law and representation.

But events had turned. That fall, the wheels of the Sandy Lake removals were set in motion. Ramsey refused to pay for provisions, so Warren had paid for supplies and canoes with his own money and credit. Julia came along to help and care for her brother. The bands were told that to collect their annuities, in goods and money, they must go to Sandy Lake—and to see if they liked the country. If so, they were to remove there next spring with their families. The entire process made no sense to the Ojibwe, they had no intention of staying. They would go if Warren were there to speak for them, and they needed their payment to live, and to buy supplies from the traders. They would head north up the Chippewa River, a 300-mile journey.

Though he fought against thinking about it when awake, the memory of what had happened in 1850 was still vivid when he dreamed. Some things remained trapped in memory. Dozing in the stage, they turned in his mind like a panicked animal.

He and Julia began with them in twenty-five canoes, gathering other bands as they went, portaging to the Saint Croix and then north from lake to lake up to the shore of Superior, walking all day, paddling the rivers, eating biscuit and wild rice at night, cooking the next day's gruel, constantly hunting game. Still, around the night fires the council men told Warren that they would not remove. They wanted their treaty money, as promised, but they would not leave their homeland.

After two weeks, they reached Iron River and the rapids that emptied into the tip of Lake Superior, where they met with the La Pointe bands. His group now numbered over 700. They gummed the seams well and followed one by one after the lead canoes mastered by men who had run those rapids all their lives. They all gathered on arrival at Lake Superior and told him again they would not remove. They knew their entire country by heart, as did their forefathers. They knew their lands and the lakes and rivers that gave them their living, the game, the fish, the good waters, the rice they gathered.

There in the cold by the big lake Warren was down with a hemorrhage that worried the old chiefs. Julia made him poultices, brought him tea and herbs to ease him in his tent. His Ojibwe friends treated him with much kindness, and the men built him a sweat lodge and gathered balsam boughs.

He declined, feeling too weak to withstand the heat. All he needed was rest before going on. They camped there on the sand point and the Ojibwe laid their nets, pulling up whitefish and trout. Warren lay in his tent, feverish, waiting for his strength to come back as it had before. Outside, the midés sang and drummed and rattled day and night. A painted and horned man burned a sage and cedar smudge, chanting, invoking Mishibizhiw, the Great Horned Snake who lives under the water. He covered Warren's forehead and chest with a potent ash concoction that mixed with his sweat and hardened. He was given tea, sweetened with maple, sometimes thickened with rice. Julia fed him gruel with mashed fish. She washed him down with hot towels and covered him in furs to sweat again. He dreamed of snakes, copper-tailed lions, water birds and long-horned oxen, but when he awoke, he remembered nothing.

After several days there came a clear, calm sunset over the lake that Great Buffalo, just arrived from La Pointe, wanted Warren to see. He brought him out on the strand where fires were burning and the people were gathered, cooking the rice and the fish and stretching their nets stretching on racks. The painted canoes were overturned on the sand, beneath a deep blue and red October sky, the air crisp and clear and not yet freezing, the first stars appearing in the east. They heard only the honking ducks, cracking fires, and the lapping lake water. The sunset purified everything that lived. Warren felt stronger.

"Nosins," Buffalo said. "Is this the sunset we see from the island? We don't see it in the same way here."

"I wish to see it from the island forever. For all my people."

"It has not always been that way. Once the Anishinaabe lived by the big salt water."

"It was good on the island. Your father was there, my father. Now it is bad. The whites and the traders bring much liquor. The young men have lost their ways, as I feared, and the elders are fast falling into their graves. Game is scarce now, and trade is bad, we must live on what the whites give us at the payments, but the traders take it. We are left naked and wretched in our homeland. Some resort to stealing. If not, they starve or freeze. The missionaries say we must plant, farm, become Christians, live like the whites. My people ask me what to do, for they call me Chief. I am not a chief. I am but a man in search of a way to live for my people. We have always depended on the earth. Now we are weak, and must ask for the mercy of the white man. My Grandson, we have put our trust in you to deal with the whites, you have learned their ways and can speak for your relatives and defend their interests. You must be our guide in our blindness and ignorance. You must lead us out of the darkness and onto the path of life."

Warren responded: "The Great White Father is merciful. He will honor his promises to his children, the Anishinaabe. We shall go to Washington speak with him. But now we must go to the payment. It is better to get the payment in Sandy Lake than in La Pointe. The traders are not there to sell their whiskey."

"I have seen Sandy Lake. It is a forsaken place that cannot support my people. No game, no fish, the soil is as barren as this sand under our feet. We will not live at Sandy Lake. We will go to Fond du Lac for payment, no farther. Here the fishing is good. Wild rice in abundance."

"Buffalo. You will tell this to the President in Washington. He will listen. Now we must go to Sandy Lake. Tell your people we shall leave in the morning. One day to Fond du Lac, then three days portage to the agency. There we shall meet with the others, get our payments, and make a feast. The government has food for us all. No whiskey. You have my word."

Warren left much unsaid that night. Although he had learned the duplicitous language of the whites in his duties as interpreter, he was not accustomed to lying to the Ojibwe. The old chief's reliance on him as adviser for his people was complete. Many times, he had defended them verbally and in writing before instances that no right-minded white man would confront. He was family, a child who shared their binding blood but who had chosen to live like the whites—partly to honor his father's wishes, and partly to build the bridge between his mother's people and the encroaching white civilization. He was at that bridge now, suspended where his words would be tested like the vines on which the bridge hung.

He lay in darkness the last night on the sand bar, stifling his cough, unable to sleep for fear of uttering some half-truth that could be false in the end and betray the trust of the Ojibwe. Yet if he did not lead them away from their old way of life, they would be buried with it.

As dawn approached, he heard them packing the canoes. He walked out onto the strand and raised his hand. Great Buffalo and some of the elders came to his side.

"Listen to me," Warren said as he waved from the point west of the desolate strand, then across the water to the east. "Over there will be a very great city. The lake near it will be full of all kinds of vessels. Over there will be another city, but not so great as the city over here. I will not live to see those cities. Some of you young men will live to see them. I want you to remember what I am now telling you."

The old men looked out over the vast lake, the rough and treeless terrain, and shook their heads, unbelieving. Warren said no more. Julia took his arm and led him to their canoe as if he were losing his mind. The entire gathering then set off, some on foot and some in canoes, toward the mouth of the Saint Louis River.

They made on for a day and arrived at Fond du Lac, which formed a small village and trading post that was once a mission and Indian school. A few old half breeds lingered about picking the last of the pumpkins and squashes, though a good portion of it had gone to seed. They told Warren that the remaining Ojibwe had already advanced to Sandy Lake or joined with other bands. News of the disguised removal had reached them. The bands, it seemed, were scattering. They stayed for a night and began the three-day portage west the next morning.

The going was hard, through underbrush, up inclines and into dense marshes where they waded through water up to their thighs. Every man carried a pack on his back, the few women as well, plus the many canoes that they set down during the frequent poses. Warren's health was too weak to maintain the regular pace. The portage took five days instead of three. Arriving at Sandy Lake, they had to cross the water to the temporary agency and the gathering of Mississippi and Leech Lake bands waiting for the payment. The November winter was on them, the sky flint gray, the first snows coming on steadily, the temperature dropping fast. At their approach, the three thousand Ojibwe on the far shore shot off welcome fire and much excitement ensued, many jumping into their canoes and paddling forth to greet them.

Warren was relieved to see his family waiting for him—Matilda, the children and his sister Sophia were living in a tent near the agent's house. Matilda told him, however, that the agent Watrous was not yet there. The goods and rations had been ready since late August and served to feed the families already arrived, along with the little game they managed to kill. The fishing in this lake was poor, it could not feed so many. The bands in the region had moved farther south some years before. The People had been eating legalet, flour, salt pork and rice for a month.

"Where's Watrous?" He asked Matilda, "Why are they here? Have they not been paid?"

"The agent left a month ago, to collect the funds in Saint Louis. Mrs. Watrous tells us he was delayed in Saint Paul. We have no other news and there is no money. No one has been paid. The traders give them no more credit."

"Our people need to eat. We've brought game and fish, but I fear a paltry feast."

He looked out on the blanketed masses gathered around the fires, the hundreds of canoes along the banks, the meager slips of meat and fish smoking on racks. The damp cold descended from above the scrawny pines, pushing down on the smoke to form a cloud over their heads. The naked elms raised their scrawny fingers to the heavens.

"There must be three or four thousand here now. And for what?"

Warren inspected the stores and found some of the flour already rotten. A skinny dog had somehow gotten into one of the salt pork barrels and lay outside, whining and convulsing.

He told them to burn the bad barrel and cull the flour. Rations would be cut to a pound of flour and a half pound of salt pork per person, per day. There was nothing left but to survive until Watrous arrived, get their money, and buy more supplies from the traders on the way home. For now, at the onset of winter, they were trapped at Sandy Lake.

The fog lifted. The coach was stopped, and the driver proposed breakfast at Marine Mills. Warren was groggy and hungry, and the smell of coffee was good and tempting. They ate flapjacks and bacon seated in a large tent put up for the loggers and builders. A big half-breed woman who ran the mess recognized Warren from some years ago when he had come down from La Pointe with sub agent Hays for his Mississippi land survey, interpreting for him, covering 1,500 miles and talking with the chiefs. Hays had to determine whether the Ojibwe east of the river in Wisconsin Territory would cede their lands and remove west. The answer was no in 1846, as it was again in 1850 and 1851.

The woman, named Marie like his mother, was surprised to find him peaked and pale. More coffee was on her stove, but it was not as good as Charlotte's, so he asked her to heat up his tea and refill his flasks. Marie gave him another stack of flapjacks in greased paper.

"You did good for them mixed-bloods at the treaty, but the Indians won't go," she told him. "You still work for the government?"

"That's all over now," he said. "Out of my hands."

"The People still trust you. They say you had a hard time with that Hays."

"I had a hard time on the way back to La Pointe that winter, but not with him. I caught a low branch in the chest chasing a moose. Fell sick, had to stop working. It still smarts, but I'll see the doctors out east. They'll fix me up."

"Hope so. I heard different about Hays. How is your wife?"

"She and the children are all well. We live on the Mississippi now."

"You take care. Of everyone. Like always. Hear?"

"I hear, Marie."

Warren found himself again with three silent men in the coach on the way north along the river road. It was warmer this way, all huddled under buffalo robes. He drank his tea and drowsed despite the jostle. Sleep was the easiest way to travel in the stagecoach, but his was more like a half sleep.

Dysentery set in at Sandy Lake. Then an outbreak of measles, and they began to die. Hole-in-the-Day rode back to Saint Paul for more supplies that never came. Some goods were sent from Gull Lake, but the edible flour was culled off by the traders and bad rations were sold to the Ojibwe for high prices, to be taken out of their annuity money. Children especially were vulnerable. Their cries echoed over Sandy Lake. Every day three, four, seven or more perished. The sickness began to rage late in November. Warren took his family back to Gull Lake.

Sophia fell ill, she and Julia remained there with the agent's wife, and Watrous finally returned. To avoid more starvation the agent purchased supplies from the traders, spending thousands in Ojibwe annuities claims, and sent the Wisconsin bands back home more destitute than when they had come. The rivers were frozen, it was useless to bring the canoes. Agent Watrous gathered them in council and told them that next year, they would have to remove to the lands designated by the government, and Sandy Lake would be the location of the new agency.

Annuities would be paid only to those who came. Big Wolf, the Chippewa River chief, spoke for all and said they would never come back to Sandy Lake.

The survivors left their canoes and struck out on foot. Winter closed in. Great Buffalo said that they left 170 dead, frozen stiff and unburied because the soil had become too hard. Another 230 froze or starved to death on the trail back to their homes.

In his half-dreaming state, Warren was haunted by the naked elm branches stiff and stark against the cold bleak sky at Sandy Lake, the hands of the trapped and starving reaching up in supplication, the hundreds of Ojibwe dying in the freeze. Their doom was already upon them. He drank his tea to quell the nausea and escape the pain, but their ghosts never left him as the stage creaked and rolled through the fallen timber stands, up the Saint Croix valley.

Yet the fact they were still moving gave him hope.

Chapter 20: Bad River

TWO DAYS OF JARRING OVER timber and boulders, chopping
out jutting roots and bogging down in sinkholes brought the coach
to a mining site a few miles below Chequamegon Bay. It was little
more than a large clearing in the pines beneath a sharp ridge hung
with wooden trestles, catwalks, conveyor troughs, smokestacks, and
derricks. A steam-driven stamp mill under a bark roof shuddered
like a beast, pounding copper-bearing rocks into bits and tailings.
Teamsters prodded their animals hauling wagonloads of dirt and
copper ore. Dark-faced miners emerged from the shafts above with
picks and shovels, flickering coal lamps strapped to their heads. The
light was just beginning to fade. Fires were lit on clearings among
sooty snow piles.

Warren stared out of the coach, pained and wheezing from the
journey. They had been lucky, said the driver, to have a harder and
smoother road from the freeze two days ago. They made good time
and did not have to use the snow runners.

He looked over to the ridges where when he was a boy, the big
trees towered above him on his family's trips to the sugar bush, some
whose breadth was four men across. The only way into the wilderness then was by Indian trail or rushing river, through a forest still
alive with game. It was magical. That was gone now, nothing but
stumps and small pines left, some areas slash cut, the stumps burning black. Loggers and miners were scraping paradise bare, making
it their own. He peered out onto the scarred and smoky skin of it,
where soot-blackened men plodded through the mud to their tents.

The three Germans descended, bags in hand, between two rows
of tents and plank cabins. They stood bewildered until a miner who

spoke their language came up and showed them to the wooden structure that served as the company headquarters. More immigrants than Indians gathered in the smoky dusk, stirring kettles of stew or roasting slabs of meat. The main language seemed to be German, or something else, Swedish he guessed, where it used to be French or Ojibwe. There was some English too, perhaps Cornish or Irish men. Things were changing quickly now.

"This is Bad River?" He asked the driver.

"They call it that. You say you want the mission school?"

"The Reverend Wheeler's house."

"Same difference. I'll take you just beyond the bend there."

Beyond the mining site was a small gathering of log and frame houses lined up in the fashion of a residential neighborhood. Some were painted white, with green shutters, and squarely fenced, with a maple, oak or ash standing here and there, interspersed with garden plots and small fields. Just as many wigwams were scattered to one side of the lane. It was a village both Indian and white pioneer. The Wheelers had established the community of Odanah a few years ago, hoping to convert the Ojibwe to Christianity by bringing to them the ways of white civilization, farming, and education. It was a long process. Very few of the Ojibwe in the Bad River band felt inclined to join Reverend Wheeler's congregation. Rather than force them, as the government would have it, he preferred that they convert of their own volition. He was one of Warren's most loyal allies during the forced removal attempts.

Further on were lots bearing stacks of milled lumber ready for building. Visibly, it had been platted as a residential street with the intention of eventually founding a town. A general store bore large paned windows displaying hardware and advertising foodstuffs, with a newly painted sign over the porch roof: *Minnesota Mining Company General Store.*

The Wheelers' residence was a log structure somewhat larger and higher than Warren's own cabin at Two Rivers, with two additions in back to form a T. The fenced plot behind the house held a large vegetable garden, now snowed over, awaiting spring. Mrs. Harriet

Wheeler stood on her porch with his sister Mary, spry and bonnet-ed, wearing an apron over her billowing gray dress. She rushed to embrace him as he stepped from the coach. He was so fatigued he could barely stand.

"Oh, Willum, Willum, Willum! It's so good of you to come and see me!"

"Look at you," he said, "A young woman now. I've missed you, Little Sister. You look wonderful."

She gave a little twirl and smoothed her white apron. "I made it myself. Mrs. Wheeler is teaching me to sew. She's teaching me everything she knows. Even geometry!"

"As suits a young woman these days. And Geography, I hope. We must all know where we are in this world." He caught Harriet's eye and nodded thankfully.

Harriet Wheeler put her arm around Mary, proud of her charge. "A fast and willing learner, she is. Like all the Warrens, I daresay. Your father made sure of that, bless his soul. Bring yourself in here now, William. The Lord has brought you this far to us, praise be on his merciful benevolence."

The driver carried up his small trunk and satchel. Out stepped his father's old friend, Leonard Wheeler. The missionary looked considerably frailer than the last time Warren had seen him, but his eyes were sharp and his smile still strong as they shook hands.

"Are you well, Reverend? You look a bit pale."

"The privilege of age, William," he joked. "Half a century on this earth, some say it's enough. But what about you? Does winter have a grip on us all?"

"I am well, much better than last year. It's good to see you. The stagecoach lulls me to sleep. It takes me some time to wake up."

Mary was pleased to serve a dinner of smoked whitefish, pota-toes, and turnips that she had prepared herself. As Warren could no longer pay for her bed and board, he was relieved to see that she was earning

After all, she was already 17. The five young Wheeler children were lively company until their mother set them to their tasks and

228

studies, while Mary was allowed to visit a little longer to catch up on news of her sisters and Warren's own little family. He gave her letters from Julia and one from Charlotte, along with the small parcel containing another glass vial, a bag of herbs and a note of instructions.

"Ah, this package is for you, dear Brother, another of Julia's concoctions and some medicinal sweetener from Dr. Borup. You have a flask to give me?"

"Yes, two," he took them from his satchel, empty. "I dare say her remedies work wonders, a true blessing on this trip. I feel quite up to it now."

"Sassafras and maple tea, and whatever else she's come up with, probably one of Mother's Indian remedies. It will do you more good than any old doctor." She went off to the stove, leaving the two men at the table while Harriet saw to her children's' lessons.

Leonard Wheeler poked at the fire then leveled his eyes squarely at the younger man. "You know this voyage is folly in your state, William. Why not wait until spring?"

"If I wait until spring, I might never go."

Wheeler frowned. This talk was unlike him. "Nonsense."

"My book is finished, the time is right, the weather looks willing. I've traveled the lakes before, as you know, and this time it will be faster with the steamers. I can be there before mid- March. Besides, how else to provide for my family? Farming? Interpreting? It's finished, and they still owe me money. As a writer, I have excellent recommendations and prospects. And I have a book. It shall be done."

"You know I have always stood by you. I could give you a letter to a judge I met in Washington last year. Supports the Indians, wants a new treaty before the removal, and he knows Commissioner Lea."

"I want nothing more to do with Lea. That's up to the Chippewa now. They have another scheme to go to Washington themselves. With Hole-in-the-Day. All folly. Lea will send them packing. Then if need be, they'll send in the soldiers."

Warren had an urge to cough, but held it back. He took out his handkerchief, saw that dried blood still stained it, crumpled it quickly and pocketed it.

Wheeler saw this and spoke in his stead: "This government, Ramsey, Watrous, they have no more support. They will move on, statehood is next on their agenda. The Ojibwe may be forced to leave, to where I do not know, but perhaps the Lord will intervene and shed wisdom on Washington bureaucrats, and they will allow our Wisconsin Indians to remain here, or in La Pointe, or where they can hunt and fish as they always have. If they are forced to go again to Sandy Lake, even more lives may be lost. Here we have our Christian Indians, hopefully we'll have more this year. But there is much to do... and they will not all agree to live like we do. To farm, go to church..."

"The government doesn't want to deal with the Indians. They want them to disappear." Wheeler had no answer for this. Warren tried to fill the void.

"Convincing them to live like the whites is your task now, Reverend. Those who resist, God pity them."

"So you will go east, you will publish your book. No stopping you?"

"To New York. I have letters, people to meet. I'll see a Dr. Trall there, he has a new method for treating what ails me."

"The treatment for that is to go south, not north, William. You need dry, clement weather and rest. Any doctor will tell you that. The climate here is hard on us all."

"Maybe later when I have the funds and the time. I hear they've opened the Erie railroad now, from Buffalo to the city. So I must find passage to the Sault, then a boat from there down to Detroit and on to Buffalo. What do you know of the boats running from here?"

Wheeler got up to tend the stove and spoke resignedly.

"The *Algonquin* is anchored across in La Pointe. That old schooner your father knew. McKay is the master. He'll likely be sailing for Ontonagon presently, for copper ore. The fever is on them. They're breaking a new canal over the Sault, connecting the lakes, but for now there's a rail cart portage to Lake Huron. Up to you. My Indians know the way through the shore ice by the landing. Charlie—he's a Christian now—can take you to La Pointe, or you can try to catch up with the Algonquin in Ontonagon. That means overland travel. There are no roads yet."

"I'll go to La Pointe in the morning. It will be good to see the old home, my grandfathers. Time allowing, I can visit the family graves."

Wheeler sent his boy to fetch Charlie. Warren knew the man as an Ojibwe who would not remove, who wanted to stay here, his home, and was ready to live like the whites to keep that privilege. He was dressed in a logger's shirt and Mackinac coat, but under his black hat his hair was still long, and his medicine pack was around his neck. Warren greeted him in his native language, but Charlie answered in English. He declined a cup of tea by raising his hand. He would wait for Warren at sunup and take him down the river, then over the bay by canoe. Charlie took out his Bible and asked Leonard Wheeler to bless it. His daughter was sick, and he would put it in her sickbed. The Reverend obliged, the man thanked him and left.

"I bless them every time I can," he said. "We brought Charlie in from heathenism, then from the Catholics. Harriet sings with his wife and seven other women on the Sabbath. Their souls were on the very brink of perdition, now we cannot lose them. May the Lord allow that we all remain with them here at their Christian home. This year we build the new church, after ten years of petitioning the Board."

Mary came back to the table with the flasks filled and the package wrapped up again. "There's still plenty left for more preparations. Make the tea and add two spoonfuls of this mixture to the flask. The maple syrup will sooth your throat."

"It's very good warm and does me good. Reminds me of home. Thank you, Little Sister."

"Thank Matilda and Julia. She got the maple elixir from Doctor Borup."

"Then he must have some saving graces, " he allowed. "Perhaps she didn't tell him it was for me. He's another one, along with Boutwell, who'd rather see our Indians cow-tied and shipped to the desert, myself with them. They're both in with the Fur Company. Borup, I'm not surprised. But Boutwell..."

"You sound bitter, William. You mustn't be. Reverend Boutwell has known you since you were a boy, he just doesn't understand why you opposed Watrous and Ramsey in the removals. It was you who got the bands to Sandy Lake."

"You know why. They wouldn't get their treaty money if they didn't go. They would starve. The government would force them in the end, or kill them. They've done it before, to Black Hawk's people, to the Chickasaw, the Cherokee, and the Seminoles in the South. The treaty makers are politicians, they have no mercy and no honor. All this fair dealing and brotherhood rhetoric is blather. A treaty for them is a contract, and they break contracts. Washington knows nothing of what's decided in Saint Paul, much less in Sandy Lake. I wanted to avoid another Trail of Tears and find the Ojibwe a good place to live, close to their homes. All Watrous, Ramsey, and the AFC wanted was to trap them for the traders to milk their annuities and feed them whiskey. Let Hole-in-the-Day handle them. He's the politician."

Warren's face had turned red. He began to hack, wheezing to catch his breath. He twisted away from the table with his handkerchief against his mouth. Harriet Wheeler quickly set a cup down and poured in some of his tea. While Warren huddled in a corner, she turned her back and added another few drops from the vial. Then she walked over to him, put her arm on his shoulder and brought the cup to his lips. He did not resist, and drank as he could. Mrs. Wheeler saw the smudge of blood on his cheek. She looked at her husband, shook her head, and wiped it off with her apron. The tea seemed to quell the cough. No further mention was made of the incident.

As her brother calmed down, Mary suggested that she make him a pallet here in the room with the fire. It was drier, he was tired, he would sleep better.

"And finish your warm tea. Drink up now, I'll make you some more in the morning."

"Very well, Doctor Mary." He hurriedly pocketed his handkerchief. "Have you considered studying medicine? A fine profession for a smart girl like you."

"I've learnt very well at the mission school here. How could I study medicine? Reverend Wheeler says I have the wherewithal. I'd have to go east like you did, but how?"

Harriet Wheeler quickly responded: "There are fine schools for girls in the East. First, you'd have to complete a finishing school. Then go on to specialize if you should like. Things are different now, and there are fine institutions in this country, more liberal, open to educating women. The Convention in Seneca was just the beginning. So many things are happening back East. We must keep the faith, in this desolate country, that we pave the way for salvation and enlightenment."

Warren seemed to wake up at the mention of the East.

"The Oneida Institute, Beriah Green's school where I went, was open to all. We all learned and worked together. Green was a visionary, he knew the Negroes must be freed and educated. Women too, of course. It is all changing, and for the better. The Red Man has no champion, save the Reverend and myself."

"Here here!" Wheeler broke in. "And your father too believed this: to convert the natives to Christianity, you have to educate these people and raise their standard of living. But who listens to us?"

"They will listen. In time. Learning is the key. We worked toward that end—to make all men equal." Warren's tone bespoke his pride in his education in the East. He could speak of lofty ideals with the Wheelers—they too were of educated New England stock. "Unfortunately the Institute foundered during the crisis and Green buckled to anti-abolition factions. But the abolitionist movement is very much alive, and progress comes fast. I'll see how fast in New York."

"Of course you will," said Wheeler. "And I expect we'll have schools here in the next few years. Chicago, Saint Louis, perhaps even Saint Paul. I've seen it grow from a handful of cabins to a city in a decade."

Mary joined in: "I'd like to teach others, really. Not about medicine, but about history, geography, literature, languages. Perhaps I shall be a teacher, like Sophia. Like you, Mrs. Wheeler."

"A noble profession indeed," said Harriet Wheeler. "And so necessary now. These poor immigrants in the mining towns are not in the least educated, they can't even speak English as well as some Indians. And what about all our children, so willing to learn? I encourage you in that direction, Mary. For now, you must complete your lesson for tomorrow and let your brother sleep. He has a long journey ahead."

Mary kissed her brother, pressed into his satchel a package of dried fruit from the company store, and went off to her room with the other children. Warren watched her go and felt a sadness well within him. Fatigue suddenly overcame his body and slowed his voice. His smile was wan as he addressed Leonard Wheeler.

"I cannot tell you how grateful I am she's with you. You've done well by her. She's learning well, and you've instilled her with grace. My father too would be grateful." With this, he left a twenty-dollar gold piece on the table.

"Thank you, William. It will help. As for Mary's education, Lyman would have done the same, but better than us," said Wheeler. "I promised I would try."

"I can leave her in your hands, then. It brings me some peace of mind. Charlotte and Julia both are married, Sophia will do fine with her cousins for now, and perhaps come to this mission school next year? If things work out in New York, as I think they should, I'll have the money to pay for it. One book leads to another, you know, and I have more in the planning..." He faded off, lost his train of thought, and longed to lie down. Why did he feel so tired?

"Don't worry yourself, we know you're good for it."

"I...I'm sorry I can't pay you more for Mary, Reverend. My father..."

"Your father supported Harriet and me when we first came. He supported all the missionaries on the Island, beginning with the Halls, for years. Housed and fed us, built the church, never asking for a cent. And you've paid for Mary ever since his passing. It's the least we can do, William, and Mary's a joy for us."

"Would that I could do what my father did."

"Do not chide yourself. You do plenty. Go do what you must, and later you'll do as you wish."

He drained his teacup. By the time Warren lay down on his blanketed pallet near the stove, his breath came from the shallows. Whether from the affliction or exhaustion, pain was the hard master that taught him to rule his life. He turned on his side. Sleep was merciful.

§

Harriet Wheeler lay on her back in the dark next to her husband in their bedroom.

"You know he would never take that mixture of Borup's if he knew what it was. He has principles. He despises alcohol and he's right. It's subterfuge, Leonard. Of course Mary doesn't know, but Julia and Charlotte are part of it. I saw the letter."

At first Wheeler said nothing. He too had principles. But he too was tired.

"It seems to do him good, Harriet. There's not much alcohol in it. Just the medicine. He'll never make the trip without it. What difference does it make now?"

CANADA
L. SUPERIOR
COPPER HARBOR
ONTONAGO
LA POINTE
SAULT SAINTE
BAD RIVER
TWO RIVERS
SAINT PAUL
MISSISSIPPI RIVER
L. MICHIGAN
GALENA
CHICAGO

PART III - GICHIGAMI

THE VOYAGE OF WILLIAM W. WARREN FROM TWO RIVERS TO NEW YORK CITY AND RETURN.... WINTER OF 1853

ALBANY

L. ONTARIO

ROCHESTER
BUFFALO

HUDSON RIVER

NEW YORK CITY

L. ERIE

— *Lakes route: By schooner from La Pointe west on Superior to Sault Sainte Marie, by rail car over the canal, south by steamship on Lake Huron to Detroit, then northeast on Lake Erie to Buffalo, New York. Continuation by rail to Rochester, Albany and the Hudson Valley to Manhattan.*

Chapter 21: Superior

Schooner Algonquin, ca. 1851, southern shore of Lake Superior, Wisconsin Territory

THE NIGHT BROUGHT SNOW, GIVING dogs good purchase on the river trail. At the whitened shore Charlie tucked Warren's trunk and bag into a canoe and paddled him across the Chequamegon strait to Madeline Island. *Monigwunakauning*—The Island of the Golden-Breasted Woodpecker. His birthplace. And his parents' graves.

The shore ice was thin and broken and the open water was flat and silver under a windless fishbelly sky. Like the many crossings Warren had made as a boy, this one began in a birch bark canoe with an Ojibwe on placid waters, his knees on a folded blanket to bank the cold from the lake below. The big birds had all gone south, but he saw a few plovers. Weightless flakes fell on Lake Superior and disappeared. Crusts of ice were beginning to reform as they neared the island. At the dock lay the two-masted Algonquin, a low schooner painted black with her tall sails still furled.

Approaching the island, timbered low and dark, Warren's mind turned again to the indigestible grudge that lay like a lump of sludge in his innards. The words "AMERICAN FUR COMPANY" were still visible on the side of the warehouse.

When his father died, the Company still held its lock on the village and Ramsey Crooks ran it with ruthless efficiency. Warren had never spoken to the profiteer he held responsible for the ruin of his father and his ensuing depression. Lyman Warren never recovered the $25,000 allotted to him by the Saint Peter's Treaty in 1837, a sum Great Buffalo insisted on to pay down Ojibwe trade debts. Instead, the AFC confiscated the money in their name. Crooks refused to negotiate with either his father or Matilda's father, William Aitken, who lost even more. Lyman fought it in court until Marie died. Then he gave it up and carried her body back to the island in an open wagon. Three years later, destitute and insane, he was buried in La Pointe.

The house and outbuildings, the farm his father had built to raise his children, to offer shelter to the early missionaries and to so many Ojibwe in need, were repossessed by the Company and converted to suit their purposes. He and Matilda lived in an agency house on the island when he first began as a government interpreter. Even those times were gone. The La Pointe that stood now before Warren, with its warehouses, the inn, the fisheries, the new dock, and the white houses lining the beach, was foreign to him. He had come back to his boyhood home as if to another country. The dock smelt like salted fish. He felt nothing for it.

Charlie hoisted his bag and trunk on the dock, but would not take payment from him. Instead, he handed Warren a pouch of cooked rice and berries still lukewarm from his morning fire.

"I pray for you," he said. He bid him farewell and turned his canoe back to the mainland.

Warren approached the schooner and asked the sailor loading a last paquet of furs when they intended to sail, and if they would take on a passenger to Sault Saint Marie—The "Soo" as it was pronounced on the lakes.

"Master says we sail at first wind." He looked up at the pines beginning to sway on Moningwana Point. "We'll go presently."

Disappointment and relief struck him at once. He would not see his parents' graves. He would see nobody. He did not expect such a quick departure, but probably it was best. There was nothing left, no turning back. His ancestors were all gone, and his sisters and cousins had moved on, their lives were elsewhere. He had wanted to go to the cemetery, to talk to his mother and father; he had never told them goodbye. But no, he would not be visiting their graves, nor his Ojibwe ancestors, nor his childhood home. His tribute would remain in his memory. And in the act he was determined to accomplish. The boat was ready.

"The Captain then?" He asked. "He's coming up."

Captain John McKay, a tall, black-bearded man, emerged from the hold and sized the younger man up as he stood straight in his beaver hat, his black cloak, long muffler, his bag and small trunk beside him, wrapped again in sailcloth.

"You're the Warren lad, are you not? I knew your father. Sorry you lost him."

"Thank you, Sir. That was a while ago. I'm looking for passage to the Sault. Then on to Buffalo."

"In the dead of winter? There's no one out here now except those daft enough to risk it for the money. We've been lucky so far, but this weather could turn at any time."

"You're doing it. I've seen rough water. I have pressing business in New York."

He had been in only one shipwreck, with his grandfather and brother Truman in a summer squall on the Saint Clair River going into Detroit, nearly 20 years ago. They'd all been rescued from the capsized schooner, *White Pigeon*, but they lost most of their baggage. As an eleven-year-old boy, he was more than a little proud of his ordeal and felt stronger for it. It had made the Warren boys something of a reputation as they began school in Clarkson, New York.

"Suit yourself. We load some furs here, for what it's worth, then take on copper in Ontonogan. We'll sail loaded to the gunwales. There's a bunk in the cabin if you like. Five days to the Sault if all goes well, then you're on your own."

"How much, Sir?"

The Captain eyed the flapping jib and smelled the chilly wind rising.

"No charge for passage in winter. You mind the galley stove and stay out of the way. Prepare to set sail!"

John McKay was reputed in the Sault and throughout the lakes as an unsinkable man who bore no affection for the American Fur Company, commonly known as the AFC or just "the Company". He and Lyman had done business with the AFC at the height of the fur trade before they switched to fisheries. He was an astute and daring sailor and never failed to deliver his cargo. Despite the dozens of shipwrecks counted in recent years, the Algonquin had never foundered. He supplied the distant Lake Superior ports of Copper Harbor, La Pointe and Marquette with flour and supplies in the winter when the populations were near starving. Warren found it reassuring. The Captain, loquacious by calm weather, told him more as they left the little harbor and headed for open waters.

McKay had in fact bought the ship because the owner, the Boston Mining Company, owed him back salary. The AFC, however, had an interest in the ship and was determined to purchase it to replace the Astor, sunk some years earlier. He knew that if it fell into the hands of the Company, he'd never see what was owed him. He ran the boat in winter to Canadian shores, where he was ready to defend it with the help of some armed Irish miners from the Sault. They held off until the AFC caved in and sold him their share of the boat. Since then it had been a worthy investment. He got lucky. He withstood the hard years, then this copper fever struck and times got better.

The Captain related this history while steering the ship through the shallow canal and beyond the sand bar on the eastern shore of the island. Warren, in turn, told him how his own father had been swindled by the AFC, Ramsay Crooks in particular. McKay told him it was Lyman who warned him about the Company's perfidy.

"That's past now, lad. No use in dwellin'."

"Agreed. Move ahead, my father would say."

"I've read the Saint Paul newspapers, ye know. I see you set to writing articles, histories of these Indians. In the *Democrat*."

"That's what I'm bringing to New York. In that chest there. It's a book now."

"Your father got a raw deal. But you've done well for yourself," said McKay. "You've got an education, written for the papers, been elected to the Legislature and made some enemies. Not all can boast as much so young. You'll make more enemies as time goes on."

Warren smiled but said nothing as he heard this praise from a man his father's age. He had learned to temper his youthful spark, to act humble even when proud. Still, he could not help feeling that McKay's attention to his writings and short political career in Saint Paul was somehow a gesture from his father. The worthy accomplishments Warren had achieved in public life, Lyman had never lived to see. Had it been different... But then, he would have seen his son's struggles, his defeats, his failure to help his mother's people, the futility of his efforts to defy the powers that be. Worse, his father might have seen his own failure again, in his son.

He had felt insulted by the Governor's "personal contribution" of five dollars. He should not have accepted it. But after all, he was seeking advances against future sales.

Staring at the disappearing island, he had a fleeting image of Anna Ramsey, her secret and generous gesture on the street in Saint Paul. He could never reveal that gesture to his father, even if were he alive. Not to anyone, for that matter. Inexplicably, she had faith in him. There were a few. He wondered about the conflicting emotions she must have felt. A woman of strong principles, shackled by marital duty to a man who couldn't care less about ethics.

He bundled himself in his cloak, pulled his muffler up and hat down and remained on deck, drinking his tea, watching the forested mainland slowly passing in the distance. The wind picked up from the north-east. McKay, watchful at the helm, pulled close to the wind, shouting orders to his three crewmen. The shoreline seemed darker in the weak light, smoke from the mining camps formed a line above the treetops, thinner now, where the big trees had disappeared after the logging boom. Even the face of the country had changed so since he was a boy. It was scarred now, no longer perfect. And it was still a young country.

The sail to Ontonogan went without incident for the *Algonquin.* They took on half- barrels of copper ore and made for deeper waters around Keweenaw Point. William Warren did not mind the big water, but stayed put in the cabin, tending the stove fire and nodding off with his herbal concoction then sampling the thick black Irish tea, heavily sweetened, that McKay encouraged his crew to drink along with him, claiming it would see them without fail to safe harbor. They ate biscuits and pemmican, a bowl of rice per day. Warren did not fall seasick. Unlike his uncle Truman, who died on the water when still young, seeking medical help for his lungs in Detroit. The wilderness had proved fatal for some Warrens. The deep lake, by its alluring beauty, its vast breadth, its fickle weather, and sudden temper, was just as fatal.

§

Some five miles off the Keweenaw Waterway the schooner hit a squall that threatened to blow them shoreward. Instead of risking the shallows, McKay beat back to open waters as the squall deepened into a storm. The Captain lashed himself to the post and ran his ship back and forth for the entire night with only the jib hoisted and trimmed, an infernal howling in the rigging, never relinquishing the helm as huge icy waves crashed on deck.

Below, water flooded in, drenching the cabin holds. Warren's trunk came undone and sloshed about violently. McKay roared out to secure the cargo.

With the determination of the desperate, tossed like a wet puppet in the cabin, Warren managed to seize the trunk and refasten it to a timber under the deck, out of the water. He was again surprised at his own strength. Now, if only McKay could keep the ship from capsizing....

Well into the morning, the wind abated. A calm set upon them— but the ship rolled and pitched with the short swells. Below decks, shivering and nauseous, Warren retched his rations in a bucket and began to cough blood. His trunk was safe, lashed above his head. He could only hope that the oiled sailcloth had kept his manuscript dry.

By the time the swell allowed anyone to move on the frozen deck, ice had formed on the halyards and whitened John McKay's Mackinac coat and beard, but he stood fast at the wheel. He told Warren to relight the stove and heat some tea, which order he eagerly executed, and drank some of his own tea to settle his lungs. The way McKay put it at dawn, patience was better than luck at sea. He unlashed himself, stretched, gave the helm to the mate, and drank a tin cup of warm black tea.

The rigging was stiff, covered with white ice, and the deck treacherous as the Captain moved forward with an axe and knocked the ropes, winches, and sails free. Warren watched the faces of the crewmen as he worked. Without him, they would surely founder and die. All held shivering to the helm and riggings while McKay gripped a stay and hacked at the ice, the craft lurching and creaking in the swells with no wind or sail to steady their course. Warren felt certain that the man's will alone would prevail and bear them all across the waters.

It was the sight of the birds in the gray dawn, small gulls or guillemots flitting effortlessly from crest to crest, alighting on the topmast, that gave him cause to ponder the arrogance of man's bravest ambitions. The water is not our element. The fish and the birds alone can own the wind and the sea. Without the courage and knowledge of the sailing masters and the ingenious vessels that bore them, all men placed on the waters naked as they were born would perish.

The storm had made Warren feel a deep helplessness, a fear for his life that he had never felt before. He repeated to himself: No, I cannot not die now. It made him chatter and bite his tongue. His herbal tea finally allowed him to drift into a half-sleep, where visions of Matilda kept the specter of death at bay. The schooner pitched and yawled while the lake calmed.

§

A day and night passed before a west wind stirred. To the east the red-orange light of the sun broke through to color the skies and restore hope to the men in the wooden vessel. The Algonquin headed into the lee shelter of Copper Harbor, where they put in and dropped anchor while they completed the de-icing of the sails.

"The weather is still with us," said McKay. "We'll continue on to Sault Saint Marie through the middle of the lake to avoid the shore ice. Mr. Warren, would you be so kind as to make a pot of hot tea for us all?"

The captain slept for an hour or so curled up on a damp bunk. Warren opened his chest to check the state of his papers: the wrapped chapters had weathered the storm. He took a healthy draught of his own brew, lay down wet by the stove, and slept even more soundly than the Captain, for one short hour.

They all slept at intervals after heading out again with the wind shifting slightly out of the southwest. But after they had quit the Keweenaw Peninsula, past what the captain referred to as the Graveyard of the Great Lakes—50 miles of shoals lining the southeast shore of Superior—the wind gradually veered northwest and stiffened, bringing passing squalls, more freezing rain and deeper swells all day, speeding the schooner along through the lifting waves and again into the night, which was finally starry and moonlit beneath scudding silver clouds. At that pace, McKay was content, they would make the 150 nautical miles to Sault Saint Marie by the following night.

"How then will you proceed, Sir?" Warren asked. "Will you attain the Bay, then the harbor to put ashore?"

"There is no putting ashore at this season at the Sault. It's surely blocked with ice. We'll wait for light, if necessary, and come in as close as we can, drop anchor, and they'll send out the sledges and flat boats to unload. The Algonquin has no choice but to remain on the lake, in the clear, until all the ice is broken, and navigation is open. Cargo goes over the river by rail cart now. Until they finish that infernal canal they've been bantering about for over a decade."

"What about Lake Huron? Is it open?"

"What you'll find on the other side, I cannot tell you, Mr. Warren. Last I heard, there were some steamers fool enough to run to Detroit and Buffalo this winter, but few indeed. If I were you, I'd find a sailboat, steam engines be damned. Ain't a master in the lakes knows how to steer one, myself included. They know how to run aground, blow them up or ram them into hell knows what. You saw the *Independence* grounded in Ontonogan. That big prop steamer. One day that one will blow, mark my words. Damnable steamships are getting too big to handle. You may find yourself waiting a month at the Sault waiting for the thaw."

At this dark prospect, Warren's resolve doubled. There was no question of waiting. He was weak, coughing more frequently but trying to ration his indispensable tea, and anxious to get on with this voyage. Above all, he had kept his manuscript dry. His journey was blessed.

§

Things did not happen as the Captain had hoped. After several squalls had passed, the freeze lessened, and they found themselves under slight snow for another day and a night. The swell became longer, the moon lit the silver clouds and produced thousands of flickering lights on the rolling surface of Lake Superior. The heavily laden vessel rocked more gently but advanced more slowly in a weaker wind. Warren remained mostly below decks, tending the fire in the stove. They dried their clothes and strengthened their constitutions with the rice, venison, and canned peaches they had taken on from the mining company in Ontonogan.

The latter part of the Lake Superior crossing was therefore the most pleasant and restful. Warren wrote to his wife and family. This was of course a sign that the voyage was going very well and he expected to be in New York in a couple weeks. He trusted that Matilda would transmit the good news to his sisters, to the Ojibwe friends who would surely pass by to ensure their comfort and ask for news. He would dispatch his letter by the *Algonquin's* return trip, entrusting it to McKay himself.

Well into the morning of the third day on the water, the boat laid anchor among the ice flows forming within view of the Saint Mary's River. Four larger vessels were also moored there, with a small fleet of Mackinac boats picking their way among the flows to take on cargo bound for the harbor. Once McKay's crew had offloaded the *Algonquin's* furs and kegs of copper, Warren shook the master's hand and wished him well, it was one of those boats that took him to the head of the river.

§

He had been here over ten years ago, coming back from the East when it was a village of Sauteur Indians and trappers living at the pace of a trading post. In midwinter, Sault Saint Marie now looked to be abuzz like a swarm of bees. Countless boats were moored to the docks at Saint Mary's River amid stacks of timbers, lumber, and quarried limestone. Hundreds of men were excavating a series of locks skirting the three-quarter mile of rapids connecting Lake Superior side to the flatter river and Lake Huron. The digging made dark pits in the snow-covered worksite.

For centuries, cargo had been portaged and boats dragged along the Canadian side on wooden rails, by ox, horse, and capstan. The big lake was twenty-one feet higher than the four other Great Lakes. Since the opening of the Erie Canal in New York, the country was open to an unstoppable flood of trade and European immigrants. This new canal, connecting Lake Superior, would open the Northwest to a new flow of commerce, mining, big ships, and more immigrants. Excavation was finally underway.

He found a young Sauteur to carry his baggage and show him past cranes and carts and horses, piles of timbers, and dirt-hefting workmen to the office of the mason boss. There he was told that he could get to the farther side of the river by rail cart along with the shipment of copper from the *Algonquin*. Then he could transfer to a steamer in Detroit, bound for Buffalo. If he could find one.

"You can't tell this year," said the taskmaster. "It's too mild, a strange one. It's even warmer further south, but navigation is still officially closed. You could get stranded outside any harbor that won't allow passage. The boats sail at their own risk."

He used the stove to heat another flask of tea and struck out with the Sauteur boy to seek a cart. The boy was surprised to hear him speak Ojibwe. He told him his mother was Ojibwe, from La Pointe. The boy would take no payment from a tribesman.

The sky was almost dark by the time he climbed onto the rail cart, found a place out of the wind between two crates, sat huddled up, and covered himself twice over in his cloak. The cart moved forward. Once again he felt that unusual sensation, first encountered on the train in upper New York when still a boy, of rolling smoothly on iron rails. Traveling along the Sault was a far sight better than by stagecoach, even if the cart was still drawn by horses.

Beyond the harbor master's cabin a clutch of Sauteurs huddled around a fire, women tending the cooking pot, the men staring at the cart rolling past them. Unmoving, like pillars under their blankets, fixed there forever. The boy was with them. Sauteurs, bands of Anishinaabe like the Ojibwe, maintained their home here. Where would they go once this was taken over by commerce?

Warren took another pull at his tea with some hard biscuit and some of Mary's dried fruit, and took stock. His clothes had dried out some at the taskmaster's woodstove. He was hungry, and coughing less. Despite all this rough going, he was in less pain. He attributed this to keeping in motion, going forward. The tea was good too, and it helped him sleep, but now was not the time. He was moving over the Sault, making headway.

§

Coal lamps were being lit, fires were burning, voices shouting and hammers still ringing on steel. As the horse-drawn cart rolled between the moon-white rapids and the dark seam of the future canal, he watched the silhouettes of hundreds of men climbing over timbers and dirt and rock, not unlike an army of ants in the frenetic erection of their hill. It was both admirable and frightful. Day and night they labored, as if nothing could stop them. Nothing would.

At the end of the rail road after the rapids, snow began to fall. He sought shelter for the night at Fort Brady, housing a small garrison on the Saint Mary's River where the quartermaster saw the weakened man's plight and offered him an empty cot in the barracks. There was a modicum of heat as long as one of the men rose to keep the stove burning at night. He emptied his smaller flask into a tin pan, heated it on the stove, and drank it down for his dinner before he slept like a man who had not slept in four days.

He rose at dawn with the soldiers and tramped through the snow to partake of military breakfast. Thus refreshed, he went again to see the quartermaster. There seemed to be no lack of food and supplies for the workers at the Sault, who began searching for their tools under the snow at first light. The quartermaster sent him to a shipping office to find out about passage to Detroit.

The snowfall proved a blessing, as it provided enough depth for a sleigh to carry Warren and two rich-looking men in high hats to the mouth of the river on the Huron side, where lumber and supplies were still being unloaded onto smaller boats, sledges, and carts from the steamer *Albany*, anchored farther out where the ice thinned. From the two men's terse conversation, he gathered that with the beginning of the canal works, workers were still in high demand this winter. The Saint Mary's Falls Ship Canal Company chartered steamers to run supplies and men regularly from as far away as Buffalo.

Another windfall. This could be his passage. He would play his White Man card.

Warren introduced himself to the two gentlemen, an engineer named Augustus Canfield and a businessman by the name of Erastus Corning, who carried a pair of wooden crutches. The first was the chief engineer of the State of Michigan, in charge of building the Canal, and the other was the president of the stock company who supplied and financed, as he put it, "the whole mess". He would have liked to know if Warren was possibly an investor. Who else would be traveling up in this country at this time of year? He could offer him prime stock in a sure thing, as this was only the beginning of this venture. Bold moves ensure bold rewards.

"I heartily agree," Warren said, avoiding the direct question. "The canal is the key to commerce and the development of the Northwest. I've just come up from the mining country on the *Algonquin*, loaded with copper going east. But steamships are needed, and the canal is essential. They'll soon be coming through the locks like salmon in the spring. An investment is quite possible, I shall speak with friends in Saint Paul upon my return from New York, if you allow, possibly to invest as a group."

"Excellent, then. You can contact my office by telegram," said Corning, offering him his business card with an address in Detroit. He then suggested they await the boarding vessel in the comfort of the harbor tavern. "What brings you to New York?"

"A project of my own. I'm going to see several book publishers. Putnam for one, Appleton, and Mr. Redfield, on the recommendation of my editor in Saint Paul, Mr. Robertson. I am a researcher and historian, and have here the manuscript of my *History of the Ojibways*, parts of which were published in the *Minnesota Democrat*, Colonel Robertson's newspaper."

"I declare, quite interesting, Mr. Warren. I don't believe it's ever been written before, am I right? Perhaps by that Schoolcraft fellow?"

"He's one of my sponsors, now that you mention it. His work is capital, but it is not the history. This comes directly from the source.

The old men themselves. I've been many years transcribing their oral traditions. Ojibwemowin was my first language."

"How unusual, and worthy indeed, Mr. Warren," Canfield broke in. "History is in the making as we speak, and it's about time a scholar took up the story of these poor Indians seeking a new place to live. We've been studying a solution to lay out a reservation for them right here, a bit to the north. But tell us, Sir, would you accept to travel with us on the *Albany*?"

Camaraderie comes quickly among men wishing to enjoin others to their cause. By nightfall the three passengers formed the fast and gregarious bond typical of the American temperament—for the time of a steamboat journey. Warren was assured cabin passage on the *Albany* as far as Detroit, and for a modest fare, as both Canfield and Corning were themselves on board as executives of the Company, and there was plenty of room on the steamship, by far more comfortable even than the best hotel in Saint Paul. It would be a pleasure to have an author in their company, and to exchange views for the four days to come. He had won his gamble.

The grand stateroom and dining room of the *Albany* were finished in polished woodwork and brass, well heated by two tiled wood stoves, hung with organdie curtains, abounding with spittoons and parlor lamps with ample berths on the sides for sleeping, although these were empty. Warren had his own cabin away from the churning machinery, as did the rest of the small party since there were no women aboard. In Detroit Harbor, Corning would introduce him to the master of a steamer bound for Buffalo, also in his Company's hire for business purposes. They would run all winter, as long as the canal project needed men and supplies.

Aboard ship, Warren felt decidedly better, attributing his improved form to the good food and company he found among his newfound traveling companions and the men that accompanied them, all of them educated, skilled technicians and engineers. As men unaccompanied by women, they had a tendency to enjoy their Tennessee Bourbon and brandies and smoke cigars late into the night, which pleasures the younger man was forced to decline due to his ongoing "cure". Warren slipped into a role familiar to him, becoming the young intellectual of the company, recounting Ojibwe traditions and tales of fur trapping in the wilderness at the dinner table, while during the day he remained sleeping and writing in his comfortable cabin. The cook was amenable to his using the galley to make his tea.

He used the time to begin an introduction to his *History* and catch up on his correspondence. In such luxury and comfort, he yielded to the desire to write a letter he had been contemplating for days:

> *Dear Mrs. Ramsey,*
>
> *I take this time aboard the steamship Albany, bound for Detroit, to reassure you that due to the still clement weather my progress toward the East is excellent and that your investment on behalf of the new Cultural Society is indeed protected and well on its way to fruition. Steamer travel, as you know, is comfortable and faster than ever before. You will perhaps be so kind as to relate this news to Mr. Le Duc, to whom I shall post this message at the Detroit Harbor, trusting him to lay it in your hands.*
>
> *At the hotel at Sault Sainte Marie, I had the good fortune of meeting two gentlemen, both with references in New York, who occupy high executive positions in the enterprise currently building the new Canal. We spend much of our time in discussion of matters of History, the march of Civilization, Education, etc. and find we have much in common. They have afforded me not only passage on this their chartered vessel for a modicum of the real price, but assured me that they can refer me to business associates in the City susceptible of assisting me in my research and of further investing in such ventures as the Cultural Society of Minnesota. What was yesterday the wilderness is now the New World. These gentlemen are also acutely aware that the advancement of transportation and the increasing floodtide of immigrants (that I have been able to witness on this voyage), will trigger*

a land rush in our Territory, and they are keen to be in the vanguard. I have guaranteed them introductions upon my return to Saint Paul.

Your kind generosity and intellectual integrity will indeed be rewarded, Chère Madame, and for this I thank you again, this time in my own hand, for your clairvoyant gesture. You have inspired me to even greater deeds by putting steam in my sails!

Your friend and servant,
W.W.Warren

Chapter 22: Erie

HE STOOD BEFORE THE POSTMASTER'S OFFICE in Detroit harbor for the third time since his arrival. He could not bring himself to post his letter to Anna Ramsey. Mulled over repeatedly before being committed to paper, he'd never got it right. He had been searching for a way to lighten the tone and to suggest a certain familiarity—or perhaps, intimacy—without undue presumption.

He had never written a letter to a lady of society. He had written letters only to men, or to his sisters or the one recently dispatched to his wife, to whom he had never previously written because he and Matilda had always lived under the same roof, with few exceptions for his work. Again considering the last line of the letter, his somewhat silly play on words seemed appropriate. But the word "inspired" made him sweat.

Was this intimacy with the wife of the Governor, with whom he had exchanged nothing more than ideas and conversation, appropriate at all? She had, in Saint Paul, expressed her utmost faith in him and handed him a sum of money in support of his publication. A woman of judgment and means, decidedly a modern thinker. Finally, he hung all pretense, wrote the sentence, signed, and sealed the missive and addressed it to Le Duc's Bookstore. It would after all remain their secret.

He paid for a 10-cent US stamp and slid it to the postmaster under the grate. The rate had doubled because he was more than 300 miles from Saint Paul. By the lakes, more than 1,000 miles. With some 700 or more to go to New York City. Worlds apart.

Workers had cut a passage through the ice on the Saint Clair River above Detroit toward the southern exit. This allowed passage for the *Albany* coming in, and now an outgoing canal for the *Globe*, the newer steamer hired by Corning to sail to Buffalo and back. The boats at harbor formed a frozen web of masts and riggings as thick as the pines north of Warren's home, but few of the boats were moving. Only the *Globe*, under special hire by the President of the Saint Mary's River Canal Company, was loading firewood for the run on Lake Erie. The ice met a leaden line at the horizon—open waters. Dockers loaded cords of wood, barrels of copper, sacks of grain and milled wheat onto pallets for the steam cranes to hoist them into the holds.

Erastus Corning himself trotted along the dock on his crutches to introduce Warren to Captain Jones. He was paying the Captain and the Buffalo shipowners top price to sail throughout the winter and haul back shipments of tools manufactured at his factory in Albany. He also introduced his laborlooker, G. F. Fowles, whom he was dispatching to recruit men for the workforce at the Canal. The cities and environs of Upper New York State abounded in immigrant labor willing to travel for the good wages farther west. The Welsh and Cornish were good workers with a penchant for mining, and they had only two years to complete the canal.

"Speed is everything in this day and age," Corning declared while checking his gold pocket watch, "If not money." Captain Jones seconded this opinion, estimating that with fair seas they would make Buffalo in less than 24 hours.

Warren was given a first-class cabin on the upper deck and charged fifteen dollars. Erastus Corning gave him his card and a note with business addresses in Buffalo, Albany and New York, plus the names of two men in that city. "Both half-million men", who could be interested in investment opportunities, especially land, in the Northwest. He bade him goodbye, good luck with his publication, and told him to wire his office when it was released.

"Wire, Sir?"

"The telegraph, Mr. Warren. Instantaneous. Covers all the Eastern cities now, over twenty-five thousand miles of copper wire. We'll soon have it running to Chicago, even Saint Paul. It'll put pen and ink out of business, not to mention the Pony Express. Give it a try."

He tipped his top hat and bounded off on his crutches. Corning was a man in a hurry and in touch with the times. There was no doubt the canal would be completed on time. The flood of landseekers and commerce would multiply tenfold.

§

For the first two nights, the *Globe* remained at dock while the crew and steam cranes loaded barrels, bales, lumber, and cordwood until the hold was full and stable. Even steerage below decks held freight, as there were no third-class passengers and the 30-man crew slept near the forecastle. Light snows came and went, the ice stayed at bay, nearing the thaw point then freezing again at night. Warren's comfortable cabin was usually reserved for women traveling with their husbands during the clement months. This was a bachelors' run for business purposes, affording gentlemen select treatment.

He used his cabin to rest, writing in the berth by the small window, his warm tea never far, ensconced in a cold but dreamy cocoon while the harbor outside bustled with construction and freight movement. Detroit was now a teeming city, industrious, preparing for the future. This was no longer his to do. His mission, as historian, was to retrace the past.

A mixture of excitement and fatigue sometimes made it difficult to concentrate as he labored over his introduction. He wrote several drafts of his opening paragraphs, thinking of the scholars who would read it and what its effect might be. His mind would cloud, and he would sleep. He must be tired. Sleep, a loyal ally. His coughing finally abated with the comfort afforded by the steamboat. When he woke, he wrote the introduction again:

Preface
The red race of North America is fast disappearing before the onward resistless tread of the Anglo-Saxon. Once the vast tract of country between the Atlantic sea- board and the broad Mississippi, where a century since roamed numer-

ous tribes of the wild sons of Nature, but a few—very few, remnants now exist. Their former domains are now covered with the teeming towns and villages of the "pale face" and millions of happy freemen now enjoy the former home of these unhappy and fated people.

Do we not owe them our sympathy and attention? Are we not now the possessors of their former inheritance? Are not the bones of their ancestors sprinkled through the soil on which are now erected our happy homesteads?...

Hole-in-the-Day's words. But it was perhaps too dramatic, too grandiose. No, it was not grandiose enough. It was chiding. It was a plea. He was drowsy again. He lay down and fell off to sleep, seeking the image of the wisp of black hair on the nape of Anna Ramsey's neck.

§

On the 3rd of March a towboat cleared the cut through the moving harbor ice to make way for the steamer's passage to open water. The *Globe*, like the *Albany*, was a long, low sidewheeler with one stack and one mast, and could carry 6,000 barrels and up to 300 passengers in season. She was a moneymaker, as Great Lakes tours were beginning to attract curious Easterners. Even more elegant than the Albany in her appointments, it suited Warren perfectly to travel again with all the accouterments of civilization. The food, served at the Captain's table in the company of Mr. Fowles and a handful of men working for the Canal Company, was even better than on the previous leg of his journey. Succulent sauces napping the Chicago beef and pork from Ohio, fresh bread made from western-grown flour, and preserves and sweets from food purveyors in Detroit and farther south, bound for the curious markets of New York and Europe.

Once on the open water, Captain Jones showed his passengers what his ship could do on a full head of steam, pushing her to 12 knots with gunwales shuddering and the big pistons rocking the timbers. One of the younger passengers, curiously named Mr. Helm, an outsider by all indications, suggested they slow the boat to 10 knots, save on fuel and get to Buffalo a bit later. He was in no hurry. Had there not been over 200 disasters last year on the Lakes, steamers colliding, burning, and exploding?

"No worries on this ship," Jones reassured them all. "She's been inspected to the smallest bore and beam, certified by the government as constructed to industry standards, she can run with the best and never get tired." They continued on thus until nightfall, when the Captain slowed it down to a more reasonable speed, so as not to "upset the fish".

The conversation at table was not so stimulating as on the *Albany*, centering around land prices in the rising new jewel of the West, Chicago, where fortunes were apparently waiting to be made. It was suggested that no city would ever outshine Saint Louis once the railroad lines were up and running this spring. Some liked Cleveland, the more established link to the eastern cities, and one man suggested that Detroit would be the hub as the center of industry due to its harbor facilities. When Warren predicted that the far western tip of Lake Superior would be the site of two great harbor cities serving the entire Northwest as soon as the Canal was opened, one gentleman remarked that would never happen until the government finally got the Indians out and made the country safe for commerce and farming.

Warren asked, "Where do they expect to put them after they take away their homelands and hunting grounds?"

This seemed to cause a moment's reflection. The Canal men simply nodded, chewing their meat. The slim outsider named Helm, sporting a trimmed mustache, slicked back hair and a gray suit jacket over a florid red waistcoat, finally spoke up, in his slow southern drawl.

"Drive 'em west over the Mississip'. Andy Jackson got that done down south over twenty years ago, and if he was still around, he'd know how to do it up here."

The finality of this truth about the famous Indian killer signaled the close of the dinner discussion. Jackson's popularity as president approached adulation throughout the country.

Manifest Destiny was more than ever the doctrine of the whites in power and Jackson was not yet cold in his grave. Warren, at this moment acutely conscious that his Indian features could not escape notice, reflected on his father's words: Old Hickory was man you did not deride in the company of businessmen or soldiers. For some reason the reserved demeanor of the canal men, even George Fowles himself, struck him as that of experienced soldiers. Officers, certainly. Notwithstanding their inbred loyalties and military educations, they ventured very few opinions. They carried themselves with reserve, soberly even when drinking, and seemed unfailingly in tacit agreement. Helm, on the other hand, did not have the stuff of an officer. He drank freely and was rank with opinions. And he looked at Warren suspiciously.

Warren withdrew to his quarters and attempted to write, then to sleep, but both proved futile. His mind kept going back to the words of Hole-in-the-Day the Elder—*the bones and the blood of our fathers...* and to other matters that did not serve his purpose. No man could stop death, so he trained his thoughts to wander along more pleasant avenues.

Later that evening he rose to heat his flask of tea in a pan of hot water on the parlor stove. Large glowing oil lamps hung by brass chains over the bar and gaming table, casting a yellow light in the warmth of the wood-paneled parlor.

Four men were settled in for a few rounds of cards. Mr. Fowles the laborlooker was present with two of his party—Canal Company men, both wearing thick long-tailed coats and heavy boots—along with the dandyish Mr. Aloycius Helm who had announced himself as a purveyor of insurance and real estate. A bottle of Tennessee whiskey was well on its way to depletion when one of the canal party retired and Fowles asked Warren if he took pleasure in the game of poker. Reasonable stakes, just for the sake of sitting in the warm parlor. Warren always felt welcome at a card table, but he was conscious of something different: it was the first time he'd sat down at a card table with all white men, invited into their club.

He sat down in the vacant chair, with Fowles to his left and Helm to his right. The dandy held a cold thin cigar in his teeth. He offered Warren whiskey and when he declined, Helm took back the glass, poured drinks for himself and the two others and slurred over his cigar, "First time I seen a native won't take a drink. New man deals."

This was one he would have to watch. Without looking at Warren, Helm set the deck in front of him and fetched a fresh bottle from behind the bar. The game was dealer's choice, dollar ante. Warren dealt five-card draw and won the first round, passing the deck to Fowles, who dealt seven-card stud. Warren, the new man, won another hand. The game was quick at first, the coins ringing and flowing first right then left, then to Warren. Then it slowed and Helm, dealing seven-card draw, upped the ante. There were now several newly printed Railroad Bank bills on the table in ten- or twenty-dollar denominations. It was comfortable. Fowles, more taciturn than the reckless young Helm, soberly dealt five-card draw. Helm on his deal upped the ante to five dollars and switched back to seven cards.

Warren concentrated, sipped his tea, and told himself that when he began to lose, he'd quit. He felt uneasy at the table with the limited amount of funds he had in reserve. He'd been in high-stakes games before, won as much as five hundred dollars playing big games with the Winnebago, then lost most of it. But he had never lost it all. This time he could not afford to lose anything. And there was this Southerner next to him…. By all rights he should not be playing poker in his situation, but there he was.

So far, he and Fowles were ahead, along with the fourth, a big bewhiskered man who spoke even less than Fowles. Helm's stack of coins was low, he was dealing seven-card again and helping himself to whiskey. Warren began to cough. Slowly at first, then a convulsion overtook him and he had to excuse himself, rise and use the spittoon at the bar. He stood bent over, wheezing with his hand on the rail, wiping the blood trace. At the table by the stove, the play had come around to him, the three men were waiting. He found his breath and stood straight. The rest of the parlor was empty.

"I'll be damned, the Chief's a lunger," said Helm. "Never seen an Injun lunger. Ain't gonna fold on me afore I get my winnins back, now, are ye, Chief? Set down here and take a drink. Tennessee whiskey'll cure what you got."

Warren said nothing. He took a draught of his tea and put ten dollars in the growing pot. He was dealt a king of diamonds. Helm continued to deal, Warren took two more cards down— both kings— and won the hand. The pot held seventy dollars, mostly in large and freshly printed Railroad Bank bills—honored at every bank between here and New York, Fowles assured them.

The loss seemed to shut Helm up for a while. Two rounds later the dandy was still losing, and audibly complaining of the cold. The stove was firing but the rest of the room grew colder. The whale oil lamp burned bright above the table, seemingly bringing more clarity to Warren's vision. The cards were crisper, the colors brighter. Good cards were coming his way and he felt like skinning Helm alive.

"Any you gennlemen ever been on a Mississippi riverboat?" Helm asked, genial. "Hell, they make this one look like a wigwam."

Warren felt no inclination to respond. Apparently neither did the others.

"*Queen of Natchez, Southern Belle*. Palaces, done up pretty as a statehouse. And women, music, minstrels, them darkies dancin'. Ever seen them high yaller girls dancin' in Saint Louis? You ever seen that? Did ye? Almost white, with just a touch of pepper. Down there the niggers even mix with the injuns. Now why you think that is, Chief?"

Warren eyed him. "A common enemy."

"Two tens to you, Mr. Helm," said Fowles, breaking the tension. Helm persisted.

"Had me an octoroon whore once. Part injun. Some o' them Chickasaw down there black as niggers. Sheeit, they could be niggers. Once it's in their blood, they never get rid of it."

Helm looked under his hand. He was showing a nine and ten of clubs. He threw in the rest of his stack, twelve dollars. Warren stayed on the strength of his two jacks up. Fowles, with an ace and king facing up, stayed. The fourth man, with two tens, folded. It was up to Helm, who threw a folded sheet of paper on the pile.

"Deed to forty acres on the Illinois River, southwest of Chicago harbor. Worth two hundred last year, four hundred by spring. I'll make it twenty for you, just to test your hand, Chief... What was it? Walker? Cloudwalker?" Helm chuckled and took more whiskey. They all looked at the deed, then put it back in the center.

"Warren is my name. William Warren. I'll see your twenty."

"Oh, that's right. Got white blood in ye. Sets my mind at ease. Wouldn't want to get scalped now, would I?" The gambler snickered but eyed Warren sideways.

He anted up and still had maybe one hundred dollars in front of him in bills and coin. It was close but worth it. Fowles followed suit. Helm dealt two cards down, looked amusedly around the table and showed his hand. He was drawing to a straight flush, but missed his bluff. He had two pair, eights and nines, but Warren showed three jacks. The dandy scowled at him, Fowles then showed his full house, aces and kings, and reached to take the pot.

William Warren said, "Gentlemen, if you'll excuse me, I'll retire now," and began to gather his money. He was slightly ahead of himself, no regrets.

Helm's eyes watered at them as he darkened to the color of spoiled meat. He rose and took out a short-barreled, five-shot pocket revolver commonly called a Baby Dragoon, waving it now at Warren, now at Fowles.

"You cocksuckers is con-spy-ring agin' me, ain't ye? No better than this fuckin' injun here. Ye done stole my property and I'll now have it back!" He tottered, drooled, wiped his spittle, and cocked his gun.

Warren's reaction was peristaltic. His boot heel hit Helm sideways at the knee. The Southerner buckled, the pistol shifted in his hand and shot a hole in the table, sending the deed, bills and coins flying in the smoke. Before he could recock, a second shot exploded, hitting Helm square in the chest and propelling him ten feet backwards spurting blood to crash against a stack of chairs, where he sprawled and quietly bled out. The shot was so loud it set all ears ringing.

In the swirling cloud of powder and cigar smoke, Warren tried to breathe more slowly. The fourth man rested his heavy firearm on the table and looked at Fowles, who nodded. It was a Colt Walker .44 caliber revolver, a specialist's gun. He let it lie there.

The Captain's mate came running and saw Helm dead on the floor with a red hole in his chest big as a fist. A pool of blood was spreading underneath him. He looked at the men, tacitly asking for an explanation.

"This sonofabitch shot at me," said Fowles. "Benton here stopped him before he could kill us all. A bad loser, drunk to boot. Mr. Warren is our witness. And the reason I'm still alive."

The Captain came in next and observed the corpse, the three men seated, and the bullet hole in the table. Nothing had moved since the shooting. Two crewmen dragged the body out and proceeded to scrub the blood. The Captain took a brief statement and the card players pocketed their money. Fowles took up the deed and by way of thanks, split the cash in the last pot with Warren and the man named Benton. Nothing more was said of it. Fowles was the big winner, but William Warren was two hundred dollars richer, mostly in Railroad Bank bills.

The Captain held the dead man's wallet, watch, papers, and pistol along with a small tin and sack of extra powder and balls, hefting it in his hand. Fowles asked to see the dead man's papers. He looked at them, gave them back to the Captain, walked over and tossed the purported Chicago land deed, which he had won fairly, into the stove.

"Not worth the paper it's written on. It's in his own handwriting. I suspected as much. A con man."

"Why did you allow it on the table?" The Captain asked.

"I had better cards down than he was showing. Mr. Warren showed a strong hand too. I thought to shut the game down one way or the other, but got a better deal in the end. Helm lost all around. Fool wanted to lose his money, nobody disagreed. We owe Mr. Warren a vote of thanks. His quick resolve gave Mr. Benton a clear shot at this lunatic."

Captain Jones was still weighing the bag of shot in his hand.

"You have no sidearm, Mr. Warren? And you're bound for New York City?"

"That's correct, Sir. No use for sidearms."

"You defend these men and yourself against an armed drunk at a card table, and you have no use for a handgun?"

"I've never owned one. Or needed one. Fire brings fire, I reckon."

"You needed one tonight. What if these gentlemen had been unarmed as well? There's worse than his kind in the City. You take this." He handed him the pistol— surprisingly light— along with the tin, the powder and bag of shot. The gunmetal was blue-black, unengraved but for the serial number and "Colt/Patent" stamped below the cylinder, with a brass and silver- plated trigger guard. The barrel, about five inches long, was octagonal, the grip of varnished walnut. Utilitarian.

"I wouldn't know what to do with it, Captain."

Fowles spoke up: "Mr. Benton will show you in the morning. Nothing to it. We'd all feel better about you wandering around on the Bowery if you had some protection."

"But what about the authorities?" Asked Warren. He found the attention of these men flattering. The gun was still warm. "Won't the police want it?"

"I am the authority on my ship," said the Captain. "You keep that close by."

They all nodded curtly, avoiding handshakes which seemed unfitting given the dead man just carried out. They went to retire as the crewmen scrubbed out the dark stain on the parlor floor. It was a gentleman's parting.

In his berth, Warren ruminated on the killing. It was ironic that the man who shot the loudmouth was called Benton, the name of his home county where he won the legislative election in 1850, then the next year lost his seat to grafters. That set him thinking about the Warren curse again, but he pushed it out of his mind. There was no curse, just fate. Flat Mouth had told him he was a Crane descendant, destined to speak, his time would come. It was a sign. Getting to New York, publishing, it all seemed a sure thing now.

Indeed, his luck was changing. Maybe there was something working for him after all. He now owned a larger cash reserve and a firearm. He wondered how in hell he was going to carry that around. He fell asleep late, but appeased.

From the back, he watched her neck, the asymmetry between the shift of her shoulders as she walked and her evenly balanced head, the delicate chin line, the smooth muscles curving up her nape, and the loose black strands falling away from her upswept hair. She asked him if he'd like a glass of water.

He awoke to morning light feeling heavy, his nerves jangled, weak. There was a knock on his door. A steward stood there with a clean basin, a bar of soap, a clean towel, and a large pitcher of hot water. To what did he owe such luxuries? He accepted, and used it to bathe summarily and shave in his cabin.

Despite the galley coffee served at breakfast, he was untalkative as were the rest of the men. Only after a cupful of his warm tea did he begin to feel right, at least right enough for a sick man on the lakes in the middle of winter. With the kettle of water on the parlor stove, he made himself a fresh flask for the next leg of the trip, by rail. He had enough herbs for a few more brews, but was running low on the maple sweetener. He would write a note to Charlotte, asking her to send more of Julia's mixture, by express, to Doctor Trall's address on Laight Street in New York City. Normally in winter this might take a month or more, but if he sent it back to Detroit on the *Globe*, it would speed things up. A shame there was no telegraph service yet in Saint Paul. He brought out his writing materials which always gave him comfort, making him feel productive, moving ahead.

He wrote the note to Charlotte, then dozed and had a brief resurgence of the dream that had visited him the previous night, about the glass of water. Waking, he contemplated another letter to send back immediately, this one to Anna Ramsey. She might enjoy a brief missive about his progress on the voyage. But he hemmed and hawed and finally did not write it. The steward came again to his cabin and announced that they would approach Buffalo in another two hours. With him was the helpful Mr. Benton, who said if he wanted to shoot that gun, it was time.

The specialist Benton was a retired Army Captain in the hire of the Canal Company as bodyguard to Mr. George Fowles during his labor search in New York State. He showed Warren how to clean and reload the small revolver using one of his pencils and the cylinder pin as a rammer, applying a touch of grease from the tin to the shots. Although Benton's big hands dwarfed the pistol butt, Warren could get a reasonably secure grip on it. Correct loading was an exacting process, almost scientific. The dosage of powder, the tamping, seating the greased ball. It held the novice's interest more than the shooting itself, which they did on deck at 25 feet from a tin can set on the rail, neither man hitting the target. The little Baby Dragoon made a flat popping sound, not wholly satisfying, and one of the caps fizzled and misfired. Benton finally drew his .44 and blew the can out of sight. The big gun made a painful roar and a shock wave that Warren felt on his face and inside his chest. Benton showed him how to clean the little pistol and charged it again.

"Use this one up close," he said, handing him the loaded gun with the safety pin engaged. Benton had a way of never looking directly into the eyes of a man he was talking to. He looked around him, as if looking at nothing at all, or away in the distance.

"Aim low, it'll shoot high. You'll be all right. Just don't show it at the wrong time."

§

They were approaching the frozen crust covering the lake shore around Buffalo. It was snowing lightly from a sky the color of the ice. The *Globe* slowed to a crawl while canoes and tugs cleared a path through the breakup, to bring the steamer in to thicker ice cover. Warren stood wrapped in his cloak and peered across to the city of Buffalo, where its whitened hills, dark buildings and smokestacks could be seen about two miles distant. The last time he had made this approach, sixteen years ago as a boy with his grandfather, the schooner took almost three full days in clear summer weather to cross Lake Erie. This time they had left Detroit just 20 hours ago. With his grandfather, they traveled up the Erie Canal in a packet boat to Brockport, then by wagon to Clarkson—another three days moving at the speed of a walking horse. This time, in a day and a half, the railroad would be taking Warren to the limit of the continent, to New York City, and to what the Anishinaabe called the Great Salt Water, the ancestral home that the People had not seen in perhaps twenty generations. The Indians manning their canoes through the ice here were of the same stock, Algonquins. The canoes were the same as those in the lakes, those in which he had traveled as a boy, unchanged for those twenty generations and more. Speed, Erastus Corning had said, is everything.

Four other steamers and a schooner were anchored close to the ice fringe. The surface was snow-covered, and thick enough here to support sledges and horse trains for unloading. Warren thanked the Captain and disembarked by ladder to be transported ashore by sleigh in the company of the canal men. Their trunks and baggage and freight, consisting mainly of copper ore in barrels, were hauled in on flatbeds by two-horse teams.

Finally, heaved atop a pile of bales like a sack of grain, was a rolled-up and rope-tied package that contained the corpse of Mr. Aloycius Helm, a man who had declared himself in no hurry to reach Buffalo. He had apparently shown the company his Baby Dragoon revolver at the wrong time.

Chapter 23: Buffalo

A FOREST OF SHIPS STOOD frozen in the waters of Buffalo harbor, their riggings still rigid with ice. Beyond, the city's dark buildings loomed large and stalwart in the snow flurry, hiding a maze of streets in which an unwitting traveler could get lost.

Warren accepted an invitation to share a fiacre to a hotel known to George Fowles and Captain Andrew Benton. Not wanting to be taken for a bumpkin, he tempered his enthusiasm but gazed, wide-eyed and dumbstruck, at the city's blocklike monoliths, their arrogant urban temperament, and the harangue of the city that marked the westernmost point of his country's most advanced and civilized state. Nature was in retreat; he was far from the wilds of his homeland. Everywhere he looked was evidence of the hand of man.

High building facades made corridors of the avenues, towering over the few attending trees, separated by cobbled streets cleared of snow by workers making way for coaches and a horse-drawn tram filled with men bound for business meetings, women on their way to gatherings and shopping errands in the city's well-stocked boutiques. For Easterners, Buffalo represented the gateway to the Great Lakes and the West, but in the reverse direction, for a man coming from the fringe of the wilderness, the city was a first reminder that the East held the country's history and culture, the gateway to Europe and the modern world. In Warren's country, the old Northwest, the territories were striving to become part of it.

The driver took them past the Eagle Street Theatre and the Metropolitan, advertising an upcoming play with a certain Miss Albertine, *A Husband at Sight*. He had never heard of Miss Albertine and worse, had never seen a stage production except once as a boy, one summer when a traveling show—a circus really—passed through Clarkson, his grandfather's town upstate. The train would soon pass near there, but he had neither the time nor the desire to return. His grandparents were gone, and he had not kept in touch with his uncle Henry—any family he had left there was scattered. His home was now in Two Rivers, his sisters and cousins nearby, an entire world away. He had left his family standing before the cabin only three weeks ago.

This voyage was otherwise propitious, he must move on. The New York and Erie Railroad, since the previous year, now connected many shorter routes from west to east, through the Burned-over region of the state—so called because of its revivalist history, which he knew well from his earlier years as a student at Oneida. Further on in Albany, the trains connected south with the Hudson River Valley rail networks all the way to the big city. Messrs. Fowles and Benton would be taking the same railroad to Albany after their business in the region, stopping upstate to tend to their recruiting mission. Another thing he would have to do in New York: take in a stage production. Perhaps a concert. He would visit museums, libraries, galleries, and bookstores where his work would soon be displayed. He would meet and discuss with the cultured literati.

For their stay in Buffalo, Fowles recommended the newly rebuilt American Hotel near the city center, from which Warren could reserve a coach to the new Erie Street Terminal the morning. The railroad connections now ensured a continuous line to New York City. He would be there in twenty-five hours, a far cry better than the six days by packet boat on the canal, and infinitely more comfortable— some had convertible sleeping accommodations, even dining cars, and vendors sold fresh food at stations along the way.

"The rails will put the Erie Canal out of the passenger business," Fowles predicted. "Well then, what about the Canal over the Sault?" Warren wondered.

"Lake passage is imperative up north. Shipping mainly, ore and lumber. But the railways will soon cover the continent. All the way to San Francisco. Gold, farming, a new life for the masses. The canal is another kind of investment. Necessary for commerce, industry."

The fiacre deposited them before the imposing hotel, a five-story building taking up a city block, where their baggage was handled by three uniformed porters, all of the Negro race. One elderly black man impeccably dressed seemed to command the team, giving orders and recommendations. It reminded Warren, looking around, that these black people were all freedmen here in New York State, where slavery was abolished in 1827—a decade before he came to the Oneida Institute. They all carried themselves proudly. He felt a moment of awe that the principles he had learned under the tutelage of Beriah Green were in action here, as if in a new country where black people were free in a free society, or at least this part of it. He also noticed that there was not a red man to be seen in the lobby, only himself, a mixed-blood. And he was entering the hotel with a pair of white men.

Fowles showed the party to the front desk. He appeared to be on a first-name basis with the heads of staff, all white by contrast, and all delighted to see him and his guests. They proposed valet services, the barbershop, heated bathing rooms in the basement, a water closet on every floor, the latest papers rushed to their room, catering and room service with coffee and strudels to tide them over until dinner, a flock of niceties that assailed Warren's ears like deer flies. He refused it all politely.

However, feeling flush from the previous night's card game, he decided to do as the canal men did and book a good single room on the second floor. Fowles took his usual suite. André at the reception desk would also book their train tickets, first class, and hold Warren's for tomorrow morning, along with the taxi. The saloon was at their disposal, the restaurant was open at seven, the new French chef was excellent and very popular, so they had better reserve. Seven-thirty would be fine, à la française. George Fowles asked Warren if he found this all agreeable and to his liking. Warren said it was perfect. Such were the just rewards of an arduous winter voyage by the northern lakes. He would rest up.

Once in his room, he found a servant in the hall and had hot water brought up for a more thorough wash and shave. He did not feel like leaving his room. He brought out his writing materials and his drafted preface, nearly completed but still needing work, a touch here and there, and set it all on the table. He looked it over, standing, and told himself this would be a good place to work. He should get to it. But he did not. It was not yet formed in his mind.

Perhaps he should dispatch some letters. But no, aside from the one he almost wrote then abandoned, to Mrs. Ramsey, he had no desire to recontact his home. It would wait. There would be time in the train. A knock announced the arrival of his hot water.

The room servant, this time girl, dark-skinned, perhaps Métisse, but young judging from her light and fluid movements as she crossed the room and deposited a pitcher noiselessly on the marble washstand. Then she turned and opened two brass wall grates, letting warm air waft into the room. Warren experienced for the first time the innovation of central heating.

She stood to one side and tightened her woolen shawl, covering her hands folded at her waist, large eyes cast downward. Yes, she was a Métisse. Creole? From the islands far south. African, surely, and maybe part white, maybe something else… He reflected a moment before grasping the purpose of her subservient attitude, to which he was not at all accustomed, especially in Upstate New York. He was even embarrassed; the girl was awaiting instructions.

As if to comply, he gave her a rolled bundle and asked her to please have his linen laundered, his spare shirt and cravat cleaned and pressed. She barely looked up at him, but by her smooth face, full lips, and delicately curved brow, she was very young. Her eyes, luminous but shaded, told a different story. An older story. Her face was expressionless, her glance furtive and at the same time self-contained. The girl, or woman, nodded and left without a word.

He had never witnessed such deference, such self-effacement. She gave the impression that she would rather be invisible.

The hotel was vast, with servants' quarters on the upper floors, ample crisp linen, the decoration tasteful if slightly overdone, and far more luxurious than any accommodation he had benefited from in Saint Paul—the best of which would have been Henry Rice's American House where his entire family had two stove-heated rooms. Here he was alone, and the room was wallpapered, plush, bright from the high curtained window, and bigger than the suite he was afforded as a Territorial Legislator. He found the heating quite comfortable. It relaxed him, made his breathing less laborious, and afforded a general sense of well-being. It would cost him five dollars, according to the posted rates. He would indeed join Fowles and Benton for dinner downstairs, and by God, he would invite them to be his guests. He took a long draught of his sweet tea, lukewarm but passable from the heat by the vent, and fell fast asleep.

§

He woke much later to a soft knocking, most likely room service, just in time to dress for dinner. It was nearly dark. He rose and felt his way groggily to the door. He had a phrase in his mind, for his preface, but there was not sufficient light to write it down, so he tried to hold it there in his head. He would arrive in New York very soon; the book must be ready.

He stood straighter when he opened the door to the lighted hallway. It was the same woman-girl, without her shawl, uniformed in gray and white, with her hair hidden under a white turban-like cap. She held his pressed linen in one arm, and in the other hand a lighted candle in its brass holder. The flame reflected twice in her dark pupils as, this time, she looked at him directly, elongating her finely muscled neck. In this light, her face was darker, rounder, and reflected the aura of a sculpted mask, lit by her eyes and a slight rose tint of her lips.

He motioned her in, perhaps overly politely, as he was again slightly embarrassed to be waited on like this. She lay his folded clothes at the foot of the bed and lit the gas lamps on the walls. Her long forearms reflected the light like satin. The uniform was small for her strong shoulders, more obviously when she reached up to light the lamps. When she stood again wordlessly, he put a coin in her hand, apprehending the lighter beige of her palms, the pink nails, the soft texture unmarred by manual work. She bowed, thanked him with a nod, and left quickly.

He had never seen a human being quite so purely, if coldly, beautiful. He had never been south. He had known Negroes only at Fort Snelling, years ago as a boy, and at Oneida where he had assisted runaways on their way to Canada. But never one like this. She seemed from another world. In New York State, there were no slaves. There were only free black women in Buffalo. Or was free the appropriate word? He would have liked to talk to the young servant woman, to know her story, to tell her his. He felt they were somehow connected.

§

Precisely at 7:30 Warren walked into the dining room where mirrors were strategically placed to reflect the gaslight wall fixtures and magnify the shine, the ornate decor and the elegance of the company enjoying the fare. The uniformed staff, as in the lobby, was made up mostly of black people, both women and men, with obviously professional training. He did not see the young chambermaid. Perhaps she was assigned only to service in the rooms.

Fowles and Benton were seated at a round table removed from the central area, far from any of the large windows giving onto the avenue outside, where snow continued to fall lightly, lit by glowing streetlamps. The tramway and prams continued their rounds as workers cleared the streets. Men and women busied themselves with Buffalo society's evening activities: dining, visiting, concerts and theatre-going. The Maître D' greeted Warren with a rapid smile and called a waiter over to show him to his table.

He passed, as he entered the dining room, one table where a powerfully built man with a strong, dark, clean-shaven chin and brick-like brow—fine-featured with a shiny mass of black hair— was seated in company of two white men. By his dress, elegance and demeanor, and the ease with which he addressed his interlocutors, Warren deduced that here was a man of Negro or mixed origin on equal social footing with the white guests accompanying him. All three appeared successful, wealthy even. Perhaps all businessmen.

But he was the only black person seated and was served, unlike the other men, exclusively by Negro staff who addressed him with great deference. An anomaly in this room and visibly aware of it, his magnetism attracted some stares, not a few from women. People talked about him in hushed voices as if pointing out a public figure with the potential for scandal.

The restaurant was filling up. It was wood paneled under a high ceiling with a fresco depicting a vast mountainous horizon, majestic clouds, distant waterfalls, several grazing buffalo, and noble Indians (he guessed, Seneca) observing them from lush green flowering brush. The two canal men were having amber drinks and studying the large menu written in manuscript. Warren bade them good evening, admiring the crystal glasses, the white table linen and heavy silverware to either side of gilt-edged china. He gazed up at the fresco.

"Splendid," he said. "In the grand Romantic tradition, it certainly suits the venue. Even if the buffalo themselves never came this far east." The men continued to study the menu. His attempt at ironic wit seemed to fall flat. A waiter served him a glass of water with a slice of lemon, which he said would suffice for now. Fowles said they'd best take the Maître D's recommendation for the evening, to which they agreed, and ordered Chateaubriand steak dinners all around. Medium rare.

"Will you share a bottle of Bordeaux with us, Mr. Warren?" Fowles asked. "They maintain a fine cellar here."

He was being treated again like one of the club. French wine was a great rarity back in the territories. He had never tasted any, and it was not considered as alcohol among certain gentry. Out of reckless curiosity, and for the sake of his own education, Warren surprised himself by accepting. George Fowles, who obviously knew his way around restaurants, consulted the list and ordered. The waiter complimented him on his choice, and while the man went to comply, Warren observed the movements of the guests and the staff, and again studied the fresco.

The noble savages depicted against the mountains appeared to be the sole representatives of the red race in the hotel besides himself. This was nothing unusual, as Indians were not given to serving whites, nor anyone for that matter, but it was an abrupt change of demography for one having lived a lifetime in the Northwest. The dining room staff was mainly white, but black waiters and porters appeared now dressed in white. He came to wonder how the dark-skinned women, mostly young, and the few Negro men serving at the table and behind the kitchen doors, were afforded such positions in a luxury establishment. They seemed to be familiar with domestic gestures, perhaps trained to such service. In the southern states, he knew, they would be slaves, at best trained house servants indentured to their masters. But surely not in New York, the cradle of the abolitionist movement. Indeed, the only Negroes he had known as house servants were Dred Scott and his wife in Minnesota, who had won their freedom in the Missouri courts, then lost it in appeal. Now it was up to the Supreme Court. A great part of America was still made up of slave states. The nation was still fighting a bitter legal battle over slavery. But Indian rights were of little importance in the white heat of Manifest Destiny.

William Warren, mixed-blood as he was known even as a member of the Minnesota Territorial Legislature, suddenly became aware that here in Buffalo, in the company of the privileged classes dining at the American Hotel, he was being treated not like a curiosity, an educated half-breed, but like a white man. Did this sit well with him, or not? He thought not.

He still felt like an outsider, a foreigner far from his home, caught the same old charade. He would have to watch his every step, every word. His father would approve but caution him, his Yankee grandfather would remind him of his manners, Hole-in-the-Day would laugh at him, but he could hear his mother telling him again that his great-grandfather, Waub-ij-e-jauk, was chief of the Crane clan, greatest orators of the Anishinaabe. Act accordingly. Do not be fooled by white men; he was not one of them. That much he had learned in Saint Paul politics.

The waiter came, opened the dusty bottle of wine, and poured it first into a decanter before serving it to Fowles, who tasted it, nodded his approval, and addressed Warren.

"Mr. Warren, we should set the terms from the outset," he said ceremoniously.

"You will please agree to be our guest, of myself and the Canal Company, for the entire evening and your stay here at the American. It's the least we can do in return for your courageous action on the boat, which most likely saved us from a far graver loss. I shall of course recount that incident in my report directly to Mr. Corning. We owe you a vote of thanks, Mr. Warren. Here here." He and Benton raised their glasses.

Warren remembered his manners and lifted his. "I did only what any man would do, instinctively. But I thank you."

They sipped the wine, a Medoc. Deep, and rich, it tasted almost gamey, with a tang like wild blackberries. He would say nothing of his former intention to pay for their dinners himself, etiquette left no place for it. Again he looked up at the fresco.

"You know, the last buffalo I saw was just east of the Mississippi," he told them, "when I was a boy. It must have been near Fort Snelling. It was already killed, and the Dakota Sioux were butchering it according to their custom, to use the hide, the guts, the hooves, the sinews, and eat the rest for their sustenance. I'd never seen such a huge animal. Bigger than a moose."

"There were some," said Benton. "The Sioux pushed them west. A good thing for them, it made them easier to hunt. Next thing you know the Sioux got pushed west themselves, into the plains."

"Yes, by the last treaty at Traverse de Sioux. But the Chippewa were the first to drive them west, out of the Mississippi Valley."

"The Sioux or the Buffalo?" Asked Fowles.

"Both. But now they rue the loss of the Buffalo. Not the Sioux."

"They'd just as like see them wiped out," said Benton. "The Chippeway might get their wish pretty soon, but it won't be their doing."

"It is not what they wish. It is hard for whites to understand, but these peoples wish no ill will upon each other. They all want peace, and to live on their lands, close to their ancestors."

"That's what Hole-in-the-Sky said at Fort Snelling back in '27. It got him a hole in his chest in a Sioux ambush outside the barricades. Killed his daughter too. We jailed the Sioux that did it. The Colonel let four of 'em loose on the plain, the Chippeway cut 'em down on the run. Hole-in-the-Sky got his revenge. But it didn't stop there."

"You were there, I gather."

"I was," Benton continued. "I served under Colonel Snelling. There was no town yet, just a few cabins, old Pig's Eye with his liquor, the Indians, and the Fort. The Army was there to protect the settlers and keep the peace among the Indians. That was the hard part."

Warren had more wine. The steaks were served, darkly browned but running slightly red under a sauce with small round mushrooms *"de Paris"* that were again completely new to his palate. The meat was uncommonly tender, but what intrigued him most was the shape and resilience of the mushrooms that resisted under his tongue and tooth. He swirled it around in the rich sauce inside his mouth. The sensation distracted him from the conversation, and from all other weighty matters that usually besieged his mind. When he tested another slippery mushroom, he just teased it on his tongue. The sensation somehow brought him back to the wispy Irish girl who occupied much of his attention his last year in Clarkson. He was 16, out of school, boarding with Mr. Ladds and spending his father's money. She was older than Warren, maybe 19, slim. She wore her hair piled upon her head in such a way that dark strands fell down and floated about her neck. Like Mrs. Ramsey...

Where were these thoughts coming from? Was it the wine, or knowing that tomorrow the train would pass right past that brothel? He spent all his money on cards and that girl, then returned to his island home to work beside his father. Two years later he married

Matilda, who was also older than he at 20, and content to have a savvy husband.

"A touch more wine, Warren?" Fowles held the bottle aloft.

"A touch, thank you. It's very good. With the steak."

The sumptuous meat, the sauce, the wine and the opulence came together to infuse William Warren with a sense of strength and self-satisfaction that he had not felt in years. The scalloped potatoes and sautéed carrots completed this nourishment and left him feeling restored in body and spirit.

The next moment, breathing in with another sip of wine, he felt a cloud of weakness. He let his fork fall to the floor. He bent over, apologizing, but felt dizzy and righted himself. He did not want to spoil this. A waiter immediately picked it up and gave him a clean one.

There seemed to be more noise in the room. Voices, glasses, plates being shuffled, the ting of silverware. Fowles and Benton paid no attention, speaking in low tones of their work soon at hand. Warren excused himself, went to use the facilities. He coughed for a moment, spat into the basin and stood breathing. The spittle was not red. The spell passed. Must be fatigue. He doused his face with cold water and looked at himself in the large mirror, leaning on the marble counter. He was all right. It was the rich food, the excitement. He would have no more wine. But knew he would soon have to retire to his room or cause himself embarrassment. He needed a good draught of his tea, and his bed.

When he returned to the table the two men were drinking brandy and they had all been served the chef's special dessert, a dish called *Oeufs à la Neige*, a large white cloud swimming in a yellow custard and topped with an elaborate swirl of stiff gold gossamer, as if a deft hand had tossed and frozen the wind in mid-air. They all partook. It was very light and sweet and the very uniqueness of eating such a marvel brought him back to his privileged state of mind. Benton ordered more brandy. Fowles admired the ceiling fresco, and this time made conversation for Warren's benefit.

"You're right. By a stretch of the imagination, that could be the country around Fort Snelling, back in '37. Captain Benton and I met there at the time."

"Ah yes," Warren said. "The year of the Saint Peter's Treaty council. The Ojibwe sold off more of their land. They thought they were selling pine trees."

"They were trying to set up borders to stop the Indians from warring. That chief Hole-in-the-Sky was there. He was quick to rile. They'd killed more Sioux in those years, and lost a good many themselves. Women and children. Had to be stopped."

"I never understood what killing women and children had to do with what they call war," Benton interjected. "The Army'd never allow that."

"Generally speaking," said Warren. "But Black Hawk, for one, would think otherwise."

"That was not the Army that did that. Those were militia."

"The government finds other solutions. They don't call it war."

"Look here, Mr. Warren..." Benton began, looking ruffled for once.

"Gentlemen, I'm sure we all agree," Fowles interrupted, "that we deplore such atrocities and avoid them at all costs." He looked from Benton to Warren. "Captain Benton lost his wife and child out west, then left the military. A hard decision for a career soldier."

"No man under my orders ever harmed the innocent," said Benton.

"I'm sorry," said Warren. "For your family."

Benton rose, wanting a smoke, and walked out of the dining room. He strode confidently as if he were still in uniform. Warren let a moment pass before addressing George Fowles again.

"I was out of place. How did they die?"

"Cholera. Not the Indians."

"I don't suppose it makes a difference. How did he come to work for you?"

"Our paths crossed soon after that. I work as a negotiator, in land, labor, mining. Sometimes in negotiations it helps to have an extra hand, and the people I work for can generally pay for it. Benton is loyal, and as we saw on the boat, effective."

"What brought you to Fort Snelling back then?"

"Treaty negotiations. Governor Dodge sent for me."

"My own father was there. I was with him, but just a boy."

"Yes. Lyman Warren. With the traders. They wanted more money. Things heated up and Taliaferro, the Sioux agent, brought out his pistol and pointed it at your father. Hole-in-the- Sky, the great peacemaker, yelled out, 'Shoot him!' I managed to quiet things down and persuaded Dodge to allow the traders more money. But that never did set right with the Chippeway."

"You say you saved my father?"

"I wouldn't say that. My job was to get the treaty signed. I take it your father never did get along with that Indian, Hole-in-the Sky."

"They had their disagreements, but they respected each other. Which is more than I can say for the American Fur Company. My father worked for them for ten years. The money allocated to him in that treaty, for the Indians' trading debts, never went to him. You know that, I expect. The Company took it all. Ramsay Crooks ruined my father."

"A shame. Crooks drives a hard bargain, I'll allow. But the Company was failing fast. The panic hit, Jackson dissolved the central bank, the fur trade was over. A lot of reasons. Crooks would tell you that his traders ruined him."

"It was my father's money, awarded in his name. Crooks owed it to him."

"Crooks owes me money I'll never see. The Company went bankrupt."

"Owes you money? You worked for Ramsay Crooks?"

"I told you, I worked for Dodge. We both had stock in the Company at the time. So did your father, in fact, but he was also on salary and Crooks expected results. The way I heard it, Lyman Warren didn't want to work for the AFC and went off to build a sawmill when he should have been building a fishing dock."

"Crooks wouldn't pay him. With six children in school, he needed money."

"He had his salary like anyone else, and they paid a dividend even in '38. But that was the end. No more fox, no more beaver. Then someone made a cheaper hat and Europeans switched to silk. I imagine that's why your father switched to milling logs."

"They still owed him twenty-five thousand. He never saw a cent."

Fowles lit a thin cigar and ordered a brandy, with a rise of his brow at Warren, who shook his head. Fowles exhaled up at the buffalo on the wall as the brandy was set before him. He swirled the liquid in an overlarge snifter, warming it in his palm.

"Mr. Warren, the imperatives of business in New York are not the same as in the territories. As stockholders we all take risks, but Crooks is known as a fair dealer. The way I heard it from Dodge, your father overextended credit to the Indians. It was the Company's money, not his."

"Some of it, maybe. Accumulated over the years. But he fed and clothed them on his own salary. The Indians couldn't hunt without their outfits. They couldn't trap if they were starving to death." Warren began to wheeze and brought his napkin to his mouth.

"I grant you that. A matter of management. But the furs ran out. It was time to change."

"But it was you who persuaded Dodge to give in to my father's claims, and to write them into the treaty. He's the one who secured the money to clear the Ojibwes' debts. He and William Aitken, my father-in-law. And it all went to the American Fur Company, to Astor and Crooks in the end. It was a fraud. They used his signature, and you knew it. They owe him that money. You know as well as I that Dodge and Crooks are thick as thieves. You worked for them."

"I can't tell my employers what to do with their money," said Fowles.

Warren was red-faced and his eyes glistened. Searching for his handkerchief he felt, inside his jacket pocket, the small revolver. It fit easily into his palm.

As he confusedly fumbled for the trigger, Captain Andrew Benton stepped up to the table and stood there, hands loose at his side. Their eyes met. Benton looked at his hand in his pocket. This presence had a quieting influence on Warren. He found his handkerchief, used it to wipe his lips, and set the large white napkin on the table.

"I suppose not," he said to Fowles. "You can just make sure they get it."

"Exactly. That was what Ramsay Crooks expected of your father."

Fowles finished his brandy and leaned forward with a sympathetic air.

"Business sense, Mr. Warren, brings its own rewards. Some men have it, some don't. You'll surely learn more about this in New York when you publish your book. Don't misunderstand me. Your father may have been generous to a fault. But you cannot fault a man for his generosity. Now I suggest that you get some rest."

Warren took the cue and got up. At that moment he saw the young Métisse girl with her sculpted neck waft by the waiter's station with a basket of linen balanced atop her white maid's cap, lithe as a willow. Time stopped for a moment. Men in the room raised their eyes to catch the vision. Women stared more openly. She did not turn her head, but her wide eyes slipped sideways and caught Warren's. Or was it Fowles'? There was no telling.

The air before her seemed to part, and she was gone. The men who had glanced up pretended disinterest. Warren kept looking around the dining hall. The sole Negro customer, the imposing-looking gentleman he had seen earlier, had left. He had a moment of distraction, a slight vertigo, and stood immobile. He surmised that he was not used to the wine.

He then remembered where he was and looked back to his host. He could tell by his gaze that Fowles had seen him looking at the girl. Benton too saw it but remained dutifully placid. Well, nothing wrong in looking. He was among men. They all looked. But William Warren did not wish to be taken lightly, nor to offend his host. The girl had disappeared and the instant of embarrassment was ended.

George Fowles returned to the even tone with which he had tempered their evening.

"I'm glad to see you approve of the staff here, Mr. Warren, exotic as some of them may seem. She's a new girl, a fast learner. I'm sure she'll be a favorite." Fowles' slight smile was intended as complicitous. Then it left his face as he changed his subject.

"I have business tonight in Attica, my coach is waiting. We won't see you in the morning, but rest assured it is all taken care of. Everything, your train passage to New York, and anything else you should need—anything, you understand—will be provided. They know me well here. We owe you a debt we can only attempt to repay. I wish you well in your publishing endeavors and your travels, Mr. Warren. It's been a pleasure and an honor. I am sure we'll meet again, perhaps in your own home territory."

Chapter 24: The Vision

YOU CANNOT FAULT A MAN FOR HIS GENEROSITY. Was Fowles insulting his father or complimenting him? A puzzling man. When thanking him before he left the table, Warren shook his host's hand. Fowles and Benton nodded to each other and quit the dining room to enter the saloon, where they joined three other suited men in large leather chairs.

He slowly ascended the carpeted staircase amid the comings and goings of the guests, the diners, the uniformed staff and wondered what kind of accommodation he would be able to secure when alone in New York. Surely such luxury would be beyond his financial capabilities. At least this time. But what if his health should improve with the administrations of Doctor Trall? Would he secure a lucrative publishing contract that would open the writer's career he had already planned out, with three more books already in the projected scheme of things?

One day he would bring his entire family to Buffalo, even New York. He would of course have to show them the American Hotel, where it all began. And his friends and supporters in Saint Paul? Le Duc? Rice? Mrs. Ramsey perhaps, with the new Cultural Society. Maybe even his old friend Hole-in-the-Day would like to see this place, and unleash his ironic wit on the buffalo fresco in the dining room.

When he finally lay down on his clean bed and turned out the gaslights, leaving the curtains slightly open for the snowy moonlight to shine through the window, he was still entertaining these thoughts. He propped himself up on pillows to make for easier breathing. In fact the room was warm, he felt quite well and did not feel any need for his tea. Maybe it was still the effect of the wine. He lay there and let pleasant thoughts feed his being as the excellent dinner and drink had fed his body.

Despite his one lapse, and a moment where he let his bitterness over his father's ruination carry him away, the evening with George Fowles and his adjutant Benton had balanced out quite well. He even felt indebted to Fowles, he had to admit, for his candor when revealing his connection to the AFC. He was most likely right about Crooks: it was simply business, big business, and his father's talent was in the territories, dealing with the trappers. The goods and most of the money his father advanced to the Ojibwe had come from the Company, but on his account, against his earnings. He could not have done otherwise. The Company made its money from Lyman Warren's efforts. He earned it for them while expanding their trade. They should have accorded him equitable recompense for his diligence at the treaty negotiations, as Lyman was the one who finally won those thousands for the AFC... perhaps unwittingly, used as a pawn by Dodge and Fowles. Where were the limits of fairness? Ramsay Crooks fired him and ruined him in the courts. They still owed him.

Sleep evaded him—he felt groggy but somehow excited, his mind vacillating, unsteady. He got up, looked out on the snow lit street, now nearly deserted. The gas streetlamps gave off an odd golden glow in circles on the ground, somehow reassuring. Below he saw a four-horse coach draw up to the hotel. George Fowles gave some instructions to Captain Benton and the hotel manager. They loaded his bags, Fowles boarded and off it went in the night. Where to, did he say? Attica? Somewhere down the line. He could not wait for the morning train. Business never waits.

The moon came and went behind the cloud bank, which in turn brought the occasional flurry of snow, slowly accumulating on the pavement below. How strange it was to be in this warm and luxurious room looking out on the cold winter in Buffalo, far from his forest home, far from his family and their fire, as if the world outside were not his concern.

He took a draught of lukewarm tea from his flask by the grate. The taste was a comfort, but it was almost empty. He must make some for the long train ride tomorrow. Courtesy of Fowles and the Canal Company. How unlikely, that a man who knew Ramsay Crooks was paying for this hotel and his passage to New York. Most importantly, he reckoned, Fowles was sincerely convinced that Warren had saved his life on the boat, which had earned him his respect. The respect of men in such positions, he could not afford to neglect.

Leaving the curtain slightly open, he went back to bed dressed in his shirt and underclothing and closed his eyes, still unwillingly ruminating on his father's fate and his fear of repeating it, caught in a train of thought from which he always had difficulty escaping. Yet the part of him he had always counted on to dispel such nonsense, the "go-aheadativeness" that had been his since his childhood, tried to prevail.

He was at the beginning of a new life, and saw now that there was no point in dwelling on the past failures and humiliations suffered by himself, or his father for that matter. Lyman had written his personal apology to Crooks, acknowledging that he had always treated him fairly. He went soft in the head. It was after Marie died. The image came back to him now: his father driving her coffin back to La Pointe, hunched over with his elbows on his knees, his hat and boots muddy, with the fogged eyes of a man already gone from this earth. William himself was heartbroken, but his father seemed demolished by her death. Over the years he had faced continual defeat, building a civilization in the wilderness, fighting to accrue stature, land, education for his children and those of his dead brother, the support of the church. In the end he had nothing to show for it but debt and his dead wife's body in a wagon.

Why was he dwelling on such sorrow in the dark of night? The wine? Drunkenness brought despair. This is why he'd wanted to rid the Ojibwe of liquor.

After his wife's death, Lyman had at least had the wherewithal to go to the sawmill and gather his books, some four hundred titles, old and new. Warren had read every one of them, copying down whole passages to learn how to write. That was his father's legacy to his son. His children must go on.

With this, he began to feel the vortex of sleep drifting in and out behind his eyes. You never knew exactly when the blackness struck, but this was what he wanted. To beat death back into the oblivion from which it came.

Sleep was almost upon him, still drugged but not blacked out, when he perceived the door of his room opening, quietly, then closing. His heart jumped awake. He saw a shadow approaching the bed and heard the rustling of fabric. It was a woman. Her arms went up, her maid's cap came off and in the moonlight he saw a mass of black hair falling over her shoulders. At first indiscernible, black against black, she came forth in her maid's dress and said to him, in French, but with a strange accent, perhaps the Caribbean:

"On m'envoie pour vous. Vous voulez de moi ?"

Wanted her? For what? He was captivated, groggy. *"Pourquoi?"* He said. Then, to his utter disbelief and stupefaction, she took off all her clothes. Save one item: a single strand of colored beads around her waist. He was dreaming. Was she his dream animal? She stepped into the ray of moonlight alongside the bed, casting a shadow darker than herself, so bright was the moon's reflection off the falling snow outside. She stood like a long- haired totem, her sculpted head and shoulders high, slightly sway-backed, arms falling easily as the limbs of a hemlock, shining like burnished wood. Her breasts were small mounds, her blank face had the roundness of youth, almost childlike. Eyes half closed, she did not smile.

She stood there by his bed emanating something like balsam, or the essence of a plant he had never smelt, mixing with a stronger scent.

He recognized that scent as fear. He had smelt it as a boy, flattened in the bush with his young Ojibwe friends. And later from Elijah, the black runaway he had kept in his room at Oneida. Was she frightened of him?

His hand went to the beaded strand around her waist, where her muscles thrived like moving water. She felt solid, real. The geometrical design on her belly, circles of raised scars around her navel, formed an ornamental burst on her dark satin skin. He thought of the pain she must have endured for those marks, and whence it came. Africa. Maybe the islands. A mere girl. For a moment he thought again of the spirit dream his Ojibwe grandfathers told him about, which he had never experienced. But then he was appalled: his dream animal was a slave.

What could a child, a black slave, mean to his life?

He asked her name, but she would not speak. She breathed deeply and made a throaty humming sound. A song without words. He looked up into her face and thought: *she's younger than my sister, little Mary.* This thought suddenly sobered him up.

"Who sent you?" He asked. *"Où est ta famille ?"*

She fell silent. Warren stood up and grasped her arms. "Who sent you?"

Her body tensed, set to spring. She looked at him in defiance, wide eyes narrowing, and bared her teeth. *"Laissez-moi ! Laissez-moi !"*

"I won't harm you," he said, and let her go. *"Je suis ton ami. Indien, moi. Qui t'envoie?"*

"My Masta," she stammered. "Masta send me. *Cadeau pour vous,*" she said. A gift. She was someone's idea of a gift. Whose? She was a child.

He stepped around her, took up her clothes and told her to dress. When she turned, he saw that she bore more scars on her back. Shallow, but unmistakable.

"Tu n'as pas de famille ?" The scars. How was this possible? She was not a field slave. "My Masta send me. *Cadeau pour vous. Vous ne voulez pas?"*

"You go back. Tell your master you did what you were told."

"No! Masta whip me! I never go back to Masta! Tonight, I go to freedom! *Vous ne dites rien.* You Indian, you help me. No tell Masta!"

"Je ne dirai rien," he said. What did she mean, to freedom?

She dressed quickly and turned to leave, holding her shoes in her hands. She said nothing more and would not look at him, but now on her face was a new determination. She searched the hall outside, and fled. Warren lay back down, still testing his theory of a dream animal.

No, it was no dream, no vision. The girl was indentured, sent to him for his pleasure by her white master. Tonight, she would have become a whore. Worse, maybe she already was. He knew now who her master was, loath as he was to believe it. Who else could it be but Fowles? Who else would send him this gift? And now, she said, she was going to freedom. But how?

He recalled the words of the mentor he'd found as a young man, Beriah Green at Oneida, where his compassion became a duty: There is no baser sin than the crime of human slavery.

His heart was racing. Oblivion came much later.

Chapter 25: The Railroad

MORNING FOUND HIM WEAK IN the dark hotel room. The pain had swollen in his lungs, his head was fogged, his joints ached. Somehow he had slept, briefly. The illness, the constant proximity of death wore him down like a bludgeon. He heard horses on the street, voices, then nothing. Some days were worse than others. This one did not bode well.

He reached for the tea flask he kept next to him in bed, now grown cold. He drank, thirsty for its quick relief, then wrenched himself up. After his third attempt, he sat propped against the bedstead. He usually slept sitting up with his board, his writings at his side, but that night he rolled and lay flat which made him congested. He lit a candle, swallowed the cold dregs of his tea, breathed slowly, and waited for the weight to lift from his chest.

In his heated room he may have blacked out for only an hour or so. Time was hard to judge. The night was inhabited not by the animal dreams of his childhood, but by regrets and fears and shuddering flashes of consciousness, intrusive and useless to his purpose. Longing for dawn, he had fallen into a welcome abyss. Now he crawled out.

The tea, even cold, brought a slow warmth that was now familiar. He gained control.

The heady, foreign scent of spice still lingered in the room. He was assailed by the memory of the black girl sent that night for the purpose of his pleasure. That was no dream. His host had said at dinner: you could not fault a man for his generosity. Fowles was speaking of himself, announcing his gesture of gratitude for the incident at the card table. Warren felt pity for the girl, a touch of shame for himself, and insulted that anyone could take him for a man who would accept the offering of a whoremonger, one who would abase a child and a slave. The iniquity of it had killed all desire. The taste of disgust lay thick on his tongue. He wanted to flee this hotel and leave Buffalo behind him. Would he be spared again this day, for the long train voyage to New York City? He must. He touched his wooden writing case, for strength.

With great effort, he lit a candle, dressed, and packed, went downstairs and took an expedient breakfast in the small gaslit parlor near the kitchen, with ample amounts of coffee which made him feel as if he could move fluidly once again. A fresh roll calmed his stomach. The dining room was empty except for a few staff. He did not see Fowles, nor his burly adjutant. He had seen Fowles's coach leave for Attica. He may never see them again.

Nor did he see the round-faced Métisse girl, which was as he expected. He hoped she had not come to harm and avoided thinking of what her future would be. Slavery was illegal in New York State, he could have Fowles arrested. But the girl was too frightened by her master. She would never testify, and even if she did, her testimony would most likely be discarded. Fowles surely had influence in this city.

Besides, this was not his fight, he reasoned. His was to advance the cause of the Ojibwe, as their historian. To publish his *History*, he must finish his preface before presenting his manuscript in New York. Let the Yankee abolitionists take up the cause of the Negro. He would champion the Ojibwe. Yet somehow he felt ashamed he could not help the girl.

The colored kitchen boy, smiling in his pressed uniform, heated some water for him. Warren tipped him over generously before he left the table in an absurd attempt to ease his conscience about the girl he could no longer help. He wished he'd found out her name, then he would leave her something and maybe she would be all right—they did not have it so bad here. Then he chastised himself for thinking that there was any justification for his failure to act. He knew what the girl's fate would be. Her only escape would be to flee.

In his room, he used the hot water to make the pint flask of his diminishing supply of herbal tea, carefully dosing the maple sweetener: two teaspoons. Searching his bags, he realized he'd left the smaller flask behind, probably on the boat, empty. Getting forgetful... No matter, he still had the one. He had maybe four teaspoons of maple elixir, and would use it sparingly to get to the city. There, Trall would help him, and with the grace of God maybe even cure him. He had read that miracles were possible, and with the new water cure techniques and dietary innovations, all afflictions could be treated. He would come away stronger, a publishing contract in hand, ready to continue his work. He drank more tea and felt better. Miracles.

Shortly after seven, at first light, he descended from his cab and entered the new railroad station, Erie Street Terminal, a long dim wooden building swirling with woodsmoke and steam. A hissing black and brass locomotive with six steel wheels taller than himself was building steam to pull the cars, five in number, through the rivers and ravines of the Mohawk and Hudson Valleys, then south to the metropolis. The first-class car was painted green, like the boiler of the locomotive, and placed forward, behind the mail car just after the huge black tender stacked with split logs. To finish the panache, the cowcatcher was painted a bright red. William Warren walked up and spent some minutes inspecting the new machinery until he was gruffly warned away from the powerful steam blasts by a bearded fireman perched in the cab. Having approved the technology to his satisfaction, he prepared to enter his future in appropriate pomp and style. A uniformed porter lifted his chest and bag and he boarded.

Presumably a light-skinned Negro, maybe of mixed-blood, the man introduced himself as the conductor and asked to check his ticket. This done, he looked carefully at Warren and his luggage, as if to assess him. The passenger's tired smile soon won him over and he welcomed him aboard. This conductor was young, probably no older than himself. It was surprising to him that a black man should be in such a position of authority on the train lines, but this was the modern world, and he was pleased to be a part of it.

He was ushered to his reserved seat in the first-class car of the New York and Erie Railroad coach that he would occupy all the way to Albany. The benches were of varnished wood with ample cushions provided. He was shown that they could be converted to sleeping compartments for overnight travelers, but for the day journey they must remain as benches. The conductor put him at ease by helping him in every detail, spreading his cloak out for him, fetching him an extra pillow, explaining the ventilation system in the arch-roofed car and the lack of toilet facilities: there would be stops along the line, and there was a compartment next to the conductor's vestibule with a chamber pot for emergencies. He outlined the itinerary on the newly opened line up to Rochester, then following the Mohawk River and the Erie Canal east to Albany. There would be a change of trains there during the night, to take the Hudson Valley line south to New York City. The conductor spoke fluid English in a soft voice which, like his own, had some musical intonations. Also, he noticed as the man busied himself with his luggage, he had a rather thin, hawk-like nose and high cheekbones under his conductor's hat, producing a handsome effect not unlike the features common to certain Native American peoples. Intrigued, Warren ventured a query.

"Excuse my inquiring. You are of Native origin, surely. As I am. Mohawk?"

"No. Iroquois. By my mother. And you, Sir?

"Anishinaabe. Ojibwe, or Chippeway as some whites say. By my mother. I was raised by her people on Lake Superior, then came here for my schooling. Oneida Institute, near Utica. Our peoples were once enemies, but that is all history now."

"Ah, yes...history." The conductor answered first in Iroquois, then in his perfect English. "Oneida. I attended two years, probably before your time, it was in the early years. It's gone now. Abolition has fallen under fire. The Reverend Green lost support...The struggle goes on. But your father is white, mine was black. He died."

"My father was a New Yorker from Clarkson. He died too. Some years ago."

"You're going back to Clarkson?"

"No. There's nothing more for me there. I'm on to New York City."

The conductor looked out on the station platform then busied himself with readying the seats, which were arranged face to face, in blocks for four or six passengers when traveling by day. At night some could be converted for sleeping.

"Enjoy your trip then, Sir. I'll be at your service up to Rochester, about four hours from here. If all goes well. There'll be three other passengers traveling in this car. For anything you need, anything at all," He hesitated a moment, then looked at Warren more directly. "Please tell me." He then stationed himself at the coach entry, directing passengers to other cars.

Warren was tempted to tip the man generously, as he had done at the hotel, since fortune smiled upon him, and he had extra cash. But something held him back and he did not tip him at all. It would have offended the man's pride, as they were on equal footing, educated according to the same principles and convictions, and in this instance the conductor had an official capacity. More than this, something told him they had more in common than their mixed origins. He could not put his mind on it, but there was an innuendo in the man's tone of voice. An unspoken complicity, perhaps because of their shared experience in one of the most progressive institutions in the country, schooled under the uncompromising Beriah Green.

He wrapped himself in his cloak, shivering for no good reason if not his ever-present fatigue, as the wood stove at the other end amply heated the car. The varnished benches, the green and gold sashed curtains and brass fixtures, as well as the dress and demeanor of the passengers on the platform, indicated the good will and solicitousness of the railroad toward its first-class passengers. Warren, with his cloak, his boots, his trunk, and flat-crowned beaver hat, was quite visibly a visitor from the western territories—even though he was still, strangely, the only passenger shown to this first-class coach. But, he told himself, he was traveling among the elite. And he was an author, speeding his manuscript to New York City. He looked at his belted trunk and rested his hand upon it.

He remained alone in first class until one more passenger stepped in and took a seat further down the aisle. Warren started and stared. It was the large black gentleman he had seen in the hotel dining room. Standing, removing his high-crowned hat, he was even more of an imposing figure, his creased brow serving as a sort of buttress above his broad face. He was again well-dressed, in a purple greatcoat expensively cut, his collar high and bound with a neatly tied cravat. He carried himself with the pride of a man in his prime, yet he appeared tired as he let himself fall heavily into his seat.

The young conductor came with his bag, making him comfortable with even more deference than with Warren, although with less fuss. He seemed to know the habits of this passenger and what he wanted. The gentleman thanked him using his first name, Thomas. There was no tip. He looked out the window, searching the station, then back at the sole other passenger and caught his eye. They nodded to acknowledge each other's presence, but the other passenger showed no sign that he had ever seen Warren before. He probably never even noticed him in the dining room last evening.

The train waited, hissing steam.

The conductor, Thomas, busied himself tending the baggage, the wood stove, smiling but businesslike with other passengers on the platform.

At one point he came back into the coach and put a newspaper in Warren's hands: the March 4th, 1853, edition of *Frederick Douglass' Paper,* published in Rochester, featuring an article on the famous Mrs. Stowe, who owned a fine granite house in Andover, Massachusetts referred to as "Uncle Tom's Cabin". It likened the authoress and friend of humanity to Shakespeare or Burns in a prolific volley of praise that produced an unmitigated impression of saintliness. He wondered if Douglass had wielded the pen himself. It was one large sheet of small print, with no advertisements, also exhorting Negroes to *Learn Trades Or Starve.*

Thomas, closing a window, glanced in the direction of the elegantly dressed black man, then back at Warren. He tapped the paper, pointed at the man, and left the car.

So that was him. Frederick Douglass, the famous author, orator, and abolitionist. He had read his autobiography, obtained from Le Duc's bookstore in Saint Paul. He suddenly looked as he had imagined him, a bull of a man, thick-haired and proud, but with fine intelligent features. And an escaped slave, self-educated. He had a white father he never knew, but he thought it was his black mother's master. Warren had heard much about him since Oneida: his anti-slavery fight, his championing human rights, temperance, women's rights, eloquently and vehemently. He was the most famous Negro intellectual in the country, even Europe. Warren knew that he had moved to Rochester, where his paper was first called *The North Star.*

He could hardly believe his good fortune. He found himself in the very crucible of literary and philosophical debate in the east, traveling with the publisher of the most influential progressive newspaper in the country, a published author himself, a thinker, a leader of his own people. He must find a way to speak to him. They had much in common, to be sure, and he may have some suggestions for a younger author. Why not just go up and introduce himself?

He was about to rise when Thomas returned carrying the bags of two more passengers. Warren covered himself in his cloak and watched to see where they would sit. Again, to his surprise, they were colored. One was a rounded middle-aged woman, small in stature but with a face as strong as Douglass'. Her brief smile revealed some missing front teeth. The second one younger, taller, thinner, dressed in an ample traveling coat and large bonnet, her dark face half-buried in her shawl. Her supple movements, even hidden by layers of thick cloth, revealed a youthful grace.

So far in this new first-class coach, there were but four passengers: himself and three Negroes. Then there was the conductor, another mixed-blood. An interesting configuration. The two women were both dressed in the stylish manner that befitted the class of Frederick Douglass himself, high-hatted, gray-cloaked, and with their shawls pulled high up on their shoulders. Thomas seated them facing Douglass, who rose. Perhaps his wife and daughter. Did he have a daughter? How old could she be?

Douglass apparently knew the older woman, embracing her in greeting, and shook the gloved hand of the younger, bidding them to sit. So, she was apparently not his daughter. The women kept their hats on, their shawls pulled up. They were seated with their backs to Warren, who was further up in the car but facing in the same direction, toward the rear of the train.

Their words were few, but Douglass loosed an impatient sigh as he checked his pocket watch and looked out on the quay. He patted the older woman's hand, as if to reassure her. The train was a few minutes late in leaving, which seemed to cause them some concern.

The agent on the platform finally yelled "All Aboard!" The train jerked forward, huffing steam, then a bit faster, clanking and hissing, then rolling smoother on the steel rails. Warren marveled at the ingenuity, the power, as the tons of steel heaved forward. People were standing back on the platform, waving as the train rolled by.

Except for one. A large bewhiskered white man running alongside the train, grasping his hat in his hand, his coattails flapping behind him as he searched in the windows of the passing train cars. His open coat revealed that he was carrying a holstered pistol at his side, but he wore no badge that one could see. He was just approaching the first-class car, huffing and looking in through the windows, when Warren recognized Captain Andrew Benton. At that moment, he heard a high cry from the young lady sitting by the window Benton was approaching. She sank lower in her seat beside the older black woman.

Benton was now being outpaced by the train, falling behind on the platform. He could not tell if Benton had seen him—Warren was farther away. Finally, the big man stopped, threw down his hat, and put his hands on his knees, heaving, to watch the parting train gather momentum. He grew smaller as the train pulled ahead. It soon left him behind.

Warren sat pondering. Was Benton for some reason looking for him? Or perhaps Fowles, on the same train? No, Fowles would be here in first class. Besides, he had left by coach for Attica last night.

The two women riding backward in the far end of the car had switched positions with Douglass, so they faced forward, and the older one had removed her hat. She was comforting the younger passenger who was sitting still as a cat, her face covered by a handkerchief. Douglass sat forward, his hands covering his brow, head shaking. The older woman appeared calm, resolute, as she was now trying to reassure Douglass, patting his knee, whispering to him.

The younger woman then sat up straight, sighed deeply, took the handkerchief away. She looked at the ceiling with her wide, nearly slanted eyes, and violently removed her veiled hat, as if it constricted her unbearably. Warren stared openly.

It was the young Métisse girl from last night, the one he first thought he dreamed about, his spirit animal. She was twisting to check the exits, as if seeking a way out. Her springy black hair fell down, just as it had some hours ago in the confines of Warren's hotel room. She seemed doubly frightened now, her eyes flashing with the rage of a cornered animal. Warren brought his coughing under control, found his handkerchief, and drank from his flask of tea, trying to make himself inconspicuous as he spied on the threesome and strained to listen.

The girl was speaking French in that strange, melodious intonation. Neither Douglass nor the woman seemed to understand what she was saying. She finally spoke out loudly, insisting that she had been seen.

"Il m'a vue ! Il me cherche ! Il me dénoncera ! Je connais les hommes blancs!"

"Who? What are you saying?" Douglass was rasping loudly, exasperated at the young girl's panic. "No one saw you leave! You're safe. Calm down, my dear, you're in good hands."

But the girl would hear nothing, she only protested more desperately. Warren began to understand. He rose and went to their seats.

"Excuse me, Mr. Douglass, Madame, Mademoiselle. But I can be of help. I speak a bit of French." He looked at the girl, who recognized him and stiffened, as she had the night before when he grabbed her arms.

"Je suis un ami," he told her. *"Tu le sais bien. Tu me reconnais. Je suis Indien. Qui t'a vue?"* She seemed to loosen, enough at least to cooperate.

"L'homme blanc au pistolet, sur le quai. Il m'a reconnue ! Il va me dénoncer!" She plunged her face into the handkerchief again as the older woman held her shoulders.

"There was a man running alongside the train," Warren told Douglass. "With a gun. She saw him and apparently, he saw her. She's afraid of him. And she has good reason to be."

"And who are you?" Douglass growled. "You were with George Fowles, at the hotel. I saw you last night."

"Fowles is no friend to me. The man she saw outside the coach is called Benton. He was also at the table last night. He works for him. If Fowles is her master, if he owns this girl, it is illegal in New York, and he should be arrested. My name is William Warren. Believe me, I am your friend and admirer, Sir. I knew Beriah Green."

He turned again to the girl. *"Comment t'appelles-tu?"* This time she answered.

"Marie." To compound his urge to help her, she bore his mother's name.

"Où vas-tu?"

"Freedom! No more slave, moi! Freedom!" She would volunteer no more, but laid her head on the shoulder the woman beside her, crouching in her shawl.

Douglass faced him. "I saw no man outside. She's simply distressed."

"You could not see him, Sir. You were facing forward. But she did, and Benton saw her. He will tell George Fowles. Will you please explain to me what she is doing on this train?"

Douglass was immediately wary. "There was no way anyone could know she is on this train. We have agents in the hotel, and no one saw her leave. How do you know the Reverend Green, Mr. Warren?"

"I attended Oneida Institute, studying under Green, some years ago."

"And you never heard of the Anti-Slavery Society, or the Underground Railroad?"

"Of course I have. I know very well who you are." He showed him his copy of his newspaper. "But I never dreamed that you yourself would—"

"We are taking this young woman to her freedom, Mr. Warren. This is Mrs. Harriet Tubman, also experienced in these matters. We must get her to Rochester. Then to a boat to Canada, where her sister awaits her. She will be safe at my house, but she's still frightened. This is not the first time she has attempted to escape."

Warren thought: The scars on her back. The price for getting caught. But Fowles had been careful not to scar too deeply and spoil the merchandise.

Douglass pressed on. "Now you tell me. How did you know about George Fowles? He owns part of that hotel. How did you know he kept her there, as his slave?"

"She's already tried to escape? From Fowles?" He asked, deliberately avoiding Douglass's question.

"No, not until today," said the older black woman, in a flat southern drawl. "She been sold three times. She was caught in Louisiana, tryin' to get to me," There was a matronly tenderness in the woman's gravel-hard voice. "Her sister made it through. The rest o' her family already dead. She don't know who her daddy is, but you look at her you know he weren't no Negro slave. Maybe Indian, Seminole or such, maybe not."

Douglass interrupted. "They said my father was white, that he owned my mother. She was Negro and part Indian. I barely knew her. Those born into slavery sometimes never know, Mr. Warren. But black or mixed-blood, the whites say once a slave, always a slave. Marie escaped, just like I did."

"George Fowles," said Harriet Tubman, "he buy her from a Creole brothel last year. This missy got spirit, say she scratched one white boy bloody. Creole madams bring up their girls like they was aristocracy. But they couldn't use her because of them scars on her belly. Her mama done that. Men don't cotton to it. Think it's voodoo. Maybe it is. Fowles bought her and bring her here. She was waiting for us all the time."

"How can Fowles get away with that? Slavery was abolished years ago in New York."

"He ain't gettin' away with it. We makin' sure of that. We got her sister to freedom already, just across that Lake Ontario." Tubman stroked Marie's hair as if she were a child. "But one thing you ought to know, Suh. Fowles bought her in Louisiana, where it's legal. Since they pass the Fugitive Slave Act two years ago, it's illegal to help a slave escape, even in this state. We all riskin' jail. But we gonna get her to Canada, to her sister." She smiled down on the girl's face. "She waitin' on you, baby."

Then she addressed Warren again. "Why don't you set here next to us, Mistuh Warren? Speakin' that French with you seem to calm her down."

Marie closed her eyes and, like a child in her reverie, brought her thumb to her mouth and suckled. She lay her head on the woman's lap, and the woman raised her finger to her lips to shush the men. There Marie drowsed, or pretended to, and the conversation ended.

The train cranked steadily ahead, the car smoky from the wood stove, sometimes at impressive speeds on the straights. In the curves, the coach rocked, and the rumble was deafening. For Warren, it was unnerving. It seemed to him that this compression of distance and time was risky. Railroad disasters were as numerous as shipwrecks on the lakes. What if they hit a fallen tree, or a deer on the tracks?

Frederick Douglass sighed heavily and walked down the aisle, glanced into the next car through the window. The fogged image of a white woman in the next car, wearing a smart flowered hat, appeared through the smudged glass. She was a good ten feet away, with the two platforms and couplings between the cars. Douglass stared across at her a moment and put his hand on the flat of the window, almost as if to touch her. The silhouette nodded, then he turned and closed a window against a sudden rain of sparks from the smokestack. Thomas came out of his vestibule with a tray of glasses and a bottle of lemon water, pouring some for the woman and the girl, while Warren declined, preferring a draught of his tea.

"Everything all right, Mrs. Tubman?" Thomas smiled broadly.

"Everything just fine, Mistuh Thomas. You just keep that door closed and locked. How's that lovely wife o' yours?"

"Just fine, Ma'am. Just two cars down. Long as she keeps that door closed and locked."

"It's a wicked world, my boy. You get the chance, you give her my regards."

Douglass returned and sat with them. He appeared impatient and ruffled and spoke directly to Warren.

"No one knew Marie was on this train this morning. No one but Harriet and myself. How could Fowles's man know that? Could Fowles be on this train? Or was Benton looking for you for some reason?"

"Frederick, stop your frettin'," said Harriet Tubman. "We got a conductor in every car."

"No. Fowles is not on the train," said Warren, deflecting again. "He left on business last night, by coach. I saw him leave. Benton stayed behind. There's no reason he should be looking for me. Maybe he was tipped off, or he suspected her. He may have been instructed—"

"And do you know just where Fowles went last night? What else do you know, Mr.

Warren? It's important."

"If I remember right, he said Attica."

"Attica? God help us, that's the next stop!" Said Douglass. "We're only ten miles away, maybe less. We'll have to take precautions."

Douglass was cautious, but anger made men unpredictable. Warren was even less inclined to tell them about the incident in his room, about the girl's being sent to him by Fowles. To what end? And it would only upset her and arouse Douglass's suspicions even more. She was such a child, her life lay ahead. She might be part Indian. Was that the connection he felt?

And there was another possibility. Benton, as Fowles's right-hand man, probably knew that she was sent to his room last night. And he knew Warren would be on this train. He may have discovered her gone in the morning, suspected that she'd fled with him, and come looking. If that were the case, Warren was indeed the reason, although unknowingly, that she was found out. Bad luck. He tried to calm Frederick Douglass.

"Fowles doesn't know she's run off. Even on horseback, Benton couldn't reach Attica before this train does."

"Oh, but he could. If for some reason we stop, he could. And there's another risk. A telegram. Benton could send a wire. To warn Fowles ahead of time."

"Are there lines to Attica?"

"There are lines everywhere. Good God, man. Where do you think you are? Antarctica?" Of course. Corning had told him: just wire him. This was New York, not the wilderness, and telegraph wires followed the train lines. What if Fowles did know she was on the train? His opportunity to approach Frederick Douglass about his *History,* about publication, was slipping from his grasp. It would not be foremost in the man's mind at present. They may soon have to face George Fowles.

The train was on a straight stretch through a pine flat when the steam whistle blared and a sudden jolt announced the slowdown. The steel brakes screeched and the smell of hot iron and sparks entered the coach. A minute later they were stopped on the tracks, the engine huffing and pinging in the midst of snowmelt, smoking timber, blackened stumps, and lowlands, a flat scorched earth just cleared for the passage of the rails on the new line, where under the gray freezing drizzle the train shone like a jewel in the ruins of the forest.

Thomas bustled through with a shovel in hand and spoke to Douglass.

"A small washout, some track to clear. No worries, ladies. Please remain on board, the country is inhospitable."

Douglass rose. "I can help, Thomas. It may go faster."

"If you please, Sir. For safety's sake, you'd better remain with your company. We have ample hands."

Douglass reluctantly agreed, telling him to make haste. They had to reach Rochester as soon as possible. Thomas left, locking the door behind him.

§

Warren thought of volunteering despite his fatigue, but he feared a coughing fit, and this made him feel embarrassingly useless. It would not be a good moment to risk disablement. Besides, he may be needed here. The wait made everyone nervous. Douglass paced in the aisle while Harriet Tubman assumed a stoic pose and observed the desolate landscape, her arm still around the sleeping Marie.

Warren made a decision. He went to his assigned seat and took from his bag the small pistol Andrew Benton had loaded for him and taught him to use. He checked the cylinders, tamped the lead balls, and put it in his coat pocket.

Twenty minutes passed like hours, Douglass watching from the open window. Then the train rolled forward again. Thomas announced the first stop in Attica, in about ten minutes. Warren rose and drew Thomas aside.

"In Attica, how long do we stop?"

"No more than two minutes. We're behind schedule."

"You keep the doors locked?"

"At both ends. Anyone coming in must come with me."

"I'll be at the far end. There may be a white man in Attica, George Fowles by name.

Wearing a gray hat."

"I know who he is. We all do. We have five conductors on this train. We'll watch out for her. There may be trouble."

"Can you fetch the police?"

"Attica has one sheriff. There won't be time."

"Are you armed?"

"No. Mr. Douglass won't allow it, and he's the stationmaster. None of us are armed." Thomas looked at Warren and spoke softly. "There are times I wish I were."

"All right, listen to me. I can trick Fowles. You make sure he comes to my end of the car, and leave the door unlocked. He won't get on this train."

He went back to sit with the three other passengers. The girl was curled in Harriet Tubman's lap. Mrs. Tubman, silently stroking her charge, conveyed an air of determination and resignation that belied a preternatural patience, the likes of which he had seen only in his Ojibwe ancestors. She bore a certain likeness to Flat Mouth in the way she held her head and looked away in the distance. Up close, she was not that old, she just looked wizened. She did not demand sympathy and respect, as did Frederick Douglass—she had already earned it. Harriet Tubman was an old soul.

"How old is Marie?" He asked her.

"Her sister say maybe thirteen, fourteen. Barely outa the cradle. 'Cept she never had no cradle. What this child seen, Mistuh Warren, I hope you never learn. Family come on a slave ship. Her own mother cut those scars on her belly. Spose' to mean she ready for child bearin'. African girls grow up quick."

"She will if you get her to freedom," said Warren. "Whatever happens, you both stay with her. I'll deal with the man in Attica."

Douglass cut in. "That's not your job, Mr. Warren, it's mine."

"If he's there, I can hoodwink the man, I'm certain. He knows I'm on the train, he won't be surprised to see me. Let him come to me. Outside. I won't let him on this train, I assure you. Our main concern is to get you all safely to Rochester. From then on, it will be up to you, Sir." He gave Douglass a glimpse of his Baby Dragoon. "I am sufficiently armed for this purpose. Fowles may be too, but I can get the drop on him, don't worry. I am merely a helper along the way. You must all go on. It's important for Marie, for your people. For all of us."

The woman appeared to have no quarrel with this, pragmatically nodding her approval.

Douglass weighed Warren's last phrase. He finally nodded, and sat with his arms crossed.

The train slowed. Ahead was the small wooden structure serving as the Attica train depot with a covered platform aligned along the tracks. Waiting there was one man in a gray hat, no baggage, holding the lapels of his gray coat. Douglass saw who it was and put his own greatcoat over the prone girl on the seat opposite. Her mouth was slightly open, like a sleeping child's.

Warren rose, went to the far door, and leaned out. The train stopped. He waved to George Fowles, who strode down the length of the platform, smiling slightly, even leisurely. Thomas was further down, watching. Three passengers stepped from a car ahead, but no one boarded. Several faces, black and white, looked out from the second-class cars observing any comings and goings on the platform. Douglass's big face was visible behind the window of the first-class car, scowling. Fowles glanced at him, seemed to ignore him, and addressed Warren.

"Why, Mr. Warren. I'm glad to see you made your train. I am on my way to Batavia this morning, just up the line. We'll sit together." He came forward to board the car.

He stepped down and faced him on the platform, Fowles was some ten feet away when Warren drew his pistol and aimed from his waist. Fowles stopped short.

Warren looked into the face of his adversary, knowing he understood exactly what this show of arms was all about. If he was shaking, he hoped it didn't show. He had never aimed a gun at a man before with the intent to use it. Douglass looked down from above through a partly opened window just a few feet away, between the two men. From Warren's vantage point, he saw that Douglass's hand was under his coat pocket, his thumb on the hammer of a firearm. The stationmaster, contrary to his orders to his conductors, was armed and ready.

"So," Fowles spoke easily. "You've taken up with the Negroes. I thought you might have a taste for them. They say she's part Indian. Does it run in the blood?"

"Mr. Fowles," said Warren, "You are a slaver, a child exploiter and in this state, a criminal. God will condemn you if the law doesn't. But you will go no further this day."

Fowles grinned. "So I was right. You decided to take the girl with you. This is how you show your gratitude? She has to work out her contract. This is kidnapping and abetting a fugitive slave under federal law. I'll have the police on you."

"You have no right to police protection. On the contrary, Mr. Fowles. Indenture is a crime punishable by New York State law. You shall not come aboard, there is nothing here for you. In this train there are only free individuals."

The train whistled; Thomas yelled out the departure. Fowles's expression turned to a grimace of impotent rage. He reached for a pistol in his belt and made a sudden move forward, gun in hand. Warren fired at the boards between Fowles's boots, but missed. Fowles winced and dropped the gun, grabbed his leg. He was shot in the foot. Blood leaked from his boot.

Warren cocked again and aimed higher.

"That's the second time this gun has been fired at you. The third time won't miss."

The train jerked forward while Warren grabbed the handle by the door. His fatigue seemed to have left him. He pulled himself up, amazed at his lightness. Fowles fumed, sat on the platform, and held his leg, grimacing.

"This will cost you, Warren. We'll find you. I paid 2,500 dollars for that girl!"

"My father lost ten times that to crooks like you. All that girl has to lose is her life. And you won't get that!"

He remained on the coach step with the pistol drawn while the train belched smoke and gained momentum. He watched George Fowles grow smaller on the platform. They were well underway by the time he saw Benton ride up on horseback. Fowles gestured furiously for him to follow the train, but the Captain doffed his hat and shook his head. After the hard ride from Buffalo, his horse was heaving and hanging its neck. It was no match for the steam locomotive on the wide-gauge track.

William Warren pocketed his Baby Dragoon and went back into the coach, the taste of victory keen on his tongue. He had shown the pistol at the right time.

Now they had to stay one step ahead of the telegraph.

Chapter 26: Rochester

THE TRAIN WAS MOVING AGAIN with its inexorable mechanical force, unperturbed by the dealings of men left behind on
the platform. Harriet Tubman was relieved but still cautious, protective of her ward. The girl, Marie, seemed to withdraw into herself,
never rising from her guardian's lap, eyes closed, with an occasional
twitch like a wary wildcat even in slumber. She once opened her
eyes to look at Warren, silently, then let them drift closed again.
Tubman fell off into a profound sleep.

Perhaps she feels out of danger, thought Warren, but he did not.
He could sense the tension in Frederick Douglass, sitting next to
him on the bench. He felt he should still warn them.

"Fowles may yet come for her," he told Douglass. "We've raised
his ideas by taking Marie, and now I've shot him in the foot. He's
not a man to take it lying down. You must know that. You were
backing me up from the window. So, you carry a firearm."

"No, I do not," he replied. "My position in the Anti-Slavery Society precludes recourse to armed violence, Mr. Warren, as a tactical
principle. But I have been pursued all my life by armed men, and I
find it sometimes useful to answer in kind. This gun belongs to Mrs.
Tubman."

Hearing her name, the woman roused. "I ain't never used it 'cept
once," she said. "My passengers sometimes gets cold feet. I show
'em my pistol and tell 'em, you get free or you die. I ain't never lost
one yet."

Warren noticed the deep scar on her forehead.

"I'll keep the pistol until Rochester," said Douglass.

He then rose and pulled Warren down the aisle, out of earshot, where he faced him with the full force of his brow.

"What did Fowles mean, 'taking the girl with you'? Gratitude for what? He thought you were kidnapping her, not us. What are you hiding here, Mr. Warren?"

"It's fortunate he did think that, or you would have had to shoot him. He still thinks I helped her escape, not your organization. Benton didn't see me at the station, he only saw Marie. So he wired ahead to Fowles, no doubt. Fowles too was looking for Marie, but saw me waiting, and I was able to lure him my way. To stop him."

"How did you know she was indentured to him? You knew that when you proposed your interpreting services earlier."

Warren felt cornered.

"Yes, I knew. She told me herself, last night when she was sent to my room, by Fowles himself. But I had no idea she would be escaping with you and Mrs. Tubman this morning."

"Sent to your room?"

"She's a chambermaid."

"But she was sent for another purpose, wasn't she?"

"As a sort of favor. You know what I mean. But he misjudged me. I sent her away, Mr. Douglass. I have a daughter myself, and three younger sisters in my charge. The very thought of it sickened me. Everything about men like Fowles is an abomination, they have no conscience. He was also instrumental in the ruin of my father. So call it an old family debt that I settled there on the platform."

"Well, at the same time, you've helped her, and helped our cause. You're now a conductor, Mr. Warren, whether you like it or not."

"A coincidence."

"False modesty, but I thank you. Keep the pistol handy. We could still face trouble."

"The telegraph? Could they get a message to Rochester?"

"They'd have to get to Batavia to send it, unlikely before we reach Rochester. But we must stay alert."

No sooner had the two men sat back down than Thomas opened the vestibule door and out stepped a woman whose demeanor, dress and dark hair heightened by her fair and unweathered skin gave her a demure air despite her obvious fury. She glared at Douglass and at William Warren.

Thomas shrugged, looking apologetic. "I couldn't restrain her, Sir. She insisted on speaking to you." She stood not two feet away from Warren, who could feel her heat.

"Frederick." She demanded. "A word, please." Her accent was British. "You were to remain at your post!"

"A word in private please." She strode to the middle of the car, Douglass followed. Warren sat at his seat and sipped tea from his flask while their altercation transpired in hushed tones. Douglass then brought her back to Warren's seat and presented Miss Julia Griffiths, an associate, who had volunteered herself and several others to serve as train lookouts on this trip to Rochester. An indispensable ally, he added.

"I represent the Rochester Ladies Anti-Slavery Society, Mr. Warren. We are opposed to firearms in all circumstances and cannot have you or anyone else compromising our legitimacy by shooting up train depots."

"A necessary exception," said Douglass. "Mr. Warren did in fact save the mission by keeping Fowles at bay. We still have Marie."

"Be that as it may, we cannot have such displays in Batavia and especially not in Rochester, where our people provide protection, and without recourse to firearms. We despise theatrics, Sir, it attracts the press and the authorities. I must demand that you refrain from further gunplay. This is not the far west." Where had he ever heard a woman speak so imperiously?

"Miss Griffiths. Rest assured there will be no further need," said Warren. Nothing was said of the pistol Douglass was carrying.

She and Douglass sat alone in an empty seat, not speaking, both looking out on opposite sides of the moving train. Warren moved to accompany Harriet Tubman and Marie. A few more whispered words passed between the two abolitionists, then Douglass finally stood and roared:

"Goddammit, Julia, you will do as I say! And I shall say no more!"

She returned stiffly to her car. Douglass remained by himself looking out a window, where he continued to huff.

There was one more stop, Batavia, before the last leg to Rochester. The line was flat and straight, they would make good speed, so there was no danger of being followed. Thomas came and told Warren they owed him a vote of thanks for putting his life in danger.

Warren did not tell them that his own safety was of little concern to him because his days were numbered—his life was either a risk or a gift every morning. He was thankful for the chance to gull George Fowles—a small revenge on the men who had caused his father's ruin. Nonetheless, he felt he did compromise the safety of the escape mission.

When Douglass returned to the bench, Warren felt he should further warn them. "Fowles will be coming along the railroad lines," he explained. "With his man Benton. He's a laborlooker, working with Erastus Corning on the new canal through the upper Great Lakes, recruiting canal workers, miners. Corning has business interests here. Fowles could use his connections to get to you."

"Mine is a safe house in Rochester, Mr. Warren, and we too have connections. Marie will be gone by tomorrow morning, and in Canada tomorrow night. You know that you're heading straight for Corning's home territory, don't you? Albany. He's been Mayor there and covets the Senate. He owns most of the railroad lines you'll be traveling on today. All the way to the Hudson Valley."

"Corning is in Detroit now. I know because I left him there."

"But the man you shot is right behind you, with connections ahead of you. You run with dubious company, Sir."

"Well, Mr. Douglass, is that not the case as we speak? I've never until this day been pursued for kidnapping. Or accused of shooting up a train depot."

This drew a smile, at last, from the grave abolitionist and from the stalwart woman still with her arm around the runaway slave, who since they left Attica had fallen into a deep sleep.

The stop at Batavia depot was quick and efficient. No new passengers. Miss Griffiths, looking colder, walked past them on the quay to turn and reboard the second-class car. Warren saw her dark hair coming undone at the nape of her neck. Thomas yelled out the departure. With no washouts, they would arrive just before noon.

Douglass, though obviously preoccupied, seemed disposed to talk. He informed Warren that the Rochester Ladies' Anti-Slavery Sewing Society was indeed a group of white women, Miss Griffiths being one of the founders and an author herself. They advocated rights for women, the vote especially, of all races. They were very good at raising funds, he added, and generously supported his newspaper and the Underground Railroad. Several people, whites and Negroes, including women, were keeping watch this train. There would be more in Rochester, waiting on the platform, all part of the Anti-Slavery movement, defending all oppressed peoples.

"Freedom rings far," he concluded, quoting himself.

Warren knew that the wide support of Douglass's cause was owed to his honesty, his eloquent speeches and writings, and to his popular biography, published in Boston. This provided him with the opening.

"Sir, you should know that I am fighting to advance a similar cause for the Ojibwe, my mother's oppressed people. In my bags I have my manuscript, a history of the fast-disappearing Ojibwe people, compiled from the narratives of their old chiefs that I have collected and written down all my life. I aim to publish it in New York City, in hopes that it will awaken the new owners of this land to the plight of the red man, from whom they have wrested it by war and decimation.

"You asked last year, *"What, to the American Slave is the Fourth of July? A day that reveals to him the gross injustice and cruelty to which he is the constant victim."* When I read that speech I thought: the same is true for the red man. The original inhabitants of America have been dispossessed of their native lands and decimated. They are just as much victims of the ruling class, in the colonies and in the Americas. The whites are intent on one thing: their own dominance.

Manifest Destiny is their supreme manifesto in this country. The enslaved blacks are there to serve the whites, but the red man must disappear."

Warren had never expressed it in those words so clearly, although he had felt it. Today he felt somehow inspired by the presence of the notorious radical before him.

"Unless we act, unless we educate," said Douglass. "That speech was delivered in Rochester, our destination. Not on the Fourth, but on July 5th, in commemoration of the Abolition of slavery in New York in 1827. You are a historian, Mr. Warren?"

"A writer and interpreter, historian by choice. I lay no claim to academic training in the discipline, but I have studied their history at length. And I am the depositor of the knowledge the Ojibwe chiefs have entrusted to me. I speak the language fluently, having spent my young life among them in the wilderness territories."

"Self-taught, then."

"Not so much as yourself, nor so extensively. As I told you, I did study under Beriah Green until the Institute was closed. My articles have reached the public through newspapers In Minnesota, where I held office in the Territorial Legislature. My sponsors encouraged me to publish them as a book. The first of a series, should I be grant-ed the time to write them. I hope to open the ears of America to their plight, Sir."

"A laudable plan, Mr. Warren. You must come back to Rochester and tell me more about this. I trust you have people to see in New York City? In the publishing world?"

"Some. With letters of introduction. I was wondering—"

"You're very fortunate. I find the search for publishers tiresome, and must depend on others to take such details in hand. It's a strug-gle every week to publish my newspaper. I seek funding where I can, even abroad for future publications. America is a poor market for human rights causes. At any rate, when we get past this hurdle and you finish your business, come back to my office, and give me news of your endeavor, perhaps write an article for the paper. One good turn deserves another. It will afford me a chance to read your treatise."

The great statesman had a way of closing a conversation definitively. This was all the encouragement Warren could expect from Frederick Douglass, who was by all indications in a foul mood, perhaps due to his recent altercation.... He fell silent for the remaining hour, closing his palm over his eyes, momentarily the image of a browbeaten man. Warren was hard put to contain his disappointment.

He let the sleepers rest, went back to his assigned seat to eat a roll, and took a draft of his lukewarm tea. He still felt the excitement from the gunshot running through his veins, and could not sleep.

§

The Rochester station was an open pass-through structure forming a dark roof over the tracks and platforms. The conductors were at the peak of their vigilance. Frederick Douglass and Harriet Tubman faced Warren and shook his hand, in what struck him as military style. The young runaway, however, when her hat was finally pinned into place by Harriet Tubman, turned and gave Warren the benefit of her wide smile and whispered *"Merci, monsieur."*

Somehow, somewhere in her troubled life, she had learned grace and perfect manners. It would benefit her as she went on to freedom. Marie was the second slave he had helped on their way to freedom in Canada. He hoped this one would make it—unlike Elijah, whose fate was still unknown.

Would that he could have done as much for his own people. He had tried, but unsuccessfully. All he could do now was speed their spoken words, their *History,* on to publication. Then he would perhaps be able to say he did something for the Ojibwe.

He stayed on board surveying the departure from the open window. Several women got off the second-class cars and joined the group of blacks and whites waiting on the platform, to form a protective huddle around the steps descending from first class. They numbered about twenty, all elegant citizens of Rochester. As Douglass, Harriet Tubman and the girl Marie stepped down, they all moved as

318

one body to the end of the platform and onto the street, then out of sight behind the station depot. They met with no opposition.

The only exception to the group movement was the white woman, Julia Griffiths, with her high hat, now covered in a long royal blue overcoat with her hands in a fur muff, proceeding by herself in the opposite direction. It struck him that she carried herself with the same poise as Anna Ramsey, with the same fair skin and dark hair done up under her hat—with a few strands, he knew, straying loose at the back of her neck. She had descended from the train as a woman alone, ignoring Douglass and the silent procession surrounding the escaped slave girl.

Frederick Douglass had remarked that abolition was not so much a matter of public opinion, as he once thought, but of politics. What would public opinion have to say about this woman? Why was he so distracted in the train? Was she the great man's mistress? Perhaps. And perhaps she was a married woman. As was Anna Ramsey.

Warren sat, now alone in the first-class coach, while a butcher boy came through selling sandwiches, cakes, sweetmeats, and apples, with some newspapers. He bought a more recent edition of *Frederick Douglass's Paper,* this one with further articles on Harriet Beecher Stowe, and exchange of letters, and an installment from a novel written by Douglass himself—as well as sufficient victuals to see him through the day, or at least on to Utica or Albany, before the night trip through the Hudson Valley.

As the train pulled out of Rochester, he drank deeply from his flask of tea and again pondered the lady walking away from the station alone. He allowed that such high-blooded women were supremely intriguing, but demanding. As the train left Rochester, he thought for a fleeting moment of nearby Clarkson, where his thoughts and passions were those of a young man, now extinct for him after twelve long years. Exhaustion then overtook him in like a landslide and buried him in merciful sleep.

When he awoke in late afternoon, the train window was clouded with ash. Mist and rain had stunted visibility in all directions, the land and sky were the color of milk. This seemed to suit his state of mind. The flask of tea was cold, but he drank nonetheless, for the comfort more than the thirst. He was alone in the first-class car, but for another black conductor busy in his vestibule. He took out his writing kit.

Dear Mrs. Ramsey,

The final leg of my rail journey to New York City affords me a moment to keep you abreast not only of the progress in my travels which has been unexpectedly enhanced by events I shall presently relate, but of recent developments in the East which I am certain will be of interest to you. At this time I am in transit from Rochester to Albany on the newly improved track consolidated into the New York and Erie Railroad system, speeding soon through the Mohawk Valley. Although still bare and awaiting Spring, the orchards, the valleys, and the river are indeed beautiful, the towns and farmhouses well established, venerable church steeples all painted white, the fields well cultivated and now being tilled for the season. The very image of industry and ingenuity. We have occasional glimpses of the Erie Canal, by which I traveled over a decade ago when studying in Whitesboro, a town we shall later pass by, and where unfortunately my revered school, the Oneida Institute, has closed its doors after a valiant struggle for the abolition of slavery and for equal rights for all races, women and men, which of course continues elsewhere throughout the East. This canal, I am told, may soon lose traffic due to the much faster and more efficient train system.

Indeed, we shall make the city in 24 hrs, whereas in my youth it took a week. Can you imagine!

Quite fortuitously when dining at the hotel in Rochester, I had the good fortune of meeting Mr. Frederick Douglass, whose writings and reputation as spokesman for universal freedom and equality you certainly know—most certainly his biography as a freed slave and his North Star paper, now Frederick Douglass' Paper of which I shall send you some copies. Currently he has interviewed Mrs. HB Stowe, you will recall.

He is a powerfully built man with a stentorian voice and keen intelligence, at the same time elegant, poised, in short a gentleman who commands attention and respect from all. As we both boarded the same train this morning and had the occasion to talk, he graciously invited me, on my return, to his home in Rochester where we shall discuss my work and possibilities of publication through his connections in Europe.

Fortune seems to be shining on me during this entire travel. A number of women from the Rochester Ladies' Anti-Slavery and Sewing Society who support his work and paper were also aboard. One associate I met, a Miss Griffith (a very interesting woman indeed, very independent-minded like yourself, an Abolitionist from England) is publishing a work she has edited entitled Autographs for Freedom. Mr. Le Duc will surely be in the know and can order it for you. If not, please advise me and I shall bring you a copy from New York. You shall have it then by my return in the late Spring.

There were some ramifications to our meeting this morning, which I shall relate to you more at length in person, reflecting the reality of the anti-slavery movement in our present time. Although unlawful in New York and other states, slave owners still pursue their ends ruthlessly and with complete impunity throughout the country. The reason for this, as you know, is the lack of opposition due to divided public opinion.

Many Northerners think that owning slaves is a venerable economic practice, no business of the law. However, as Douglass has said, abolition is more a matter of politics than of public opinion. Through politics shall we prevail, and through knowledge and enlightenment. The work is long and arduous, but you would be pleased to see that free individuals of all colors live and work alongside the white Anglo-Americans in the state of New York. Such will, I hope, be true of our own Territory when the moment is ripe for statehood. Would that such enlightened thinking benefit the Red Race as well. We have enslaved them as much as any Negro and we now inhabit their lands. Where to find justice and equality if not in the burgeoning new nation? When will we give them their due?

Here his mind wandered and he laid down his quill. He took to watching the hypnotic swoop of the telegraph wires as they dipped and rose between the poles along the tracks. Were Fowles's words racing along them now, alerting Corning's men further up the line? Were they already waiting for him somewhere?

He absently wondered if he should include any mention of her husband, the Governor, in his letter. He would have liked to call his attention to these matters, but was loath to refer to Governor Ramsey in this, a private communication. He would rather just be talking to Anna. He could see her intelligent features light up as she listened to his account of the runaway slave girl. He must be careful not to make himself out as a hero, but surely it would be a moment to savor. Perhaps he would tell it to no one else.

Anna Ramsey would be the only one to understand the import of the Underground Railroad, and why he should be risking his life to publish his *History of the Ojibways.* His mother's people, his people. Maybe she was the only one to understand that.

Chapter 27: Black Angels

HE CAME AWAKE JANGLED WITH A SENSE OF URGEN-CY. He could think of no reason why, but it jerked him to his senses. The train passed over a trestle bridge under which a barge was being poled by men and pulled by a team of horses on the bank. The passengers and crew lay flat on the deck as the barge passed under. The old world trudging below, the new one speeding overhead. The water of the canal reflected the clearing sky, but the blue was deepening. Afternoon was waning. Soon he would have to write by lamplight, nearer the vestibule, comfortable by the stove. One thing led to another in his mind. He brought out the draft of his Preface to write in the margin of the first page:

"We do not fully understand the nature and character of the Red Race. The Anglo-Americans have pressed on them so unmercifully—their intercourse with them has been of such a nature, that they have failed to secure their love and confidence. The heart of the red man has been shut against his white brother, who has never deigned to look inside that heart."

This was not wholly appropriate either. Although it was true. He would have to review his prose, which he often judged overly emotional, to adopt a more scholarly tone. After all, was he aiming to outdo Schoolcraft or Fenimore Cooper? He resumed:

"Much has been written concerning the Red Race by missionaries, travelers, and some eminent authors, but the information respecting them which has thus far been collected, is mainly superficial, gathered through the intermediary of careless and imperfect interpreters, and the accounts

of unreliable sources. Notwithstanding all that has been written respecting these people since their discovery, the subject is still vast, and the tribes are fast disappearing. Some are already wholly changed in character through forced contact with an evil white population set upon exterminating them with dependence upon the demon whiskey. Their history will soon be a blank. Under the present conditions of the red race, there is no time to lose."

Imperfect. But it needed to be said. He would mitigate the dramatic tone later, in the final draft. Too intense for history. He did not want to be taken for a temperance fanatic, nor a hater of the white race. It was important that he set the tone right. What is in play here is the survival of the Ojibwe history, the rites, the true biographies of the chiefs, the mythology, and the few remaining Anishinaabe themselves. Urgency, and sympathy, but without soliciting pity.

He lay down his pen, lost in the swing of the wires outside his window. It was darkening fast now. He nodded off.

§

Someone shook him. The conductor, a more portly and older black man, had lit the lamp near his vestibule, stoked the stove, and come to ask his passenger if he needed anything. Warren hardly heard the man, although the train was stopped at some station. UTICA, said the sign on the platform.

"I beg your pardon? Are we not near Whitesboro?"

"Yessir. You're going on to Albany, then New York City?"

"Yes, but--I used to know someone in Whitesboro."

"That so? You need anything, Sir?"

"Some hot water, for tea. I think I have enough left..."

"That kettle on the stove is hot. We got no tea. Coffee, sir? You look a bit pale."

"I have my own tea. Thank you. I can make it."

"The train takes on water here and leaves in forty minutes, if you need anything at the station, stretch your legs outside. The door's open. We got two conductors outside too."

"Conductors?"

"Orders from the station master, Sir. You safe on this Railroad." The man smiled broadly and winked at him. "Nobody bother you out there. We make sure."

Warren descended from the train in a slight fog. Two men, dark-skinned, were stationed at either side of his car. They looked his way briefly and nodded. Douglass, he then understood, had wired ahead and given instructions for his protection. He wondered if they were armed. Then he touched his pocket and remembered: he was.

The conductors followed discretely as he bought some dried fish, bread, and an apple from a vendor on the platform, found the privy, and boarded again. They checked every passenger coming aboard, then locked the doors. Douglass ran an efficient organization. He found his seat and dozed, reassured. And too fatigued to worry.

Whitesboro. The Oneida Institute. It was not so far, yet now a distant past. He tried to remember how he was as a boy when he and his brother Truman first came east for their education, staying with his grandparents in nearby Clarkson. He was learning English fast, determined to pass up all the other boys, and won a prize for drawing the best map of the United States. A year later when he was twelve, he wrote his first letter to his father:

"So I was put in a higher class of which I was the smallest of them. It was pretty hard to keep up but I did keep up all the way through the book...And in spelling I can spell any word, but now I am studying Latin with 5 boys. The master says who will beat will have a premium and my Grandfather says he will make me a pair of pumps if I shall beat them and there is no question but I will beat them..." And then his post scriptum: *"I have wrote this letter without any help but excuse me for bad writing. Do not expect such bad writing next time."*

Then Lyman came east on "business" (which, they found out later, was to sell his Clarkson land to his brother, Henry). Seeing the boys' progress, he enrolled them in the Oneida Institute in Whitesboro, a grand experiment in interracial education, and affiliated, as was the Warren family, to the Presbyterian Community. The next year the girls and his mother came and they all stayed at the Warren residence, the girls attending Clarkson school while the boys continued at Oneida, working and studying. They first heard of the Underground Railroad from Beriah Green himself, who made them swear to secrecy. Twice he harbored a runaway slave in his room. He never knew if Elijah made it, but he never told his parents. A year later Green broke with his church supporters and lost favor, surviving on charitable donations. It lasted another year, enrollment waned and Oneida had to shut down.

Young William went back to Clarkson. Lyman sent him the last of his money and encouraged all the boys to defray some of the costs by finding some manual work. He was fifteen when he learned to risk that money on cards and spend it on what he pleased. He stopped writing home, where Lyman Warren's financial difficulties had worsened. He could no longer pay for his children's education or board, and they were living on the goodwill of their grandparents and credit from the schools. His father wrote a final letter. He heard his words as if he were next to him:

"What is the matter with you? Have you no Ink, Pens, or Paper in that country?"

He snapped awake, unaware that he had dozed off again. Lyman Warren sat across the aisle in his leathers and feathered hat. His father eyed him sternly, sucking on his pipe. He mumbled an answer.

"I owed the money to my tutor for room and board, Father, I had to work—"

"You're no good at lying, William, never were. You spent the money on your footloose life. Cards. Then that bordello. Young and stupid. A man must learn to be honest, first of all with himself. Why in the hell did you ever come home?"

He was sixteen and rotten with guilt when he left Clarkson without telling anyone, not even his father, and went back to Lake Superior to face the music and help his family. It was all he could do while the girls and Truman stayed on to finish their educations. His father, strapped for cash, was still irate. It was the beginning of the end for Lyman Warren. And the beginning of everything for his son, William.

§

He awoke again. The train was still in the Utica station. He dosed his herbal leaves and maple mixture into the flask and walked to the stove. His legs felt heavy, he moved slowly. There were now five other passengers in the first-class car, all of them white and well-dressed, some dozing, the men mostly stouter than those in the territories. People who ate good fare and never went hungry.

One rather stern-looking woman was watching him fill his flask with some disapproval. She was sharing a basket meal with her husband, whom earlier he had seen behind the vestibule nipping deeply from his own flask. Now he was slowly chewing his sandwich, collapsed on the bench, looking blankly out the window at the station, the unhappiest and most uxorious man he had seen since his departure from the territories. The woman rose from her seat as the conductor called the departure, and approached Warren, jutting her sharp chin forward.

"Are you aware, Sir, that consumption of alcohol is unlawful on this train? It will soon be outlawed throughout this State."

"A laudable development, Madame. But I am making tea, not whiskey."

"Hmph."

"And I support your Temperance cause wholeheartedly, under certain circumstances. Would you also be opposed to slavery?"

"An abhorrent practice."

"Then I suggest, Madam, that you free your husband from your tyrannical grip."

She actually gasped. "Sir, you are drunk! I shall call the police!"

At this juncture, the train jolted forward and the woman fell properly on her backside. The husband looked around briefly, the open flask in his hand, his cheeks puffed and eyes wide. The wife was fortunately hooped and cushioned by her ample petticoats. The husband capped his whiskey, sighed, and made as if to come to her aid, taking pains to appear solicitous. The woman began to protest and insist on police intervention when the man told her raspingly to shut up unless she wanted to spend the night in a jail cell with him. This seemed to work. The man took another swig without comment from his wife.

Warren returned to his seat. The incident changed his mood. In disarray on the floor of the coach, the woman had hurriedly covered her rounded calves of a whiteness that Warren had not witnessed since his long-past nights at the bordello. Beyond that detail, his accuser bore no resemblance to his very first taste of a woman, the Irish girl whose name he could not recall.

The train creaked out of the station, leaving the gaslit depot behind, then the streets of Utica with its flickering lamps in the windows of its hotels and houses.

Warren ate his frugal dinner and drank his warm, sweet tea. They were soon out in the dark night, where the countryside was invisible with no stars above. The great steel machine rolled steadily ahead, sounding the tracks with regular blasts from the steam whistle. They advanced more slowly at night, he reflected—you never knew what might lie ahead.

The Irish girl's name came back to him: Eunice. It was not a whore's name. Incongruous, not a name he would have imagined at his young age for a girl of the night. When he saw her for the first time they were both intimidated. Warren had been encouraged by well-intentioned upperclassmen to imbibe in strong liquor, but was not drunk in the least, or so told himself. He had won at cards that night and felt confident. Introduced by the Madam, he found Eunice to be shy, coy, a novice like himself, and hopefully understanding. Upstairs in the low lamplight she undressed and asked him what he wanted. He had not the faintest idea.

You decide, he told her.

He only wanted her to keep her hair up, a bit disheveled as it was with the dark wisps trailing on her nape, because he found her neck beautiful. From then on, over the two months until he left, Eunice kept her hair up when he came. By the end of their tryst, it always began to fall down. He was perhaps a bit in love with her. He

328

left more money than she asked—young men can be imprudent that way. Then when he was broke, just before going home, he snatched a few coins from under her mattress. He regretted that, telling himself that one day he would somehow pay it back. But now that was over, he would have to live with his unconscionable theft. Futile as it was, calling up her image—her white neck, her piled-up black hair—never failed to thrill and console him. Those last months in Clarkson were so vivid they seemed like years. The softly floating strands loose on her neck haunted him still.

§

It was much later when the conductor shook him awake again. The lamp burning at his side was the only light in his coach. There were no other passengers.

"Albany comin' up, Sir. Got to make ready for the connection to New York. Hudson Valley train on another track. Just a short walk. You be comin' with us. Car number two. You need help, Sir? You all right?"

"No." His writing materials had fallen out from the leather pouch. He gathered them up. "Yes, fine. Thank you."

He was dizzy and slow, half asleep still, and his weariness was intolerable. But mostly, the pain was at bay. He kept moving, packing, forcing himself, careful not to falter. The conductor was watching him as the train pulled into the dimly lit station.

"I'll carry that trunk over for you, Sir. My man outside carry your bag. We walk over together, you between us. It'll be fine. You can lie down in that Hudson Valley train. They got nice comfort, make into a pallet. Nobody see a thing. We set you up, don't you worry."

"Very kind, I thank you." Warren was scouring the quay for possible enemies. They would be looking for him, examining the coaches.

"You a friend of Thomas and Mr. Douglass, you a friend to me. One helpin' hand deserve another. You best carry that hat now. Keep low. We don't want no one to notice."

The conductor nodded knowingly at him and took his trunk from the floor. The uniformed colored man on the quay, introduced as his new conductor for the New York train, took his bag and held his arm. He was escorted like this across the quays, a large black man flanking each side of him and he, bent over in his black cloak, hidden by the mist. The walk took only a few minutes but to Warren, it seemed interminably long. The men carrying him could have been angels. Black angels. In the dark night Warren felt almost invisible. He hoped it was true.

Inside the waiting train, the new conductor, a younger man, brought in a hurricane lamp and settled him into a fold-down berth above the benches in the first-class coach, which again was empty. He slid the trunk under the bench and turned down the lamp. It went dark inside the coach, the only dim glow coming from the platform lamps outside.

"You got a load o' number nine coal in that trunk?"

"Mostly paper actually. It's a book. It will be once I get to New York, and it's printed."

"Well, you tell them to print small. People ain't gonna wanna buy no book this heavy!"

Not buy his book? That was impossible. He had it from the best counsel that it was a valuable contribution to the history of the country and its first inhabitants. The curse of loss that had ruined his father would not garrote William Warren.

"Yes, they will buy it. It will be lighter."

"Just joshin' you, Sir. What you call that book?"

"A *History of the Ojibways.* My family's people, to the west. I must get it to New York."

"They buy it. You ask Mr. Douglass." He locked the doors and settled into his vestibule. His tea, lukewarm, was about half gone. He was congested, his breathing was shallow, but he could rest. He calmed himself to quell the urge to cough, then lay down on the pallet suspended from the wall as the train began to move about midnight. Then he saw two shadows in the mist on the platform outside.

Two men, hatless, were running heavily alongside the tracks. They seemed to be scouring the quays, but his coach was dark and out of their reach. He saw them stop, shake their heads and disappear as the train left Albany Station behind. Lying flat and low in the darkened coach, he trembled. He would never know if they were Corning's men, sent on Fowles' orders. Nonetheless, he felt like a hunted man.

His heavy cloak weighed upon his lungs, but kept him sufficiently warm. He was, in fact, transpiring. A bit feverish. He could smell his own fear. The conductor on this Hudson Valley line kept the stove stoked. As if to touch home, he put his hand on the trunk containing his writing materials, thinking he should write to his father, to tell him....

But no, that he could not do, Lyman was dead. To stop thinking about him, and to align his more sanguine thoughts, he borrowed the hurricane lamp, sat up and began a letter to Matilda. He wrote slowly and falteringly as the train rolled on:

> *My Dearest, my Wife,*
> *This missive finds me on the last leg of my journey to New York City, in the new train along the Hudson River, more powerful than our own Platt or Mississippi as they run past our warm little house that protects you and the children from the cold and darkness that must surround you now. Soon the Spring will come. Here it is night, and in the morning I shall reach my destination where my doctor awaits me eager to begin treatments, and where I shall forthwith and most certainly find publishers just as eager to pay me and publish my manuscript. (If you have trouble reading this letter, ask Julia to help you). You understand as I do that this is essential to our welfare.*

He paused. Would her understanding ease her hurt at his leaving them alone? What could be worth such abandonment? He was not abandoning them. He would succeed.

It pains me to be absent during the sugaring, but Alfred and Cordelia have learned well and are able to tap our maples with you. Mind that little Tyler stays warm. Hole-in-the-Day will send help from the tribe as well. He promised me. He will also send rice, and game from the hunt...

The train continued into the night. Through the window, he perceived some dim lights from a town on the riverbank, then again the train sank again into the darkness, heading south along the Hudson. He saw sparks from the smokestack speed by, like fireflies in a windstorm. His father appeared again, sitting and writing a letter. Lyman had taught him about will, about never giving up, about caring for your family, your responsibilities, your people. Go forward, never back. But then...for him to finish insane, desperate, broken, in sadness and in ruin. Was the struggle futile? Was it all vanity, or blind faith?

"Nothing but bad luck and bad men, William. The hardest part is admitting defeat. Give it your best, you'll never hold it against yourself. You'll do fine." Lyman spoke no more, and went back to his letter. He did the same.

My Dearest, this train has brought me close to my father's home in Clarkson and my beloved school, Oneida. It has been a journey through my past to reach the future. I have not dallied. It strikes me as I move forward to secure a livelihood for us, that my own father made this journey as a young man thirty years ago, but in the opposite direction, and in the Spring of his life. What New World awaits me in the greatest City in our country?

I shall write again as soon as I am established at Dr. Trall's Institute at 15 Laight Street. Please send news of you and the children. Alfred should be able to write to me now, in his own words and yours. I think often of you, the boys, and Cordelia.

Affectionately, your Husband, WWW

He folded the letter, and heated his wax on the stove. Unsteady on his feet, he sealed and addressed it to his home in Two Rivers, Minnesota Territory. He would try to send it from the station in New York City. One more draft of warm tea and he lay down on the improvised pallet wishing it were a mattress of fresh meadow grass.

The conductor covered him with his cloak and wiped his brow with a cool towel. "You feel all right, Sir? You sure you don't want some hot coffee?"

"No, no. I have what I need. I just want to sleep. Please."

"You want sometin', you just holler." The conductor left the towel there.

His blood swirled inside him, coursing through his ears, drumming in his temples, but the cool towel gave him solace. The comfort of black angels was something he had never felt before, and he was grateful. The train rumbled and shook through the night, but exhaustion overtook him regularly, allowing him to sleep, even though it did not feel like sleep.

He was a boy. The night was dark, fraught with running footsteps encircling the encampment, the only light falling cold from the moon. Voices whispered and shouted in the forest beyond, twigs snapped around him. He hid low to the ground with his small revolver in hand, short of breath as he scoured the darkness to see the enemy. He knew not who they were, neither his friends nor the attackers. Shots were fired and arrows flew at him and stuck in the cedar trunk behind which he cowered. He was afraid of being scalped. It must be the Sioux. Someone behind him bolted to another tree and was shot down. It was an Indian. He feared it was his friend, Gwii-wisens, and yelled out. A shadow fired at him, he saw the lead ball fly past him in a hissing arc. He tried to run but seemed paralyzed. His lungs constricted in panic. He cried out for his father, trying to escape the dream, but found he had no voice.

When he woke in the moving train, sweating and choking, Warren was alone in the dark but for the hurricane lamp in the conductor's booth. He was homeless, fatherless, voiceless, and now a hunted man.

PART IV
MANNA-HATA

— Hydropathic and Hygienic Institute, 15 Laight Street: 5th Ward near St. John's Park. Canal Street across Broadway to Five Points, Mulberry and Orange Streets, 14th Ward.

Chapter 28: Safe Haven

Dr. R. T. Trall's Water-cure Establishment in New York.

Manhattan Island, New York City, mid-March 1853

A NEGRO PORTER HELPED HIM from the train to the taxi line with his trunk and bag in tow on a handcart. Early morning, barely light, Warren stumbling, seeing nothing but a moving blur of black and gray. The thick air smelled of coal smoke. He ached all over and despite the cold, he was perspiring. Once out of the terminal, he was unsteady on his legs and lost. The porter held his arm. Another angel. This world was full of Black Angels.

"Are you all right, Sir? You need somethin'?"

He stood tottering, coming around. It passed. It must pass. This porter was no angel, simply a kind man. You could hear it in his voice. William Warren was not dead.

"Thank you," he said. He paid the man and stood for a time unmoving, collecting himself under his cloak and muffler. He felt heavy, yet light in the head, and breathed slowly, tasting the air. It did not sting his lungs, but it was bitter, close, thick with coal soot and something indefinable, stagnant, rotten, that he could recall from no other place he had ever been. The city's bowels hung in the air.

The Chambers Street Terminal was no more than a roof over a rail yard, open on all sides as in Rochester. But the noise was constant, and the air was colder, laced with black coal dust, the morning fog so thick he could see no color except the gray buildings and a line of black cabs, their dark horses waiting. He sat on his trunk, wheezing, his head empty except for a vague expectation of his arrival at his destination—an address unknown to him in a city unknown. He had no visual image of the place. Instead, he saw himself, but from a far vantage point, as if from a distant lamppost.

He was outside the terminal, hunched over, a lone man sitting in a cloak and hat, a herd of people rushing past him. Fearing he might be bowled over in the throng, he at once lifted his head and straightened up, suddenly re-inhabiting his own perspiring and painful skin. A sip of tea from his flask would be welcome, but people would take him for a drunkard. That would not do on his first day in New York City.

He shook himself awake. Hundreds of people appeared and disappeared. The streets around the terminal were gutted, rails upended and jutting out of the ground, bricks and dirt piled high amid stacks of timbers and unlaid steel. They were rebuilding the tracks. A dozen men at once hefted one long rail like a lone cadaver and slowly carried it to its place. They laid it down and turned to hoist another while the sledge men hammered down the spikes. The sound seemed to come from far away.

Beyond this, he discerned a wall of buildings in every direction, sometimes an open space where one had fallen, or another was being built. A city in the throes of becoming, not unlike Saint Paul, but on a vaster scale. The surrounding avenues were tremendously wide, the new buildings vast and high, the facades imposing their girth above him. Everywhere around him, demolition, digging, and construction were heaving up the innards of the city and changing the face of the streets.

As a foreigner here, he should not let his guard down. He looked around...no one was following him or lurking about, no one looked at him. He felt invisible in the throngs. People did not walk, they hustled, they ran, heads bent. A newsboy in front of him hawked the morning paper without looking at him, then got lost in the crowd. He was the only one sitting, an obstruction among the throng, a stump they had to avoid. The yelling, the rushing, the knotted tenseness of the harried masses outside the station suddenly overpowered him, and he felt in need of protection. He should reach his destination without further delay. He would take a private carriage. Directly.

He approached the smallest cab, a one-horse runner covered with a canvas top. It looked economical. The driver wore a black stovepipe hat and spoke in an incomprehensible murmur, but perked up considerably when Warren announced his destination on Laight Street. The man secured his bags and comfort, addressed him as Sire, dusted himself off, and drove amid the turmoil in a circuitous route through the thinning fog. The cab soon quit the high brick and stone facades of downtown to a quarter with smaller streets lined with wooden structures, strewn with piles of refuse, offal, blackened snow, and dead horses left to rot. Makeshift board houses were hammered up shoulder to shoulder. Coal soot was everywhere.

Advancing in thrusts and stops, the driver took several turns, avoiding street fires, paving works, overturned carts, cracking his whip at rag-poor children who assailed his passenger in tongues rough and unfamiliar, where speech was of nothing but money, spoken through outstretched hands. Through the din and clatter of commerce, New York emerged as a squirming mass of humanity where nothing, not even the buildings, stayed in place. As the fog thinned he caught glimpses of dank avenues teeming with soot-covered hod carriers bent under burdens, barrels of beer and rum and whale oil, women in threadbare shawls hawking oysters, painted prostitutes old and young, armies of vendors pushing wares and services, vying to undercut a rival's prices. They clattered over rocks and cobblestones past a great variety of houses and buildings, some half burnt down, garden plots swampy and rank with human offal, two dead mules, and a scourge of scavenging dogs fighting in a pool of blood before a butchery.

This part of the city was in constant flux, being demolished, burnt, and built up at the same time. Hardly fit, as the hack told him, for a gentleman such as himself. The stench was worse than in Saint Paul. Warren felt a sudden tang of nostalgia for the familiar odors of woodsmoke, humus, and evergreen, of his home near the water in Two Rivers. But there was nothing he could accomplish there now. Here in New York City, he was at the threshold of the new world even though, on this bleak morning, it appeared more like a vision of hell.

They emerged from the pandemonium and crossed back over a wide paved thoroughfare called Broadway, lined with opulent buildings many of which imitated Greek temples. The driver described it as "an old injun trail", the longest in the city, center of luxury and finance.

Past Saint Paul's Chapel, they passed a large, graceful building that took up a city block, faced with granite, Doric columns supporting the entrance.

"The Astor House, Sire, just across from City Hall and the Park. Best hotel in the city for years, until they opened the Metropolitan just behind there, and the Saint Nicolas uptown. A palace. Gas lighting. Got central heating in every room, they say. Over a thousand rooms. Things get bigger and bigger. They'll soon put Astor out of business."

Warren doubted that. John Jacob Astor had made his fortune in the fur trade before he was born. The pelts sold in Europe for a dozen times what he paid the trappers for them. When the furs dissipated and the money flow slowed, Astor sold the business to Ramsay Crooks, took his trading profits, and bought up land in New York City. He now had the biggest fortune in the country. The luxury hotel, built not twenty years ago and soon to become obsolete, was a testimony to Astor's business acumen. He owned the land, he would build something else. Lyman Warren, who died as penniless as the Indians, was like so many of the old fur trade— an anonymous contributor to Astor's fortune.

This was more like the New York City he had imagined—a great concentration of wealth, a throbbing world market center where vast fortunes were made and spent. At this early hour it looked empty save delivery wagons and street cleaners washing down the sidewalk, hauling their buckets and ladders. There was a bustle of activity before the *New York Herald* offices on the near corner, a mass of delivery boys hollering for the morning edition, cabs lining up to pick up reporters. It was magnificent, the flow of words coursing through the city like the flow of blood through a living being. One publishing house, he recalled, maybe two or three, had their offices on Broadway. He would soon return here. He must have his coat cleaned.

They crossed the great avenue, heading north and east, then the cab turned again toward the rising sun onto paved streets lined with trees awaiting their Spring moment. Here the air began to clear, the sun pierced through and opened up onto Hudson Park, a landscaped square with symmetrically laid alleys and walks, winter cottonwoods, chestnuts and catalpa trees, hedges, and trimmed bushes still bare, bordered on all sides by flower beds that men were now turning and planting. On Varick Street, men with carts were carrying off piles of offal and rubbish. The Park was bordered by stately townhouses of red brick and brownstone. The older houses were built in the Victorian style for people who probably did their shopping on Broadway.

The driver took his passenger for a tour of the Square, pointing out the highlights. They had come through lower quarters, and now emerged into this neighborhood, heralded as one of the most elegant quarters of Manhattan. St. John's Chapel dominated one side. A pity, said the hack, that the railway lines were being laid on Hudson Street to one side of the park, making the old neighborhood a bit noisy…. Warren then realized that the Hudson Valley train, himself in his coach, had rolled right past the Square this very morning, drawn by teams of horses in an effort to reduce the noise and smoke for the residents. The terminal where the cab began its tour was not far away at all. He was being promenaded like a tourist. The hack blathered on.

"Bloody train is chasing the posher people out of the old city to up north where the mansions are going up. One might think oneself in the old country here, with a bit of the look of old Dublin. When they put the rails underground, we'll get our city back."

He reined in the horse and stopped the cab in front of number 15 Laight Street, which in the sudden sunlight appeared to Warren as a paradise found— the Hydropathic and Hygienic Institute of New York, R.T. Trall M.D., proprietor. A clean, square stone and brick building three stories high, adjoined to a like building of four stories with windows all around, newly painted gray shutters, and a sidewalk with recently planted trees. It took up a good portion of the city block. The driver charged him a dollar, which was exorbitant, but this included portering fees for his trunk and baggage that he deposited at the front desk of the impeccably clean lobby A sign beside the door also announced rooms for rent. The floor was of white polished marble framed in a border of pale jade green. He had found his protection.

Within its hushed but resonant walls, the Institute was peopled by soft-shoed, efficient-looking women in long gray dresses, high-buttoned black shoes, and white aprons, some in medical smocks. One of these, young and slim as she was with her jet-black hair under a white cap, looked at Warren with the large, dark, shining eyes of a night bird. Her skin looked as fine as pink silk and almost perfectly transparent, just barely covering the delicate muscles of her face and neck. She had well-plucked eyebrows drawn closely together under her knitted brow, expressing an open concern, not unlike maternal pity. Her lower lip seemed on the verge of trembling. Under her blazing gaze, fatigue made Warren slightly dizzy.

She bade him sit down and asked his name. He answered mechanically. Ah. He was expected. Did he have a good trip? Doctor Trall would be notified and receive him shortly. Would he perhaps like to freshen up a bit? No thank you, I'll wait.

He hoped the dizziness would leave him, that he would awaken.

He sat on an upholstered divan, stylish, perhaps European, and was immediately brought not a glass, but a full pitcher of water. The water tasted good, clean. About twenty minutes went by, during which he tried with difficulty to stay alert and breathe slowly, as he felt his lungs gurgling deep down, and this was not the time to cough. He did nod off once. Some persons passed, men and women, sickly-looking patients in white robes, accompanied by more nurses

A door down the hall was opened from the inside as if by a ghost, and the prim young woman with bones like a bird's escorted him to the Doctor's study, where she entered with him, sat at a small corner desk, and brought out a pencil and note pad.

The Doctor entered from a side door, preceded by his high balding forehead and dark patriarchal beard, introducing himself only when standing behind his desk, bent slightly forward with his fingertips splayed on the blotter as if flattening an invisible map. Some formalities were written down by the woman, whose name was Miss Park. She was then dismissed, and let herself out as Doctor Trall himself finally sat, brought out a sheet of paper and questioned his patient.

"Symptoms?"

"Well, Sir. Some coughing, fatigue. Congestion. Occasional bleeding."

"How long?"

"About five years. It began when I was injured one winter, in a fall."

"Where?"

"In the woods, Sir, on horseback."

"Where were you wounded?"

"Ah. Here, Sir." He touched his sternum. "There was some internal bleeding, they thought it was from my stomach, but after some time it stopped. Then it began again."

"Take off your shirt and lie down here."

"I've been traveling for a long time, not bathing. I apologize for—"

"I'm a physician, no need to apologize. You're carrying a fever. Lie down."

He obeyed and showed Dr. Trall his bird-shaped scar. The doctor then felt his bones, sounded his chest, his heart, his lungs, then his glands. He examined his teeth, his "rheumy" eyes, his tongue which he declared whitish. He tested his joints and explored the flexibility of his internal organs. Warren did not complain but winced as his hand pressured his liver. As he washed his hands in a bowl the Doctor told him to sit again in the chair. All this time Warren kept from coughing, but with difficulty. Trall wrote his notes, then lifted his head and looked straight at him for what he thought was the first time.

"You've sustained multiple fractures of the ribs and a crushed sternum. Those heal with time. Internal injuries naturally follow, congesting the organs. I suspect some infection. It is undoubtedly painful. Do you take spirits?"

"No. Never," he lied. He figured the red wine that one evening in Buffalo was as good as never.

"What do you know about the Hydropathic and Hygienic sciences, Mr. Warren?"

"They refer to treatment by water cure. Hygiene being health."

"How did you hear about this Institute?"

"In the newspapers in Saint Paul. An article spoke highly of your approach, Sir." He watched Trall write this down.

"Do you know what hygienic means?"

"Er...healthy. That is, sanitary. Having to do with health, I believe."

"Mmm. Are you married? Children?"

"Three. Yes, we are married."

"How often do you have relations?"

"Relations?"

"Sexual."

"Ah. Well, not often these days, Sir." This was true, and Warren regretted it, looking down at the Persian rug under his feet, showing some wear, but clean. The entire room was very tidy. "We have one child on the way. That was the last time, some months ago," he lied again, but it was mostly true. "Fatigue. My health has not been well."

"Half the battle is won, Mr. Warren."

He brightened and sat up straighter. "I beg your pardon?"

"Sexual intercourse and poisons drain our healthy fluids and spirits, upsets our balance and prevents the body from absorbing the essential source of our good health. You engage in neither, which is a great advantage for your cure. Bowel movements?"

"Of course. When convenient. Or imperative."

"It's not always easy in the wilderness, is it?"

"No. We use the occasional purgative. Herbals, mainly."

"Mmm. Diet?"

"Diet, Sir?"

"What do you eat, mainly?"

"Mostly what game I can hunt, venison, bear, rabbit, fish occasionally, and rice. Wild rice. Biscuits. Some turnips, squash, carrots. When in season. We live by the Mississippi river."

"That will have to change. Your cure here will consist of a healthy diet of vegetables only, no flesh. Our bread is made of whole grain unbleached flour, as recommended by Mr. Graham. Regular exercise is mandatory. We shall have to rid the afflicted organs of all impurities. Medications?"

"Medication, Sir?"

"Potions, elixirs? Anything you take for relief, as it were?"

"Just an herbal tea my sisters prepared for me. It seems to do me good, warm, and sweetened with a bit of maple syrup." He coughed only slightly, bringing out his handkerchief and trying to hide the blood stains. Sitting in the Doctor's office, he felt soiled, unclean, though he had bathed and changed his linen only two days ago. Or was it three? He noticed the encrusted soot on his coat, his soiled cravat. There was dried blood on his lapel, gray ash on his broadcloth trousers and mud on his boots. He wiped his lips and held his handkerchief stiffly, balled up in his hands, wary of having to cough again. Trall saw this, and nodded.

"What's in this tea?"

"I don't really know, plants from the woods. The women in my family are quite knowledgeable with respect to native Indian remedies, herbs and roots." Warren brought out his glass flask with about three fingers of tea left in it, the last of his mixture.

Trall uncorked and smelled it, frowning.

"We'll have to analyze this. Valerian, meadowsweet, peppermint, surely. Perhaps licorice. The main pillar of the cure in this Institute, Mr. Warren, in addition to a strictly vegetarian diet which will be prepared for you, consists in taking in large amounts of pure water. We have it delivered daily from springs across the river. Hygiene extends to the inside of the body as well as outwardly. This spring water is also used for your prescribed soaks and baths, filtered and purified here in our facilities by our specialized staff. The Preissnitz method is described fully by me in this issue of the *Water-Cure Journal,* which I put at your disposal. What is this maple syrup?"

"I have no more, just these few drops." He handed the doctor his vial, with some apprehension that he could not explain or justify to himself. In truth, he was loath to give up the last remnant of his sisters' remedy. It had sustained him throughout his journey. The sweet mixture had become a kind of touchstone. Trall smeared the remaining drops of syrup onto his index finger and tasted it. Then he abruptly rose, crossed to a table, took a mouthful of water, and spat into a bowl. He returned to his notes, head bent.

"And you put this in your tea?"

"Yes. I made the syrup myself, from our trees. Pure maple."

"Then surely you recognize that this mixture is not pure maple."

"The tea alone is a bit bitter. They go well together."

"Does it help you sleep?"

"In fact, yes. And it seems to ease the pain. And the coughing."

"A suppressant. And if you do not take it? Nervousness? Delusions? Fright?"

Warren hesitated. "I...I can't say. I've had it with me since I left my home a month ago. Thanks to my sisters who saw me safely through to Lake Superior. They gave me sufficient quantity to last the journey. Until now, when I put myself in your hands, Doctor."

"Mr. Warren, in my hands you shall soon improve. For the past month, with this syrup, you've been ingesting a disguised tincture of laudanum. A mixture of opiates, drugs, and alcohol. It is very fortunate that this is finished." He corked and handed the empty vial back to Warren, who sat wordless, slightly dizzy again and inclined to cough. He summoned all his self-control.

"It explains your haggard coloring, the veil over your dilated pupils, your congested liver, your fatigue. It has certainly done you more harm than good, and you will surely feel the symptoms of lack for the next few days."

"Some say I've got the consumption, Doctor. That there is no cure."

"Ignorance. Bigotry." Trall stood and began pacing, hands in his vest pockets and eyes raised as if seeking inspiration, or an audience.

"We'll begin immediately with a bath and a wet sheet packing to induce sudation, lukewarm in your case. Twice daily. With sitz-baths to improve your lungs, a revulsive for the head and chest. We must correct the morbid and restore the healthy secretions. The article explains it all from the scientific approach. You shall have your own lodgings and take all meals here at the Institute, and avail yourself abundantly of the hygienic facilities in addition to your prescribed regimen. Hygiene, Sir, as you divine from the name of our Institute, is capital. The city outside is a hotbed of typhus, cholera, venereal afflictions, and epidemics of all sorts come from the four corners of the world, and a breeding ground for rats and vermin. This Institute is a spotless haven immune from that iniquitous wound, a pure sanctuary. We all work to keep it that way, and to eradicate any infection, with no recourse to so-called medicines, drugs, or quackery. You will find every modern convenience at your disposal, throughout the Institute. I have cured every ailment of this nature from the ague and the croup to pneumonia, Mr. Warren. I shall cure yours, have no doubt." He paused by the sideboard to wash his hands with a bar of soap, rinse them in a separate basin, and dry them with a clean towel. He then turned and continued, addressing Warren head on, hands behind his back.

"You have come all this way to entrust yourself to me, to confirm the benefits our hydropathic and hygeio-therapeutic methods. I commend you, Sir, you are a forward moving and modern thinker. Be prepared to stay for a minimum of eight weeks, then we shall take stock. My secretary will see to your registration, the staff will give you what clothing you need here for the cure, and maintain your personal laundry. Everything will be provided for the overall fee of twenty-five dollars per week, fifty percent payable upon registration, the balance after one month. Miss Park!"

The woman entered immediately with an armful of clean linen and stood by the doorway, intensely, waiting at attention. Warren rose and asked, without hesitation, "Sir, may I have my flask? It's rather a sentimental item."

Trall assessed his patient, then poured a finger of the tea into a glass, corked the flask and handed it to him.

"My herbal specialist will analyze this. You may finish the rest, Mr. Warren, but just this day, then we'll boil the flask. I suggest parsimony with the last of it, reduce the dosage gradually. We are not inhuman here. The first few days will take some mettle, but it's nothing that a man of your constitution cannot deal with. We can duplicate the tea for you, but for sweetener you must rely on our pure honey. Drink three pitchers of pure water per day, take all meals here in the Institute, nothing else. Miss Park and her staff will see to the administration of your treatment. Welcome to our establishment." The Doctor did not shake his hand, but nodded cordially.

At the registration desk, Warren signed the documents drawn up and paid $100 in gold coin for his first month. He then asked if there were "facilities" he could use.

He was shown to a large, white-tiled vestibule with a sort of privy in the corner, and a large porcelain basin equipped with the accouterments of modern plumbing such as he had seen at the hotel in Buffalo, but more sober and utilitarian in design. The privy was a heavy wooden contraption, a kind of chair with a hole to sit on and a chamber pot inside. The water at the porcelain basin ran hot and cold and drained through a hole into a lead pipe that disappeared into the wall.

Once alone, he urinated, rinsed his sweating face, and was over-taken by a wracking fit of coughing that lasted a full minute or more. He spat a large quantity of bloody phlegm into the bowl and rinsed copiously, then drank two swallows of his precious tea. His head spun. Leaning over the washbasin, he waited, then felt it's calming fingers pervade his body.

Laudanum. They were all in league to fool him—Julia, Matilda, Charlotte, even Mary, perhaps even Mrs. Wheeler. And it worked. They got him here. Bless their devious little female hearts.

There was a looking glass over the basin, and it caught him short. He understood the concerned expression on the transparent face of Miss Park. He was peaked, lined, eyes blackened below and red around the rims, his face sallow and void of color or expression, his long hair dull and grayed with soot, matted flat against his scrawny neck. He had changed much since he'd had his image taken in Saint Paul, even since Buffalo two days ago. He looked like a walking ghost and for a brief moment, he felt like weeping aloud. His own ravaged face was the price he had paid to get here. It made him wary of walking out and confronting the young woman who was herself a picture of rosy health, with her shiny black hair done up under her cap, and her starched white apron.

He had no choice but to trust his recovery to the good Doctor. He must build up his strength. He must be able to go forth into the city, confident and promising, and meet the men in the world of publishing who would finally open the gates to his future career, to his family's survival, to the recognition and legitimization of his mother's vanishing people, the salvation of the Red Man's history. He would write to Anna Ramsey, to Matilda again, to Rice, to Le Duc, and the news at home would spread, that he was safe and well in New York City and soon to be acknowledged as the writer and historian he had become.

He began to shake. He was going to weep. He sat on the stool, hoping that he had spat up enough blood to keep still and breathing to regain his composure. Time lost its meaning.

Please forgive my tardiness in responding. My affairs have taken a brighter turn and required my full attentions.....And the children?...It seems just yesterday we....

A knocking on the door. It was an unfamiliar voice, a man's.

"Mr. Warren, Sir? Mr. Warren, is everything all right?"

The man's voice, again with a foreign accent, a sort of brogue like the hack. Warren was sitting on the closed seat of the wooden toilet, his chin in his hands, staring at the door, asleep with his eyes half closed. He did not answer. He was deep in thought, composing a letter to his father, indeed to his mother, to reassure them. That they were both dead did not matter.

"Mr. Warren? Is everything all right? Are you fallen ill, Sir?"

He fell off and crumbled onto the tiles, unable to answer. The door opened.

"He's feeling poorly," said the voice. "Call the Master."

"Who?" It was a woman's voice. He looked up and saw Miss Park, indeed several Miss Parks, with her small head and concerned look. The man's voice grew insistent.

"Go fetch your boss, Woman! The man is ill."

"Ill?" The young woman drew near and gave him a little slap on the face. "He's sick!" Said the brogue. "For the lovva Mike! Call the Master!"

"All right. Clean him up. Bring him up to his room, number twenty."

Warren thought that Miss Park possessed a kind of ethereal beauty, but she quickly left him there on the tiles and ran off. He could see no man, just the white of the tiles moving around him. Someone, something, lifted his body from the floor as if he were weightless. He uttered something in the old language, Ojibwemowin, wanting to speak to his mother... Then he fell into blackness.

Chapter 29: The Cure

THERE WAS MURMURING, WHISPERING EVEN. He was lying prone on a high table in a darkened room where the air was oppressively close and uncommonly warm, with one window showing daylight through closed curtains. Immediately he felt the pain in his chest and limbs and the urge to cough, to which he succumbed, only to find he could not move his arms nor turn over on the table. He was wrapped entirely in a warm wet sheet and belted down. He began to gag when someone unfastened him, caught him under the wrapping and turned him on his side, where he could cough his blood and phlegm into a metal dish. A man in a gray smock held him as he hacked and spat and struggled to breathe, comforting him in a low and not unpleasant voice tinged with the brogue that he recognized from the moments before passing out. This lasted for a long few minutes, then he rested, heaving on his side while the room spun and transparent stars swam before his eyes. His throat burned, his tongue tasted of the bloody phlegm.

"There now, that's the stuff. Spit it all out."

"Help me up. I must sit. Please open the window." He struggled to get out of the wet sheet.

"Can't do that, Sir. Doctor's orders. But we'll set you right in no time." The man freed his arms and exposed his chest, propped him up on pillows, and let more light in from the window.

He breathed while his vision steadied. The wetness was unpleasant, but warm. On a small cart beside the bed was a long red tube attached to a large syringe, and a white enameled dish of dark blood.

Warren realized he was naked underneath. The room was tidy, sparsely furnished, wallpapered, containing a high bed, a desk by the wall with his travel bag and writing satchel, a chair, a lamp on the desk. His clothing lay cleaned and folded on his trunk, his hat and cloak were hanging on the wall. The bird-shaped scar on his chest, he noticed, was redder than usual. But then, he was not at all accustomed to seeing his bare skin. He looked at his arms and chest. He had lost some flesh, some coloring. He had never had much body hair, his Indian blood prevailing, but he had never seen himself looking so white. His mother would have called him skin and bones.

In the corner by a table was a woman writing in a notebook, whose presence made him very aware of his nakedness. He recognized Miss Park.

"How do you feel, Mr. Warren? You've been asleep for some time." She had a hard accent, she pronounced it "Mistah".

"Much better, thank you. How long?"

"Three days. Drink this please." She handed him a glass of very cool water, which compared to the iron-laced water of the Lakes region, tasted pure and smooth. It felt wonderful on his tongue and going down his throat. He quaffed gratefully before he lay back and began to shiver.

"Dry him off, Billy, and feed him," said the woman. "Then bring him downstairs." Miss Park was obviously accustomed to giving orders here. She turned and went out the door.

He was given a warm bathrobe, helped to the dry bed, propped up again.

While the man wheeled out the wet table and went to fetch him something to eat, Warren assessed his physical state. He was, admittedly, as weak as he had ever been. Of course, he had been asleep for three days. He ached all over in his bones, his muscles, in his lungs, and his abdomen growled, yet he was hungry. More than that, he was still thirsty. But not for more water. It was a nagging thirst, for something else. His eyes searched the room and settled on his satchel on the table by the window.

He rose and made his way, using the chair as a cane, to his belongings. His wooden writing chest containing his manuscript was still belted, set on the floor with the closed travel bag and leather satchel with his papers and sundries. It was all safe. Apart from his pressed clothing and unmuddied, polished boots, no one had tampered with his belongings.

Inside the satchel, he found the last of his tea in the flask. It had been thoroughly cleaned on the outside, the glass shone and the cork was new. The Doctor was good for his word, he'd left him the dregs to finish. He uncorked it and drank the last of it, almost a whole mug full. It was not very palatable, somewhat nauseating, cool, but it was what exactly he wanted. And now it was gone. He wanted more. He recognized the familiar taste of the liquid inside: bitter yet sweet with maple, pungent with the forest. Now he was keen to the slight aftertaste of something untraceable, carried by the sweetness of the maple, his own trees, his family's labor over weeks in the sugar bush, and the long winter voyage that had taken him so far from his home to a heated room in this enormous city that was to be his proving ground.

A dizziness grasped him, forcing him to sit on the single wooden chair by the desk. As if in a dream, he saw himself drinking from the warm flask under the buffalo hide in the sleigh alongside the Mississippi, in the stagecoach north through the Saint Croix Valley, below decks through the storm on Lake Superior, and onward...over Lake Erie to the hotel in Buffalo, the Métisse girl's face, Fowles shot in the foot, the resolute stride of Frederick Douglass at the station in Rochester, and the last interminable miles alone with his own resolve, writing on the lid of his cedar chest, reclining by his manuscript, brewing his last batch of tea on the wood stove, rolling steadily toward New York in the train through the dark Hudson Valley when even the memory of hunger had left him and he ate nothing, perpetually sustained in a state of waking sleep by his precious elixir. He could not recall those last hours spent trying to seize a dream just beyond his reach. Nothing palpable came to his memory—it was all a fog. Until the memory of dawn on the train, when he could distinguish the barges and steamboats on the wide river, then farther on, the belching smokestacks announcing the entry to the great city. That was when he had risen again in the slow-moving train, and forced himself to walk.

He sat, thinking about returning to the bed, expecting to sleep again, but he did not. After a few minutes the pain subsided and he found it easier to move. Although weakened, his vision and mind sharpened and he had the encouraging notion, for a few fleeting moments, that he was in his familiar body once again and in full control of his mental faculties and his destiny. This was the purpose, he reasoned, of following a cure. To be sure, the three remaining fingers of his sisters' laudanum-laced concoction had set him right again. Not a moment to lose.

He rose, opened the curtain wide, the mass of branches telling him that he was high above street level and that spring was not far off—the buds on the maples and lindens were peeking out. There was sunlight. Maybe it was morning. He opened the window and found the air still cool. The noises of the city—carriages wheels and horses on cobbles, hammering on boards, iron clanging, distant yelling—all seemed at a safe distance. He closed the window, turned to the satchel on the desk and extracted the tools of his work.

Instead of taking to bed and using the lid of his chest as his escritoire, he sat at the small table and by the light of day drafted a letter to Henry Schoolcraft in Washington, telling him he was ailing and the times were too pressing to see him now, but thanking him for citing his work in his last volume of his *History of Indian Tribes* and asking for a copy sent to his New York address, by express. He also told the scholar of his endeavors, his recently finished manuscript, his future plans for further volumes on the Midewewin, Ojibwe chiefs and mythology, and the urgency of gathering and publishing all this information quickly while the old men were *"fast falling into their graves."* His intention was to ensure publication as soon as he was strong enough. In the meantime, he wondered if he might have any suggestions for publishing or for his future work, giving his return address as 15 Laight Street in New York City.

The man called Billy returned with a bowl of barley soup, dark bread slathered with honey, and two apples. He introduced himself as William Daniels.

"Me father called me Billy, and it stook." He would be his personal nurse and valet, if he allowed, for the duration of his stay here at the Institute. He would see to his every need. Warren asked what day it was. It was March 19th, said Billy.

"Well past the ides! Heh!" He volunteered spontaneously that he was still paying the price of a prolonged Saint Patrick's Day and needed to calm his nerves, if Mr. Warren would excuse him. He turned to the wall and took a swig from a pewter flask, then pocketed it underneath his gray smock, which buttoned high and was ample enough to hide anything. "Just for medicinal purposes, you understand. Miss Park would not think it appropriate, I'm sure. Nor the Master."

Warren said nothing. Instead, he dated the letter March 19th, stamped and addressed to Schoolcraft in Washington, and asked Billy to post it for him that very afternoon.

"Sure thing, Sir. Count on Billy!"

He took his meal which he found very satisfying, lingering over the bread and honey, before his guardian took his arm, gave him warm slippers, and showed him downstairs where he walked him on a "constitutional" around the corridors to glance at the dining hall, the two long white-covered tables empty after breakfast. Boarding house arrangements. He would be quite comfortable eating alone in his room, where he had work to do. Billy walked him twice around the ground floor, passing Miss Park who briefly looked up from her administrative duties, stuck out her smooth white hand and firmly shook Warren's, bidding him good day. That was the extent of his exercise for the morning.

"Is he drinking his water?" She asked Billy, without looking at him. He was.

Besides the efficient nurses, male and female, they crossed paths, slowly, with several white-robed and slippered patients, all wearing white or gray. Only one Negro patient, he noticed, in the establishment—an elderly man with a huge gold ring. This was a marked change from Upstate New York, and the Black Angels on the trains. Here, everyone was white but him.

Some of the patients nodded but were mercifully as un-loquacious and inwardly mournful as Warren himself. His robe and slippers were the same, he was one of them: a mute patient. It was not customary for him to shun conversation—he had the reputation in Saint Paul's American House of being an incurable tongue-wagger. This made him wonder what had become of his old self. His guardian, however, greeted everyone cheerfully and had a gift for drawing a smile or comment from even the most recalcitrant.

Billy finally shuffled him into a small room entirely tiled in white but for a row of blue-colored accents with a Greek design suggesting a line of square waves on a long blue sea. There was a sort of cutout barrel seat in the middle of the room—a roundish wooden affair, a large tin bathtub, and numerous pipes, basins, sinks, and water fixtures crisscrossing the walls. The room had two open windows, near the ceiling, through which the sounds of running water could be heard, like an incessant waterfall inside a stone cavity. A diffused gray daylight entered through these windows, as well as through the transom on the corridor. The effect was both warm and cool, relaxing, even pleasantly soporific. Other rooms in the lower level were dedicated to the cure and apparently occupied by other patients undergoing watery administrations. He doffed his slippers and felt the warm tiles beneath his feet. The Roman baths, he had read, were heated in this way—through the floor. A hallmark of advanced civilization.

"Now Sir. You're to sit on the stool there and contemplate if I might suggest, what a great relief it will be once the good Doctor has rid you of your ailment. It's a good place to read if you're given to that... there are books in the library." He watched Billy as he fussed over a stack of towels and saw the man really for the first time.

Billy was solid, fair-skinned, sanguine, clean-shaven with a mass of curly black hair and sharp blue eyes fitted into his sturdy head like stones, but which darted around him in constant movement. Two pink scars were in the final healing stages, one on his chin, and one over his black left eyebrow. His wiry build beneath the smock belied a latent strength born of hard labor and frugal living. He was a full head shorter than Warren, but compact and surely twice as strong. It was clear he was Irish, but Warren had to wonder what his life had been like—they were about the same age. With his large squarish hands, also scarred, he unfurled a hose and filled a basin in the bench hole with cold water.

"They call it a sitz bath. It's for yer health, Sir. Bum in the water. You might find it a bit cold at first, but you get used to it. I'll leave you to it."

Billy left him there. He lifted the bathrobe, sat, and applied himself to his cure with all the assiduousness he could muster. It was no greater a shock than a dip in Lake Superior in summer, only more localized.

He thus spent a not unpleasant time with his posterior soaking in the water of the sitz bath, cooling down after the overheated room, and he allowed that he did feel a refreshment in his temples and inside his organs, a sort of de congesting. He sat and imagined himself talking with his New York publishers about how many copies to run at first. Just as he began to feel the pangs of hunger, he fell again into a half sleep, with his buttocks and genitals still dipped in the sitz bath. The man came to fetch him, woke him up for only a short interval while he helped him up the stairs to his room, where Warren ate another bowl of barley soup and lapsed into welcome oblivion.

§

It went like this for several days, with the relief that time became an empty concept since he was never awake for more than a few minutes at a go. At first, when awake, he felt that nagging thirst. He was nervous and shaky, uncommonly hungry. He ate the tasty though monotonous fare quite heartily, and welcomed sleep as he welcomed the cool drinks of water and tea given to him by someone of the female staff—sometimes by Miss Park herself though not often—and the continuously faithful Billy, who at one time even carried him in his arms up the stairs to his sickroom. Billy even took to shaving him in the mornings, if the patient was sufficiently awake to sit up. He was accompanied to and from his baths, induced sweats, and cool sheet wraps.

If Warren noticed any change in his state, it was this total list-lessness, an indifference to his own inactivity, and a profound weakness that caused him not to long for sleep. Miss Park attributed this to his total exhaustion. A strange phenomenon it was, as if he were looking at himself, an unfamiliar self that inhabited his ailing body, from another corner of his room. He would have fits of guilt and chide that other self for laziness and lack of will, only to lose this inspiration and sink again into sleep. Time went on, or it did not, unaccountably. He awoke hungry, and since he felt too weak to make the trudge to the dining hall, he was brought the Institute's ample vegetarian fare on a tray. His fever lessened.

He became so absent-minded that he neglected for days to open the only mail he had received at his new address: the response to his from Henry Schoolcraft, himself in bad health in Washington. It was an encouraging note, urging him to publish by contract to ensure a just share of the profits, and lauding his work as that of a genuine laborer in the field of Indian history, all of whom are public bene-factors. The old scholar signed off with every wish for his success. Warren had been hoping for the name of a publisher, but at least he had the master's recommendation. He added the letter to his file of encouragements and went to sleep.

Still too weak to venture outside and take action, to see the pub-lishers face to face, he was conscious of being impeccably clean, moving from room to room and wrap to wrap, to steam rooms, to bathtubs, sitz-baths, plunges in tepid water, and once to a dousing with a pressurized water jet that he could not abide, causing him to flee naked as day into the hallway, which no person in the Institute seemed to think unusual. Billy brought him his robe, calmed him down, saw him to his room, and offered him a drink from his own flask, regretting that it was only local swill and not the heavenly whiskey from the highland area of the Old Country. Warren thanked him but refused, preferring a drink of herbal tea.

It was then he realized that the tea, made now by the Institute staff and sweetened with honey, left something to be desired. He seemed to have slept through most of the symptoms of lack that Trall initially warned him against—the nightmares, the nervousness, the shaking, the sweats. He spent many waking hours under induced sudation, trundled in a special bed wrapped in lukewarm sheets and rubbed vigorously by Billy or another of the men on staff, so he probably had nothing more to sweat out. Thus he could conclude that he was not, objectively, addicted to the drug.

This being said, the pain in his chest was ever-present during waking hours, as was his coughing despite his efforts to quell the fits. They were even somewhat more frequent, but this did not perturb his principal observer, Miss Park, who noted it all on her daily checklist. Dr. Trall, she informed him, considered that any expectoration was a manifestation of the cure's progress, proof of the elimination of the poisons within his system. The tendency to sleep long hours was a reflection of a deeper-than-usual state of exhaustion; his body's resources were acutely depleted, in need of purification and fortification. He was convalescing well. Which he could verify, Miss Park offered, by reading the literature at his disposal.

This was all detailed in Doctor Trall's articles and in his *Hydropathic Encyclopedia,* a text, available here in the library, used by his students. Miss Philomena Park was proud to be among his numerous women students, not only here at the Institute but prior, during her literature studies at the college for women in Mount Holyoke. The text was also a favorite among medical students at such higher learning establishments as Princeton and Radcliff. Mr. Warren would do well, moreover, to subscribe to the highly informative *Water-Cure Journal and Herald of Reform,* to which the Doctor was a regular contributor. Miss Park could make the arrangements when convenient, before his departure.

The Doctor came to see him once during this time, giving him a quick once-over and ordering him to continue treatment but to double the intake of grains, lentils, beans, and bread smeared with honey. The herbalists had managed to duplicate his precious tea for him according to the Doctor's prescription, with a double dose of Valerian, Saint John's Wort, and honey, but without his even more precious elixir. The kick in that concoction, Warren recalled with some fondness, had seen him through a month of hard travel in wintertime.

As he accumulated sleep and food, his fever came and went. He came closer to his senses only to realize that he was still exceedingly weak and enduring considerably stronger onsets of pain and congestion. He might have gained a little weight, but his shirt still hung loose on his neck. He was not the kind to complain, and he reasoned that the less he talked about it, the faster the pain would go away.

Only when he began to encounter long sleepless spells in his room, overtaken by a nameless fear that caused him to swallow hard, grind his teeth and endure a shaking fit that undermined completely his stoic reserve, did he resolve to draw Billy into his confidence one morning as he served him his breakfast of cereal, dried fruit, and milk. With his usual panache, Billy flung open the curtain announcing with a Praise God! that it was Spring. The trees were greening outside his window and the air, after a night's rain, smelled fresh and warmer. The morning light dispelled Warren's nocturnal discomfort, allowing him to assume his normal posture sitting up in bed and a more melodious tone of voice. Decidedly, he had always preferred daylight to the black of night.

"Billy, how long have I been here?"

"Almost three weeks, Sir. This be the fourth of April."

"All this time I've never seen the world outside."

"It's about time you seen the solarium. That can surely be arranged."

"I must get out. I have business to attend to in the city. Can you help me?"

"You mean to see the publishers? About your book?"

Warren looked at the man, inquiring without speaking.

"You've been talking a bit in yer sleep, Sir."

"Is that so? What have I said?"

362

"Not much. Sometimes in tongues, as they say, but nothing embarrassing, I assure you. Always the same. About the book. I imagine that's what's in the trunk."

His small chest lay unopened in the corner of the room, still belted, the lock intact. It looked like the most decrepit article—scarred and beaten, one side cracked—in the entire room, which was otherwise quite new-looking.

"Then I've revealed to you my entire life."

"Oh no, not at all, Sir. Rest assured. Just about the Indians, the history. And for Billy Daniels, it's always mum's the word. That's why the Master trusts me with the patients, Sir. Reliability, Discretion, Service, and Punctuality is me motto!"

"Then perhaps you can begin by running a personal errand for me?"

"No trouble, Sir. Anything within me power."

"I want you to go to the druggist and fill this vial. Tincture of Laudanum."

Billy uncorked the vial and sniffed it loudly. "There's a bit of rum to it, but that's not all," he said. "There's something sweet."

"Maple syrup. But I doubt you can find that here. I made it myself from my own trees back home. The main thing is the laudanum."

"Well, Sir. That's against the Doctor's policies, you know. It might take a bit of doing."

"That's why I'm asking you, Billy. I can pay. And I can trust you."

"Of course, no question. But is it best for you, Sir? At this juncture?"

"It's the only thing that stops the coughing and pain. It does me good. I'll need it if I'm to accomplish what I came to do, go out and publish that book. And return home."

"Home, Sir? That's what I couldn't understand. Sometimes you mention the island, the lake, the river, the cabin. Where is yer home, if you'll forgive me asking?"

"Beyond the Great Lakes. Minnesota Territory. Indian country. A paradise."

"Ah yes. They told me that when I paid for me passage. Then I got here and there was no more talk of paradise. This city is the end of the line. The good Doctor was a Godsend, I'll allow. He took me on as his boiler man and it's been two months. Still, I ain't put aside enough for passage to paradise, though. The missus says the only way I'll ever get there is by negotiatin' with Saint Peter at the pearly gates. I tell her it's more likely I'll have to deal with Lucifer himself!" He genuflected and winked upwards at the ceiling. Warren surmised that Billy must be on good terms with his Catholic God.

"They tell me the trees out there are taller than the Cathedrals of Europe."

"I suspect that's true, Billy, though I've never seen Europe. I hope to someday, Paris especially. Do you suppose you could bring my manuscript to an address I'll give you, a publisher named Appleton here in the city?"

"Of course. All them book people have their publishing houses over on Broadway and Varick, just a stone's throw from here, Sir."

"I'll have the package ready for you tomorrow. As for the vial, I need it now. To sweeten my tea, as it were. Hand me my coat, will you?"

Taking his purse from his bag and feeling the inside pocket, he found everything intact. He still had his roll of newly printed Railroad Bank bills, the 250 dollars in winnings from the steamship card game, sewn into the lining. The deerskin pouch in his trunk held another 100. He still had to pay that much for the remainder of his cure and board at the Institute. And he needed to keep some for expenses and for the trip home—the new train line to Chicago, he expected, then a steamship up the river to Saint Paul. A smaller pouch in his inside coat pocket served to carry what he called his running money. He handed Billy Daniels a coin.

"Will this do?"

"Oh yes, Sir. I should think so." Billy pocketed the coin and pulled out his own pewter flask. "Would you mind, Sir?" He swigged without waiting and held up the open flask. "Perhaps a snort for himself in the interim? Medicinal?"

"No, I'll wait, thank you. You're certain that will be enough?"

"Sure thing. A fiver'll get you anything you need in Five Points."

Chapter 30: Allies

BILLY DID NOT COME BACK that day. The male nurse who escorted the patient to his wrap that morning said he was on an errand that would probably take him the entire day. Warren's consternation at this absence, which surprised him, made him take up his pen after his nap in the afternoon and draft the letter to D. Appleton and Company, to whom he would entrust his manuscript for review, to be delivered by Billy on his return the next morning. The Appleton brothers, fully engaged in publishing, had a large bookstore on Broadway in what was called the Appleton Building.

"Trusting that the subject, original as it is, should interest you, I must impress upon you the urgency of my submission. I have traveled far, possess only one copy of the manuscript, and have only limited time in New York, during which I am undergoing daily medical treatment. Could Mr. Appleton please apprise me of his opinion before the end of the month? I am aware of the inconvenience, but must know soon if publication is feasible for the company, or if he has any alternative suggestions. I include a letter of recommendation from Mr. William Le Duc of Saint Paul, as well as one from D. A. Robertson, editor of the Minnesota Democrat, where extracts of an earlier version have already been published."

Writing this letter, he imagined himself talking directly to these gentlemen at their offices in the Appleton Building. He felt somewhat intimidated, as if he were no more than a backwoods scribbler addressing powers that reigned high in the celestial circle of intellectual literati in New York City. Packing the volume, he realized that the draft of his preface was shoddy in appearance, having been penned during the voyage, and merited further concision and explanation. His was the only first-hand history of an Indian people in existence. His information must be considered true, from the mouths of the old men themselves, despite discrepancies that might arise when compared to their history as recounted by white scholars, which although incomplete could be dated more accurately. Had checked and cross-checked with the old men, but there could be mistakes, as they were given to conjecture. This haunted him. And the prose was imperfect, hasty, and contained awkward passages and faulty grammar. He did not have time to have the whole manuscript edited. How could he explain this haste, his own amateurism, this lack of perfection, of writerly diligence? By recounting how his family was in need, and the pale rider was close on his trail? How could he, under those circumstances, convince these gentlemen to champion this unusual and incomplete work issued from a young and unknown hand who might soon leave this world? He was driven to add a page to the preface before concluding his cover letter:

"The following work may not claim to be well and elaborately written as it cannot be expected that a person who has passed most of his life among the wild Indians, even beyond what may be termed the frontiers of civilization, can wield the pen of an Irving or a Schoolcraft. But the work does claim to be one of truth, and the first work written from purely Indian sources, which probably has never been presented to the public. Should the notice taken of it, by such as feel an interest in the red race, warrant a continuation of his labors in this broad field of inquiry, the writer presents this volume as the first of a series..."

He went on, in his preface, to explain as he did to Schoolcraft his intention of writing further works on the Ojibwe beliefs, religious rites, on their spiritualism, the Midewiwin. The writer also proposed, *"...if his precarious health holds out, and life is spared to him..."* to present a collection of mythological traditions that may be termed the *"Indian Bible"*.

Wasn't this phrase too maudlin? Or misplaced? No, it was not misplaced. It would be in every way akin to the Bible. But the bit about his life being spared? And there was more, the second work, the myths and Manabosho stories, and finally the lives of the great chiefs. It would take a lifetime. He had the will and the wherewithal. The only thing he might not have was the time.

He left off, set down his pen, and felt nauseous, heavy in his limbs, overcome by vertigo there in his chair. He slumped back for a few minutes, then slipped like a landslide into a vertiginous sleep, thumped onto the floor, and lay there embarrassed and puzzled, watching tiny spots whirl before his eyes as if he were under a stream. Suddenly, he felt the rushing water of the stream envelope his body.

The cold and the fright at not breathing shocked him awake. He emerged, took a trembling deep breath, and felt his heart beating strongly. Perhaps too strongly. It was a dream, only a moment. He felt like he might be dying. But he did not die. He lay there breathing.

He hoped no one saw this lapse. He soon realized this was ridiculous because he was alone in his room. This got him up. He was fine, it was just a spell. No one would know.

Where was that damn Billy, with his flask?

He rose slowly, awaited balance, drank a glass of purified water, opened the window, and looked out on the reddening dusk over the city roofs.

With the coming of spring, the heavy coal fire scent of the city air had receded, chased by a fresh tang of sea wind, which that evening renewed his senses. He heard the clinking of a mason's hammer below, the echo of steel on steel, of human strength on stone, the relentless cadence of one man's industry in the bowels of the city heaving around him. Warren had come here to be a part of it, to labor in building the knowledge underlying man's endeavors. He was once again certain that his writer's hand was as strong as that mason's arm.

He was merely feeling embarrassed by his precarious health and his perhaps disproportionate ambitions. After all, he was not yet at death's door and didn't want to give them that impression. He explained in the letter that he would rework the preface before publication. But the tone was meek; he lacked the confidence to propose his writings with the authority required for publication. He did not want to beg. That too would be a faulty strategy. He felt exhausted and must stop writing or risk ridicule.

Outside the window overlooking the burgeoning trees, the rooftops and scaffoldings, gaslights were being lit in the street below, and he could see windows of distant four- and five-story buildings taking on an amber glow while the sky above turned from smoky blue to flint. He lit the oil lamp on his desk, rearranged the pages of his preface, and signed the cover letter.

It was done. His legs would no longer carry him, but he persisted in making a neat pile of bound foolscap and setting it beside the lamp. The whole, with the manuscript wrapped in canvas and deer hide thongs, contained his future. He lay down and looked at the volume, forming a squared package. It was ready to venture out in the world, if worse came to worse, without him.

There was a knock at his door, fast and sharp—not Billy's. "Mistah Warren. Are you quite all right?"

"Excellent. Please come in."

Miss Park came in as the light was fading, with his dinner on a tray. She did not wear her white nurse's cap this evening, but rather piled her black hair high on her head. This was distracting because it exposed her youthful neck. A few strands had escaped along her nape, dispelling her usual air of perfect efficiency. Warren found that this recurring motif, as he met different women in his travels, opened a side path to the unbridled parts of his imagination. He knew it to be one of his weak points, a rather pleasant one, but he must not dally.

He asked her, as she busied herself with the curtains and picking up linen, bending and stretching her slender waist, whether she could please wrap this pile of documents in brown paper for delivery the next day. Billy Daniels would act as courier. He handed her the address. "Providing Mr. Daniels is available," she said. She had a precise way of speaking he could not place—her "A"s were hard, and sometimes she rolled over her "R"s like a wagon wheel, then she didn't pronounce them at all.

"If he's off on a spree, we may not see him for days. Delivery to Appleton publishers? Am I to conclude this is a manuscript, Mistah Warren?"

"Yes, it is. A History. The Ojibwe. An Indian people in the Northwest. A rather rough and ready story, all in all, but true. From the mouths of the old men themselves."

"I see. The Indians. Poor things. We had no idea you were a writer."

"I'd mentioned it to Dr. Trall in my letter."

"I was not informed."

"This is my first book. Parts were published in newspapers."

"You know, do you not, that you must knock on every do-ah in this city, Mistah Warren? New Yo-ahk is rife with writers. Publishers are very much involved in municipal ventures nowadays, tourist guides, the Crystal Palace. They don't gamble much on newcomers. Appleton has an active scientific branch. Ah you familiah with the George Palmer Putnam house?"

"A prominent publisher. Governor Ramsey of Minnesota has recommended that I look him up."

"He's published Poe, Cooper, Irving, even some Ojibwe writer in fact. Was it Copway or Copwell? And prominent women, Wetherell, Susan Ward. I would imagine he'd be looking for something to rival the success of Mrs. Stowe's novel about the Negroes. I could work out an interview for you."

Warren looked at her incredulously. "You could do that?"

"Of course. He's currently considering some of my own work."

"Your work, Miss Park? May I ask..."

"Nothing saleable." She approached suddenly and looked him square in the face, folding a towel.

"Poetry," she announced. She stretched her neck, pushed her head a bit forward, and asked with a triumphant air, "About time, don't you think?"

Her birdlike features sharpened, and he felt cornered. "Time?"

"For a woman's voice, Mistah Warren. A woman's ideas."

"Absolutely. A poetess I know in Minnesota publishes in local newspapers. Mrs. Julia Wood. She sometimes uses a pen name, Minnie Mary Lee. Fine sentiments, as I told her just..."

"Sentiment, Mistah Warren, is precisely what undermines the state of women in this county. We need ideas, analyses. We need the minds and votes of women to further the pressing issues of a progressive country. Abolition for one. Women's suffrage for another. Equal rights for all men and women created equal. It's in the Constitution, but coming from a man's mouth it's only so much poppycock. I don't suppose you know the works of Elizabeth Barret?"

"Er, the classicist, Barret Browning? Thomas Browning's wife?"

"She was accomplished and known in England before she ever met him. Now they call her Elizabeth Barret Browning. Exactly what I'm talking about. Can't a woman exist on her own without the legitimization of a man's approval?" She shoved his soiled linen into a cloth bag and drew the string, forcefully.

"I should hope so, Miss Park. But society being what it is..."

"Society is a men's club in both senses of the word: a bludgeon and a covey. We've put up with it long enough, the hour has come. They know this in Europe. We shall fling open the Gates of Perception! Georges Sand will soon be usurped by the Baroness Aurore Dupin. Mahk my words, Mistah Warren. Now, do you want my introduction to Putnam?"

"I'd be most grateful. And if fortunate enough to secure publication, the entire Ojibwe people will be in your debt. My mother's people are the cause I espouse."

"Laudable, Mistah Warren, but do not patronize me. We speak as two writers seeking to turn the tides of oppression. On equal footing. I shall prepare your package and if that no-good layabout comes back, I'll have him deliver it. But not to Appleton, to Putnam."

"Excuse me, but I've already prepared and included the letter. I have recommendations to the Appleton Company. I'd like to proceed..."

"Suit yourself, but you're baahking up the wrong tree, Mistah Warren. Appleton will send you sailing."

§

He spent another night he would qualify as sleepless, pondering the poetess's talent for mixing her metaphors. But in reality, he slept, if only lightly and in spurts. He coughed but without bleeding, endured his ration of pain and discomfort, drank cold tea, and sat up by the window watching the gaslights go out in the neighborhood, hearing voices shouting far off over the rooftops, rising up from the brick and stone and mortar world below. The train creaked and rattled past the nearby park, drawn by teams of clomping horses. He thought he heard shots, then the clanging of a bell. Then calm. Strangely enough, there was not a night bird to be heard. Occasional gulls cried out in the latest hours, but he could not see them. The moon was at first a dull luster behind the clouds, then all light disappeared. He let himself dream of his home and found that he missed Matilda and the children. He missed his Indians, his canoe, his log home, his adversaries and friends in the wilderness and in Saint Paul, where he was well-liked by people who counted. He would have liked to talk with his old companion Gwii-wisens, now become the flamboyant Chief Hole-in-the-Day the Younger. Old Flat Mouth, was he still alive? He missed them all, but this he knew was part of his characteristic sentimentality and he would not bow to it, just savor it.

By far the worst of his night fears was the worry that Billy would not come back, as Miss Parks had intimated. He desperately needed an ally, a runner. In his weakened state, he felt he could not depend on his own legs to go out into the city and sell his manuscript. He could do it on paper, by writing to the publishers and submitting the book for consideration, but he found the streets of the crowded city intimidating, even dangerous. In the back of his mind lurked Fowles, following him on crutches, or Corning's armed henchmen waiting to grab him. But this was unlikely; New York City was immense. He dispelled it as another irrational fear that came in the night to haunt him.

Also, he had but little faith in his appearance, fearing that in person he would falter, behave sickly, and fail to produce the image he wished of a young and productive writer with great plans for future volumes. He needed someone to deliver his letters, his papers. And to find him some tincture of laudanum, the elixir that had gotten him through the hardest part of his journey. He could not impose on the rigid character and duties of Miss Park for this service, although she was more than willing to help contact publishers. Billy would be better as a runner, and he would get him what he needed.

The morning brought relief. He slept through the last two hours of the night when the pigeons began cooing, then his personal valet came in bright and bustling as usual with a fresh pot of tea and breakfast on a tray. Billy deposited the tray on the table, reached under his gray smock, and ceremoniously set Warren's little vial beside it, now filled with a dark liquid. Then he set down a larger flask with an amber liquid inside. The man said nothing, just beamed at him. Warren tasted it.

"Maple syrup. And good. You're a magician, Billy."

"They make it upstate. When you ask around Five Points, you find what you want. I figured it would do you good. Touch of home, ye know? Now, Sir, I suggest you make your concoction and hide that vial. Plenty of sneaks around here."

"I must owe you something."

"Not a penny. Now I'll deliver that package. Miss Parks wrapped it up nicely, bless her nitpicking little soul." Billy briskly turned and left.

"Many thanks." He poured some syrup on his bowl of oatmeal and milk, a bit into his tea with a few drops of the other. He first had to test its potency. How could Miss Parks ever doubt this man's dependability?

So he came to make his own doses of tea sweetener. The strength of the laudanum tincture, based on what smelled like a sweet sherry, was about equal to the one Julia had made, which could have been diluted with the watered-down rum the traders sold to the Indians and loggers in the Saint Clair Valley. In any case, the maple syrup from upstate New York—every bit as good as his own—carried the day. He drank only one cup of his tea and deduced there was less alcohol and perhaps more opiate in this one, and it was every bit as effective. With surprising speed, the mixture quelled his congestion, relaxed his pain, and restored his ability to reason, act and move around with more agility and fortitude. This illusion of control would last until it lulled him to sleep again. The leaves outside his window took on the fresh green hue of early spring to filter the sunlight dancing on the walls of his room. He was slightly dizzy, but functional.

He shaved himself that morning, looking into the small round mirror above the desk. His cheeks were a bit gaunt and colorless, but he had gained back some weight and declared himself stronger. Then he tucked away his pharmaceutical necessities in his trunk, forming an implicit collusion with Billy Daniels that he found satisfying, as a stranger in a strange city is pleased to form a useful bond with another stranger.

Billy returned in time to escort him down to his water-cure administrations, but the regenerated William Warren took pride in being able to negotiate the stairway and corridors without leaning on his nurse's arm. In his lukewarm sheet wrap he took a restorative nap, then a stroll around the corridors, even venturing outside for the first time (Miss Park was absent from her station in the lobby) to view the gentle Laight Street, its cobbles, passing carrioles and urbane strollers in their top hats and city dresses taking the air beneath the trees before lunchtime. He looked up at the branches, remembering that they were just greening upon his arrival. This was the first time maybe in a month that he had viewed them from ground level. The window of his third-floor room was now almost obscured by linden leaves. He had wasted precious time.

Waiting for the return answer from Appleton, he assiduously exercised by walking, mounting the stairway, and practicing a modicum of calisthenics as indicated by Billy Daniels with the patience of an experienced trainer. He forced himself to eat slowly and well in his room—for he still could not face the dining hall—and occasionally ventured into the glassed-in solarium on the top floor to nap with a cup of tea and feign reading a book from the Institute's library. In addition to the army of scientific journals and publications by Trall and his fellow hygienists, he found *Harper's* and other magazines, travel brochures, and literature on the city of New York as witnessed by such notable writers as Washington Irving and Edgar Allen Poe (fascinating), even a travel log by Charles Dickens, whose opinion of New York was entirely negative: the lot of the poor was worse in America than in England.

Perusing a library or bookstore was always a pleasant experience. He enjoyed being surrounded by books, imagining the very weight of the paper and the work that went into publishing them, setting the type letter by letter, binding the copies... It was a tribute to the mission of the writer, and the essential work of the publisher and printer, those who evidenced the intellectual activity that comprised a body of knowledge and literature. This restored his confidence that soon his own work would be bound and waiting among the books he loved to touch and read. The traditions and knowledge of the Anishinaabe people would stand among these pages, as Flat Mouth said, forever. His efforts, and their history, would be part of the bookish smell of knowledge.

Abiding thus with his ruminations, his water-cure administrations, and his soothing tea made him less nervous, but in his soul, the empty hours of waiting caused a mute anxiety he was forced to endure. He allowed that unlike his Ojibwe friends and forefathers, and his Métis- French grandfather Michel Cadotte, he had never been a patient man. Matters must move forward, forthwith, and when they would not move of their own volition, you must push them to happen. Events must be provoked, work must be accomplished, progress must be prodded into being. This must be his father talking, his white Yankee upbringing, his European—or perhaps it was now better referred to as American—blood. His time was short and he could not predict when the publishers he had to contact would answer him. Perhaps he should have done this differently. He should have gone to Appleton himself, manuscript in hand, impressed upon him the necessity to read it immediately and decide one way or another. He chided his lameness. There was no time for this waiting game.

§

It was one short week later, on the day he was authorized to go out alone to take a walk around Saint John's Square, that Billy came up running to find him sitting on a park bench, observing the exotic species of flowering bushes the landscapers were planting. He informed him that a note from Appleton was waiting for him in his room.

It was enthusiastic but disappointing. They were impressed by the work and certain it would be of interest to a growing public in the Territories, but the company was fully invested in ongoing projects and unable to propose a direct contract without advance orders. However, in view of Warren's excellent references and support in his home territory, if their friend and excellent book dealer Mr. William Le Duc would order a thousand copies for his Saint Paul bookstore, they would print and deliver them.

This took him aback. It seemed implausible, not to say impossible. How could Le Duc sell a thousand copies of any book in a Territory that could boast maybe a few hundred literate inhabitants? It was ridiculous. Just a roundabout way of saying no. However, this first refusal did nothing to shake his resolve, as he was satisfied that Mr. Appleton had taken the trouble to glance at his work and to answer quickly. He penned a thank you note and requested that they return his manuscript to the hands of his courier. Billy executed his task with due alacrity and brought the package back that afternoon. It was wrapped exactly as it was when Warren had sent it; he wondered if they had taken the trouble to read it thoroughly, or if they had only read his cover letter. He would probably never know.

Next in line, he decided, was Redfield, again a business acquaintance of Le Duc. The following morning, he redrafted essentially the same cover letter but addressed it directly to Justus Starr Redfield, who according to Le Duc had just published work on the discovery of the Mississippi Valley with narratives by Father Jacques Marquette, Allouez, and Hennepin. Warren's work tied into this same history but from the Indian viewpoint, and could very well interest him, although he was relatively new in this field. Warren expressed the same urgency, for the same reasons, and dispatched his man along with the manuscript and letters to the Redfield publishing offices.

He then wrote the same to Putnam, but used another and more direct approach. Along with his summary, he included his letters of recommendation, the one especially from Alexander Ramsey, and the mention that he had been in contact with a New York poetess, Miss Philomena Park, who had mentioned that a personal interview might be more fruitful for both parties. He could bring him the manuscript in person. His time in New York was limited and coming to a close, he added, but he would be available for an interview for approximately another week or two and he would be honored to discuss the work with him directly at his office.

Miss Park was as good as her word, and handed him a sealed and, he detected, lightly perfumed note enclosed in a small envelope the color of a robin's egg, with her name and nothing else embossed on the cover flap, to the attention of Mr. G. P. Putnam. The red wax seal depicted the sole letter "P" in an elaborately scrolled design. The complete effect was unmistakably feminine. Despite decorum, he felt the inclination to ask her about the content of the note, and he did. She looked at him sharply and set her chin.

"I requested an interview for you, as you asked. I could hardly praise the merit of a book I've never read, now could I?"

"I have but one copy, and it's now in Redfield's hands. Nor have I had the pleasure of reading your poetry, Miss Park."

"Nor will you until it appears in print, Mistah Warren. No one will."

"Then I hope it is soon. Thank you for the note." He included it in his own larger envelope to Putnam. It was a risky move, but what else could he do with only one manuscript and so many people to show it to? He must also write to Harpers & Brothers, but decided against overextending his solicitations.

377

D. A. Robertson, back in Saint Paul, had indicated that Judge C. F. Daly could possibly help him, and had written him a letter to that effect which he had given to Warren before his departure. He wrote to the Judge requesting an interview, included Robertson's recommendation, and waited.

The cruel and fickle month of April breathed on, with colder rain showers outside and water-cure within, a bit of sun on occasion. He walked in Saint John's Park on good days but could not yet risk a lone foray farther than two blocks from his room. Billy walked with him once as far as Broadway, teeming with shoppers and businessmen, where he looked for the Appleton Building but tired before he made one block in the crowd. Shuffling along, fascinated and frightened by the brightness, the flashing glass, the marble columns and uniformed doormen, and the richness of the window displays, he was bustled by a newsboy and faltered, holding himself up against a lamppost. He was simply dizzy, he said to Billy, but in truth, he could hardly breathe. His man had to support him again, serving as a human cane, and he had to pay for a cab back to the Institute.

The cure continued, his cough and fever abated, but still, he felt weak one day, then passably functional the next. Usually, he took a book or magazine from the library and favored his naps in the solarium on rainy afternoons. With the elixir, his and Billy's secret, his sleep had returned. One evening, Billy stole into his room with a lascivious wink and produced from under his smock a lidded tin of warm beef stew, which the convalescent devoured with undisguised pleasure and confessed his willingness to purchase more on another evening if Billy could manage it. He did, twice, and for no charge— as it came from the restaurant where he sometimes served tables in the evening. The Irishman was a man of many resources.

Warren then toyed with the idea of writing letters home, for which he had thus far little inclination because he had no good news to report, and he received no word from anyone in his homeland. Especially not Mrs. Ramsey nor Le Duc, who had his address, as did his family. He wondered about the effect of the letter he'd written to Anna Ramsey, dispatched at Detroit almost two months ago.

Whatever had come over him? Delirium? Some unnamed long-ing for another woman, another life? No, he had but one wife, Matil-da. And one life, the trajectory of which he now could resume in short order because it was perhaps nearing its end. Now he was try-ing to save it. He did not write home. He did not want to dismay his family, nor his sisters, nor anyone relying on him. His maple sweet-ener ran low and he began to fret.

§

Then the letter came from Redfield, returning his manuscript and saying he was very impressed with it. Indeed, he was willing to discuss how he could participate in publishing the work but at a later date since he would be traveling for business over the next few days. Possibly he could receive him towards mid-May. This too, Warren found unsatisfactory but was encouraged. At least he had his manuscript back.

That night his cough took a turn for the worse, and he resorted to a good dose of his tea more than once to calm his nerves. He was finally induced to sleep, but woke in the morning, feverish, with blood on his nightshirt. For some obscure reason, he felt ashamed and was counting on his trusty valet to cover for him. No one must know about this aggravation. It would pass. It had before. But he had to hide the blood. He would not look at it.

Along with his breakfast, Billy brought in an envelope, deliv-ered by courier that morning, from George Putnam. He would be pleased to receive him in his offices, but would it not be a more efficient use of time if he could first peruse his *History?* It would not require more than two or three days, and they could meet on Friday next, the 29th of April. He included his regards to Miss Park.

It had worked. And he had the manuscript to send. He sat up in bed and asked Billy for the lid to his chest and writing materials.

"Oh, worry me," said Billy, seeing the blood. "What have we here? A little tussle last night caught him unawares, that it? Can't have this sort of thing. You change into this clean nightshirt, Sir, and let me take care of this. Nobody'll be the wiser. Eat your breakfast, keep your strength up, then you can write your missive."

Warren had heard this same admonition from his own mother. He found it amusing to a point, coming from this rough-looking young man. But had he slipped back into childhood that much?

"You'll be wantin' me to deliver the package again this morning? To Mr. Putnam?" Uncanny. Billy seemed to be able to read his every intention in advance.

"Yes, if you'll be so kind, I'll just dash off a note to him and away you go. And Billy, give me my coat and take some money before you leave. I'll need some more sweetener soon, by tonight in fact. Do you suppose you can handle that?"

"Rather that than handle me wife. I'll be back tonight, but after dark, maybe midnight."

"And this Friday, can you help me out about town? We have an appointment."

"Fine, Sir. But don't you want me to get that coat cleaned for ye? And the trousers and cravat? You do yer best when you look yer best, they say."

"Right you are. Spare no expense." He held out two five-dollar pieces, but Billy took only one.

"This'll do fine. No use carrying extra money about in this city. With all the grafters and hustlers about, it'll disappear in a shot. And don't be givin' no dollars to the hack drivers. Fifty cents is more than ample. They'll be takin' ye fer one of the wealthy and put out the word you're a prime target for the gamers and the barkers just lyin' out there like snakes in the shade. But don'tcha fear, Sir, don'tcha fear! You'll be in no danger walkin' with Billy. I can spot 'em a mile away."

During the day Warren rested, received only the lightest administrations from the staff. He ate lightly and drained the rest of his tea sweetener. Both in bed and in the solarium, he made a point of sitting up, as lying prone would congest him, running the risk of another hemorrhage. His aim was to heal the wound that broke in his chest the night before. He took his sitz-bath assiduously seated on the barrel stool, followed by a warm water wrap in a chair. He did not plunge into a cold bath this time, but sponged down the sweat

380

with cool water. The treatment as prescribed by Doctor Trall, he was eager to admit, was comforting to both body and morale. Perhaps, he told himself, this was all he could hope for at this point.

As he was nodding off in the solarium sitting in a wicker lounge chair, a copy of *Harper's Monthly* on the floor beneath him, Miss Park came up with a ledger in hand. She sat primly beside him.

"How are you feeling, Mistah Warren? The Doctor is satisfied with your progress, glad to see you up and about these last two weeks."

"I suppose I'm doing all right." His voice was very quiet, even to his ears. She noted this down in her ledger.

"Would it be convenient to settle the second half of your bill this afternoon? That would take care of everything up through mid-May. Then we'll take stock of things and see if you require a longer stay."

"Of course. For the bill. You have the regards of Mr. Putnam. I received word today. I sent the manuscript and have an appointment on Friday. You have my sincere thanks, Miss Park."

"Entirely welcome. Should you need accompaniment, I could make myself available to go with you."

"Ah. How kind. Actually, Mr. Daniels has volunteered to help me along, if need be. I know how busy you are, and he appears to know the city very well."

"Are you certain that Mr. Daniels would be the person to give the right impression in a publisher's office? The man is barely literate."

"Well, just for the travel. He doesn't have to come into the office."

"But I could. Putnam knows my family. And he has my manuscript."

"I see. And you might want—"

"Two birds, one stone. We could both walk out with a contract. You have to push these people, Mistah Warren, or you never get anywhere." She leveled her round eyes at him with her thin jaw squarely tensed, her brow lowered, determined. She would not take a refusal easily.

"You will excuse me, Miss Park, but I feel it might be better to go this first time on my own. I'll surely mention your manuscript and your need for an answer post haste. Even though I've never read it."

She snapped the ledger closed and rose. "Very well. Go with the Bowery rat. I'll be at my desk until six tonight. For the payment. Good afternoon, Mistah Warren."

He went to her lobby desk at ten minutes before six to hand her a one-hundred-dollar bill on the Railroad Bank and wait as she wordlessly wrote out the receipt. She thanked him on the part of the Institute. He thanked her for the receipt and climbed back upstairs reflecting on the possible consequences of having contradicted the will of a woman like Philomena Park.

But he had a friend in Billy. Having saved a last draught of sweetener for the evening tea, he slept well in the first hours, then woke to find the Irishman shuffling slowly about his room looking for a match to light the lamp. When he found it and turned to Warren, his face was almost unrecognizable. One eye swollen shut, with a bandage over the temple under his broad cap, the other just a slit, his lips cut, twisted out of shape, Billy looked like he'd been run over by a team of horses.

"Good Lord, man. Have you seen a doctor?"

Billy attempted a smile and brought out the bottles he'd promised, deposited them on the nightstand by the bed, then produced his own flask, holding it delicately as both his hands were swollen, and drank deeply. He tottered and moved with difficulty to sit in the chair, sighing. He seemed completely at ease and, incongruously, happy.

"It was a good fight," he said. "Didn't turn out as planned, but Billy got his man, and he got his money."

"What are you talking about?"

"I was the underdog, Captain, bets against me. Just the odds I like. Floyd outweighed me by twenty-seven pounds. Had to show him a thing or two about footwork, take a few punches meself, but me luck was with me. One roundhouse here, to the chin, and the bugger was down. He tried to get up. I rang his bell again with me left—all I had in it—and he was out. Man's got a soft chin. Aye, Cap... Soft chin." He drank again.

"You're paid to fight?"

"Winner takes all. A month's wages in 10 minutes."

"And if you lose?"

"Depends. Floyd did pretty good, likely. He always does. Wants a rematch. Told him I'd think about it."

"You're in no shape, Billy. You should see a doctor. Why risk a rematch?"

"Missus fixed me up. We got ice downstairs, from the fishmonger." He took a swig of his flask while Warren mixed his own elixir, poured some into a cup of cold tea, drank it down and poured another. With his good eye, Billy watched this exceptional deviation from Warren's rationing habits. He noted his dark mood and attempted to introduce a more hopeful topic.

"Now then. Are we set for Friday, Captain?"

"I am Captain of nothing, Billy. Except maybe my own soul. Even that is doubtful."

"We think alike, Sir. Our soul don't belong to us. But as Captain, we set its course."

"And where does it take us?"

"Where we hope to land," said Billy. Warren raised his cup and they both drank. Billy reached for the laudanum vial. "With permission, Sir?" Warren nodded. He poured a few drops into what whiskey remained in his flask.

The low lamplight conversation that night was muted, couched in secrecy as the two drinkers each sought their own relief. Such moments, when the will still shines alive beneath the fog of men's bravado and self-denial, lead to camaraderie in thought, and sometimes in self- revelation. They did not get drunk, they got friendly. And more talkative.

Billy, it turned out, was one of the lucky few that survived the early potato famine and emigrated to America with the thousands evacuated from Drumcliff by Gore Booth, who mortgaged his Lancashire estate to finance his starving tenants' crossing.

"The man was a saint," he owned, "And condemned as a devil. In truth, I owe him my life."

But thousands stayed in Ireland and died of disease or starvation, including his mother and all six of his brothers and sisters who succumbed to typhus. He never found out what happened to his father, who went off in search of labor one day and never returned. Billy was a hearty boy, and lucky. Booth had him trained as a steam mechanic in Ireland and unknowingly sent a skilled worker, not just a peasant, to the promised land. Canada first, then he worked his way to New York, where hundreds of Irish, now maybe thousands, had grouped together in the Five Points district, where they could count on better food and lodgings and were paid twice as much or more for their labor than they were in Ireland. Of course, the Americans expected four times more work than in the home country, but this was all the same to Billy. Still, the missus sewed shirts, she cleaned and served table, as did he, to save what they could for their dream.

"And what might that be?" Warren asked.

"Land. In the West. I want me own farm, Captain. Missus wants her own house, now with the two little ones. Another on the way... Anyway it works the same here as in Ireland. You want a good life in the promised land, you don't get it by workin'. You get it by ownin'."

"Farming? And you know how to work the land?"

"Both of us born to tenant farmers. Then the famine. Potato blight. Course, we never had nothin' before that 'cept rent to pay. And the smaller the harvest, the higher the rent. Nothing left there for anyone now. New York's a good town, but it's not for mine. Land here belongs to John Jacob Astor and he's not sellin'. He owns the land and the leases. Won't grow a thing but bricks, stone, and money. Out west, they say the earth is so ripe you can spit tobacco juice and grow a field. That true, Captain?"

"You're a trained mechanic."

"Aye. I can ply me trade where it's needed, put aside for the farm."

"You have to make a claim, Billy. This year they expect thousands like you."

"Forty acres. At a dollar and a quarter an acre. We almost have it."

"You can stake out 160 acres in Minnesota Territory on warrant or scrip. And they all know it, all those families coming off those ships down there in the harbor. Germans, Swedes, more Irish too, I'll bet. Europe is spilling its thousands of poor on New York, all bound for the promised land."

"Every man has a dream, Captain. Even you I'll wager."

"My dream is wrapped up in that package you delivered today, Billy," He looked over at his writing materials on the table. "With your help, I'll plant it in Mr. G. P. Putnam's office on Friday."

§

The next days of waiting went by painlessly for Warren, helped along by sleep and the precious suppressant. During that time, Billy Daniels—whose real name, he confessed, was O'Daniel but he dropped the Irish O' in New York to avoid association with the scourge of the labor market, who would work for less than a Negro freeman—healed fast. He lost his swollen features and regained every bit of his agility and strength, which he put to the service of helping his patient in and out of warm and cold baths with the delicacy of a nursemaid, notwithstanding Warren's six-foot stature. This could be explained, he mentioned to Warren when he brought him some pork and beans one evening: he was a good deal thinner than when he first arrived.

He resolved to eat to keep his strength up. In truth, he did not have much of an appetite since his digestion had become difficult and unmanageable despite his vegetarian diet. He did not say this to Billy, nor to the Doctor, nor to Miss Park who in any event appeared quite miffed and was not speaking to him.

On Friday Billy paid special attention to his patient's bath and dress, gave his hair a trim and worked to restore what had visibly become a lackadaisical morale. He went so far as to shine his boots. "Always shine the heels as good as the toes, Captain. Ye want to impress them just as much goin' out as when ye come in."

Warren was told he had better brighten up or miss planting day. To do honor to the man dedicating his services to a doubtful cause, he made the effort to stand up straight. It took a bit of muster, but he could still put on the dog. In the afternoon he took a nap sitting up in his bed fully clothed. Just as he took a final draft of tea before venturing out into the streets, Billy showed up and produced a small jar of rouge to give him some color. Then a bit of powder for the complexion, "To tamp the shine, Cap. Gives a healthier luster. An old stage trick." He attached his high starched collar and tied his silk cravat for him.

Billy gave his charge a once-over and nodded. He himself then shed his gray Hydropathic Institution smock to reveal a suit of clothes of light tan striped wool, highlighted by a yellow and red striped cravat and an embroidered vest over a clean white shirt. He sported a low-crowned top hat with a shiny silk band. All of this, he owned to Warren before leaving, he gleaned from the wardrobe at the Bowery Theater, where his missus often played and he himself had strutted a few times on the planks.

Warren looked at his face in the little mirror, seeking to recognize the man he used to be, speaking before the Territorial Legislature, publishing in Robertson's paper. He had become something of a sensation at the time. It was known and obvious that he was a part Anishinaabe, their defender, a born storyteller and fine orator. Was this man still alive? He must be. But no one in New York knew this. Here, he was a complete unknown. In the glass he saw a skinny, sad-eyed clown.

"You've made us up as a pair of actors, Billy."

"Smile, Captain. All the world's a stage. The bard himself knew that much." Billy's talents were legion indeed. He may as well give it a go.

As they came down the stairs, they met Doctor Trall himself, a rare sight in the hallways, who complimented the pair on their appearance. Trall was duly impressed and approved of an afternoon walk. He inquired as to their destination.

"An appointment with Mr. Warren's publisher, Doctor sir. A Mr. Putnam, over near Broadway. Thought I'd show Mr. Warren some of the sights afterwards, time permitting."

"Putnam? You have dealings with George Putnam, Mr. Warren?"

"My manuscript is currently in his offices, being considered for publication. A historical work." Warren drew himself up to his full height and smiled, as if he were, like his escort, playing a role on stage.

"I see. I am represented by another publisher. More in the medical field. However, please give Mr. Putnam my regards. I wish you well in your endeavors, and if I can be of any service in that regard during your stay, please don't hesitate to ask. You're looking very well, Mr. Warren. And I should like to know more of this manuscript. Indeed."

The Doctor shook his hand and nodded to Billy. Warren deduced that Doctor Trall had forgotten about his first letter, in which he'd mentioned his writings. The man had no idea who he was, or what he had accomplished despite his illness. He must be too absorbed in his own work.

The pair walked out into Laight Street. It was a glorious afternoon, and mercifully for Warren, Miss Park was absent from her station that day. He was not of a mind to face adversity.

Chapter 31: Manhattan

THE TRIP TO BROADWAY DRESSED for business raised his mood. It was his first foray into the metropolis. He felt propelled like a log in the rapids, caught up in the chaotic flow of the strangely impersonal humanity encountered on city streets, which piqued his curiosity. In all these thousands of faces, each one had a story unknown to the others. Now he was on his way to the publishers, who purveyed all those stories to the world.

Billy led him just around the corner from Hudson Square to Canal Street where they waited only 10 minutes before boarding a crowded horse-drawn streetcar and heading south, where the rails turned onto Church Street. Still weak, he was crushed and jostled by insistent and upright bodies seemingly indifferent to such intimate contact. Warren felt again that he was being spotted as a country man, a stranger who did not know to use his bulk and feet to butt in, claim his place and be squashed with the other travelers like so many fish in a barrel. Billy, no longer a misplaced immigrant, assumed his bourgeois stage costume, raised his chin, and slipped right in, keeping a firm hold on Warren's arm.

New Yorkers here dressed in style—the men in long coats and high hats and the women in wide crinoline dresses and sporting all manner and style of elaborate hats, parasols, muffs, and collars. There was a heady smell of mixed perfumes. Nearly everyone was standing up clutching their purses and watch fobs as the driver sold tickets through a hole in his glass partition. For all the attention they paid to their appearances, these Manhattan city dwellers spoke not a word to each other, and seemed to put considerable effort into looking straight ahead at nobody or reading a newspaper (the men) or magazine (the women), glancing distrustfully right and left, taking an offended air if perchance you caught their eye.

Soon the gentility of the neighborhood gave way to a commoner crowd, where gentlemen strollers took their time to compare the wares of the women and girls perched in doorways or leaning out windows with wide painted smiles and direct gazes. One of them saw Warren staring, rolled out her tongue at him and wagged it. Some men got off the streetcar here, preferring to walk, while the prim women looked disapprovingly ahead and held their children close to the collar. After passing the New York Hospital it was time to step down and walk, turning toward Broadway.

Here was the city. The constant shouting, the jostling horses pulling overloaded carts of baggage, boxes, merchandise, trunks, fruits from the ships; fragrant hot breads and roiling steam mixing with acrid coal smoke. Everywhere were men, women, and children hurrying to spend their money in the shops, great stores and theatres that seemed to gain in luxury and stature in the downtown area, the heart of commercial Manhattan. The very buildings became grander on magnificent Broadway. He righted his posture in imitation of the richer inhabitants and strove to blend in with the strutters of the East Side. Everywhere he looked, huge, printed advertisements on brick or stone buildings stopped his perspective. Above, the sky was a uniform gray. The street noise rattled his brain.

Arriving before the offices of G.P. Putnam Broadway, Publishing Company, Billy straightened Warren's four-in-hand cravat, newly pressed and shiny, then tightened his own which was slightly limp, the color of lavender. He would take a turn by the old brewery nearby, and meet him back here in an hour. He would wait if need be. Not to worry. It was five sharp.

Warren renewed his effort to stand at his full height before entering—he was lucky to be taller than most men, and should use this to his advantage. His dress was elegant, his shirt clean and waistcoat pressed, his long cloak and hat lending him a stately aura reserved for a man of letters on business. In his satchel he held his letters of recommendation and the recent encouragement from Henry Schoolcraft containing a caveat to do nothing without a contract. He felt, all things considered, sufficiently armed for the interview. Behind the marble stairway he found a corner and had a last draught of his tea. Fortunately, the office was only on the second floor. He ascended slowly.

He sat waiting in the book-lined antechamber, hearing voices behind closed doors. It was a welcome change from the anxiety of waiting and the boredom of being bedridden. If only he could abstain from coughing for the whole interview. His one clean handkerchief was already bloodstained from that morning, and he was carrying a low fever. He composed his breathing, concentrating on the calm afforded by the smell of the countless books on the high oakwood shelves.

A clerk entered, a thin balding man in a brown waistcoat with silver spectacles. The employee's manner revealed no enthusiasm for his profession, nor any sign that Warren was the eagerly expected new author of the day. He offered a magazine, *Putnam's Monthly,* December issue, suggesting that it may be of interest to him. It was Mr. Putnam's latest venture, promising for the future. This one featured a serialized novel by a young woman recently in vogue *(Perhaps he had read Miss Wetherell? Charming woman, and a gold mine for Mr. Putnam...)* Plus an article by Mr. Washington Irving, who in fact lived just around the block.

Warren thanked him somewhat over-enthusiastically and fingered the magazine. The paper was thinner than that of a book, but it was handsomely printed.

The door to the main office opened again. It was George Palmer Putnam himself, ushering out a young woman stunningly dressed and behatted, carrying a parasol and a small round purse. She was attractive, rosy-cheeked, but Warren was not in the state of mind to make acquaintances.

"I assure you my staff and I shall give your work the utmost attention, Miss Bryant. You shall hear from us in under a fortnight. Most interesting indeed." He shook the woman's hand, and she thanked him demurely before floating out on her wide petticoats.

The publisher then turned, smiling behind his dark beard, and extended a thin but firm hand.

"Mr. Warren? Most pleased. I've finished reading your work. A prodigious effort, Sir. Please come in."

On the large side table in the editorial sanctum, Warren recognized his open package and manuscript, bundled in chapters with thin leather straps. Putnam bade him sit, crossed behind his cluttered desk, and folded his hands. It was one of the few occasions when Warren found himself unable to speak. His breaths were shallow.

"Mr. Warren, my staff and I approve heartily of your manuscript. Fascinating. Monumental. Congratulations. It has the stamp of excellent research and a lively pen, which values I hold dear. The histories read like veritable adventures, and it's crammed with curious information. It will certainly be of great scholarly and commercial interest. Unfortunately, my overburdened company cannot risk fully investing in the venture at this time. But I'll tell you how I am going to help you."

"Sir?"

"Very original, this record of the aboriginals' oral history. Essentially, we're listening to the Ojibwe tell their own tale, but in a learned and lively voice that holds one's interest unceasingly. One wonders how you managed this. You must be more than proficient in the language."

"My mother's people, the Anishinaabe, as they call themselves. I spent my childhood among them. But my father, an educated man from upstate, read to me in English as a boy. Our family descends from the Mayflower Warrens. I was born in what most call a cabin, but my father had the largest library in the Northwest."

"Yes. And you were a Government interpreter. Widely respected among the Indians. I can understand that. Governor Ramsey speaks well of your skills as an orator and your term in the Territorial Legislature."

"An elected office. Were it not for some parties' dubious conduct at the urns, I would still be active in the Legislature. However, my intention is now to follow the path of authorship." He cleared his throat. Putnam, his gaze direct, put his fingers together, giving Warren the impression that he had his entire attention. This was the moment.

"This book, Mr. Putnam, is the first of a series of works I am qualified to undertake. If you are disposed to publish this first volume, as I explained in my letter, I will continue the series with a work on the lives of the prominent chiefs, then the rites and secrets of the Midewiwin society, what we call the medicine men, leading up to what could be a very amusing book on legends and hieroglyphs, in short, the entire cosmology—though not necessarily in that order. On this, I defer to your professional editorial and publishing experience."

"Absolutely, Mr. Warren. I have no doubt but that you shall succeed, and brilliantly. You must be familiar with the poetic works of Mr. Copway, your...er, fellow tribesman."

"Published by yourself, Sir. I have perused it in your office. Quite admirable indeed. My own intention, my very duty, is rather historical in nature. Scrupulously transcribing and elucidating the oral traditions of the Anishinaabe before they disappear with the old men upon whose memories I rely. I have neither the ambition nor the talent for works of the imagination."

"Mmm. Well, in this age, we seek both of course, Mr. Warren. We have to sell books, and there is a lively demand for accessible fiction. Especially serialized."

Warren suppressed an urge to cough. A slight dizziness momentarily overtook him. As luck would have it, Putnam suddenly rose and spoke looking out the window behind his desk, appearing to study the flow of potential readers on Broadway. The tightness in his chest subsided as Putnam spoke to the street below.

"At present I am engaged in printing and reprinting several pillars of our country's literary edifice, with whom you are undoubtedly familiar, as well as the entire catalog of the confounded industrial exhibit. The Crystal Palace has mobilized the great part of our working capital..." He abruptly turned back toward Warren, illuminated by an idea. "...along with the magazine you hold in your hand—an interesting approach that helps us survive in this cut-throat world of publishing. You say your work has already been serialized?"

"Partly, Sir. In the *Minnesota Democrat,* thanks to Colonel Robertson, at an earlier stage. It was he who initially suggested I gather the articles in book form."

"It is an eventuality we may consider, but I tend to agree with Mr. Robertson. What you have here is a book, Mr. Warren, of grand proportions. I am simply uncertain that we can interest the current American public in the *History of the Ojibway* Tribe at this juncture. I am sure it would be of interest to scholars, and to the Indians themselves—should they one day learn to read. Where the general public is concerned, many other issues pervade the budding New World imagination. Time will tell. As I told you, I am prepared to help you. I cannot invest, but you will find others to invest. What I can do is offer to have your manuscript stereotyped and printed in, say, 1,000 copies. The expense for you would be some 350 dollars. All rights revert to you, the G.P. Putnam publishing house would take no profits. I can act as seller here in New York City, and if there's a second run, who can tell? What say you to that? Do you think you could raise the capital? Surely, Mr. Warren, with your references in the Territories…"

William Warren grabbed his handkerchief and twisted in his chair, wracked by a violent cough that brought sweat to his entire body. He attempted to answer the man standing at the desk, but a darkening fog crept over the room.

Putnam crossed to the table to pour a glass of water from a decanter and set it in front of him. He returned to the window and resumed his survey of the street below, discretion itself. As if appeased by a visiting spirit passing through him, Warren's breathing eased, daylight returned and he recovered enough to drink from the glass, attempting a smile. He wiped his brow and quickly hid his handkerchief.

"Please forgive me. Our winters are harsh in the Northwest."

"Yes. Here as well. But with the advent of modern heating methods… Where exactly are you living now, Mr. Warren?"

"My house is just north of Saint Paul on the Mississippi. I was born and raised— with the exception of my years at the Oneida Institute—in La Pointe on Madeline Island, the home of my mother's people. My father exercised in the fur trade until—as long as he could. It was there I began collecting the stories from the old Ojibwe...."

The fog was gaining. As he closed his eyes, Putnam crossed to the long table where he turned over the first pages of the manuscript as he spoke to his own subject. Warren heard the publisher's voice as if from afar, behind a wall.

"Interesting. Young writers from the Northwest Territories are coming into the light and their observations are of precious value. The lands will soon be thrown open entirely to settlement by these multitudes you see outside, arriving from Europe. Their futures await them in the Territories, which will shortly attain statehood to form the largest market in the world. The real future of this country lies with the settlers, don't you think, Mr. Warren? What you refer to here as the "onward resistless tread of the Anglo-Saxon"? There is an idea, my man, a truism. Perhaps you could expand a bit more on that theme in your introduction. What will the Indians leave for the white settlers? What awaits *them?* Don't you think?"

There was no answer. "Mr. Warren?"

Putnam looked up to find his interviewee slouched over in his chair, eyes closed, hat and satchel on the floor. He walked over and touched his forehead. Warren slid from the chair onto the rug, unconscious.

Putnam jumped for the door. "Robert!" He cried into the hallway, "Fetch me some salts, and a physician!"

He ran with the bare-skinned Ojibwe boys past Grant's Point, up to the Indian cemetery. The pointed roofs covering the graves reminded him of his initials etched in the wet sand: WWW. There two boys stopped at a grave house and left some wild rice in the wooden bowl in the small doorway. He drew close and stuck in his hand to touch the darkness under which no grave could be seen, but where an Ojibwe lay buried with his bag of medi-

cine, his soul departed on his voyage to the Spirit land. He turned his hand
around inside, seeking to touch the dark void.

He jerked awake from the dream with no remembrance of it. His lungs ached. He was sitting on a bench, propped up on cushions between two square packages in George Putnam's waiting room. On his right, his own manuscript had been gathered, stacked, and wrapped in brown paper, set neatly beside him. On his left was a stack of books tied up with string. One was Putnam's prize publication, *The Wide Wide World,* by Elizabeth Wetherell. There was the Copway book, the *Life, Letters and Speeches,* and others from among Putnam's publications, copies of his new magazine.

He remembered the decorum required in the place where he had apparently fainted, and made a move to rise. Billy's hands held his shoulders from behind him, keeping him down.

"Not too fast, Captain," he whispered. "Catch your breath and take a drink." He handed him his flask of tea.

"Do ye more good than a quart of this other." Billy's close breath had the stuff of whiskey to it.

"What happened? What time is it? Where's Putnam?"

"He's got another live one in his office. I got worried and came up to see. About half past six. Good thing I did, they were about to call a doctor. I told him I was from Trall's Institute, you were takin' the cure and you'd be right as rain soon. Question of dosages. He knows Trall, so we just let ye rest up here. Drink up now."

Warren obeyed, dizzy, and slipped his flask into his pocket. Putnam came in with an elderly man. The two men were chuckling as if at a private joke among old friends.

"Ah, Mr. Warren!" Putnam exclaimed, relieved. "You're feeling better, I see. Excellent, indeed. Allow me to introduce you to Mr. Washington Irving, a friend and neighbor of mine who just stopped by."

Warren slowly rose, so entirely intimidated by the renown of the white-bearded figure before him that he could say nothing more than "It's an honor, Sir."

Billy bowed and stepped back.

Irving, gracious, told him "Likewise."

"Mr. Warren has some Indian histories to recount," Putnam went on. "Fascinating stories of the Northwest tribes. And he can wield a pen with the best of them, present company excepted of course. We just may come to a preliminary agreement, a sort of trial run to see how it goes."

"I look forward to seeing it in print," said Irving. "You are in good hands with Mr. Putnam. The fairest dealer in New York. Good evening, gentlemen."

Putnam was visibly relieved to see that Warren was conscious and now in the care of his manservant. He bid them both goodbye after reiterating that his offer stood firm, with one hundred percent of the profit inuring to the author. Mr. Irving himself received a healthy percentage of all retail sales of his revised works, and he was quite satisfied. A good system, rather innovative, for legitimate writers. It remained to be seen how the sales would go for his *History*. Warren thanked him for his time and the gift of books, assuring him he would consider his offer and answer shortly.

The interview exhausted Warren's meager capacities. They returned to the Hydropathic and Hygienic Institute by cab for which he paid 50 cents only, on Billy's insistence. It was ten times what he had paid for the streetcar. Billy carried the books and manuscript up to his room for him, set them on the desk, and congratulated him on the fruitful interview.

"Ain't no business of mine, Captain, but pray tell why we brought your book back here. What was the deal?"

"Three hundred fifty dollars to print a thousand copies, Putnam handles sales, I get all the profit. A reasonable deal, I believe. But I have only one hundred fifty to my name, Billy, and I still have to get home. I'll have to see another publisher."

"Aye. Or raise the money."

"Raising funds is not my strong point, especially not here."

"Anything to sell?"

"Just my own name, worth nothing as of this date."

"Well then, I might have a proposition, Cap. I'll look into it, tell you tomorrow.

Meanwhile, you get your rest. I'll bring you up some barley soup."

But when Billy returned, Warren was sound asleep. He left the soup on the nightstand, with a round of sausage hidden at the bottom of the bowl. He ate it with gusto around midnight, drank a cup of tea, and blacked out again.

§

Adversity may be his best ally, he reflected the next day as he folded and addressed his letter to Judge Daly. For Warren, it was a source of new energy. He did not view Putnam's proposal as a reason to despair, but as another path to take. It meant he had faith in the book, but could not risk his own capital in the commercial venture. All the profit from his own book sales had a good ring to it. It was certainly better than Appleton's proposal which would have cost him a thousand, for only a percentage of the profits. He recounted as much to Judge Daly, and asked his views on the subject, and if he hadn't any other publishers to recommend in New York.

Billy returned later that Sunday, with a busy and excited air that Warren had not recognized before in his aide-de-camp. Early afternoon, time to help Warren down to his sitz bath. He settled him in, pulled up a stool, and spoke in a conspiratorial whisper.

"Captain, we've got our plan. The rematch. Me and Floyd is all set up for Thursday. We want to leave time, a few days, for the odds to climb. I'm still the underdog, by two to one for now. Floyd's the favorite, going in at no value. But the big blubber head has been limpin' around the taverns all despondent-like, and word has it he's gone a bit soft in the head since I knocked him down. We let this thing ride a couple days and we'll be four to one, mark me word. This time, no beatin' round the bush. I'll knock him out before the end of the third."

"I hope so for you, Billy. Is this all legal?"

"That's the last thing we want. The law gets wind of it, the whole thing's over. But don't you worry, the bettin's secure. We all know the man who keeps the score. Now, here's the strategy. This game is small potatoes. There ain't no Yankee Sullivan stakes on a match like this one. We bet alone, best we could get is two to one. But we pool our money, a hundred from you, a hundred from me, along with my supporters, it'll pay twice that. We both get four back on our one, plus our initial one. You publish yer book; I go west and stake me claim. It's a sure thing, Cap. Come in with me!"

Billy slapped him on the knee, leapt up and danced back and forth in the bathroom, shadow-boxing and growling.

"I'll flatten the bastard, so he won't know what hit 'im! One shot at that soft chin o' his! Just one!"

Warren looked on, incredulous but fascinated. Truth be told, he loved a good bet and was disposed to believe that Billy was one. Of course, it would be risky, gambling always was, and if he put in a hundred he would have only fifty left, barely enough to return to Saint Paul. He might find a good card game before he left, and he suspected Billy could tell him where, but one hundred on one match...

"How can you be sure to get those odds?"

"We wait, Captain. This morning the betting started in the grocery, when Catalpa announced the rematch. By noon it was two to one. Floyd came in drinkin' and rantin', sayin' he was gonna dirk me one right there. Me, I backed off, opened me hands, and took no drink. Nothin'. In trainin', ye understand? The lads saw that. Tomorrow it'll be three to one. By Thursday, we'll have our odds. But even three to one's good."

"Billy, I can't do that," Warren announced.

Billy looked crestfallen, wordless for once.

"You'll bet yours, won't you? Even if I can't go in?"

"Sure. But we could make a lot more by poolin'."

"I can't. I'm sorry. But good luck. And stay in training."

§

Two days went by while Warren rested and pondered. He wrote some short letters home, one to his friend William Wood, one to Matilda saying basically the same: he was making headway, some houses were considering his work, and there was no doubt but that he would succeed.

He decided not to write to Anna Ramsey until he had an answer to his previous missive, which now seemed ridiculous to him. What had come over him on the boat? It was unlike him to be so boyish, so unthinking in his intentions. The governor's wife was a business associate, an investor on behalf of the new Cultural Society, and their communications should remain within those bounds. He chided himself for his foolish romanticism, keeping this foible a secret among others that he reserved for the depths of his guilty conscience. He hoped the letter had never reached her, that it had got lost in the mail, that the lady would never suspect him of misplaced attention He hoped, in truth, that her answer would never come.

Billy, meanwhile, was taciturn, less visible, but concentrated. By all appearances, the man took his training seriously. He came in sweating from his run in the morning, all business, walking sprightly on the balls of his feet, pouncing up the stairs several times a day to deliver linen and water jugs, move furniture, busying himself, always leaving early to "do the run". He reported that indeed, by mid-week, some bets were coming in at four to one. There was more money on Floyd, as he was the favorite, but it paid peanuts—barely two to one. Himself, he'd wait to bet until Warren made his decision.

"But my decision is made..."

"Yessir. I understand. We'll just wait and see."

Miss Park, whom he saw daily, seemed to have softened her attitude toward Warren. He actually caught her smiling once, as she arranged some flowers that Billy had brought to his room. (Wisteria cut from the solarium, he'd said. And a few roses from the park.) She remarked on how well he was doing in his cure, and that he had gained back some weight and color since his outing the other day.

He spent most of the time, when not bathing or submitting to some form of water administration, sleeping and dreaming in the solarium, or strolling slowly in the dappled shade of Hudson Square. His restorative tea, with its secret maple sweetener, was never far from his reach. Taken regularly in modest rations, it held back the coughing, eased the pain, tasted like home, and seemed to do him good. A more copious dose (only at night) ensured sleep, during which he dreamed of himself in incongruous situations that he never remembered upon waking, so muddled was his mind, so slow and heavy the awakening, so far away the certainty of purpose with which he had begun this journey. The dreams were not beneficial; they did nothing to alleviate the anxiety that overcame him before first light.

What if he should falter now and die, an old man at 27, a father of three, on the cusp of his career as a published historian, yet still destitute? What could be said of his life? Had he accomplished anything he set out to do? Had he saved the Ojibwe from decimation by the liquor sellers, the greedy traders, and the malicious politicians who wanted nothing more than to take their treaty money and watch them die out? Didn't Ramsey say that in another generation there'd be none left? No, he had been able to do nothing to further their cause. Had he fulfilled his promise to his family, his mother, to Flat Mouth, Great Buffalo, and Hole-in-the-Day? To others who had backed him and sent him on his way? No, he had not.

Had he reversed the curse that killed his father, to be squashed by fate, by failure, by the rebuttals and refusals of avid men in power? No, he had not.

Had he signed a contract with a publisher? Had he entertained several competing offers? No. And given the state of his health, prospects looked dim. Objectively, he had done nothing of all this. He would die and leave his family behind, in poverty and ignominy. His book would remain a stack of paper and wasted ink.

His nightmare, Failure, sat perched across the room on his bundled manuscript, festering and heaving, its ugly wart-ridden eyes staring him in the face like a gargoyle.

He must find a way. He must raise the money. A drowning man, he reasoned, reaches for the first branch he sees.

When his attendant came in that evening with his dinner with a timid "Evenin' Sir", he stepped lightly across the room to the table. Warren let the seconds pass, then broke the news.

"Billy, I'll go in with you," he said. "Tomorrow we'll bet two hundred. I'm sure you'll beat him." Billy set down his dinner tray, beaming.

"Now I will for sure, Cap. You know me secret strategy, it canna fail. No doubt about it. Me and the missus thank ye for this, sir, ye won't regret it."

Warren brought out the last two fifty-dollar bills from the poker game and extended them to Billy. "Put the money in tonight, then."

"Oh no sir. That would be jumpin' the gun, and not good form. The way we work it is, I'll give you my hundred, and tomorrow just before the fight, you place the bet with Catalpa. The fat man with the bowler hat. You'll see him behind the bar down at the saloon, tell him I sent you. You can trust him."

"I'll have to come down to the saloon? Where do you fight?"

"Out back. That's the way it works. It won't take long. I'll get in close, one rounder to the jaw, and Floyd's down by the third. You collect the money from Catalpa, we meet here later. Besides, I'd want you there for luck. Yer a blessed one, I can tell. I knew you'd come through for me." He took out another small flask of the dark liquid that Warren recognized and slipped it into the nightstand drawer.

"Additional fortifications for tomorrow. I seen you was almost out."

"A man of foresight. Thank you, Billy."

"It's me thanks you, Captain. You won't see me until tomorrow night. Rest up. Be at Hope's Well on Mott Street at six. About a block from the Bowery Theater. Someone'll be here to accompany you, help you along. Don't you worry. Billy's seen to everything."

Chapter 32: Five Points

Five points, by George Catlin, probably from 1827. Collection of Mrs. Screven Lorillard, Far Hills, New Jersey.

WARREN TOOK STOCK THE NEXT morning after his sitz bath. He seemed all right. Weak, but able. He told himself he felt sufficiently capable of venturing into the city again. In any case, the money had to be raised and he had set things in motion. Everything he had, his family's future, every penny of faith his friends had entrusted, was hanging now on Billy. He must follow his choice.

A good portion of the morning was spent reading and sleeping in the solarium, having made a fresh flask of laced maple sweetener, which he planned to put into an uncustomary cup of coffee that he requested for his noon meal. Coffee always seemed to wake him up.

The man from the kitchen was doubtful that they had coffee, but he would see. It was brought to his room later when he was napping, by Miss Philomena Park. She wore her white cap, under which a few soft strands fell astray. Today she had a demure, effortless smile. She closed the door, glancing at him from the corner of her big round eye as if trying to size him up, then put the steaming coffee pot and cup on the nightstand. The welcome aroma made him sit up straighter on his pillow. His sister Charlotte loved coffee.

"Coffee is not offered at the Institute, Mistah Warren. For obvious reasons. But I managed to hail a boy on the street."

"You've compromised yourself. To what do I owe this favor?"

"You'll need to remain alert. We shall be penetrating into a den of iniquity."

"We? Miss Park, am I to surmise—"

"That's correct. At five shaahp I shall accompany you to the place of meeting and introduce you to the proprietor. You will meet me outside on Canal Street, where you and Mistah Daniels took the streetcaah to Putnam's office. Put your pistol in your pocket. Hold the money close."

He had never suspected this. But of course it made sense. She knew more about him than he about her. "So. I am afforded the protection and guidance of the fair sex. What more do you know about the arrangement between Billy and me?"

She handed him a small leather purse containing a roll of bills. "What he has told me. This is our share. Put yours in with it and place the bet as agreed, with Mistah Catalpa. Then you pick up the winnings after the match. I, as a woman, am not allowed in the betting circles, nor am I allowed to witness the fight. I shall leave you to it."

"Your share. So, you are Mrs. William Daniels, unless I'm mistaken."

"You aah mistaken. We pooled our savings for this, but we're not married and never shall be. As far as Doctah Trall and anyone else here knows, we are not even acquaintances. I ask that you respect that secret, for professional reasons. All Trall knows is that Billy walked in off the street one day looking for work. I recommended him to Trall and he allowed him a trial period as a sort of do-all man. A good thing. If not, he'd waste away in the Bowery washing windows and playing the rat dogs. Of course we'd met previously. Through the theater. Occasionally. Put him on stage and he cleans up quite well. I suppose he gave you the song and dance about his being a family man."

"Two children? And one on the way?"

"One on the way now, is it? Dream on, O'Daniel. Pure invention. There are no children, or none that I know of. The man has a perverted imagination. But he's a hard worker, he learns fast, and he can box. He's worth his word when he's not drunk, which is a sight better than the rest of the lot. They'll rob you even when they're sober, most of them..."

"Tell me one thing. How is it that an attractive woman like you, from a good family, educated, independent-minded, an actress and poetess at that..."

"Precisely, Mr. Warren. Independent and proud. O'Daniel— well, now he says Daniels—he's the same, but he's like all the poor Irish in this city, a pawn in the system, manipulated by Tammany Hall to stay right here and vote for them. Billy wants to get out. I've...tried to help him. Taught him to save his money. And he will get out, go west. With the grace of God, so shall I. But as a woman I can't do it alone."

"And he can. Is that it?"

"He has the stuff for it. I saw that the minute I saw him on stage. Stepped in as my leading man one night. He makes you believe in him. Billy O'Daniel puts his mind to it, it's as good as done. He's what you call a scrappah, Mistah Warren. Nothing deters him. You'll see that for yourself tonight. Drink your coffee. It'll get cold. Now if you allow, I have duties. Canal Street, five shaahp."

He sweetened the coffee generously, drank an entire cupful, put the remainder of the pot in his pint flask and rose in a fighting mood to dress properly for an evening out on the town. It would be his first. He reloaded his Baby Dragoon, hoping he would never have to use it, and remembered Benton's useful words: don't take it out at the wrong time.

§

The interview with Philomena Park was edifying, but it left him with as just many questions unanswered. What of her family? They must be well off. Why wouldn't they help her, if going west was her wish? Had she been disowned? Why would she pool her savings with Billy but never marry him? And the theater? What kind of theater would have an unknown Irish immigrant play her leading man? And most intriguing was the present moment. It was entirely incongruous that Miss Park, Philomena, should escort a man into the Bowery. Surely Billy had cronies to do such work... He looked out his window, past the trees, away to the endless rooftops of the city. The sky seemed lower, threatening rain.

He read in a New York guidebook that the Bowery, the iniquitous carnival slum of New York between Five Points and the East River, operated according to established custom. Those who could not resist "slumming", as the sport was called, had best observe certain practices. Women were excluded from the all-male saloons unless they plied a privileged trade: prostitution. But New Yorkers also loved the theatre, of which there were many, with crowds of high-class swells mixing with local low life just as in Shakespeare's day. Entertainment was the primary business. You could get drunk at an oyster bar, see *Macbeth* at the Bowery Theatre or a jealous fireman's murder drama in a cellar next door, where you would find ample female company to round out a night of slumming.

The guidebook also recommended not carrying any cash or valuables there, not engaging in any of the rampant street gambling, card games, magic tricks, or dog fights, as they were all rigged to hoodwink the unwary tourist. Muggings, knifings, pickpocketing, drunkenness, extreme poverty, and filth were common, so watch where you stepped. Stay in full view of the public, avoid dank cellars and alleys, and do not count on help from the police officers, as they were few, mostly corrupt and disinterested in your plight unless they could turn it to their own profit.

With these caveats in mind, precisely at five, he met his valorous guide, smartly dressed with parasol open, as befitted a young woman of standing. She handed him a lacquered black cane with a brass knob representing a fat-nosed bulldog, pointing out that it was on loan from the theater but quite solid and effective in case of need. He was expected to use this theater cane as a war club? Hole-in-the-Day would have a laugh if he saw him now.

They boarded the crowded streetcar to descend Canal and got off on the opulent Broadway, now somewhat familiar to him, where they left the neo-classical business temples and began to walk east. She did not make small talk. She hardly spoke at all, but smiled when she advised him to put more purpose into his gait, as if he were rich and owned the city. Their destination was not "faah", she said. The sky darkened and it began to drizzle.

Thus they proceeded through the streets into a denser cluster of tumble-down wooden houses with little stoops and boardwalks, canvas awnings and storefronts, interspersed with taller brick tenements crowded to the cracking point. Wagons, refuse, human derelicts, and fly- ridden dead horses littered the streets. The stench was putrid, churning, hardly breathable.

"This looks like a frontier town," Warren said, "Almost like Saint Paul twenty years ago."

Miss Park kept walking, answering straight ahead. "It was a frontier town, not long ago, over a filled-in lake. Then the tanneries and slaughterhouses gave way to these wooden two-stories to house New York's immigrant masses. The difference is that here, it was built by landowners. Slumlords, we call them. After the anti- abolition riots nearly razed the area, new industry came in, the populations exploded. Landlords sold their holdings, new owners divided the houses and leased rooms to immigrants on short- term contracts, and a slum was created. More brick buildings like those went up to pack in more immigrants, who were all dirt poor when they left Europe. Here they're free to become even poorer, pay their money to slumlords and protection rackets. Just around the corner from Broadway, the richest boulevard in the country. The Astor brothers got rich, and now are getting richer, but on luxury, not poverty. Better business."

"John Jacob Astor," Warren said. "Once employed my father, in fur trading. I'd heard that all the money he made on furs, he invested in New York."

"He's building up those big hotels north of here." She pointed with her parasol. "These slums were created when his brother Heinrich sold this land in 1825. He'd inherited it from his father, a German butcher. The Astor men were good with money. John Jacob sold his furs to Europe and China. Then put the money into New York land. It takes money to make money."

"Those furs were trapped and tanned by Indians," said Warren. "Even far out west. He paid them a pittance for them, trinkets. Then the furs ran out, but Astor had created a personal fortune. When he invested in this city, he didn't need the furs anymore, nor the Indians. He controlled the fates of thousands through his business dealings. Including my own father. Astor sold his fur business to Ramsay Crooks in 1830, one of my father's best years—just before the fall."

Wending his way through the crawling tenements, his nose cringing, his eyes keen to the squalor that living can bring, he reflected that History is as indifferent as God. This sour affirmation led him back to the regret he felt for his father, for his impotence in the face of powerful forces that he had spent most of his life battling. The Warren curse? William Warren admitted that, despite his mixed-blood, he was luckier than most. His father had ensured him a better start than the poor immigrants, who continued to fight no matter how great the forces against them.

In Five Points, the pavement turned from brick to mud. Warren recognized the noise and pandemonium he had seen on the first day in the city, when the hack drove him through on his guided tour, whipping the children and beggars away from his cab. East of Broadway, both men and women were clearly of another cut: dirty, dark-eyed, more direct. Everyone looked drunk or drugged, even the battered children. Some wore rags, some a poor imitation of colorful finery, while all their feet, shoeless or shod, were muddy. The misty rain smelled of smoke.

Miss Park trod fearlessly on, Warren with his cane at her side. Both men and women eyed them both as if assessing them from head to foot. In the space of ten minutes, they had changed worlds completely. Stench filled the streets, permeating the mist.

"We're entering the tenth circle of Hell, Mistah Warren. What you are about to see is humanity at its most...abject. Look lively, and hold on to our money."

He took his cue and looked straight ahead, occasionally hefting his cane and feeling the weight of the small firearm in his trousers pocket. Advancing through the human ruins, Miss Park did not alter her gait, nor the haughty way she held her head. She lost her concentrated air. Her eyes softened, her severity disappeared and seemed to wax into something more ambiguous, a mix of heightened tolerance, disinterest, and disdain. Her black hair was raised and hidden, her collar high. The hat on her head was of dark red silk, a smaller version of a man's flat-crowned top hat with a purple ribbon flowing behind. She wore it at a jaunty angle proper to a horsewoman of the upper classes. The result worked like a shield: the ragged throngs seemed to step aside and clear a path before her, like peons before nobility.

They walked on into a long market street abounding with food for sale, and waste. The crowd thickened, languages and accents were foreign, voices grew rougher, the air itself grew denser and pungent with offal and filth. Blacks and yellows of every age and ilk mixed with the whites, as numerous as the Red Indians in Saint Paul, some street minstrels playing music for coins thrown into a hat, some dancing before the small string bands, women or girls selling corn bread or hot biscuits. Less lively were the drunkards, with their filmy eyes and crumbled features, men and women tottering in and out of the saloons and groceries. Some lay inert against the walls or under makeshift barrel shelters in the alleys. Harlots in their doorways or sitting on stoops bared their arms and bosoms for him and beckoned him back, mouthing sweet nothings but not speaking—he supposed out of deference to Miss Park, who advanced undeterred.

He followed his guide, avoiding horse carts, refuse, dung, burning garbage, and buckets of human waste from tenements emptied into the muddy street. Miss Park glanced at him.

"There's little danger here," she said. "We're close to the 6th Ward Police Station, just near Tomb's Prison. A murderer was hanged there in the courtyard just this morning. The thieves keep their distance."

If she said this to reassure him, he still felt an undercurrent of danger in the faces around him and grew wary. It was obvious that he was a stranger, that his Indian features and frontier dress singled him out. None of the men wore long cloaks and wide-brimmed hats, and none of them walked with a fashionable young woman from a higher class. He felt they were targets, while Philomena Park appeared nonplussed by the roil of humanity around them.

But she was not indifferent. They both stopped at the sight of a smoking ruin where a small crowd was huddled. A volunteer fire brigade of what she called "Bowery B'hoys", young men dressed in plug hats and red shirts, shouted and exhibited their bravado. Some were guarding the pump and fire plug from another rival brigade while their pals hoisted a ladder and buckets to the second floor, dousing the last of the flames. A fight between the two brigades broke out and demanded more of their attention than the fire itself.

In the street, children were crying and women wailing, raising a great hullabaloo about whose fault it was and where to go. Men, women, and children were climbing the rubble, evacuating burned furniture. Someone threw a soaked straw mattress on the bricks, where it continued to smoke. A passerby offered five cents for a blackened table, but the woman would not sell. Others were scavenging but no one seemed to care.

Warren penetrated the side alley past the rubble and looked into a tenement courtyard, strung with laundry with a reeking privy in a corner. He saw two men make off with the two spoked wheels and an axle of a half-burned wagon. One was older, long-haired, bearded, fur-hatted, and dressed in fringed buckskin with a sheathed hunting knife at his belt, a throwback to the frontier. His sharp blue eyes looked Warren straight in the face as he hurried past, brandishing the wooden wheel as if proud of his plunder. The other, who also caught his eye as he passed before him, was a giant Red Man, a good head taller than Warren, his massive shoulders covered in a wool blanket he recognized as government issue. He had seen piles of them distributed at annuities payments in La Pointe. The giant's dark red skin and heavy features, his slightly slanted eyes, and especially the tattered moccasins on his enormous feet, beaded with puckered seams, told Warren he could be Anishinaabe. The pair disappeared, the Indian's beaded braids flailing behind him as he loped through the streets hefting the wheel and axle.

Warren joined Miss Park under her parasol. She was observing the scene with the concerned expression she reserved for the suffering.

"Where will they go?" He asked her.

"Not faah," she replied. "Like everybody here, especially the women and children, they have no alternative. They'll crowd in with others like them, ten or twenty to a room. These are mostly Irish, they're used to it. It was pretty much the same back in their stone hovels in County Sligo, but with nothing to eat. They find it bettah heah, Mistah Warren. At least they can work, or prostitute themselves. Some look for a way out, to somewhere. If they don't die first."

They walked on. Her dark sense of realism silenced him.

The vision of the giant Indian perturbed him. He was so strangely misplaced, out of his natural habitat, the woods of the Northwest. How could this be? And the frontiersman— possibly an old trapper? For a fleeting instant both those specters had looked at him with a kind of recognition, as if they knew something about him, that he too was a stranger, and they were all stranded here with just one goal in mind: getting back to their home, where they belonged. Unlike these immigrants adrift in New York City, they had such a home. Somewhere.

He stepped into a mess of liquefied excrement, whether dog or human he could not tell, but certainly diseased. This forced him to clean his boot with a stick, then rinse it in a yellow puddle before a soiled tenement stoop. A small boy lay there asleep. This place, this city, this forced concentration of humanity, was filthy, unhealthy, unnatural. Trall had called it a breeding ground for vermin and disease of all sorts. There must be something to Trall's insistence on cleanliness. He felt far from his Laight Street haven of hygiene, filtered water, clean linen and peace. And even farther from his pinewood cabin in Two Rivers.

Yet for all its poverty, the street was rampant with offerings. Every man, woman and child had something to sell or to buy, like the little sweet corn girl selling it "hot from the pot", alongside brassy-voiced fishmongers and fruit vendors. A man played a fiddle, a child jigged barefoot and passed a cup. Whiskered men in sooty coats watched luridly as a young woman with a swing in her gait and a low neckline dropped in a coin. An elegantly suited and top- hatted Negro man lithely tap dancing on the boardwalk was chased off by a vigilante with a club.

Foodstuffs and opportunities to spend money abounded, yet the people, these new Americans just off the boats from Europe, had the look of the unclean poor. If most in these streets were Irish, there were also Germans, Jews, Swedes and Finns, Negro freedmen and more—those who called themselves Natives: whites born on American soil. Their faces were drawn with soiled wrinkles, their eyes dark in their sockets, their hands caked with dirt. Warren had difficulty associating such abundance with poverty. Greens and potatoes in overflowing bushel baskets, strawberries by the cartful, trays of fresh bread and biscuits, barrels of sausages, meats, and fish, all hawked by haggard people with the drawn features of the destitute, or the hopelessly drunk. Bars and breweries lined the streets catering to an exclusively manly world of drinkers and gamblers, while stores strung with hams and garlic, pickle barrels standing open, offered the dram to women as well as men.

He had seen the poverty of the Ojibwe, the Sioux, the Menominee after the fur trade disappeared. He had seen it and lived with them through starvation, sickness, and epidemics that all but wiped out most of the tribes. The Ojibwe had nothing left except what they could hunt, gather or make from what the earth gave them. They were poor, but had never wanted to be rich like the white man is rich.

Despite their suffering, the sons of nature had never lived in such dejection as this, in the tenements of Five Points, where these people—at least it appeared so to Warren—had a roof over their heads and commerce was afoot, yet poverty reigned.

The Indians had always known how to live in the forest, how to hunt, make their deerskin clothing, decorate their lodges, and teach their children through stories how to continue that way of life. When they could no longer clothe their children except with trade cloth, when the whites paid for the last of the furs with alcohol and the game ran out, they became desperate. They drowned their grief. They lost their way of life, and with it their will to live.

These immigrants, just off the boat, must have another kind of grief to drown.

§

Philomena Park led him into Mott Street where a steady stream of men milled up and down. A good many deviated into Hope's Well saloon. A small sign was tacked above the door decrying the motto of the establishment: *Restore All Hope, Ye Who Enter Here.*

Except for the first word, Warren recognized the reference to another kind of inferno. Save this single distinguishing feature, the building was nondescript; it could have been a tenement like any other. His guide raised her chin, assumed a dignified air and, to his surprise, took Warren's arm.

"I trust you feel quite up to this, Mistah Warren. Women are generally not tolerated in such places. It can get rathah raucous inside."

"Things get raucous where I come from too, Miss Park. Shall we?"

Inside, a large panel hung from two chains: "*Hope's Well—service at the bar. No credit.*" The intolerable din from the herd of men suggested a fight somewhere. The bar ran the length of the saloon— one long, dark room lit by smoking whale-oil lamps also hanging from chains, reaching back to a smaller vestibule with a door to either side. One door was closed and latched and gave onto the alley, with a huddle of customers clamoring to get outside. It was guarded on either side by two giants with arms crossed, a pair of statues before a palace, glaring over the heads of the crowd. One was a muscular black man, unshirted, his cannonball head bound with a red bandanna and shining in the lamplight. A wide red sash around his waist held what looked like a cutlass. Next to him, Warren recognized the giant Ojibwe, who had shed his blanket and now wore a buckskin waistcoat, a bear claw necklace and copper bands around his massive wrists. Like the giant Negro, a red bandanna circled his huge head. They both towered above the men clamoring around the alley door; no one had the heart to challenge their authority. This formidable pair, the Indian and the Negro, seemed to be cut from stone—immovable.

The other door was open, with a stairway leading down to a cellar where men came and went with mugs of beer and cigar stubs. Many of them appeared quite young, some swells or B'hoys banding together, but others were older and rougher around the edges, the kind Miss Park referred to as Bowery rats. Although still light outside, it was dark enough in the saloon to warrant several overhead lamps that cast a yellow pallor through the smoke. A few card tables left only standing room for the crowd, drinking and growling insults.

When Warren entered with Miss Park, some men gaped for a moment and the murmur subsided. He kept his hat and put his weight on his cane while she folded her parasol. When they walked toward the bar, the crowd parted, momentarily leaving a path for them in the half-light. A few the older men took off their hats in her presence—apparently, she was known to some in this place.

There were three bartenders. They skirted the bar to approach the one at the far end, a fat man in bowler hat and a gold embroidered waistcoat. His face was round, his fine hair clipped short, his mouth too small for his head but well formed, almost feminine. He motioned for the men at the bar to clear a space for them, which he offered with a sweep of his hand, a narrow smile and a patronizing bow.

"Well, well. Miss Philomena Park. If you please, come forward. Delightful to see you again, it's so rare we are blessed with the presence of a ravishing star of the stage."

"Likewise, Mistah Catalpa, delighted to be heah. This is my associate, Mistah Warren."

"I've been advised." His accent was genteel and unmistakably Southern, as were his manners. He kissed her hand and shook Warren's. The man had hands softer than a woman's. "Mr. Warren. Welcome to Hope's Well. Mr. Daniels has advised me of your coming. Just in time, I might add."

"Then you know of our business." She said, nodding at Warren, who produced the envelope and laid it on the counter.

"Yes, Mademoiselle, perfectly well. In my opinion a wise placement." He counted the money and slid the envelope into a locked strongbox bolted under the bar. Then he wrote out a chit and handed it to Warren. "May I offer you refreshment? Courtesy of the establishment. So infrequently do we have the pleasure..."

"Gin, please. Thank you," she answered firmly.

"Yes. Coffee, if you please," said Warren. Catalpa motioned to his barman; the drinks promptly appeared. Why did he tend to imitate this man's speech? He never said '*if you please*' in this affected manner. Perhaps because this southerner stood out as a gentleman in a crowd of ruffians. Warren wished to distinguish himself in the same way.

But he would not have the chance. A cry rang out as the saloon crowd made a rush to the alley door. The two giants, the Indian and the Negro, frisked every one for weapons—there was already a boxful of firearms at their feet. Catalpa took a shot of gin himself and squared his bowler on his large head. "All bets closed!" he shouted, "*Rien ne va plus!*" and pocketed the key to the strongbox.

"I'm afraid I must ask you to leave us now, Miss Park, as per our protocol. The alley is no place for a lady."

"I'm perfectly aware," she said. "You now deal strictly with Mistah Warren, is that cleah?"

"Perfectly, as you say."

"There is no question of this lady stepping out of here without protection," Warren protested. "I can't allow it." But this had already been arranged.

"This officer of the peace will see to her safety," said Catalpa. A suited man with a badge, waiting by the bar, tipped his hat. "As for you, Mr. Warren, our most able guardian of the establishment, Monsieur Morlay, will accompany you to the match."

The old frontiersman in his leathers and coonskin hat stepped up beside him, the huge knife tucked into his cloth belt. He nodded at him, spat brown juice into a spittoon and said, "*enchanté*". Warren deduced that they had been followed along their route to the saloon by the Indian and the Frenchman. He looked at Philomena Park, who was undoubtedly known to the establishment and a recognizable personage in Five Points.

"We shall meet again shortly," she said to Warren. "Make sure you are accompanied back to the Institute. Pay Morlay something extra if necessary."

She left with the New York City Marshall at her side, while Catalpa made for the alley door, Warren following with his bodyguard Morlay. At the door, he stopped for the frisk. The Indian looked at him from under his bandanna.

"*Toi, armé?*"

"*Oui,*" Warren answered. "*Un pistolet.*"

"*Toi, vas-y.*" The Indian nodded him through to the alley. For some reason, he was allowed to keep his sidearm. Then he understood that Billy must have pre-arranged all this. Or was it Philomena? In case of trouble, he was a privileged guest, unsure that he enjoyed the status.

He and Morlay joined the huddle of fifty or sixty spectators outside.

"Chief Bob White, a good man to have on our side," said Morlay in his heavy accent. "He kill a man in a bear hug. Nobody want to fight him."

"Where's his home?"

"Canada. Chippewa. Used to be a slave, now a free man."

A yell rose up as a space was cleared and the fighters were escorted to the center.

Chapter 33: Hope's Well

THE RUMBLE IN THE ALLEY heated up, the noise almost deafening. Cigar smoke was as thick as in the bar, bottles and flasks were tipped freely and money was still changing hands. A shroud of daylight filtered down from above the rooftops, leaving the alley darker than the street in front of the saloon. From the clotheslines above hung two oil lamps, already lit, and casting a yellow light on the space in the middle of the huddle. There was no rope to form a ring, only the rough circle allowed by the crowd of betters. The two bare-fisted boxers faced each other.

Billy, bare-chested, was dancing up and down, shadowboxing, black curls bouncing as a pair of trainers rubbed him down. He saw Warren and broke into a wide smile, raising his hands over his head already in victory. Across from him, surrounded by a group of men including Catalpa, was the opponent, Floyd Spilth, frowning, stringy-haired, draped in a large towel, glaring, immobile except for the chewing motion of his chin and the tongue that darted out to lick the drool from his lower lip. Where Billy was lean in the waist, Floyd's gut protruded. The Hope's Well favorite was more than a head taller, massive-shouldered, square-jawed with small dark eyes housed deep in their blue-black sockets. He looked without wavering at Billy as if trying to burn a hole in him. The crowd was shoving him forward, urging on their champion.

Warren's hopes dropped at the sight of this meaty-looking specimen whose long arms hung heavy and bowed inward. It was not just his size, but what he had inside him. Warren saw that the match was grossly uneven for Billy Daniels, a blithe and kind individual, a dreamer with not an ounce of malice in his soul. And as the underdog, he was going in at four to one: it was next to impossible. How he had ever beaten Floyd Spilth in a first match, Warren could not fathom. It must have been his Irish luck. He had better be right this time, the opponent's glass jaw was his only hope. Otherwise, Floyd would pummel him to the mud. And both their futures with it. If Billy lost, Warren's money and any chance of publishing his *History* would vanish in the smoke of the alleyway. That, Warren told himself, was impossible.

The giant Indian, now with three feathers upright in his bandanna, leaped out into the space before Billy, spread his arms like an eagle, and launched into a stomping and whirling war dance. He let out a series of whoops that made the onlookers step back and gape while he rushed Floyd with downward chopping gestures with a phantom tomahawk in his hand. Morlay himself then joined in the dance, whirling in, and mimicking the same chopping gestures but with his big knife in his fist. The old trapper was probably of mixed-blood and as wild as Chief Bob White. Warren was tempted, as he had been as a boy, to join in the dancing. But decorum took over and he satisfied himself with whooping and raising his fist in the air.

There were no announcements. Catalpa rang the bell, and the circle suddenly went clear. The trainers shucked Floyd's towel. He spat tobacco juice on the ground and advanced, his bare fists raised in the classic forward position. Billy came forward dancing, his arms loose at his sides, and turned two whole circles around the bigger man, who followed him with his eyes, then attacked and missed three times while Billy feinted and danced again.

"Stand and fight, ya Paddy sonofabitch!" He yelled. "I'll rip yer fuckin' head off!" He missed again.

Morlay was by Warren's side. "Ain't nobody faster than Billy," he said. "He run the Native ragged, then he hit him. Once. Maybe twice."

"Why is the big one called a Native?" Warren asked. "He's white. Only Indians are native to this soil."

"Floyd's gang over there, all Natives. They say it's political and divine. Because they be born on American soil, they say it gives them the right to run things here. They forget where they came from. Now too many immigrants, Irish, Polish, German. All Billy's people Irish, except me and the Chief. We Canadian. The Nigger, he come up from Georgia, Underground Railroad. Now he a freedman. No more slaves! We all free here, *Mon Capitaine!*"

There was a shout. Floyd had tripped going after Billy and was on his knees by the edge of the circle. As he got up Billy moved in and crowded him with a volley of punches to the body, but couldn't get near Floyd's head—the bigger man had his face buried in his arms. He took the belly punches standing, unmoving, looking for an opening, then the bell rang. The first round had lasted just over a minute. The boxers retired to their corners for a wipe-down. More money changed hands in the crowd.

"*C'est privé, ça,*" Morlay explained. "*Petite monnaie.* Small change. The real money is in the box."

"Why did he ring the bell?"

"London Prize Ring Rules. A fighter goes down, round finished. A fighter stay down, fight over. Billy got a hard head. No worry."

The second round was a repeat of the first, Billy dancing around Floyd, taunting him, feinting a punch, backing off, Floyd giving chase, Billy moving like a shadow. Until one of the Natives from Floyd's corner shoved him roughly back into the center and Floyd's right connected. Billy went down, nose bloody, and Floyd fell upon him with all his weight. A shout of protest went up among the Irish, but Billy rolled over and got up, feeling his ribs. The bell rang. Again, it was just over a minute. The fighters rejoined their corners.

"That's illegal, Morlay!" Warren exclaimed.

"Not in this fight. The rules allow. Tom Hyer fight Sullivan, the big ape fall on Sullivan six, seven times. Beat him into the ground, seventeen minutes."

Warren took a drink of his flask, feeling the pain for Billy. A blow like that would surely kill him now, as it almost did when the branch hit him in the woods. But it didn't seem to affect Billy so badly. He sat on the stool with his head back as his trainers cleaned him and the Chief danced around him, chanting his praises. Billy looked over at Warren and winked.

When the third round ended the same way, he began to worry. Billy could not get to Floyd's chin. He had to stand and fight. He was struck three more times and began to hug the Irish side of the crowd, avoiding the Natives, while Floyd pursued him with the stealth of a hungry wolf. Still, Warren thought, the beast was slowing down. Billy was younger, in better shape, and could take the punishment while he waited for Floyd to tire and open his guard.

Billy finally got his punch in, splitting the flesh above Floyd's left eye, then a left to the jaw. Blood sprayed the Native Party men at the sidelines and the crowd roared. Floyd went down on all fours. But he got up again. He was shaken, groggy. Catalpa rang the bell to end the round. Floyd was helped back to the corner, where his men called in a bloodsucker and formed a huddle. The smell of man sweat, alcohol, and adrenaline were sharp in the ring.

"One more like that, Billy, and you beat him," Morlay told him.

"He canna see me now, the bugger. He canna hit what he canna see."

The huddle around Floyd broke up and left only the fighter, sitting and brooding at Billy with just one eye, the other swollen shut, his bloody fists square on his thighs like hammers. The bell rang and they came forward, fists raised.

Floyd led with his left, and Billy dodged. He blocked the next left jab, staying in, close but not too close, looking for the opening to the jaw. They turned around, the crowd yelling for a hit. But Billy would not come close enough. Daylight faded, and now the glow of the lamps hanging from the ropes above formed the only ring the fighters had. The crowd was half-hidden in the shadows. The round went on, neither fighter was down yet. But it was sure that one of them would be, would have to be.

Floyd attacked with a series of jabs from the left, striking once, backing Billy into the Native side. He reached the line of men at the edge of the space and tried to come forward, blocking the jabs, when Floyd hit him with a roundhouse right that sent him reeling into the

Natives, who flung him back. His knees buckled and touched the mud, but he did not fall. His eyes were already closed when Floyd's right fist came down like a sledge and hit him again behind the ear. The crowd howled as he toppled sideways like a cut tree.

Floyd stood over him and spat a tooth while the referee knelt and felt Billy's pulse. A small pouch fell from Floyd's right hand, dripping like a cut of meat. In the mêlée, someone jumped in, picked it up, and fled.

The bell rang for the last time as the crowd went berserk. Billy was down. He did not get up.

§

Now what use was it? He'd lost it all. And there was Billy. Did he get him killed?

It was Chief Bob White who carried Billy in his arms through a maze of dark alleys as the drizzle thickened, stepping soundlessly through puddles and piles of jetsam as if over fallen branches in the forest. Warren followed on his cane, Morlay at his back. He could not bring himself to abandon the unconscious Billy. This disaster never would have happened, he was convinced, had he not agreed to take part in the bet. Now that everything was lost for both of them, he wanted to be sure that the downed fighter received medical care. If he lived.

They penetrated through narrow passages until they reached a space too wide for clotheslines, with piles of wood scraps and rubble from burnt or fallen buildings forming a mound of ruins. The night sky opened above them. The moon made an appearance through the shifting clouds, casting a cold pallor on the maze in the clearing.

Fort Mulberry, as Morlay called the makeshift courtyard, was a demolished lot amid the tenements, brothels, and saloons of Five Points, not far from Hope's Well, between Mulberry and Orange streets. There was no access from the street, only through alleys and narrow passageways cleared through the rubble piled up as high as twenty feet. Warren was certain he could never find his way out alone. Once inside, the clearing had the appearance of a hunting camp set up on the quick, with a few wooden lean-to shelters and a wide circle of sailcloth canopies where barrels of stores were piled. Clothing and drying meat hung on ropes and stick tripods, two lanterns were set up on barrels and a small fire burned in the center, smoking and hissing in the drizzle. There was no one in plain sight, but he saw movement in the shadows under a canopy and an occasional dim light in a tenement window. If there were people in there, Warren felt certain that they had few candles to burn.

Despite the chaos of the detritus surrounding it, Fort Mulberry held a certain military order. It was not unlike an outpost in a battlefield that required a constant presence and attention to detail. Barrels were set up to catch rainfall, the ground was cleared. At the far end, lit from inside by lamplight, was a large wagon with a rounded canopy covered with patched-together sailcloth. Warren had seen these covered wagons driven by settlers heading west, but for one difference: this wagon had only its two front wheels, the rear section being held up on trestles. The two wheels and axle scavenged from the fire that afternoon lay beside it, apparently intended for mounting on the covered wagon. Scattered about were boards and staves, pots and spikes, pieces of tables and chairs wired or nailed together, tin washtubs, a rusted-out boiler, and miles of half-rotted rope salvaged from New York harbor.

Inside, the wagon was clean and well fitted out, with shelves and stores, pots and pans and wooden spoons hanging, a few benches, and two folding cots, much like a country cabin. A few wooden crates formed steps to access the back, a sort of formal stoop, with an awning over it to make a small porch or veranda. Someone had made it homey. The only element missing was a team of horses. The sole animal in Fort Mulberry was a small, battered rat terrier that did not bark, but greeted them faithfully and whined with genuine concern when he saw Billy unconscious in the Indian's arms. He was introduced as Beaver, the best moneymaker in the fort.

Chief Bob White hefted Billy inside the wagon and laid him down on a cot, cleaned the dried blood from his face and hands, and covered him in blankets. Then he told Warren, "Get me a bucket of coals." His language sounded strange to his ear, from north of Lake

Superior, but Ojibwemowin. The Chief knew that Warren under-stood his language. Maybe Billy had told him.

He went to fetch the coals, scooped into a bucket by a boy about fifteen who was tending the fire and carrying water from a nearby barrel. The boy was scrawny, long-haired with blond fuzz on his face, and spoke no English, nor any language Warren could under-stand.

"This is Eamon," Morlay said. "He don't talk, but he understand sign language. His sister talk for him."

He brought the coals to Chief Bob White, who lit a stick of smudge tied with grass and blew on it, fanning the smoke up and down Billy's prone body. He then concentrated on his head, where he shot the smoke in with his breath, inhaled to suck out the afflic-tion, which he blew up to the top of the canopy. He took his med-icine pouch, shook it over him, and chanted in tones that Warren recognized as Midewiwin ritual, the meaning of which escaped him even though he spoke fluent Ojibwemowin. The Chief's dialect was from farther north, and Midé chants, still secret, were in a coded part of the language he had no access to. He could find out from the old men who trusted him, back home. If he got there.

He heard voices outside—Morlay's, then a rumbling bass and a woman's voice. Miss Philomena Park stepped up into the wagon, still dressed in her finery but carrying a small satchel, accompanied by Dubois who ducked through the opening with a block of ice in a bucket. Chief Bob White terminated his rite and gave his stool to the woman, who lifted Billy's eyelids and examined his pupils by candlelight. She felt his heart, his ribs, and his battered cranium with her hands. He was more bruised than cut. There were no open wounds. The Indian had cleaned him properly.

"He's swollen up. But he's alive. That animal must have steel fists."

"No. Fist of lead," said Morlay. "Bag of lead shot in the right fist. Someone slip it to him in the corner. Floyd hit Billy twice, he drop the bag. Morlay seen it. Old Bowery trick."

"That's illegal," said Warren. "Why didn't you speak up?"

"Too many men. A boy pick it up and run. Natives, they stick together."

"He didn't need to hit him twice," said Miss Park. "He was out on the first blow. It was a sting. Spilth lost the first match just to lure Billy into a rematch. We were all clipped. Somebody's made a lot of money. Chop me some ice, would you Dubois? And wrap it in this." She produced a clean towel from her satchel, one of several from the Institute. The big Dubois chipped at the ice block with a short dagger. She applied the ice pack to Billy's head and covered him with blankets.

"We'll have to wait. There's no more bleeding, but he's lost a bit through his nose. I can detect no fracture. Leave me with him for a while."

The men gathered around the fire, deferring entirely to the judgment of the woman they all appeared to obey without question. This was another source of perplexity for Warren, who sat on a crate among them. This band of rough men, all of them foreigners to New York, had a bond together and a visible respect for Philomena Park that bordered on veneration.

There was one other female, young and blond and thin as a wisp, apparently the sister of Eamon. They looked like twins, but she was almost a year younger. Irish twins. She dressed like a boy, smoked tobacco in a pipe, and partook of the whiskey bottle being passed around. Her name sounded like Aynit, but Chief Bob White called her Little Fire. All their family, she said, had died on the boat to America, or here in Five Points. Eamon himself almost died last year, but survived the fever. He just lost his voice.

Warren took none of the whiskey but sipped openly on his flask, wishing it were his tea instead of coffee. It kept the pain at bay, but it kept him awake while his true urge was to lapse into oblivion to escape the torment he felt sitting powerless in these ruins, Billy on the brink of death, the money lost. His book, the *History*... Publishing money lost on a gamble.

The rain had passed and left a circle of moonlight over the dark tenements crumbling around Fort Mulberry, sometimes disappearing behind a fast-moving silver cloud. Many nights like this he had spent around the fire on the island with the People, telling them stories of King Arthur and Merlin, about Nasredine or tales from the Arabian Nights, and listening to the old men tell of Manabosho's tricks and their own heroic acts. Sometimes the drum would come out, the men forming a circle around it, and their chants would travel far through the dark trees and over the water. Those nights were rich with laughter and magic. But here in the bowels of America's greatest city, the sadness around the small fire brought them the only warmth they could find under the cold moon. It quelled all the laughter these wandering few had in them.

He went back into the wagon where Miss Park was still observing Billy under the lamplight. She avoided—as they all did—talking about that night's defeat by tending to matters directly at hand. From her satchel, she brought a metal box with an array of medical instruments. "I don't want to bleed him, but I may have to. There's no need for you to stay, Mistah Warren. You should return to the Institute." She gently applied the iced cloth to Billy's head. "Is there anything you need?" He did not want to leave.

"No. Save a real physician. I'm trained as a nurse, not a surgeon."

"What about Trall?"

"He'd peach to my fathah and it would all go to hell. Trall must know nothing."

"Nothing about what?" The woman's secrets unnerved him. "About this place? About you and Billy? What is all this? What are you? A poetess? A nurse? Or a concubine?"

"That's quite enough, Sir!" She rose and turn as if to bite him. He recoiled.

"Forgive me for insulting you in your own home, but I must know."

"You are not forgiven. This is not my home. I live with my aunt. My childhood home is in Boston, where I shall never return. What you see here is all the home those people outside may ever know."

"And what is your role here?"

"I serve as advisor and spiritual guide, Mistah Warren. And I care for them. Until they can finish this vessel and strike out for the West. I help them seek their dreams."

"This wagon? They'll never get it out of these ruins. It's too big and there's no path to the street."

"Look around you, it's all crumbling down. The slumlords will tear it down or burn it then they'll simply roll it out and away they go. They must be ready."

"And you'll go with them? With Billy?"

"That remains to be seen." She turned back to the wounded fighter.

"This is madness!" Warren exclaimed, surprised himself at his outbreak.

"Then we're all mad!" She cried back. "Madness is what makes this country! Is it not mad to leave your home, escape your trap, and cross the ocean to a place unknown, to end up you know not where? To change your fate from hopeless poverty to hope in the promised land? Whatever has been accomplished without a little madness, Mistah Warren?"

"But this plan is devoid of reason. They've built their wagon inside the trap they live in. It's desperation, not madness."

"Is it not desperate to leave your family alone, to travel thousands of miles across the lakes in mid-winter, risking your life, cold and sickness upon you every step of the way?"

"There was a reason."

"To publish a book? You strike me as a little mad yourself."

"I also wanted to seek medical help. You know that."

"You're fooling no one, Mistah Warren. It's the book, isn't it? Was it worth it?" He said nothing, but his eyes wavered as they met her glare.

"It was a desperate choice." She lowered her voice. "A bit mad. I can admire that." Then she stood to face him. "But you have a family waiting, Mistah Warren. Go home. Before it's too late."

From outside the wagon came a wafting of voices humming in the night, then the piercing wail of a lone fiddle. The low melody was as simple and sinuous as a dirge, sadly beautiful, and ancient. Warren looked out at the band of men hunched over on stools and crates around the fire. Eamon, the young boy, held his fiddle against his hollow ribs, wresting and bending the notes as if torn from the depths of the ruins around them. His sister Little Fire stood beside him, her face lifted, watching the sparks getting lost in the stars. In her strange, hard accent born in the stony fields across the sea, she slowly sang:

> *I'm just a poor wayfaring stranger,*
> *Traveling through this world below.*
> *No more sickness, no toil, no danger*
> *In that bright world to which I go.*
>
> *I'm going there to meet my father,*
> *All the loved ones who've gone on.*
> *I'm just going over Jordan,*
> *I'm just going over home.*

The boy fiddled, the girl sang, the men hummed, they fell silent. Then they played it again. When the Indian chanted in the high ranges, it sounded like an Indian song. But it was the same song. Dubois had a voice as deep as his chest when took a verse with his eyes closed, bringing gospel into the bowels of New York City. When one went silent, the others carried on, alone or together. Nobody wanted the song to end. Inside the wagon, William Warren hummed the tune lowly, as did Philomena Park, with her hand on Billy's arm.

The fiddle played into the night while Little Fire sang the beauty of her home. The men retired under their canvas shelters. Just the three of them—the poetess, the defeated fighter and the would-be historian remained in the covered wagon. She stayed close to Billy's side, changing the ice pack when it melted. Warren would not return to Laight Street that night, they decided. He could go with the Chief at early light. One of them must go back, to avoid any suspicion from Doctor Trall. As for herself, she would come back later that day. If need be, she would get help for Billy in the morning. There was nothing they could do but wait for the swelling to go down.

He rationed his flask doses and eventually found short fits of sleep on a bench in the wagon, fearing the worst for Billy, enduring the inevitable onslaught of his own demons, the specters of failure and ruin. Now he had gambled it all away, how could he go home? It was impossible. He'd been a fool to gamble, to risk it all on one fight, on Billy, who fell to a leaden blow in a fixed match. Desperate acts are not admirable, as Miss Park so poetically suggested, they are simply desperate. He ruminated on that desperation all night long. He could not think of a way to reverse it. Perhaps you had to be a bit mad.

"Indians love to gamble," Chief Bob White told him in the morning. "White men hate to lose."

It was first light, just before dawn, Canal Street was still empty, and the gaslights were being shut down. They spoke in Ojibwemowin.

"The Indians have nothing more to lose," Warren said. "All they had, white men already took it," said the Chief.

"Not everything. They can't take the Indians' hearts, Bob White. What's your true name, your Anishinaabe name? *Mayagi-bine?*"

"I lost my first name. Back in Manitoba, when I was a boy, a white man hanged me from a tree, left me to die. I freed my hands, climbed up the rope and waited in the tree. He came back, I jumped him, killed him. Now I'm wanted back there for murder. Can't ever go back. That man took my heart."

"Why did he hang you?"

"Never told me. But I kept the scar." He tugged at his bear claw necklace and showed Warren the white ring around his neck. "Morlay give me that name, Bob White. Some kind of bird."

"What about Morlay?"

"He bought me from a Sauter band as a slave. Went trapping in Québec. Came down here to sell the furs, get more money, he said. But they freed the slaves here, long time ago. Morlay said, fair's fair, you're a free Indian. No more money in trapping, we stay here. Now go west. California. Gold out there."

Warren doubted Chief Bob White would go west for gold, since gold never meant anything to the Anishinaabe, no more than a wheat farm did. To Morlay maybe, but even then...maybe not. What is worth looking for when your life disappears? Some questions were best left unanswered. He did not pursue the subject.

"Dubois too, he's a freed slave?"

"Free here, but he can't go back to Louisiana. He stole a chicken. Chain gang waiting for him. He came up here with his wife on the Underground Railroad. Antoinette, Creole woman. Strong and pretty. She found work, then the white man raped her, hurt her bad. Dubois like to kill that man, but she won't let him. She says go west. Be free."

"And the twins? Little Fire and Eamon?"

"Billy find them singing on the street. They sleep together. Crazy. Same blood, same clan. Anishinaabe never marry in same clan. We have different ways. By Anishinaabe law, if I was Dubois, I kill that white man."

"Maybe, but that man didn't kill his wife."

"She had a baby in her. Baby died. Now she can't have no more baby. Kill for kill. Bob White, he kill the man."

"And you'd be right by Indian law. But by U.S. law, they'd hang you again. Hang twice?"

The Indian looked at him sideways with a crease between his eyebrows.

"Maybe Bob White think twice."

They walked up Canal Street and as far as the Hydropathic and Hygienic Institute where Chief Bob White left him and began his loping run back to Fort Mulberry.

William Warren plodded up to his room exhausted. He undressed. The relief of being alone allowed him to cough and hack up blood for as long as he dared. This lasted some minutes while he spat into the chamber pot. Then he sat on the edge of his bed, urinated copiously into the pot and poured himself a great dose of elixir to escape his feeling of hopelessness. He did not want to think about the fate of Billy, or his *History*, or his promise to the Ojibwe, or his family.

As the light was coming up outside and the birds in the lindens were well into their morning songs, he let himself lean back on the pillow. Sitting up with his legs stretched out before him, his feet seemed very far away. He sat on the edge of the dock his father had built on the island and stared down into the clear water. Dizzy, aching, fearing he might drown, he faded into the drug's pale imitation of sleep.

Chapter 34: Money

WHEN HE WOKE, HE LONGED TO SLEEP AGAIN. The light was painful despite the filtering curtain, his mouth trembled, his head felt twice its weight and he had difficulty focusing. He fumbled for his tea. He had neglected to hide the flask before the laudanum put him out, and there it stood on the nightstand. He coughed up a bit of phlegm, but it was not bad. Unwise, this lapse in his vigilance. The cough suppressant was still working, but his tea flask was empty. His legs ached from the walking the night before. On the table with his tossed clothing were his breakfast and a pot of Institute tea, lukewarm.

Shaking, he filled his flask, poured in more sweetener, and partook of his bowl of cereal. Since witnessing the catastrophic fight in Five Points, he had eaten nothing. Was Billy still alive? He wolfed down the brown bread and honey and eagerly drank a cup of tea. Laced with laudanum and maple syrup, it provided some relief from the pain and dulled the pounding in his head. His father had advised him: take care of the body, the mind will follow.

He would begin slowly. Clarity gained ground as he smoothed his clothing. He began to move, although still unsteady on his legs as he shaved with cold water from the basin. Again he wished he had some coffee. He would resume his regular water-cure schedule this afternoon. Now he needed a plan of action. Returning to established habits, he assessed his situation. Billy was defeated. He had lost his money. That was a fact. What was left?

Someone had emptied and cleaned the chamber pot. It was not Billy, nor Miss Park since they were not present, he was certain. The room attendant had therefore seen the blood he'd coughed up the night before and would make a report. A minor hemorrhage, but Trall would be inquiring as to his state of health. He would have to present his best foot forward to give him the notion that his cure was working wonders, and William Warren was in fine enough fiddle to leave the Institute and begin his trip home, even with the meager funds he had left.

This much was true, he reasoned. The vegetarian diet did him good. Although he missed the meat and felt weaker for it, he felt less bilious and slept much better, all things considered, with fewer coughing fits. That must be the sitz baths and the lukewarm body wraps. But then again it could be the laudanum, as it had worked since he left Two Rivers. He felt all in all "purer" with the absence of "morbid secretions"—Trall's nemesis. He attributed his fatigue to the drug, a necessary side effect. And he had lost some weight. He must be sweating it out, as the Indians did in the sweat lodges—the theory behind the techniques was not that much different. As long as he had his tea and laudanum sweetener, he would be all right, but that was no concern of Trall's and it was better that he know nothing about it. Now foremost in his mind was reaching his home. Unlike the displaced vagabonds and the Irish twins at Fort Mulberry, he had a home, and was now most anxious to return there, to his family.

He had made inquiries and found that he could now make the trip faster by railway. Reading the *New York Daily Times* in the library, he found that the Water Level Route along the Lake Erie shore was now operating, due west all the way to Chicago. There seemed to be many contenders on this route. One advertisement, in particular, caught his attention in the April 21st edition:

CHICAGO AND ROCK ISLAND RAILROAD OPEN TO LA-SALLE AND PERU (100 MILES) and there connecting with first-class steamers for St. Louis, and New Orleans, and intermediate places on the Illinois and Mississippi Rivers... Passengers leaving New-York by the Morning Express trains of the Erie and Hudson River Roads, will reach Chicago in time to go immediately on. Those leaving New-York by the Evening Express trains

may rest all night at Chicago, and leave the next morning at 8
o'clock. Time from St. Louis to New York and Boston, over the Erie
and New-York Central Roads, 75* hours; and to Philadelphia,
over the Cleveland, Columbus, and Pittsburg Roads, 68 hours.

It was the speed that astonished him: three days to Chicago. One drawback: he would have to go back through Buffalo on the New York and Erie line, recently consolidated by Erastus Corning, who could still be in Albany or even on the same train... But this was unlikely. They ran several trains per day, and he would take the evening Express. There was also the risk of crossing paths with Fowles and Benton, but he reasoned—or hoped—that they were back in the Sault by now putting the new labor force to work. He would not take the lake ships, nor would he stop in Buffalo. He would connect at Dunkirk or Erie to the shorelines, direct to Chicago. It would cost him maybe ten dollars first class that far, then maybe fourteen more to Chicago. If he understood it right. There would be several changes along the line including a switchover to standard-gauge tracks in Erie, but nothing he could not manage. He read also that the mail ran with daily regularity on the railway lines. No longer dependent on the boats and stage lines, a letter would reach Chicago in even less time, a telegram even faster. This new concept, speed, was everything. Since he left home three months ago in February, the speed of travel had multiplied five, maybe ten times over. The new world was here.

In Chicago, he would board an Illinois River steamboat and connect with the Mississippi to Saint Paul. The new train line to Galena was held up, but the steamers were fast and many. It would be much less exhausting, warm, and comfortable all the way. With fifty dollars left to his name, he could pay for the voyage and expenses, but little else. He would have to use his good credit once home to convince Rice, Le Duc, and maybe some other Saint Paul supporters, to finance the printing of his book. And to feed his family. But he had set things in motion, and publication was now a sure thing. A matter of money and time.

To feed his family, yes. A surge of guilt overtook him at the thought of not being there, at least to supervise the work. Hole-in-the-Day's band would be helping them now. They were finished with the sugar-making, they must be breaking ground in the field. He wondered if George had been able to help Matilda with the plowing. The People sent by Hole-in-the-Day would be helpful in the sugar bush, but they were hopeless when it came to farming in spite of all his tutoring and encouragement. Farming was another "benefit of civilization" they neither valued nor understood—they'd rather be hunting. The women had heads on their shoulders, they dug and planted as you showed them. The young men, in truth, would rather be warring, their preferred summer occupation until just a few years ago. He too should be hunting, or fishing to replenish the stocks while awaiting the harvest. He thought of his children.

He finished dressing, for what purpose he did not know. Fatigue overtook him and he sat, his writing quills and ink before him in their pouch on the desk. The manuscript was still sitting at his feet, wrapped in brown paper. There were his plans, his dreams. He opened the window to watch the warming air waft through the spring leaves and hear the birdsong. Instead, he heard hooves on cobblestone, the hansom cabs and trash wagons passing below, iron clanking, foreign voices shouting, and masons' hammers. The city growling. The city, man's rational creation, now took on a wild life of its own, indifferent to his plans and dreams. Something much bigger was afoot here. The future overtook the world like a landslide.

Suddenly he felt engulfed in mud. Nauseous, he had to sit on his bed and breathe easily. His thoughts became disconnected. This something bigger countered his will in everything he undertook in public life, in his work as interpreter, in politics, in his struggles to help the People. He had spent his life fighting for the survival of the People. Warren knew he thought of the Ojibwe as his people, despite his Yankee blood. Perhaps his fate was more linked to theirs. Their roots, the bones and the blood of their ancestors, were anchored in their soil, in their history there, in what the whites called America. Indian country, until they took it from them.

Modern life foiled him. It would ruin him. So he turned to the past, to writing, and wrote his *History*. It was not big, it was not fast, but to the best of his knowledge and in the memory of the People, it was true. He had wanted it to be the bridge between his two families, white and Ojibwe. Now his *History* too was beaten. It lay there inert, a bound package at his feet, unable to speak for lack of listeners. The years, the stories, the hopes of the People. Gone.

He suddenly lost what was he thinking about. He was going soft in the head. He was a dying man. Planting, fishing, hunting, that was all past. A way of life lost. He felt like writing to his cousin George or talking to Matilda, whose patience had always helped him through these moments of doubt. Would he see them again? He had exiled himself to reach this city. His family, his life, were now two thousand miles away and he sat weakened and nearly penniless on a strange bed. What else did he have to hope for? The book. To accomplish his mission, for the People, to keep his word to Flat Mouth. To leave something behind, for his family. Before it's too late.

His plans seemed blocked, at least for now. Would he have the strength to do this? He must see other publishers. He must see Redfield when he came back to the city. Had he read the entire manuscript? Had Billy delivered it? Where was Billy? His mind was working slowly. Billy lay unconscious in Five Points. Or dead. Or maybe not. This meant waiting. He had no more time to wait. He must get back to Two Rivers. He was dozing off. He shook himself awake, or he would fall to the floor again. His weakness astounded him, then disgusted him.

It was then that he saw the letter left on his desk that morning, from Judge C. F. Daly. He eagerly broke the seal and opened it. A short missive in response to his own. The Judge was much impressed by his *History* and the recommendation of Colonel D. A. Robertson, who had sent him a published clipping from the *Democrat*. He would like to help, but his work and appointment schedule was full for the moment. In the interim, if feasible with Putnam, Warren should indeed invest in publishing his own work. He recommended two New York investors who could possibly provide a solution, William Wickes and Timothy Lyons, and gave him their office address. He would put in a good word, and Warren could contact them directly. Good men, keen on investment, they could be instrumental in financing the 350 dollars required for printing. Daly was certain that a great number of persons here in New York would be interested in purchasing it, and a first run would be sold quickly, the return considerable. He should by all means consider this solution.

Of course. Judge Daly was right. Raise the money, that was the plan. Wickes and Lyons were the same men recommended by Le Duc that day in the bookstore. Investors. Why hadn't he thought of it? He had, but gambling on a prizefight was not the right way to invest. Daly had the right solution: a loan, a sound business proposal. Sales would ensure repayment of the funding, the returns would establish his reputation and allow him to continue his works, perhaps with more hydropathy in a more clement climate while writing. It was perfect. He would not wait for Redfield; he must set the plan in motion today.

He took up his quill and wrote to Wickes and Lyon requesting an interview on behalf of Judge Daly and Le Duc, to discuss an investment opportunity. It was imperative that they answer directly because time was of the essence, he was leaving the city very soon and must handle all business matters before his departure. He folded and sealed it with his diminishing wax. And there was little ink left in his bottle. Everything was diminishing. This note must leave immediately, he must find a courier. He would ask Trall. It was almost noon.

As he descended the stairs, he came face to face with Miss Philomena Park, whose face betrayed the fatigue of the night, giving her a softer air, a bit puffy, more mature. She wore the same clothing, but her hat was in her hand and her hair slightly undone. Despite her hurried pace, she appeared in control of her person, if not of the situation.

"Mistah Warren, can we please speak for a moment in your room?"

"I was just on my way to see Doctor Trall. How is Billy?"

"No change. Please, we'll discuss this in your room."

Once the door closed, she brought out a purse and handed Warren two fifty-dollar bank bills. He stared at them.

"This is your half. At least we covered our initial wager. Billy and I have the same, I assure you. It's called hedging. I put a hundred on Floyd Spilth, who by the seventh round paid two to one."

"How is this possible?" He asked incredulously. He would not touch the bills, he felt incapable of accepting them. She put them on the desk, no nonsense.

"We went to collect this morning. Chief Bob White and Dubois accompanied me to Hope's Well. Catalpa and I had an arrangement, but Billy must not know. Not now. I'll keep his money for him until this blows over, then give it to him when he needs it most. I'll invent some story."

"So. You're not only his muse and banker, you're his manager."

"I had a strong intuition that the fight would not go as we'd hoped. A good number of these Bowery fights are fixed. Catalpa holds the keys. I'm certain he's the one who slipped Floyd the shot pouch. But a bookmaker has to be good for his word, so he paid out on my hedge bet. All the money on Billy is pure profit for Catalpa after he pays off his pony, Floyd Spilth. Billy was drawn into the trap when Floyd intentionally lost the first match. He has no glass jaw. They suckered him into it. They call it business, Mistah Warren."

"You seem to know the rules pretty well."

She took a comb from her bag and, standing before the small round glass above the basin, proceeded to put her hair up, pinning it up with combs. The unabashed intimacy of the gesture, her standing with her back to him, ingenuous, her nape exposed, charmed him utterly. She leaned at the waist and pinched her cheeks to bring up the color.

"Working the stage in the Bowery, you find out things. Some things you don't want to know. But there it is." She powdered her nose, rouged her lips, and applied a touch of kohl to her eyebrows and lashes. The makeup kit looked like the same one Billy had used on him before his Putnam interview.

"A dangerous place for a young woman," said Warren, deepening his voice. Why should he deepen his voice? It was completely involuntary.

"I do not intend to play the Bowery all my life. And I use a stage name. You might say I lead a double life."

"More like four, I'd say. Manager, Nurse, Poetess, Actress..."

"An artist must survive. A woman these days must assume many roles." She turned to him and stood straight, slightly smiling. "Then again, at some point, one must make one's choice. Don't you think?" When she smiled, she was more than pretty. She had a radiance, her eyes lustered, her pupils deepened. One was drawn not only to her reasoning, but to the lips that spoke it. But for Warren, that was not a good thought to pursue. He snapped out of it.

"Tell me about Billy," he said, anxious to change the subject.

"The swelling's gone down. He's still unconscious. I'll check on him later."

"You're not worried?"

"Of course I'm worried. He should stop fighting. It'll kill him next time."

"Thank you for your...prudent management. You took a risk as well," he said, looking at the money she laid on the desk.

"Hedging. Mistah Warren. Never put all you have on one horse."

"Yes," he said, still holding his letter in his hand. One horse. "I was going to ask Doctor Trall to see about delivering this letter. It's about my book, and it's important."

"Give it to me. I'll see to it." He did so gladly, as he was in no hurry to see the good doctor. She looked at him with the motherly crease between her eyebrows. Even that crease became her. "You look tired."

"I'm better than Billy, for sure. Just a bit ragged."

"I'll send up your lunch, and arrange for your treatments. You should rest, Mistah Warren. You have one more week at the Institute. You can continue if Trall recommends it. Have you thought about that?"

"It depends on the answer to that letter." It was a half-truth. In his present state of mind he had no intention of staying any longer, come what may. "It may produce a more immediate and business-like solution for publishing. You might call it hedging my bet."

"Very well. It will be delivered this afternoon. Good day, Mistah Warren." I'll keep you abreast of Billy's progress." She left him, her hair still a bit undone.

§

Trall came to visit him in his room that afternoon and caught him asleep.

"Please come in. I'm just resting." He checked. His tea flask was tucked away in the drawer, a pitcher of purified water in its place on his nightstand.

"Remain on the bed, Mr. Warren. I'll just check your pulse," said Trall. He did this and sounded his chest and heart. He wrote in a notebook and made no comment.

"Any congestion or bleeding?"

"Occasionally, but minor. Less than in the beginning."

"You're carrying a fever. Most days, in fact. According to this record."

"I can't seem to get rid of it. Some days are better than others."

"Yes. How does the diet suit you?"

"Excellent, sir. And the baths and sweats are very beneficial in reducing congestion, as you said. I intend to pursue them at home."

"Highly recommended. It must be clement weather now in Minnesota, the summer highly beneficial to your health in particular. You have the intention of returning, then?

"Yes, I must."

"Another two or three weeks here would be better, Mr. Warren. After that, I recommend that you continue your cure in familiar surroundings. Your family. The psychological benefits can also speed your recovery."

"I'm afraid my presence is required at home. Travel is faster now, I can go through Chicago by rail."

"Ah. What about your book, then? Have you made arrangements?"

"Several possibilities, I believe. I have a good offer that I must follow up, but that can be done from my home."

"While you still have the manuscript here, I should like to have a glance at it, Mr. Warren, with your permission. It would give me pleasure to read a bit of your history, time allowing."

"I'm flattered, Doctor. It's there by the desk. Please take it and read it at your leisure, I won't need it until Monday."

"Splendid. Thank you." The Doctor picked up the package on his way out. "In the interim, Mr. Warren, you shall continue your cure for this last week and drink water copiously. Eat hearty. I'll have the kitchen add an extra portion. Strength for the voyage. You'll leave the Institution in ship shape. Be well."

Thus the weekend passed, waiting, sleeping, sitz bathing, anxious dreams that he made no effort to remember. He read the newspaper, some magazines, nothing more taxing for his eyes or his mind. On Monday a theatre review caught his eye, about a new drama that had made its debut on Saturday night at the Bowery Theatre.

"The curious Wilderness Untamed was penned by Rose Bachelor, a young Bostonian lady who plays the main role of Sacagawea, the Indian maid so indispensable to the Lewis and Clark expedition across the continent, upon which the drama was based. Among the many characters was a giant Indian in full regalia playing Sacagawea's brother. A brawny Negro billed only as Dubois plays York, Clark's slave. The plot hinges on a far-fetched love affair between the slave York and the Indian maid, who escape to found a multi- racial Utopia on the far side of the Rocky Mountains.

"Billed as 'An Alternative History of Manifest Destiny', the theme, undoubtedly strongly displeasing to an enlightened public, would have been routed off the stage had it not been for the twenty popular Bowery B'hoys who played the Shoshone tribe. The cos-

tumes and final battle scene were thus marvelously exciting, inciting the active participation of many inebriated locals—all of Irish extraction—in the audience.

One wonders if the final message of this militant spectacle is not to dispatch all Negroes and Indians to the Far West where they can all fall in love and live peacefully on reserves. Perhaps we should send the Irish with them so we can all enjoy a more peaceful evening at the theatre."— G.G.

Warren wondered how a theatre critic in New York could avoid being tarred and feathered. He easily recognized some members of the cast as the Fort Mulberry crew, right down to their dog Beaver who played Seaman, and regretted that his fatigued state kept him from attending an evening at the Bowery Theatre.

§

Philomena Park returned that afternoon. She wore her smock and white cap and assumed her duties as administrative nurse. At the same time, she brought him another vial of the amber liquid that both sustained him and weakened him. She put it directly into the drawer beside his bed.

"Courtesy of Fort Mulberry," she explained. "Billy is awake. He said you might need this."

"Thank heaven. I was wondering... "

"I'm sure you were. It's highly addictive, being an opiate."

"No. I still have some left. It helps. I'm worried about Billy."

"That he might not wake up? We all had that fear. In the end he's a bit woozy but it's nothing he can't stand. His speech is...not quite right, and his balance a bit off. It's like being drunk, without the euphoria of feeling in complete control. I don't expect you know about that, being a prohibitionist."

"Where necessary, yes. Alcohol is killing the Indians. What's left of them. Is that not the ultimate goal of Manifest Destiny, Miss... Bachelor? Isn't it? Rose Bachelor?"

Her eyebrows arched, and she smiled. "Ah. So you've found me out. How, may I ask?"

441

"A review of your play in the paper this morning. I see you've recruited the Mulberry contingent as your company. Commendable. I'm sure it was magnificent. Congratulations are in order."

"We'll see. The critics despise it. Too radical. Only ticket sales will tell. We might have to ban alcohol in the theatre. When they get out of hand they destroy the scenery."

Warren was mixing his elixir with the syrup.

"There's a bit of alcohol in that, you know," she said, but not accusingly. "A little. A necessary vehicle. It won't kill me."

"No, I think not. I mean, I hope not..." She said, turning away. She was silent a moment, as was Warren. Something unspoken, or unspeakable, hung between them and made them both embarrassed. It was he who spoke first, sitting up in his bed and feeling like a damned invalid.

"Will Billy be back? I may need him to help me again. Before I leave."

"I'll tell him. Knowing him, I'm sure he'll want to make it up to you."

"For what?"

"For your loss. He feels guilty. I didn't tell him about the hedge bet, nor the winnings."

"Then I'll invent something, that I held some money back, that I didn't lose everything."

"He'll still feel that he owes you something."

"He owes me nothing. It's my own doing. And you erased any debt."

"But you can't tell him that. Think of something, a favor. Make it good."

§

The next day, Billy came back looking battered and shamed. Philomena Park brought him in, then left them both alone. He shuffled about the room looking for something useful to do. He wore his gray water-cure smock but still had his cap in his hands. One eye was closed and bruised, his nose swollen and bent, most likely broken. His one good blue eye was cloudy and looked not directly at Warren, but askance.

"Sorry, Cap'ain. I let you down," he finally said, slipping him a tin of beef stew. "Been restin' up. Feelin' limpsey. Few days, Billy back to his ol' self."

It was true, his speech was slurred. He was shaken. He sat down. Maybe he was even a bit drunk. Warren couldn't blame him.

"Good to see you, Billy. There was nothing to do for it. You were tricked and took a fall, a bad one. Obliged to you for the stew."

"Morlay's doin'. Uses herbs, he says. Cooks like a Frenchman, that man. Says he is French, but he's part Indian. They're all good men. Even the girl."

"They are. They took good care of you. Philomena, especially."

"No woman better. We ain't married, y'know. A secret. Maybe someday."

"She told me, Billy. The secret's safe."

"I ain't got no chil'ren. 'Cept them two twins. They got nobody."

"The way I see it, you all have each other. Pals stick together."

Billy got up suddenly and began to circle the room, fretting, bumping into the bed, the desk, then stopped, caught his head in his hands and stood fast.

"I let 'em all down! Sonofabitch caught me unawares. I couldn't get to his chin. They was pushin' me into him. Then he caught me widda lead fist. I've a mind to waylay the bastard. Catalpa too. Now he's braggin' he wants to take on Tom Hyer, but Hyer won't fight for less than ten thousand. Floyd's small pickins'. Ain't in his league. Fuckin' low-lifer. He'll never fight in this city again. They're talkin' of runnin' him and Catalpa out of town, ye know..."

"We were all dirked, as you say in this town. Don't worry about me. I still saved a hundred back, to tell you the truth, and that will get me home. I'm a prudent gambler."

"Damn right y'are," he said. "I shoulda bin. The boys is all askin' about ye. Bob White says Injuns are tough buggers. Born to lose, hard to kill."

"We'll see. This one, just part Indian, still has some hard road to travel."

Billy rose and turned to leave, slowly, then remembered: "Oh. And this came for ye." He handed him a letter. It was from Wickes' office, by post. Billy stood waiting, shifting his feet and worrying his cap.

Warren looked up from the short note. For a moment, his face lit up.

"Billy, can you come with me downtown? Thursday at three? Looks like we're in business again."

There was still hope. Sure, he could count on Billy.

The possibility of another avenue opening up awakened his spirits and his vitality. It appeared to have the same effect on Billy, who redoubled his efforts for the next two days to have Warren's clothes cleaned, trimmed his hair, shaved him carefully, and brought him a meat dish one evening and then something called oyster chowder. It was deliciously fresh, with bits of cracker and tangy spring parsley. He remembered tasting it once as a boy at his grandfather's house, with oysters brought up fresh on the Erie Canal. This was New York, the taste of the salt sea. He would have to tell Matilda about it. This special taste you could not find in the lakes. The Indians on the island ate them raw, as apparently, they did in France. He swirled it over his taste buds and burst the tender bits one by one. The tastes seemed to carry both the depths of the ocean and the crest of the wave.

He reflected with some regret that during all his stay here, he had not seen the ocean, just forests of masts by the piers on the two rivers embracing Manhattan Island, the harbor rats, the dank dirty waters around the wharf, and once by the Bowery the women selling shellfish, cockles and oysters and lobsters still alive and wagons full of cod still jumping. There would be as much to see again, he told himself, in the waters of Lake Superior and the thousands of lakes and streams in his homeland.

On Thursday, Billy looked passably better, dressed again in his theatre finery, and walking straighter. He escorted Warren to the interview with Wickes and Lyons, staying close at his side, carrying his charge's leather case half empty, as he had left the manuscript with Trall. These were not publishers, Warren told him, they were money men, but they had yet to agree—it was not, as they say, in the bag. He walked with his bulldog cane, slowly, and when caught in the crowd on the sidewalk, put his left hand on Billy's shoulder. During the slow walk, he pondered what the two men would require as security, as they would perhaps not be interested in a cut of the book sales—it was admittedly not common business practice and, all things considered, a gamble. Would they gamble on a book? What else could he offer?

Climbing up the stairway to the first floor, he became winded and had to stop to catch his breath. But he was well primed on coffee and painkiller, determined not to pass out on a chair again. He was announced by the secretary and straightened his back. Billy Daniels waited in the outer vestibule where he endeavored to impress the young lady at the reception by pretending to read the newspapers.

The suited businessmen were waiting with Judge Daly's recommendation on the desk.

"Mr. Warren, glad to make your acquaintance. Judge Daly speaks highly of you, said Wickes, the older, rounder man.

"As highly as he does of your new Territory, Sir," said Lyons, balding but sharp-looking. "It appears that all these immigrants arriving on the boats are racing west to have a piece of it, start their new lives."

"They say the Mississippi valley is a garden unlike any other, full of beauty and richness," Warren ventured, recalling the words of the poetess, Julia Wood. "I've written the history of the original inhabitants…"

"Yes, the Judge mentioned that. Congratulations on your coming publication."

"Thank you, Mr. Wickes, but you see…"

"But that you might need help financing." Efficient, to the point.

"Not without guarantees, which I can provide," he replied, in kind.

"Of what nature?" Asked Lyons. "Have you any tangibles, property perhaps?"

Warren had already thought this out. He had made a claim. Land he had wanted to keep for his family. It was the land of their Ojibwe ancestors, truth be told, treaty lands sold by the US government. He had paid to keep part of his roots, and might now lose it. But it was inevitable, he had to risk it. And there were deeper roots at stake: their history.

"I have a claim of two-quarter sections of valuable land next to my own. I can have delivered to you to one of those parcels, 160 acres of land on the upper Mississippi, in the form of a legally transferred deed from the land office of Minnesota Territory, upon my return. It is worth 400 dollars at this date. It will certainly double by the end of the year. One hundred percent pure profit."

Warren perspired, wiped his brow, and calmed his breathing as Lyons showed Wickes a list of current land prices on his desk.

Wickes nodded and smiled at Warren. "We could advance half that, Sir, the other 200 upon presentation of title to this office."

"I should of course reserve the right to name the repurchaser, and am prepared to buy back at the stated price." He could hardly believe his own words, but he must succeed here. His future, and that of his family, depended on this day.

§

Billy saw Warren come out of the meeting with a wan but satisfied smile.

"We have to pass by that bank on our way back to Laight Street, Billy. And keep a keen eye out. I have here an envelope containing a bank draught for 200 dollars."

He had signed his written bond to William E. Wickes and Timothy Lyons promising to deliver the deed to 160 acres of land on the Upper Mississippi in four months:

Know all men by these presents that I William W Warren
of the County of Benton territory of Minnesota am held and
firmly bound unto William E Wickes and Timothy Lyons of

446

the City of New York and State New York in the final sum of
four hundred dollars, which sum well and truly to be paid

I bind myself, my heirs, executors, and administrators
firmly by these presents. The condition of the above obli-
gation is such that if the above bounded William W Warren
shall procure or cause to be procured a good and sufficient
deed executed to William E Wickes and Timothy Lyons of a
quarter of a section of government land lying in the county
of Benton territory of Minnesota and remit the same to them
within four months from date then this obligation to be null
and void, otherwise to remain in full force and virtue

Wm W Warren, Esq
- New York. May 11th, 1853

The sum, 400 dollars, was twice the face value of the offered land at $1.25 per acre, a very desirable tract in Benton County that he wanted to keep out of the hands of liquor traders.

In writing the bond on their desk, carefully but falteringly, Warren recalled the words of his friend Hole-in-the-Day: *For the Indian to live like the white man, he must want what the white man wants, and value what the white man values. This will bring change to the land. We cannot stop it, but we can resist, claim our share, and survive.*

The businessmen agreed to his right to name a repurchaser. That condition was owed to the Indian in William Warren. The white man in him sold it to them at twice its face value. The buyers were counting on reselling the land at a good profit.

Once on the street, it was Billy who could not contain himself and exploded with joy. "Ye did it, Captain! The book's as good as gold now!" He even threw his top hat into the air.

Warren walked on aided by Billy. He stepped lighter and hoped it was true.

Just down the avenue from the investors' office, he withdrew the two hundred in cash from their bank. This raised his operating capital to three hundred fifty, and he had another two hundred coming once back home. But first, he had to get back to send them the deed. He would have to settle his bill here and get back home safely, which would take up some of that capital— only then could he send Putnam the $350 to print 1,000 copies. It appeared never-ending, but the plan was going to work. His *History* would be published. At last.

§

Back at Trall's Institute, Billy Daniels had to carry him up the stairs to his room. He was fevered. Billy came back with a basin of ice-cold water and cooled his head for the better part of the evening. Warren felt more than grateful for this meticulous care and knew now how necessary it was. The walking, the tram, facing the crowd downtown, the loan negotiations, finally selling his land claim, it had all been exhausting. He laid out his plan to Billy Daniels. He needed a special favor.

He would pay for passage for both of them if Billy would help him make the trip back to Saint Paul. He feared that the travel, even by first-class rail transport, might finish him. He couldn't carry his baggage, and he knew there would be transfers to make. A stagecoach, perhaps, and a stayover in Chicago. The trip might take over a week, and they would finally reach Saint Paul by steamboat. One look at the number of boats arriving in New York Harbor, and the thousands of European immigrants pouring in, and you knew that the newspapers were not exaggerating. They all had intentions to go west. The Sioux and the Ojibwe had been "pacified" and sold their lands, which the government had now opened for auction, ready for the great white tide of immigrants arriving in Saint Paul this year, even at this very moment. It would be time for Billy to look at the land he wanted. Maybe even stake a claim, then come back for Philomena. And whoever wanted to come, in the wagon. When it was ready. Billy kept silent and pondered.

Warren felt uneasy when he mentioned the wagon. He did not want Billy to suspect his true thoughts, that the wagon was pure delusion, that there was no chance of getting it out of the slums of

Five Points, much less rolling it all the way to the West. They had no money, not even the horses to pull it. They were deluded dreamers, the Chief, Dubois, Morlay, Billy, and the whole crew at Fort Mulberry. The Irish twins were adrift in the folly of it all, just a couple of poor immigrants, motherless children who wished they'd never left home. They had no idea what it took to strike out west and farm the land. He hoped Philomena would talk sense into them all. At least into Billy, who was at that time leaning on the windowsill watching the light fade, pondering his future. He still gave no answer.

Warren reconsidered. Practically speaking, his main concern was reaching home intact, completing the land deal, paying Putnam, and seeing the book in print. Money would soon be coming in. But he was so weak at this point that he was unsure he could make the trip without Billy. Another option: he could prolong his stay in New York, write to his lawyer friend William Wood and ask him to send the claim warrant. Or borrow another two hundred to finance the printing, start the book sales rolling and gain strength for the return. He would continue the cure another month, reduce the laudanum, stay rested instead of gallivanting around New York... He was in good hands, and he should allow the water cure time to take effect, here in the summer weather. The trip, he feared, would be exhausting.

Billy suddenly pounded the windowsill ever so gently with his fist, stood at attention, and faced him.

"Y' know, Captain, that wagon ain't nothin' but a pipe dream. I'll go."

"What's that?" He hadn't expected this.

"I'll go west with ye, help ye out. It's the best way, long as Billy's here, got two able legs and hands. At yer service, Captain."

"What about Philomena, the others?"

"I figure every man for himself. Philomena's the one wants that wagon; it was her idea. Woman's a bit daft, no practicality."

"Really?"

"She wants to start a community, she says. A kind of town, out west. A *Utopia*, with *Esprit de corps*, as she says. She's writin' a play about it."

"A poetic spirit. She has some interesting ideas," said Warren, cautiously.

"Best go stake the claim first, I say. Then I come get her, if she'll have me. The others can follow if they take a mind to. But they can have the bloody wagon and take turns pullin' it for all I care. I dinna want no part of it."

This made up his mind. Billy was willing to be his traveling companion. He would invest the cash, pay their passage and expenses, and arrive home safely to get on with his business, his convalescence and writing his future books. He had a vague hope, unmentionable to anyone, that publishing his *History* would be the thing that cured him.

§

The next morning Billy was dispatched to the Duane street office to purchase two tickets on the Monday morning train to Buffalo and Chicago. Philomena Park thought the plan was excellent, and went with him to make sure he got the tickets right. Billy told her he couldn't believe his good fortune. He came to New York in steerage, but he'll leave in first class. He almost kissed her in public, but she sidestepped him.

"Just make sure that Mistah Warren gets home in first-class shape," she replied. "He has much to do that only he can."

Trall came for his final visit and pronounced him improved, but in need of surveillance and continued cure. The Doctor would have to fend without Billy Daniels at the Institute for much of the summer, an inconvenience, but he was reassured that Warren would be accompanied for the trip. He wanted his patient to go home in better health than when he came. He would do well to eat hearty. When the Doctor handed him back the manuscript, praising the few pages he had read—he knew many erudites and scholars who would want a copy as soon as it came out in print—Warren asked if he could leave the manuscript in his hands here at the clinic, along with some of his letters of recommendation, to be dispatched to his publisher, George Putnam, later this summer. He had entire confidence in both the Doctor and Miss Park to see to its safekeeping. Moreover, she was well acquainted with George Putnam. If the Doctor was agreeable, he would return to continue his cure at a later date and, in the interim, might he use 15 Laight Street as his New York address for future dealings with his publisher? Trall was pleased to be of service to his patient, the future historian.

It was all organized. Warren asked Billy for more oyster stew that night, even though he had difficulty keeping it down. He knew he needed it to go forward.

Chapter 35: Homeward

THEY GATHERED IN THE PARK where broadening leaves formed a green canopy over Hudson Square on the morning of departure. The sun was just brightening at 6 o'clock, the treetops catching first light, the flowering bushes deep and lush below. It did not compare to the wild forests around the Warrens' cabin near the upper Mississippi, but walking—on his cane now— under such an abundance of spring leaves made him long even more for his home.

Billy Daniels, who had spent the past two nights sleeping on a pallet with his eye on the patient in his room, carried his bag and writing chest. It was considerably lighter this day as the small trunk was empty of his manuscript and letters. It contained only some newspaper clippings, theatre reviews, recommendations from Dr. Trall, and a small rolled-up and wax-sealed packet of poems which the poetess had told him were experimental and meant for his eyes only. Philomena Park, dressed for her day shift at the clinic, had come early to Laight Street to meet the sendoff party from Fort Mulberry. It made an unlikely site at dawn in Manhattan.

Morlay was in his beaded leathers and raccoon hat, Chief Bob White wore his hair in thick braids, festooned and feathered, a copper chunk on a leather thong with his medicine bag over his bear claw necklace. He had one arm crossed and his blanket folded in ceremonial style. Dubois sported a three-point hat borrowed from the Bowery Theatre, his long knife carried in a wide sash closing a bosun's tunic. The blond Irish twins both had their wide wool caps on, and they'd found some shoes in the street. Eamon was holding the dog, Beaver.

Doves and pigeons and smaller songbirds rose to the occasion, reminding Warren that the maples and ash and hickory and birches shading his log house were waiting for him like this, but it would be even more beautiful. He was feeling up to the trip, fully dressed in his hat and cloak, his breathing shallow, walking slowly but erect on the bulldog cane that Philomena insisted that he keep, as it matched his character. He greeted them all. They had come bearing gifts for the trip.

What Warren did not know was that Philomena had spent the previous evening around the fire at Fort Mulberry, reading to them passages from the manuscript of his *History*. She chose from his preface and the chapter on the origins of the Ojibwe, the people who call themselves Anishinaabe, or "Spontaneous Man", and whose word for their Great Spirit, *Ke- che-mun-e-do*, had no equivalent in the English language, but embodied the pitying, charitable, overruling, guardian and merciful Spirit, the one who watches over the people like a caring parent, vigilant against all harm. Chief Bob White knew this and felt embarrassed. He rose and did a pivoting dance step on one foot as if he knew not where to go. The Ojibwe never mentioned the name of the Great Spirit except in ritual and veneration. He offered some tobacco to the fire. But the others sat mystified, and listened to her story of William Warren, his knowledge passed down from the disappearing old men, of the people he loved, of what he had come here to do, which he now had to finish by returning home. Billy would go with him to help him through, she told them, because the illness was on him. Once in the Northwest, with Warren safely home, Billy would look for land and stake a claim. Then they could all go west.

Little Fire had baked a shortbread for the trip. Eamon handed him a small fossil shell from the coast of Ireland. Dubois gave him a vial of amber liquid. Morlay gave him some maple syrup made by an old Lenape man from the trees just north of Manna-hata. Chief Bob White offered a tied-up bandanna with some tobacco, a bear's claw, and a small arrowhead, telling him something inaudible in their common language with his big hand laid on his shoulder. Then he shook his hand. They all did. The Irish twins both embraced him.

Finally, Philomena Park handed Billy a purse of coins, their group contribution toward a section of farmland wherever he might find it. Billy understood that he was being assigned a mission. He was confounded and mute, but suddenly advanced and kissed her squarely on the lips, which provoked a small round of applause from the crew. She turned away, trying to hide her blush, looking askance at Warren with her curled index finger to her lips. He smiled, bowed to her, took her hand, and kissed it.

"Godspeed, Mistah Warren," she whispered. "Keep an eye on Billy."

Billy loaded the trunk and bags into the waiting cab, and they boarded while Little Fire sang the tune about the wayfaring stranger in her eerie child's voice—the second verse this time to honor Warren's request, so he would not forget it. The horse clopped away as she was still singing, then Eamon's fiddle kicked up the tempo and the cab surged forward. Billy waved and shouted his vow to be back soon.

§

About an hour later, as the train left the station and wended its way north along the Hudson River piers, past the forests of tall-masted ships and black belching steamer stacks, the hordes of shouting immigrants with their carts of trunks, furniture, pans, and children crowding the docks and rails, all of them looking for a new home in the enormous land beyond the city, the song was still in William Warren's head. He drew out his note paper and wrote down the words while they were still fresh in his mind.

I know dark clouds will gather round me,
I know my way is hard and steep.
But beauteous fields lie there before me,
Where God's redeemed their vigils keep.

I'm going there to meet my mother,

She said she'd meet me when I come.
I'm just a goin' over Jordan,
I'm just a goin' over home.

Before they had left the city, Billy opened the purse Philomena had given him—on behalf of them all, as she intimated—and found five twenty-dollar gold pieces. He had in his charge not only a sick man, but the round sum of one hundred dollars constituting all the savings that the Mulberry crew had been able to scrape together. He was incensed, and stared at the coins in disbelief.

"This don't mean I'm a rich man, Captain. It means I'm answerable to them miserable vagabonds. Feminine company excepted. They gone and put upon me the duty to find their bleedin' paradise."

"Knowing you, you'll do it, Billy."

Nonetheless, the full purse did have some effect on his demeanor. He put the coins away deep in his Bowery Street Theatre waistcoat, dusted off his lapels and straightened his cravat by his reflection in the window. Once satisfied, he sat up straighter and assumed the distant, nonchalant air affected by the better-dressed men in the first-class car. Warren had once told him, sincerely, that he was a man of circumstance. Now he felt like one.

The composition of the train, heading north and west on the express schedule over the same Hudson River line, was different from the one he rode last March. The wood-fired locomotive was bigger and black. The women's first-class car was the last, just behind the men's first-class. These two cars toward the rear, both arranged and decorated to recall an upper-class sitting room, were spacious and for now, reasonably empty. Then came a second-class car of wooden benches that was fuller, and finally two converted boxcars with little or no seating space, only wooden benches along the sides. Closest to the engine was the one they called, erroneously, the "emigrant car", a windowless mail car which also held human beings. They were both full to cracking with Germans fresh off the boat and, according to the porter, all from the same town in Germany. Now arrived in this country, they were officially "immigrants". Most of them left from

Jersey City via the Pennsylvania line in special trains that hauled only immigrants, but there had been too many, hundreds of them, so this Hudson River express had also to pull the displaced Germans. Apparently, the railroad officials considered such transitory people not yet arrived in America. They could still be treated as aliens.

The comfort in their first-class car left nothing to envy. It was new, with velvet- upholstered seats accommodating two gentlemen, a carpeted aisle, curtained and brass- appointed windows, four spittoons, and a separate necessities compartment with a closing door. The central wood stove was not lighted and a breeze wafted in from the windows that the conductor opened on request. Water and refreshments were available, but to the conductor's regret there was no dining car because of the immigrant problem today, which added extra length and weight. The stations in Albany and Rochester, where vendors were abundant and the fare excellent, would have to suffice until Buffalo. The porter would take care of everything. The gentlemen would have to rough a bit it on this trip.

Warren was relieved that they were not standing or lying on the floor with the Germans in the head-end cars. He anticipated his fatigue and decided to sacrifice the expense for both him and Billy. Besides, he was used to first-class travel now and not of a mind to settle for less. The porter, a uniformed, gray-haired man (a paleface on this trip, he noticed), told the two mutton-chopped men in front of them that there was little risk of engine smoke or sparks toward the rear of the train, so the windows could be opened, and ventilation would be better here. Safety came first. As for the risk of any vermin or disease, the head-end cars were crowded but isolated from the rest of the train. The immigrants got what they paid for. Also, in case of any obstacles or mishaps along the line, the front cars served as a buffer. Rest assured, gentlemen, first-class passengers are in able hands on the Hudson River Line.

"Buffer?" Billy asked him as the porter left.

"If the engine explodes or derails, they're the first to go."

This hardly reassured Billy Daniels, who thought the train was going too fast. As they left the city limits, skirting the river, he envied the slower barges and steamers crowding the Hudson. At some points he would stand and look down at the water's edge, then sit and cover his eyes. Then he suddenly elbowed Warren and pointed out to the water, where a huge white- headed bird plunged and lifted a fish from the river to fly off west, heavily wafting his great black wings. "Ain't never seen a bird that big," he expounded. "Wouldn't want to fight him." An American bald eagle, Warren told Billy, could outweigh him. They will see many where they are going, but sighting the loner at the start was a good sign for their voyage.

§

Warren's eyes were closed much of the time. He took the offered coffee from the porter and sweetened it from his flask, traveling as much in his mind as he was in this train. The Hudson Valley was peaceful, the river calm, the round hills green and wooded, and the farms were lush. They were not out of the city long before he began to spot the birds, big and small. Plovers and kingfishers, diving ducks and guillemots sped over the surface of the river, the herons and sandpipers in the shallows, while hovering above, were the raptors. Vultures, small peregrines, and a big red-tailed hawk. If he were lucky, later he might see another bald eagle. He spotted a few long-tailed ducks and what he thought were wild geese high in their V formation headed north to Canada. He did get lucky and spotted his clan bird. Two sandhill cranes on the edge of a marsh, their long necks dancing. The mating season.

It was odd to be without his manuscript. He had entrusted his meager life's work to safekeeping at 15 Laight Street. What could be done from now on depended on his diligence, the speed with which he could accomplish his business. He should have written to Matilda to tell her he was coming back. He should have written to Le Duc, to Rice. But now maybe he would be there as fast as a letter would travel. He could not overdo. His breath was short. He must not get winded, he feared a bleeding fit in his lungs and could not afford to lose much blood. The laudanum was a godsend.

Chief Bob White's request that morning as they bade farewell was that he bury the arrowhead when he reached home. For the

Chief, William Warren was an Ojibwe at heart. He must offer the tobacco to Ke-che-mun-e-do over the Misi-ziibi River. That way, they might see each other again in what was now their home, Anishinaabe country. For there in Manna-hata, he knew, they were in the country that their Algonquin ancestors had inhabited since the beginning, from lower Canada all down the coast from Plymouth to Jamestown, before they followed the Megis shell toward the setting sun. Bob White must return there, as must Warren, because this eastern country was now claimed by the palefaces. The bear's claw was for him, for protection. May it give him the strength to do what he must do. He would once again be looking for the Megis shell, heading west like his Ojibwe ancestors.

Documented history, as Warren had read it, told the same story, but differently. Looking over the Hudson as the farmland turned to forested mounds and green hills, past the occasional town of neatly painted houses with white churches, with steamboats churning the waters, he saw a lone canoe with two paddlers, each with a feather in his headband. The canoe was going slowly upriver and appeared to him as a black shadow, a silhouette against the silver skin of the wide river. He wondered from what band those natives could be—one of many hundreds. Perhaps some disappeared tribe of Algonquins, maybe Mahicans.

§

The train made a stop in a place called Poughkeepsie, a rich-looking town with stately houses painted in different colors with white trim, the garden trees already tall. All the people at the station were white and looked content. Even the children were well-dressed. There was one Negro couple. The dark-skinned woman was dressed elegantly but not allowed in the first-class women's car. She had to travel with the men in second class and took this as a matter of course. The man, quite professional looking with his newspaper, boarded to sit beside her. They did not protest—apparently Negro women were not considered first class. On the northern line, Frederick Douglass had sat in first-class with two Negro women. Warren was certain he would have protested this discrimination on the

458

Hudson Line. He wondered if, as a mixed-blood, he was actually allowed in first class. His Yankee side must be working for him in New York. He also wondered if Yankee was not originally an Indian word. He would look it up.

Some other whites got on, some got off, the whistle sounded, and the train wound its way along the bank. The name of the town sounded familiar. It was Algonquin to his ear, maybe Lenape. U-ppu-qui-si. Something about a reed-covered lodge and little water. The country was named by Indians. He was rolling on iron rails through the heart of a country that was home to native tribes since the beginning of time as they knew it. Their bones and blood made up the soil on both sides of the river that reached the sea at Manna-hata Island. He had seen practically no signs of these Indians, save the two silhouettes canoing upstream. Where were they? What had he learned about the New York Indians at Oneida?

Over three centuries ago in 1626, the Manates sold the island of Manna-hata to the Dutch for a handful of trinkets and moved west of the Bronx River. All the bands of Algonquins in New Amsterdam and the surrounding country, the Lenapes, Canarsies, the Matinecooks, were pushed out early by the whites, while the Mahicans, who lived along this Hudson River, were all but wiped out by smallpox. The original peoples in the east numbered in the millions before the whites came. The first European explorers and settlers never knew how many they had destroyed. The Five Nations of the Iroquois and the Hurons traded furs for muskets from Dutch traders and fired them on their enemies, the Algonquins, who were pushed westward and vanished from the great salt water. Firearms changed everything, but the East was still Indian country.

From then on, the old men tell it. The Anishinaabe warred against the Mohawks, the Iroquois, and migrated west to war against the Sioux and pushed them further west, out of the Great Lakes, then out of the Mississippi valley. Hole-in-the-Day the Elder told Lewis Cass and William Clark, when they were negotiating boundary lines between the warring tribes of the Northwest, that the Ojibwe took their lands from the Dakota Sioux the same way the Great Father took this land from their British King, by conquest. He liked to remind white men of that. The Ojibwe drove them from the country by force of arms and had inhabited it ever since. No more than a handful of warriors were left to fight for their homeland. The chiefs wanted peace for their people, not war. Warren could see it coming. The palefaces would push them into the plains with their treaties, their settlers, their bibles, their whiskey, and their guns. They would push them into reservations, force them to farm, cut their hair. They would abolish their language and traditions, take their children from them, destroy their culture, their history, their very existence, until they disappeared from the face of the continent. It was inevitable. Only the names would remain—the lakes, the rivers, the valleys, mountains, and islands, from Manhattan to the Alleghenies to Shenandoah, Chicago, Michigan, Minnesota and Missouri, beyond the great plains of Dakota country, Omaha and west to Chinook country on the Oregon coast. Even the memory of their culture would die. Unless he published his *History*. For their stories to live on. The whites could not kill their stories.

§

He and Billy shared Little Fire's shortbread and dozed and took in the country of the Hudson Valley, the tall oaks, ash and dogwood, the occasional burst of flowering redbud. How rich and green it must smell to walk among those trees, to feel the soft loam under your moccasins. Warren had missed this spring spectacle on his night journey from Albany to New York City when he was unconscious most of the time, having abused the dosage of his tea flask.

Philomena was fully aware of his subterfuge and told him how to use it with knowledgeable parsimony. "An ounce of prevention is worth a pound of cure, Mistah Warren, but do not over prevent."

He had learned since to ration it better, to abide the pain, support the congestion and suppress the coughing, but not pass out. At night he would take a dose amounting to some thirty drops of laudanum tincture. That would take care of it. And he must eat something to avoid gastric distress, although food was hard to keep down. Take care of the body, and the mind will follow. Had he told his children his father's advice? There was much left to tell them.

§

The stop in Albany made him uneasy, as they had to switch to the New York Central line, Erastus Corning's new business venture. Back into enemy territory. As they approached, he saw the city as much larger and busier than he could have imagined that night last March, built mostly on a hill, with a large port where the train station joined with river and canal freight coming in from north and south. Riverboats of all sizes and shapes filled the Hudson, big steamers heading up to the docks, as well as sloops and barges. Once in the station, the first-class passengers were told to remain seated until the platforms were clear.

Time passed slowly. The Germans in the emigrant cars had to change trains carrying everything they had, which caused some panic. What seemed like two hundred people suddenly poured out of the cars into the station, running and jostling, herding children, not knowing where to go, unable to ask for lack of English. "Buffalo!" They would yell, "Buffalo! Erie!" They were easily recognizable in their cloth coats and linen shirts that hung to their knees, men as well as women, and the roundish caps the men wore over their blond hair. They carried baskets of food, bread loaves sticking out, several of them with huge rolls of sausage in their hands or tucked into aprons or pockets.

One tall man with a ginger beard and a revolver in his holster carried himself with a calm that set him apart. He surveyed the pandemonium and hailed a conductor, with whom he spoke English when he presented himself as the guide and interpreter for the group of immigrants. A stationmaster came with some officials and deputies to sort it out. The interpreter stood on a bench and spoke to the group, who listened with an awe they might reserve for a pastor or messiah, and lined up to have their papers checked by the officials. This took an interminable half hour, during which time Warren feigned sleep in the car, next to the window on the platform, one eye on a keen watch for Erastus Corning's men.

Finally, they were all channeled into the two emigrant cars on the right train. The baggage car, a boxcar at the head end, was quickly filled with furniture, trunks, baggage, and boxes bound for the West. The remainder had to be sorted, labeled, and left on the platform, hopefully to be shipped later to Chicago or Saint Louis. People were leaving their lives behind them, going to where they had nothing waiting. The porter gave the sign to Warren and his aide that they could now board the Buffalo train.

First-class baggage was handled by the porters, but they had to switch platforms, which meant a short walk through the throng of passengers. Warren held close to Billy with his cloak collar up and his hat in his hand to remain inconspicuous, walking slowly, glancing around him. He was hunched over on his cane. He must look like an old man. So much the better. He would not want to cross paths with Fowles or Benton, nor with Corning. This was irrational, he knew, as there was little chance for such a coincidence. But it could happen. His luck was bad at this point. What could he possibly do—shoot them? The small pistol was still in his coat pocket, but he regretted not having cleaned it and reloaded the chambers before leaving New York.

Then he thought: this fear is absurd. Some years ago, even some months ago, he would not have felt it. But now he had lost that confidence. Somehow the feeling crept over him that his life was in mortal danger, and his heart began to pound. If he should die now, here in the Albany station, all would be lost. He felt a weakness coming on. He must resist. Reaching the first-class car, he stopped short, stood wavering, and dropped his hat. Some drool fell from his lip and he wiped it quickly.

Billy saw him falter. He caught his hat and took his arm while a porter helped him mount the footstool to the boarding steps. His aide set him down into the first seat and went to ensure that his baggage was on the train. The wagon so far was vacant. Warren, thankful for the isolation, pulled his cloak over his head and took a large swallow of his tea, indifferent now to whoever might think he was a drunkard. He coughed a little and spat blood into his handkerchief. This sort of thing, he should avoid.

A few gentlemen began to arrive in the car. The bad spell passed. The fear was leaving him. He would make it. Billy returned with some hot sandwiches and pie from a vendor's cart on the platform, inquiring after his Captain's state.

"In fine fiddle. Just a passing cramp. Makes you a bit unsteady."

The train left on schedule. There was no sign of his enemies, and he was assured that in Albany, no one was looking for him.

This train was longer, ten cars in all. As the tracks entered the Mohawk Valley and headed due west, there was much construction where the tracks followed the river, then the canal, slowing down their progress. Billy ate his sandwich while Warren picked at his. Billy marveled at the forests, the bluffs, and the well-tended farm-lands where huge cows fed on the thick grass, feeling he was at last penetrating into the heart of the promised land. Even the sheep here, he told Warren, were fat as barrels.

"Barrels of what?" He asked him, seeing he had found a quart bottle of beer in the station and was enjoying it thoroughly. Billy gave him a wink and offered a swig, which he took to honor their camaraderie.

He was grateful for his traveling companion. He felt safer again for no rational reason other than that he was not alone with Billy by him—he would make it home. Or maybe it was the bear's claw that he carried in his pocket. Perhaps, he thought, it was also because he was nearing his old haunts again, those glorious days of youth now past, the home of his father and grandfather. It was a place where he was young and strong—Oneida was a seat of learning, of growth, where he found the world so much bigger than his home on Made-line Island, bigger even than the Great Lakes. Beriah Green's school opened his mind to a world where all men were equal upon the earth and under the kingdom of God. Those ideas he brought back with him to the new territory that was to become part of a new country. He was hopeful, energetic, stepping with certainty and daring into the world of men.

He daydreamed of those days as he dozed along the ridges, through the tunnels, through the towns and forests, the train winding its way slowly as the afternoon passed, the evening waned, the cliff-dwelling birds multiplied at feeding time. He spotted another bald eagle, several red hawks, another formation of Canada geese, and kept an eye out for another crane, the bird that meant his voyage home was blessed. By his cabin, along the Mississippi and the Platte, they came in by the thousands, thick as buffalo on the prairies. He wondered if he would see any buffalo on this trip—maybe on the plains, after Chicago. Sometimes they came far north, into the lakes by Saint Croix. He daydreamed, as he lolled, of animals in the big trees and grasses he knew when he was a boy. Tall white pines and firs, too broad for him and Truman and their cousins to put all their arms around. He had seen them being cut down by the lumberjacks, leaving high stumps. Fields of stumps where the first peoples had husbanded those trees for thousands of years.

§

Nightfall. The train reached Rochester. There was a stop announced for the train to take on water. The passengers could stretch their legs. Billy spotted an open tavern and went for refreshment, but Warren said he would stay put. They opened the doors and windows on the emigrant cars but forbade the people to leave the station. There was not a black person in sight this time, save the porter in charge of second class. He wondered what had become of the Negro couple who boarded in New York. He wondered about Frederick Douglass, whom he had intended to visit on his way back, to discuss publication in Europe. He would probably never see Douglass again. In the short time of the stop in Rochester, the train unmoving, he became impatient. They were wasting precious time.

The train arrived in Buffalo after midnight. The immigrants all disembarked and were directed to the harbor, where a steamboat waited for them. They looked exhausted, but on they plodded with their baskets of food. The weather held; silver clouds passed before the half moon.

The express train continued to the Pennsylvania line, where all passengers changed trains to a six-foot gauge line for twenty miles, then at Erie were asked to disembark to change back again to the smaller gauge line if they were continuing on west to Cleveland, Detroit, or Chicago. It was the middle of the night, but the station terminal was navigable by gaslight. Billy escorted his charge to the Cleveland train scheduled to leave in four hours, at 8 o'clock. He hoisted Warren into the train and arranged him as comfortably as allowed by the upholstered but rudimentary seats, where he dozed sitting up, his habitual sleeping position. His weakness was alarming to his guardian, who tried to feed him a little more of the shortcake and take some cheese he'd found at the Rochester station. They had been traveling for 24 hours, with another two days and nights ahead of them before reaching Chicago.

Along the southern shore of Lake Erie, time again became meaningless, a state to which he succumbed as if to a balm. At times the water was there, to the north, with boats unmoving on the horizon, water birds black and gray on the shoreline, loons and ducks skimming away, frightened by the train's clamor. The tracks entered some low sandy hills and he dozed again. Sleep was never deep.

Billy every now and then would disappear. He had found some card partners in second class, but would not venture into the emigrant cars. The conductor came through announcing stops—Cleveland, then smaller towns to take on water, wood. Vendors would sell a bit of sausage, a loaf of bread, perhaps some cheese or a can of bean soup. Detroit meant a change of trains, again in the middle of the night.

They went on through the woods of Michigan, the flatlands of Ohio and Indiana with the big water on the right. And the birds... the birds... Warren saw an entire stand of cranes in a bulrush marsh just below a bare sand dune, beyond which was the northern sky reflecting the silver blue of Lake Michigan. They rolled on, coming closer night and day.

Chapter 36: Reckoning

THEY REACHED CHICAGO ON THE afternoon of the third day, only a few hours behind schedule, where Billy himself declared it was time for a rest before going on, in a real bed. Warren concurred and directed the hansom driver to an establishment recommended by both Henry Rice and Le Duc called the Sherman House, not far from the station, not far from the lake, close to the canal connection to the Illinois River.

The elaborate brick and stone buildings were magnificent, enormous, larger, and newer than in Manhattan, the streets paved with cobblestones, while next to some were lots of wooden houses or log cabins. Bridges were under construction along the Chicago River. Billy recognized the accents of the workmen, mostly Irish, but some were German, some Polish, the stonemasons Italian, the underground diggers mostly black or yellow. Thousands were pouring into the station from the trains and boats arriving by Lake Michigan or up the river from Saint Louis. Tracks were being laid through the city and along the river, tunneling was everywhere. The speed of the changing cityscape created a kind of frenzy. A colony of ants building their hill. It was the New York of the Great Lakes, no longer the muddy log-built town Warren had been told of when he was a boy. He had never been to Chicago in his short life. Nowhere in the Northwest had he seen a metropolis like this in the stages of becoming.

They found that the Sherman House, which Le Duc spoke of as a fine old Chicago establishment, was now a much improved and grand hotel, appointed in Italian marble in a rococo style even more pretentious than his Buffalo lodgings. Warren checked them into a first-class room on the first floor. At the desk, he was informed that transportation by rail, the Galena- Chicago Union line to the Mississippi, was not quite completed. It may be more comfortable to go by packet boat through the canal and connect with a steamer at the lower points, a perfectly beautiful route that would get the travelers to Saint Paul in about two or three weeks, if all connections worked well.

"But we just came from New York in three days. How is that possible?"

"Marvelous, the new railroads, aren't they?" Said the clerk. "I'm sure that in a year or two, the Saint Paul line will be open, or at least the line to Galena. They are building at breakneck pace, Mr. Warren, I assure you. But for this trip, why not take your time? The rivers are lovely at this time of year."

"I don't have the time," Warren said bluntly. "I must see the gentlemen who recommended your hotel in Saint Paul before the end of the month."

"Ah yes. Mr. Le Duc. There's a coincidence, and what a pity. Mr. Le Duc passed through Chicago and stayed with us just three days ago, on his way to New York. In fact, with the new train lines, he should be there now. Astounding, isn't it?"

"To New York?" Warren was astounded but not for the same reason. Had he stayed, he could have met Le Duc in New York and made an arrangement on the spot. He could have even seen him here in Chicago. The timing was all wrong. His plans were foiled again. Rotten luck, rotten fate.

"Traveling on territorial business, I believe, to the Crystal Palace exhibit. He left a forwarding address, should you want to wire him there. The telegraph office is just down Clark Street, but we shall be glad to dispatch it for you."

"That's a thought," he said. "I'll ponder that. But my companion and myself would first need a rest. Can you set up a separate cot in the room for Mister Daniels? I am...convalescing." He was dizzy, must be losing his vocabulary. "And he is my...my nurse and assistant."

"Of course, Sir. And all train and boat ticket offices are just downstairs, if you like.

Should you need anything, just ring the front desk."

The porters took the bags and trunk while Billy Daniels helped him trudge up the wide carpeted staircase to their first-floor room. This took time, because he would not be carried. By the time he sat him down on the bed, Warren could no longer breathe enough to walk or think, fever was rising in him, pain and fatigue made him curl his limbs. Billy went to see about some hot water.

Warren reached for his flask. Before he could open it, a coughing fit wracked his chest and a clot of blood and phlegm held back for three days on the train spewed across his waistcoat. He put his hand there and saw the same blood red palm he'd seen that winter when the branch struck him from his horse and he'd landed flush on the snow. Outside the window was the daylight of Chicago filtering through the curtains. He was still a long way from home.

§

His nurse and assistant found him like that, sitting up, unconscious, but breathing more easily and by all appearances, resting peacefully for once. He was, Billy reasoned, out cold. He wiped off the blood as best he could and soaked his waistcoat in the basin before he sent it down for cleaning. At least he was a neat invalid and didn't soil the bedclothes. A stroke of luck. This was a posh hotel, he didn't want to offend. For himself, they could have gone to a boarding house but Warren had insisted once again. Damn the expense, he'd declared. He had the money, comforts were important and certain services essential.

This gave Billy the notion of a bath for his Captain. A good sitz bath of sorts to bring the congestion and fever down, then a sweat, a cold plunge, just like back at the Institute, would do him a world of good. Unfortunately, no hydropathic establishment could be found in the city, but there were fine bathing facilities with several tubs, hot and cold water provided, here at the Sherman House.

Billy had a drink at the bar, thought it over, and ordered a tub of each, hot and cold, brought to their room the next morning. For this evening, a basin of cold and one of hot would do. And a good hot meal, brought to the room about seven, would be perfect. No sausage, if you please, just a good cut of beef. Chicago's best, he was assured. Billy also requested a pot of good hot water for tea and a bottle of whiskey—the one served at the bar would do fine.

It was indeed very convenient to be waited upon by the obliging hotel staff. Warren awoke about six that evening, weak and taciturn but feeling passably better, while young Negro and Irish chambermaids brought up the tubs, basins and waters as ordered. Billy bathed him with his usual encouraging advice and constant chatter about the grand hotel and the customers he crossed in the bar. Room service waiters delivered the steaming meal on a rolling cart under polished domes on white linen. Warren ate little, but allowed that the meat was tender and good. Billy made up for it with his stevedore's appetite, ordered pie for dessert and became a favorite with the staff as he was a liberal tipper. He was able to make a fresh pot of tea for Warren, who had ample sweetener left thanks to his parting gifts from the friends at Fort Mulberry. The thirty drops of laudanum were doled out, sweetened, and swallowed with a cup of hot tea. He sat by the window with the Chicago gaslights reflecting off the tall facades lining Clark Street.

Below, he saw a large animal with a long white head and stubby antlers walk slowly by his hotel and look up. No passers-by seemed to notice the beast. He had not seen the Windigo in many years, but he knew it was never far—it caught up with him, and now even here on the streets of Chicago. It was waiting.

Before he closed his eyes, he reflected that there was not a tree in sight. Billy Daniels, certain that he would be asleep and breathing for most of the night, went out on the town.

§

The improvised convalescence in Chicago continued for some days as Warren waited to gain strength for the final leg of the journey. The cold and hot bath plan initiated by Billy Daniels seemed to help—it established a sort of hydrotherapy outpost in their comfortable room, where meals were served and all Warren's needs were seen to. He was again an invalid, Billy assuming a certain authority as his dedicated nurse and assistant. This would cost him some cash, but he was buying time. He dressed and rose occasionally to walk around the huge city block, with his cane and his assistant by his side, then return to the lobby and sat reading the newspapers, searching for any scrap of news from his homeland to the north. Of course it would be old news, as there was no telegraph connection to Saint Paul, and no through train line as yet. But news from the East, Washington, and New York, now traveled at lightning speed over the wires.

An article in the *Chicago Tribune* forwarded from Washington and Buffalo informed him that Democratic President Franklin Pierce had appointed Col. Willis A. Gorman Territorial Governor of Minnesota on May 15th, replacing Alexander Ramsey. Many lesser territorial officials close to the Whig party had also been "guillotined". He read further that John Watrous was also replaced as sub agent for the Chippewa Agency in April, an investigation of his actions was under way. The article went on to report that the *New York Daily Times* had followed this corruption affair closely, concerning the Sandy Lake Tragedy in which 400 Chippewa Indians needlessly perished in a self-serving removal plan initiated by Ramsey, Watrous, and interested trading concerns. President Taylor's illegal removal order was revoked, and there was no more question of forcing the annuity payments to Sandy Lake—they would continue to be made at La Pointe.

So the Whigs were out, he reflected, and the Ojibwe—his Indians, as he called them— would not have to remove. For now. Perhaps Buffalo's trip to Washington last year had finally produced results. This afforded him some measure of solace. His enemies, Watrous and Ramsey, those who drew him into their plan only to use him, bringing suffering and death on the Wisconsin bands, were ousted. Like Buffalo, like Hole-in-the-Day, like Flat Mouth and all the leaders, he distrusted them completely and despised them. Watrous would get his, and so would Ramsey. Chances were that he, William Warren, would never see the money they refused him for his services. It was over. He only wondered what had happened to Anna Ramsey and her nascent Cultural Society. Maybe that too was all finished. He would find out when he arrived in Saint Paul. If...

His goal now was to see his family. Matilda and the children were likely anxious. If he reached Two Rivers, he would find the land warrant, send it on to Wickes and Lyons, arrange the money to deal with Putnam, perhaps through Trall and Judge Daly. But looking hard into the face of what likely awaited him, he avowed that his chances were slim. Time would pass quickly now, so he must take precautions. He had begun to draft a letter to William Le Duc, at his forwarding address in New York City, but had not sent it yet. He reviewed it now.

Accidentally hearing at this place that you was on your way to New York, I write you these lines.

I was so sick and feeble while in New York that I could not do anything towards getting my work under way. Mr. Robertson interested Judge C.F. Daly to help me, but he was very busy on his own affairs and I became so anxious to go home before I lost all strength, that I left the matter in his hands at his own request. He lives at No. 9, St. Clements Place.

Mr. Putnam received me very kindly but he had so much on his hands in the way of publishing that he could not take my work. He offered to have it stereotyped for me and get 1000 copies printed and bound, and act as my agent in the city for the sale of the Book, provided I pay the Expenses. I of course own the whole thing and get all the profits. He calculated $350 to stereotype it. The offer is still standing. He gave me quite a present in Books.

Appleton said that if you would order for 1000 copies he would publish the work. Redfield read the manuscript, was much pleased with it, told me to call on a certain day and he would tell me what he would do. I was too sick to call at the appointed time, and neglected it altogether.

Now Sir, if you will undertake the work in hand and publish it on your own expenses so that we own the whole concern, I will give you an interest of one half.

There he had left off. He spent a restless day considering his options in the brutal light of probable developments. He weighed the consequences of both possible outcomes of his situation, and completed his proposal to Le Duc:

If you cannot afford to do this, I want you to take the manuscript and bargain with a publisher as though it were your own. I give you full powers to act in my behalf. It will be alright between us. I want but 100 copies for subscribers who have addressed me.

Quite a number of people in New York and different points are anxious to have the book come out and the moment it is advertised there will be plenty of orders for it.

I left the manuscript with Dr. R. T. Trall, No. 15 Laight Street.

I enclose you an order for it on mine. It may be well for you to see Judge Daly, as he has some letters Dr. Trall's respecting the work which might be of use to you.

I leave the matter entirely in your hands.

Truly yours,
Wm W Warren

He dispatched the letter through the front desk of the hotel, dated 19 May, in care of A.S. Barnes at 31 John Street in New York. It was written now, and if it reached Le Duc, it would—with Godspeed—be history no matter what happened. His business was in order.

He paid for passage for himself and Billy Daniels on the train to Rockport, a distance of only 86 miles, which was the extent of the strap rail the railroad had laid so far. There was only one class, not overcrowded, and it was not frequented by immigrants, he was told, who generally traveled by packet boat from Chicago. It was still the old world up in that country. From the end of the line they would take a stagecoach to Galena, and board the first steamer available to travel north, up the Mississippi. He imagined that the river was magnificent and wide at that low point. It was surely, in the month of May, a beautiful thing to see.

Chapter 37: Mississippi Home

WHERE THE WATERS FLOW WIDE between dun bluffs, flanked by marshes and greening bush, where the trees lean toward the Father of Rivers pulled by silt and gravity, and currents swirl over root tangles and branches and shifting sands, all things are seen to change. You change with them. When the days grow longer yet seem too brief, as powerful wheels churn the surface, rippling silver at night under the moon and stars which also extinguish in their time, a man sees the Mississippi with new eyes when great change is upon him.

This is his river. Born at its source, he has paddled it, swum it, drunk it and fished its waters in summer, walked its ice in winter, fought its currents, hunted its beaver, loved its loons, and married its daughter. This night, the river is opening its arms and bringing him home, from farther upstream, from where it began. He may have the privilege of seeing his family again, or he may not. His heart has weakened for lack of breath, blood has seeped into his lungs, the fever is constant, the malady has gnawed his legs and invaded his mind, but here the riverboat is carrying him back upriver and he need not rush. Patience has won out, he is an old man, no longer fighting. He will travel toward his home as long as the river is willing. The river is endless.

§

The morning train had reached Rockport quickly, in relative comfort for about six hours, but that was only half the overland journey. There were five stages waiting and all the passengers bound for Galena crowded in, nine to a coach. They ate and continued on through the Illinois plains, Warren wedged between Billy and an elderly gentleman who slept or feigned sleep all the way, cushioning the jostling of the coach but smelling of urine, age, and decay.

The sunset over the prairie, its seas of undulating grasses reaching far to the flat horizon, reminded him of the changes at end of the day on Lake Superior when the sky turns from blue to silver to green to red to darkness filled with stars. The tall grassy plains here were endless and empty, all the animals hidden but for the chicken hawks that hovered, spied a prey, then dove. There seemed to be no houses, no farms, only an occasional settlement along the rutted road. It had not rained much that spring. The rivers and creeks were lower than usual. Someone said the flat-bottomed Mississippi riverboats had it hard this year with the shallow sand banks. That day, the 27th of May 1853, marked the beginning of William Warren's 28th year. He proposed a toast to Billy, to a long and fruitful life.

"To a long birthday then, Captain!" They both tipped their flasks. "And many happy returns like this one!" In his jostled half-sleep, Warren dreamed of running on the beach as a boy on Madeline Island.

They stopped at an outpost to have a meal of beans and bread and to rest and water the horses, then went on through the dark plains where lighting flashed over the grasslands. Further on in the night, the prairie was alight with fire to the south. Towering clouds reflected first the white lightning then the orange flames that limned the edge of the earth. Warren counted the seconds between the lightning flashes, then the thunder. Maybe seven miles. Not a farmhouse to be seen against the white light. The stage pushed on.

§

Rain finally came toward sunrise and slowed them down. There was another stop at an inn for breakfast. The prairie lands heaved into rolling hills, the red earth scarred here and there by lead mines. Then came the steep cliffs of the Fever River and the town of Galena on both sides, dug into the rock and dirt on each side of the water, just wide enough for steamboat passage. Several steamers were docked. The water journey began.

Billy helped him hobble aboard the *Dr. Franklin*, a side-wheeler that he was somewhat familiar with, as it had brought Indian annuities, supplies and whiskey for the fur traders up through Saint Paul for years. It had also carried the two thousand displaced Winnebago from Wisconsin to Minnesota in 1848, to be herded into their new reserve in what used to be Dakota land, but was now Ojibwe country.

In 1851, in signing the treaty that was Ramsey's pride, the Dakota Sioux sold those lands for 3 cents an acre, and slowly trod into reservations on the plains west of the river. They lost their woodlands, the lakes, the rivers. The government was advertising it as paradise found, excellent farming land, the big timber to the north just ready for felling. Minnesota was ready for the inrush. Speculators were waiting like spiders for countless thousands of immigrants.

The *Dr. Franklin* was loaded to the rails bearing those immigrants northward, some already on board from lower points on the Mississippi. Galena's shops were busy with men and women seeking bread, milk, cheese, whatever they could find to sustain them for the rest of the voyage. On the steamer, young pigs were being herded in the hold below decks, where there were barrels of flour from the river mills. The lower decks of the filthy, white-painted vessel were crowded, but the two upper decks were for higher-paying travelers.

Again, Warren said hang the expense. Before boarding, Billy's papers were checked and suspected. The officials required him to show his money. He did so, but one hundred dollars did not appease the inspector. Warren had to vouch for him by asserting that his assistant was in his employ. This was accepted when he produced the letter of recommendation from Henry Rice, and he was recognized as a Saint Paul notable having served on the Territorial Legislature. Billy was impressed as much as the inspector. They were given a small stateroom whose occupant had just vacated, and charged $3.50 each for the four-day voyage to Saint Paul. Warren paid for them both, as agreed.

§

At seven that evening, still light, the *Dr. Franklin* set off under a barely passable bridge canal, then huffed slowly through the narrow winding passage under the cliffs to make the seven miles up the winding Fever River to the Mississippi. Sleeping on the lower deck were some 400 German and Scandinavian farmers and craftsmen, families one and all, ranging from babies to grandparents, all exhausted, some sick, sharing their meager dwindling bread with other families, relieved and thankful to be reaching the end of their arduous voyage over seas, lakes, rivers, and rails to their promised earthly paradise. Warren watched the families falling asleep, children in the arms of their mothers, the men and oldsters curled around their belongings, tied bundles, baggage, chests, pans and ladles, a chair or carved stool, precious boxes of tools. The European immigrants were anxious to get to work and build their new homes, their farms, to make Indian country into their country, to make the new America.

It seemed odd to be traveling arm in arm with the future, he who had lived so faithfully with the past. Maybe he was a complete anachronism, out of his place and time, a fuddy-duddy, a half-educated bumpkin from the wilderness, a nostalgic invalid whose mixed-blood left him nowhere in time. They might consider his book, if it ever sees daylight, as all hogwash, useless stories of a useless time. The Indians and trappers were the past, these immigrants were the future. Who will tell them about this land, and the native people whose bones they will overturn with every passage of their plows? Will they ever learn about how the Indian lived in the forest, on the lakes, the rivers? Will they ever be told the priceless value of what the Ojibwe and the Sioux, all the tribes, were leaving them? Or would all those native generations, their knowledge, their history, and their traditions, only slide into the river to sink, to settle down, and turn to bottomland?

The sun had gone down. They were navigating a fork where the tributary fed into the big Mississippi. Both Warren and Billy were on the top deck looking out on the broad opening river as the engines came on full and the big wheels churned faster, roaring through the water with its gliding surface smooth as a pond, shaking the steamer to the timbers, free at last from the confining cliffs. The distant shores were low and soft with foliage, it was enormous and wonderful. The air was clear, the rising moon was a wounded circle, just past full, big and bright enough to silver the river and the thin clouds above. Warren sat on a chair by the railing, one hand on his cane, one searching his coat pocket. He had one more thing to do.

Billy Daniels had found no Irish on the boat. For him, that was why the officials suspected him—to their minds, Irish immigrants are too poor to be anything but thieves. Where was an Irishman going to find the money to buy land?

"You have enough, Billy," Warren rasped as he handed him two of the fifty-dollar bank notes left to him. "Here's your pay, well earned. That makes two hundred in your purse, good for a section of 160 acres, wherever you like."

"I canna accept this Captain, I thank ye. You keep it for the missus, yer children, and yer book. Ye've paid me well, here I've come to the promised land, first class all the way. Billy's come up in the world thanks to yerself."

"I'll have enough. I still have 150 in reserve," he lied. "Plus our expense account, and soon I'll be getting the 200 owed to me in New York, to publish the book. I have friends here. My family and I will be fine. This is yours, for your dream. With my thanks. I never could have made this trip without you."

"Beggin' yer pardon, Sir. I've not yet done me job, gettin' ye home. Why not keep it until we get there? It's outta place for me to have so much money. I might gamble it away here on board, knowin' me devious mind."

"You won't. And I want to do this now. Before we land." Warren shot his arm out straight, the two bills extended, and looked at him squarely. His hollow eyes shone with fever. Billy was not dumb. He should not have to explain. "Take this," he said. "Understand me."

Billy looked his employer straight on for a few moments, then cast his eyes to the deck and took the money, stuffing it in his waistcoat. He nodded his thanks again. Suddenly he stood, arranged Warren's cloak over him as he lay on the reclining chair on the top deck, then found another chair and sat by him, as he had done since the beginning of their trip. Warren wanted to stay up here as long as he could, to take it all in. They would go into the cabin later. The two men took out their respective flasks, raised them in a toast, and drank.

§

Late that night they awoke as the steamboat slowed and drew close to the shore where there was no landing in sight. There the wheels stopped churning. It was quiet enough to hear owls and nighthawks in the forest, some crickets distant in the grass. There was also some bustle among the immigrants on the lower deck. A man shouted something in Swedish, a woman wailed. Three men made shore in a skiff with a small bundle. They were gone but a half hour and came back shovels in hand. The boat put off again. There was cholera on board. A mother had lost a child.

There had been cholera in Chicago. There was cholera in the Mississippi River Valley. Warren had seen it take whole bands of Anishinaabe, who called it the whites' disease. Cholera traveled, seemingly in circles, and took you quick. He had seen all manner of death since his childhood, death by drowning and death by the knife, death by tomahawk, war club, death by pistol, death by cold and starvation in mid-winter, death by revenge and death by justice, his own father's death by failure and despair, and there was no death you could choose with a clear mind if you lined them all up to compare.

Cholera was bad, and you did not choose. You lie in sweat and thirst, moaning, while your fluids drain, your skin cracks and clings to the bone, the nose in the end grows thin and sharp until you rattle and breathe your merciful last. Children go fast, the strong suffer longest, and you are completely powerless, your life means nothing anymore. It gives you every reason to hope and pray that God will accept you, that your life has been good enough to avoid Hell, which is worse, and that the kingdom of Heaven will be merciful. The purgatory of this existence on Earth is suffering enough when cholera takes you.

These thoughts did him no good through the next days, when the boat stopped again to wood, to wind and stilt its way over a sandbar, to discharge passengers at Prairie du Chien, and thrice more to bury cholera victims. Then he reflected that these people were unfortunate, they fell sick and died in the beginning of their struggles, when they had yet not commenced their lives in the place where they had come to live them out. Whereas he had lived a full life, he judged, but he would not have the time to make it fuller. If your life is good, your death is good, Tug-aug-aun-e had once told him. A warrior wants to die fighting.

It came to him during the night that this could be the time to thank the Lord for his life, but putting prayer into words did not come easy for him. He had prayed, at the mission, in the church, a good Presbyterian, but hardly ardently. He had never petitioned God for whatever reason. This he did not speak about. Certainly not to his father who had a certain attachment to the Mission. He could only recall repeating rote and scripture to his religious tutors. So in the night, he said no prayer. Instead he watched the heavens move. The next night it crossed his mind again and he asked Billy to find him some tobacco. He came back with a cigar. Warren tore it up, stood by the rail with Billy's help, and let it fly from his hand in the light wind over the Mississippi. Then he did the same with the pouch of tobacco from Chief Bob White, an offering to Ke-che-mun-e-do.

As for himself, he found no words to say. God, the Great Spirit, needed none.

Further on there were many islands, logjams, and more sandbars, where they ran aground once in broad daylight. Stasis wore on his patience, so he took more tea and slept. He slept many waking hours, on deck, in the cabin, avoiding crowds in the parlor. His eyes were half closed, and he kept his hat on. Billy helped him between the chair on the deck and the cabin and kept cold compresses on him to calm the fever. Twice he had to carry him to the cabin, to bed. Warren wanted to see no one, but found that as the days wore on, he longed for Matilda and the children, his own brothers and sisters. Just to see that they were all right. He may get a chance to rest for a day, with his sister Charlotte, but his real rest would come at home. He hoped as they neared Saint Paul that no one would recognize him. This would not be a propitious time.

Despite his reclusive state he yearned for the riverscape. He looked out the small window of his cabin. It rained, multicolored clouds passing with spring thunderstorms, and when the sun came out, they could see far enough over the hills and bluffs to spot rainbows. The immigrants were enchanted, especially the children. There were flat boats on the river, poled barges heavy with barrels, and more and more canoes. The Indian paddlers kept a good distance away. The steam whistle, Hole-in-the-Day once told him, sounded like a moaning beast in a bad dream, like nothing that had ever been heard before. They still distrusted it.

§

It was the steam whistle that woke him. He found he could not rise alone from the cot and had to wait for Billy to come fetch him. They were docking in Saint Paul. It was time. The bags were packed and taken by the porters. Billy washed his face, dusted his hat for him, tied his cravat, and wrapped him in his cloak. Then he bent, lifted William Warren's long frame in his arms with no more effort than it took to heft a child, and brought him outside on deck to see the sun through the mist on the river.

As the *Dr. Franklin* rounded the bend, day broke in the east and turned the blue river mist to gold, Warren wondered who would be there to greet him for his homecoming. They waited while the mist dissipated, and the steamboat maneuvered its way into a quay slip. The dock was already swarming with immigrants and animals, but none from their vessel.

Below, at quay, anxious families were stopped on the landing ramp. The moment had arrived, this was the journey's end, but the *Dr. Franklin* was cordoned off by armed deputies. The Captain was speaking to an official. No one was getting off the boat.

"Billy," said Warren. "Take me down there. We cannot wait."

The date was May 31st, 1853. Even if he had but one day left to live, Warren was eager to get started.

§

When Billy Daniels came to see Warren at his sister's house the next morning, the first day of June, there was no answer at the door. A neighbor, a frail, older woman daubing her eyes with a wet handkerchief, told him that Charlotte Price had gone for the undertaker. Her brother, a young man, had up and perished in her house that very morning, bled out through the lungs. God rest his weary soul.

Epilogue:

WILLIAM WHIPPLE WARREN WAS LAID in the ground on June 2nd, 1853, in the only existing cemetery in Saint Paul, attached to the Episcopal Church, where the Reverend E. D. Neill officiated the ceremony. There was no time to spread the news. Charlotte and Edward Price were there, as was Billy Daniels, and only a small number of acquaintances. The rest of his family, Matilda, the children, his sisters, learned of it a day later. William Wood wrote a lengthy eulogy that was published on the 6th of June in the Minnesota Democrat. Matilda gave birth to their fourth child, a girl she named Madeline. Julia Warren Spears recalled later that Hole-in-the-Day, when he heard of Warren's death, was shaken. He said, "I have lost my elder brother and best friend."

§

No letters from Warren to Anna Ramsey were ever found. Alexander Ramsey himself was acquitted of corruption by a Senate committee, became the Republican Governor of Minnesota in 1860 and continued to make his fortune in Saint Paul real estate. The new Ramsey House was decorated by Anna, and stands today as a historical site, one of the most opulent manors in the city.

§

Wilkes and Lyons sent William Le Duc the bond that Warren had signed in New York and claimed two hundred dollars, but Warren was dead, and the land warrant was never disclosed.

§

No land entry was ever recorded for Billy Daniels, who found work that summer as a fireman on the propeller *Independence*, under Captain John McKay. Sailing Lake Superior in November, on the way from the Sault to Ontonagon and La Pointe, the boiler exploded and she sank, killing four. According to the *Lake Superior*

Journal of November 22, 1853, the names of the two firemen killed were unknown.

§

Matilda and the children, got on with their lives. Matilda re-married, and they lived next to Truman Warren at Gull Lake for some years, then moved to the White Earth Chippewa Reservation in along with many of the mixed-blood Warren family, who multi-plied and went forth into the modern world in different parts of the country. Some remained to marry into the tribe and others left to mix their origins even further, eventually losing their roots and ties with the once powerful Ojibwe nation. Yet the memory of William Warren and the deed he accomplished, live on in their memories. Young Tyler lived to a ripe old age, as did Madeline, the daughter William never saw. Warren's sisters Julia and Sophia outlived him by sixty years. Both left written recollections of their brother and those times in the Territories.

§

Dred and Harriet Scott, married in 1837 at Fort Snelling where they were house slaves to Army Surgeon Dr. John Emerson, fol-lowed the doctor in his posts further south until he died. In 1846 they sued for their freedom in the Missouri Courts and won, then lost in the appeal brought by Doctor Emerson's widow. For over a decade the Dred Scott case fired a nation-wide debate on the fate of slavery. The lengthy court battle was finally decided by the U.S. Supreme Court in 1857, stating that no black person was eligible for citizenship under the Constitution, and therefore had no right to lay any claim before U.S. courts. *The Dred Scott Decision* favored the southern slave states and further inflamed anti-slavery sentiments. This deepened the North- South rift that soon led to Lincoln's Eman-cipation Proclamation, the Fourteenth Amendment, and sparked the American Civil War. Dred was freed by his new owner in 1858, the year he died of consumption, known today as tuberculosis. Harriet lived on as a free black woman in Saint Louis, taking in laundry.

§

Young Hole-in-the-Day, circa the early 1850's.

Chief Hole-in-the-Day the Younger over the next fifteen years became a prominent Ojibwe leader, a warrior for peace, a savvy diplomat and dashing public figure. He lived on his picketed farmhouse with more trappings than most white settlers including plows, hoes, a yoke of oxen, a ferry boat, lumber and furniture, guns, saddles, shawls and blankets, flags and medals, gifts from U.S. presidents, livestock, and a barn. He made six trips to Washington on treaty negotiations, during one of which he seduced Ellen McCarthy, a young white woman working as a chambermaid. She followed him back to Chicago and he took her up to live with him at Gull Lake, where she got on fine with his other Ojibwe wives.

The Chief, who like his father had a propensity to drink strong liquor, gained a reputation as unpredictable. He fomented joining forces with the Dakota against the whites in 1862, then pledged one hundred braves to the Union during the Civil War. He helped negotiate the Treaty for the White Earth reservation in 1867 and said he would take a knife to any half-breed trader who came there. Yet he welcomed the entire Warren family. This did not sit right with the mixed-bloods, especially a clutch of traders who hatched a plot against him. The Chief changed his mind just before he was to leave again for Washington, but the news did not travel, the plot was under way. He stopped for a drink at a Crow Wing saloon. On his way home, a party of ten hired Ojibwe of the Pillager band confronted him near Gull River.

He guessed what it was about, stood up in his buggy and said, "You have caught me at a bad moment. I am unarmed!"

That day, for once, he had forgotten the Colt .45 revolver given to him by President Pierce. *Madwaywewind*, the leader, shot him in the head and neck with a double-barreled shotgun, another shot him in the heart. They stabbed him, robbed him of every stitch of clothes and fought over his gold watch which one assassin, professing regret, later tried to sell to Julia Warren Spears for five dollars. They took his horse and buggy and ransacked his house, threatening to take Ellen. The Chief's Ojibwe widows told them that if they did, they would incur the wrath of the whites, so they left her.

Thus ended the life of the great chief, lauded as the Peacemaker, one of the most intelligent, daring and influential Ojibwe men ever to enter the public and political arena, and loyal friend of William Warren. One of Hole-in-the-Day's daughters later married William Vincent, a grandson of William through his son, Tyler. They too lived on the reservation in White Earth.

Hole-in-the-Day's death reached the magazines and newspapers as far as New York City and a ten-cent stamp was issued with his portrait, but his assassins were not prosecuted. John G. Morrison, allegedly one of the conspirators who volunteered to go with him to Washington that day, said in 1912:

"...if we did kill anybody them days, it was no crime; you couldn't hang a man for killing ten Indians."

Hole-in-the-Day was buried as he wished, in (or near, it was later claimed) the Catholic graveyard in Crow Wing, where they put up an American flag and a small cross, even though he never got around to converting. That graveyard was resold and lost over the years.

Such was also the fate of the grave site of William Whipple Warren, which lies somewhere beneath the streets of Saint Paul, the Minnesota State Capital. No remains of either man were ever recovered.

§

William Le Duc found Warren's manuscript in New York and brought it back to Minnesota, entrusting it to Henry Rice to arrange for publication. Warren's *History of the Ojibways* was first edited and published under the initial title by the Minnesota Historical Society in 1885. It is the only book of its kind, considered a seminal work and the authoritative basis of recorded Ojibwe history. It has since been reprinted several times.

Warren's original manuscript, after the initial publication, was lost and never found.

There remain some of Warren's letters and writings, and a small marker among the trees bordering a clearing by Two Rivers near Royalton, Minnesota, where the Platte meets the Mississippi, the site of the log home where he lived briefly with Matilda and his three children. To this day there are no other houses in sight, only the trees and the birds and the river.

MIIGWECH

The following is the version of Warren's Preface as edited and published in 1885:

PREFACE.[1]

The <u>History of the Ojibway People</u>

by William W. Warren

Minnesota Historical Society Press, 1984 edition

First Published in 1885

The red race of North America is fast disappearing before the onward resistless tread of the Anglo-Saxon. Once the vast tract of country lying between the Atlantic sea-board and the broad Mississippi, where a century since roamed numerous tribes of the wild sons of Nature, but a few — a very few, remnants now exist. Their former domains are now covered with the teeming towns and villages of the "pale face" and millions of happy free-men now enjoy the former home of these unhappy and fated people.

The few tribes and remnants of tribes who still exist on our western frontiers, truly deserve the sympathy and attention of the American people. We owe it to them as a duty, for are we not now the possessors of their former inheritance? Are not the bones of their ancestors sprinkled through the soil on which are now erected our happy homesteads? The red man has no powerful friends (such as the enslaved negro can boast), to rightly represent his miserable, sorrowing condition, his many wrongs, his wants and wishes. In fact, so feebly is the voice of philanthropy raised in his favor, that his existence appears to be hardly known to a large portion of the American people, or his condition and character has been so misrepresented that it has failed to secure the sympathy and help which he really deserves. We do not fully understand the nature and character of the Red Race. The Anglo-Americans have pressed on them so unmercifully — their intercourse with them has been of such a nature, that they have failed to secure their love and confidence.

The heart of the red man has been shut against his white brother. We know him only by his exterior. We have judged of his manners and customs, and of his religion rights and beliefs, only from what we have seen. It remains yet for us to learn how these peculiar rites and beliefs originated, and to fathom the motives and true character of the anomalous people.

Much has been written concerning the red race by missionaries, travelers and some eminent authors; but the information, respecting them which has thus far been collected, is mainly superficial. It has been obtained mostly by transient sojourners among the various tribes, who not having a full knowledge of their character and language, have obtained information through mere temporary observation—through the medium of careless and imperfect interpreters, or have taken the accounts of unreliable persons.

Notwithstanding all that has been written respecting these people since their discovery, yet the field for research, to a person who understands the subject, is still vast and almost limitless. And under the present condition of the red race, there is no time to lose. Whole tribes are daily disappearing, or are being so changed in character through a close contact with an evil white population, that their history will forever be a blank. There are but a few tribes residing west of the Mississippi and over its head-waters, who are comparatively still living in their primitive state—cherishing the beliefs, rites, customs and traditions of their forefathers.

Among these may be mentioned the Ojibway, who are at the present day, the most numerous and important tribe of the formerly wide extended Algic family of tribes. They occupy the area of Lake Superior and the sources of the Mississippi, and as a general fact, they still live in the way of their ancestors. Even among these, a change is so rapidly taking place, caused by a close contact with the white race, that ten years hence it will be too late to save the traditions of their forefathers from total oblivion. And even now, it is with great difficulty that genuine information can be obtained from them. Their aged men are fast falling into their graves, and they carry with them the records of the past history of their people ; they are the initiators of the grand rite of religious belief which they believe the Great Spirit has granted to his red children to secure them long life on earth, and life hereafter; and in the bosom of these old men are locked up the original causes and secrets of this, their most ancient belief.

The writer of the following pages was born, and has passed his lifetime, among the Ojibways of Lake Superior and the Upper Mississippi. His ancestors on the maternal side, have been in close connection with this tribe for the past one hundred and fifty years. Speaking their language perfectly, and connected with them through the strong ties of blood, he has ever felt a deep interest in their welfare and fate, and has deemed it a duty to save their traditions from oblivion, and to collect every fact concerning them, which the advantages he possesses have enabled him to procure.

The following pages are the result of a portion of his researches; the information and facts contained therein have been obtained during the course of several years of inquiry, and great care has been taken that nothing but the truth and actual fact should be presented to the reader.

In this volume, the writer has confined himself altogether to history; giving an account of the principal events which have occurred to the Ojibways within the past five centuries, as obtained from the lips of their old men and chiefs who are the repositories of the traditions of the tribe.

Through the somewhat uncertain manner in which the Indians count time, the dates of events which have occurred to them since their discovery, may differ slightly from those which have been given us by the early Jesuits and travelers, and endorsed by present standard historians as authentic.

Through the difficulty of obtaining the writings of the early travelers, in the wild country where the writer compiled this work, he has not had the advantage of rectifying any discrepancies in time or date which may occur in the oral information of the Indians, and the more authentic records of the whites.

The following work may not claim to be well and elaborately written, as it cannot be expected that a person who has passed most of his life among the wild Indians, even beyond what may be termed the frontiers of civilization, can wield the pen of an Irving or a Schoolcraft. But the work does claim to one of truth, and the first work written from purely Indian sources, which has probably ever been presented to the public. Should the notice taken of it, by such as feel an interest in the welfare of the red race, warrant a continuation of his labors in this broad field of inquiry, the writer presents this volume as the first of a series.

He proposes in another work to present the customs, beliefs, and rites of the Ojibways as they are, and to give the secret motives and causes thereof, also giving a complete exposition of their grand religious rite, accompanied with the ancient and sacred hieroglyphics pertaining thereto, with their interpretation, specimens of their religious idiom, their common language, their songs. Also their creed of spiritualism or communion with spirits, and jugglery which they have practised for ages, and which resembles in many respects the creed and doctrines of the clairvoyants and spiritualists who are making such a stir in the midst of our most enlightened and civilized communities. Those who take an interest in the Indian, and are trying to study out his origin, will find much in these expositions which may tend to elucidate the grand mystery of their past.

Succeeding this, the writer proposes, if his precarious health holds out, and life is spared to him, to present a collection of their mythological traditions, on many of which their peculiar beliefs are founded. This may be termed the "Indian Bible". The history of their eccentric grand incarnation—the great uncle of the red man—whom they term Man-abo-sho, would fill a volume of itself, which would give a more complete insight into their real character, their mode of thought and expression, than any book which can be written concerning them.

A biography of their principal chiefs, and most noted warriors, would also form an interesting work.

The writer possesses not only the will, but every advantage requisite to procure information for the completion of this series of works. But whether he can devote his time and attention to the subject fully, depends on the help and encouragement he may receive from the public, and from those who may feel an anxiety to snatch from oblivion what may be yet learned of the fast disappearing red race.

Acknowledgments and Further Reading

When I began researching this novel at the Minnesota Historical Society in Saint Paul, the Newberry Library in Chicago, and a trip to Madeline Island in Wisconsin, I found a good deal information on microfilm and in collections. This increased with the development of the internet, but books remained my main source. For the record, despite my part-native roots, I am not Ojibwe, but William Warren is my great-uncle. I grew up near the L'Anse Chippewa reservation in Upper Michigan, with my culturally white family. My mother was born on the White Earth Chippewa Reservation, as were her parents and grandparents, and her grandmother Sahgoshkodaywayquay (not a Warren) was full blooded. I do not claim to be an authority on the legends and history and do not speak the language. Living in France and working alone, I could not easily access the Warren and other papers safeguarded in different libraries and institutions throughout the United States. With the publication of historian Theresa Schenck's excellent biography of William Warren in 2007, the result of twenty years of professional research, nearly everything I had to know was there before my eyes, including the letters and papers I could not reach. We met in France, and she has generously assisted me and supported my novel project from the start. For this she has my lasting gratitude.

Of the extensive documentation on Warren's life, there remained two blank pages: his years as a student at the Oneida Institute under Beriah Green, and his trip to New York to seek a cure and a publisher. The Oneida years, the transformation from boyhood to young manhood, his initiation to higher learning and abolitionism, make another story. What interested me primarily was his dedication to his work and the astonishing journey he undertook—his impossible dream—in the last winter of his life, despite all odds when dying of consumption, or tuberculosis, for which there was no scientific diagnosis or informed treatment at the time. William Warren cheated the pale rider to see his book to publication.

This was fertile terrain for a novel. We know he went to Saint Paul, to Bad River then over the Great Lakes, though we do not know how. We know he stayed at Trall's Institute in New York and whom he saw there, from his letter to William Le Duc, his last, posted May 19, 1853 from Chicago. He undoubtedly stopped there on his return, almost completing his full circle, and made an important decision that reflected his certainty of imminent death. He died some ten days later at his sister Charlotte's house, the day after he landed in Saint Paul. As he had hoped, his manuscript was found in New York. It was returned to Saint Paul and published 32 years later by the Minnesota Historical Society.

How this journey could have happened, the possible and probable events as Warren crossed the United States and ventured into the rapidly changing world of 1853, is the fruit of imaginings stirred by reading many accounts of those times. I also wanted to reflect on the man, his mind and his life. William Warren's role as a mixed-blood Ojibwe is still disputed. He was both lionized and vilified during his lifetime and despite historical evidence, his true nature and sentiments find both friend and foe today.

For the most thorough and balanced historical reckoning, one must read Theresa Schenck's William W. Warren, *The Life, Letters and Times of an Ojibwe Leader* (University of Nebraska Press, 2007), and her annotated version of Warren's *History of the Ojibway People* (Minnesota Historical Society, 2009). Among her many works on American Indian history and culture, *The Voice of the Crane Echoes Afar* (1997), as well as the edited journals of fur trader George Nelson and missionary Edmund Ely afford the reader valuable insight into to the country and minds at work on the frontier.

William Warren was the first to write the history of a Native American people as told by their own knowledge keepers, the original oral historians. Despite its flaws, it is a lively and fascinating read. Some of the other books I used are cited below. The sources available by searching the internet are now legion.

Essential to understanding the machinations behind the tragic Sandy Lake Removals and Warren's role in advising the Ojibwe is *Fish in the Lakes, Wild Rice and Game in Abundance* (James M. McClurken et. al., especially the section by Bruce M. White), published in 2000, on the background of Ojibwe claims to treaty rights refused by the state of Minnesota. The legal battle was finally won when Supreme Court Justice Sandra Day O'Connor rendered her landmark decision in favor of the Ojibwe people on March 24, 1999. This book represents the research done in support of those claims, and contains extensive behind-the-scenes information and cultural background on the politics of treaties in Warren's times.

For further detail on American Indians in the Great Lakes, the fur trade, La Pointe and Saint Paul, readers can consult several successive editions of Henry Rowe Schoolcraft's *Algic Researches* and *Indian Legends*; *Life, Letters and Speeches of George Copway (Kahgegagahbowh); Cadotte Family Stories* compiled and edited by Thomas Henry Tobola, 1974; *La Pointe* by Hamilton Nelson Ross, 2000; *A History of the City of Saint Paul to 1875*, James Fletcher Williams, 1983 edition; Thomas L. McKenney's *Sketches of a Tour to the Lakes; North American Indians* by George Catlin, edited by Peter Matthiessen, 1989, *Chippewa Customs* by Frances Densmore; *Atlas of Great Lakes Indian History*, 1987, edited by Helen Hornbeck Tanner with cartography by Miklos Pinther; *Indian Nations in Wisconsin* by Patty Loew, 2001. For background on Ojibwe notables, see the succinct works of Mark Diedrich are *The Chiefs Hole-in-the-Day (1986)* and *Ojibway Chiefs (1999)*. Also: *The Assassination of Hole-in-the-Day* by Anton Treuer, 2010, is a longer work that surprisingly describes Warren as a "trader" who gouged the Ojibwe. *Woman in the Wilderness, Letters of Harriet Wood Wheeler, Missionary Wife, 1832-1892* was compiled by Nancy Bunge, 2010; *Unto*

a Good Land, Book II of the Emigrant Novels, a historical novel by Vilhelm Moberg, 1952: *Beyond the Boundaries, Life and Landscape at the Lake Superior Copper Mines, 1840-1875* by Larry Lankton, 1997; *Indian Women and French Men* by Susan Sleeper-Smith, 2001. *To Build a Canal, Sault Sainte Marie, 1853-1854 and After* by John N. Dickinson, 1981.

The first two books my aunt gave me were *Red Shadows in the Mist*, by James (Warren) Hull, self-published in 1969, and William Warren, *The story of an American Indian*, by Dr. Will Antell, Dillon Press, Minneapolis, 1973. Both men are Ojibwe of the Mississippi band, born on the White Earth Indian Reservation. These small and dedicated books are out of print. The recollections of Julia Warren Spears can be found at the Minnesota Historical Society in Saint Paul and reproduced in Theresa Schenck's biography. A good many of the scanned manuscripts of the Warren papers can be found on-line at the University of Wisconsin site. Readers will find that some of the letters used in this book are quoted verbatim, others are fictionalized.

Among the abundant history of America and New York in the 19th century, I consulted *What Hath God Wrought, the Transformation of America, 1815-1848* by Daniel Walker Howe, 2007; *Young America 1830-1840* by Robert Riegel; *Abolition's Axe, Beriah Green, Oneida Institute and the Black Freedom Struggle*, by Milton C. Sernett; *Immigrant Life in New York City 1825-1863*, by Robert Ernst, 1994; *Five Points*, by Tyler Anbinder, 2001; *Low Life* by Luc Sante, 1991; *A Historical Atlas of New York City*, by Eric Homberger, 1994. This list just scans the surface, but they helped form the background of William's story.

I give heartfelt thanks to my family for their support and patience, to my departed mother Virginia Hope Warren and her sister Lois, who gave me the early stories and Warren documents and the desire to write this book, and to the friends who have given me inspiration, time, editing help and encouragement: Tim Anderson, Malcolm McCallum, Tyler Fleeson, Paul Belle, Paul Merrill, my sister Marisa, Theresa Schenck, Pamela Wilkie, Antoine Audouard, Iris Hart and above all my essential wife and partner, Sylvie, whose patience apparently knows no end.

April 29, 2022
Tim Warren McGlue
Le Havre, France

Lightning Source UK Ltd.
Milton Keynes UK
UKHW012327170223
417112UK00005B/489